The Sanctuary

Michael Taylor

Copyright © 2022 Michael Taylor. All rights reserved.

No portion of this book may be reproduced in any form without permission from the publisher, except as permitted by U.S. and UK copyright law. For permissions contact: Michael Taylor michaeltaylorbooks@gmail.com

The Sanctuary and The-Passage-Between-The-Worlds series is copyright to Michael Taylor

This novel's story and characters are fictitious. Certain long-standing institutions, agencies, and historical figures are mentioned, but the characters involved are wholly imaginary.

For my wonderful children. Every single day you make me proud.

"If the doors of perception were cleansed everything would appear to man as it is, infinite. For man has closed himself up, till he sees all things thro' narrow chinks of his cavern."

William Blake, *The Marriage of Heaven and Hell*

THE SANCTUARY

Prologue

Reader, be quick! There is little time to lose, come with me now to an age almost lost to the mists of time. Two old friends sit together; talking, worrying…

"Already he becomes strong." The wizard looks at his friend, worry etched into his face. "It is becoming, a problem."

She shrugs dismissively. "A few thousand followers only, I really don't see…"

"Not long ago there were merely hundreds, soon they will measure tens of thousands, hundreds of thousands!"

"You exaggerate, surely?"

"Mitra, open your eyes and your mind!" he exclaims. "You know of the Demon King's slave pits, toiling hour upon hour, day after day to churn out more of those vile creatures. How long will it be until the world is overrun?" He forces himself to become calmer. "I foresee a time when even we wizards and witches will be unable to stop him. Far into the future perhaps, but nevertheless!"

"But what can we do?" Mitra shrugs again. "Your latest attempt to kill him failed, just like the ones before." She is risking his wrath, she knows this, but it's not the time for delicacy or hurt feelings.

His face flushes a deep crimson and he cannot meet her eye; the decision to send assassins against the Demon King had been a controversial one, even though those who died had all been volunteers. He regards her for a long time while he makes up his mind, until finally, "We have to safeguard the future and give the generations to come a chance to fight this menace."

"And how do you suppose we do that?" She is skeptical. "We may be powerful but even we can't control the future."

The wizard smiles without mirth. "Perhaps we can though." He gets to his feet abruptly. "Come with me."

It is a long walk into the hills, to a desolate place far from any village or town. As they walk, the moon, full and bright, clears the horizon and night-time descends. She is tired as, at last, he leads her into a small copse of stunted trees, but her curiosity outweighs her need to rest. When they come to a clearing she gasps, unprepared for what she sees there.

It is a demon, naked and terrified, hanging by its feet from a gibbet in the center of the clearing. Its hands are tied, its mouth gagged, its eyes wild and pleading. Drool drips from behind the gag into the large copper bowl beneath its head. Nearby, a cage contains a second creature and, although it is covered entirely by a blanket, Mitra can hear the demon crashing frantically against the bars, can tell from its muffled screams that it is also gagged.

She turns to her friend, her gaze disbelieving, accusing. Her first emotion is shock, then puzzlement; her friend is no murderer, and even if he were, she refused to believe he would indulge himself in this sadism.

"What are you doing? I know we detest the demons, want them gone, but this is not the way. Look at that thing, it's terrified. Why, Cornelius, why do this? What perverse pleasure do you gain? This is not the way to revenge yourself upon the Demon King!"

He rounds upon her furiously. "You think I like doing this? That I get enjoyment from it? You think I seek to gain some kind of petty revenge over Kanzser?" He turns from her and looks up into the sky; the moon is almost at its zenith. He nods in satisfaction. "No, I'm afraid this is as regrettable as it is necessary."

For the first time, Mitra notices the knife he holds in his hand.

"I'm sorry," he tells the demon simply, then, ignoring Mitra's appalled shout, he draws the knife across its throat as she watches, open mouthed. Blood jets from the dying creature's throat into the waiting bowl and the wizard begins his spell, chanting, slowly at first, then faster and louder so that soon he is shouting, up towards the moon.

And as the huge, shining orb passes directly overhead at last, its pure white rays reflect from the rapidly filling bowl so that the entire clearing is cast with a ghoulish red tinge. Cornelius continues the spell as the light begins to spread into the trees and beyond. And now the moon itself is no longer pure white but faintly pink, turning deeper and redder as his voice begins to crack and falter. He motions his friend to follow as he makes his way back toward the open countryside. As they leave the shelter of the trees, a gale is blowing, becoming stronger and more violent by the second as if it too is raging against the moon.

THE SANCTUARY

For Mitra it is a night of shocks and here is another, for the moon is now a deep, blood red and its light bathes the land as far as the eye can see. And where before the land had been sparse, desolate, now it is fertile. Grass grows over bare earth and rock, trees grow before her very eyes, laden with fruit and berries. In the distance a stream, before only a mere trickle, is now a flowing scarlet ribbon. Mitra can see fish jumping in and out of the water, joyful, as if they too cannot quite believe what has happened. They fly through the air, competing for who can go highest, before splashing back into the water, their shiny scales glinting red like a million tiny sparks of fire.

As the wind continues to rage, a single thorn bush, its wicked spikes infused with the red of the blood moon, is buffeted, tossed this way and that, struggling to maintain its hold, its roots weakened from years of surviving in the dry, stony earth. Suddenly, four of the spikes are wrenched from a single stem and carried aloft. Three are scattered far and wide to take root in distant lands. But the fourth is flung high, up into the stratosphere, beyond the winds to where the air is still. It hangs there for a moment then drifts slowly back toward the earth, only to be caught again by the swirling winds, and borne along, barely above the ground, sometimes so low it brushes the tips of the still growing grass, in danger of becoming caught.

But whether by chance or design, the wind always gusts more strongly at the last second and the thorn, crimson in the moonlight, appears to dance along like a firefly up the hillside. And at last it is blown into the mouth of a cave, only a small cave, seemingly insignificant. The thorn lodges in a tiny crack near the entrance and there it will grow, waiting for many centuries until its true purpose is revealed.

Eventually the wind abates and Cornelius falls silent. The spell is complete.

"Why? How?" the witch finds her voice at last. "Why did you kill that demon and what happened here? What is all…this?"

"I killed the demon to make the blood moon," he gasps, so exhausted he can barely speak. "And as for this?" His chest heaves alarmingly. "It's a question of balance. Every evil act should have one of good to balance it, otherwise the world would be drowned in evil before we know it." He sinks to the ground and sits, head between his knees as he tries to relax his thumping heart.

"I get it…" she says slowly. "Because you killed the demon, you had to do something good. I understand that." She looks at him, her expression still puzzled. "But killing the demon to make the moon red? I still don't understand why."

"It's a weapon!" He lifts his head and glares at her, wishing she would leave him alone. "The blood moon is a weapon, it kills demons! In the future, should there be a need to wipe them out, we now have the means." The anger leaves his eyes to be replaced by a look of sadness and something else. Shame?

"It's quite probable that history will remember me as a murderer," he says dully.

She begins to offer words of comfort, but he silences her with a gesture. "Please, Mitra, leave me alone for now."

"But what about that one?" she insists and nods toward the trees. "Aren't you going to let it out? Please tell me you're not going to kill it too. I don't think I could stand that."

THE SANCTUARY

"I plan to let it go, but not yet, not until morning. Now please, no more talking, I must rest."

So, they sit in a silence which gradually becomes companionable until, at last, the dawn breaks over the distant mountains. As the final traces of the blood moon are erased by the morning sun, Mitra follows the wizard back into the trees and watches without speaking as he removes the blanket and opens the door of the cage. The demon snarls obscenities at him for a moment then tries to run but he stops it with a flick of his wand. It stands there, unable to move, the look of hatred frozen on its face.

"Go, tell your master what has happened here. Warn him he can never be certain if, when the moon is full, it will be white or red. Warn him that the blood moon is the harbinger of death for all demons should they be foolish enough to be touched by its rays. Tell him it will be this way until time itself ends and that one day the blood moon will rid the earth of all his kind."

The hatred in the creature's eyes should have been enough to turn him to stone but the wizard is indifferent.

"Tell your master that I, Cornelius, descendant of the original Six Wizards, have decreed this and that it will come to pass." As his voice thunders across the hills, the demon cowers in terror, no longer daring to speak its obscenities, even if it were able.

When the wizard releases it with another disdainful flick of his wand, the demon scampers away, up the hillside as fast as it can toward the cave, longing desperately to reach the safety of its own world.

Part One

THE SANCTUARY

Chapter 1

London 1964

The streets of Notting Hill were awash with noise as another busy market day drew to a close and a heady mix of aromas, some easily identifiable, others more mysterious, hung in the air. It was the run up to Christmas; there were just two days left, and the skies above were heavy with the threat of more snow. A tide of last-minute Christmas shoppers hustled to reach the tube stations before it fell again.

Among them, tired from another Saturday working at one of Chelsea's least fashionable boutiques, Ben was as eager as everyone else to get home and it was a relief when he saw the red and blue neon sign of Notting Hill Gate shining through the gathering dusk.

As he hurried down the steps of the station, he cannoned into a tall man wearing a dark overcoat and a black Fedora style hat, pulled down so that his eyes were hidden. Before he could gasp an apology, he felt something thrust into his hand. He glanced down and saw it was a leaflet or pamphlet of some kind.

The tall man bent close to his ear and spoke, "Read it, *don't* lose it and, most importantly, *be there."*

The man's breath was hot against Ben's cheek and his eyes bored into his for an instant before he was gone, lost among the crowds before Ben could even react. He stood and stared at the black hat disappearing into the distance but still just visible above the heads of the throng. He was oblivious to the people pushing to get past, some cursing him as they hurried by. When he could no longer see it, Ben turned and allowed himself to be hustled down the remainder of the steps. Then, having negotiated the turnstiles and by some miracle actually found a seat on the crowded tube, he opened his palm and looked at the crumpled piece of paper. He smoothed it out onto his knee and read:

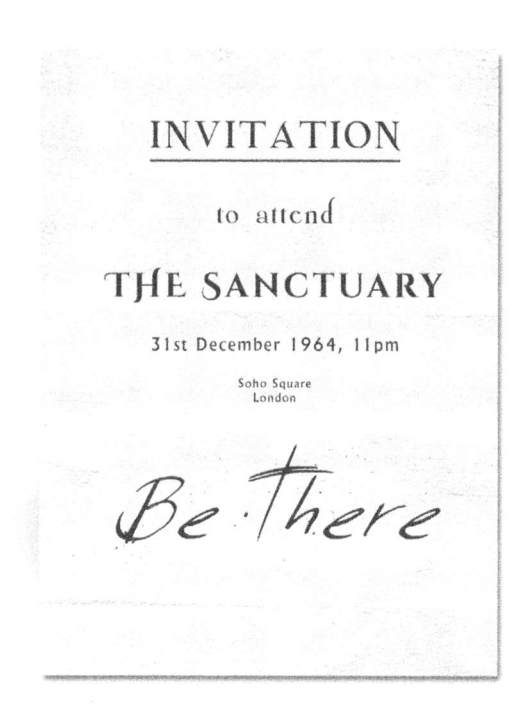

> INVITATION
>
> to attend
>
> **THE SANCTUARY**
>
> 31st December 1964, 11pm
>
> Soho Square
> London
>
> *Be There*

The thirty-first of December; my sixteenth birthday. Ben stared at the paper for a long time, wondering what it meant. He had to squint and hold it close to his nose to read the address, it was written so small. *Almost as if it needs to be kept secret,* he thought. As the train sped through the network of tunnels far beneath London, the words *Be There* seemed to get larger and larger.

Like a threat. He shuddered involuntarily.

Impulsively, he crumpled the paper into a ball and dropped it to the floor; a woman across the aisle looked at him disapprovingly, then sniffed and turned away.

The train sped onward, and Ben tried not to look at the ball of paper lodged by his foot, but his eyes were drawn downward as it seemed to stare up at him, accusingly. He kicked it away but at the same moment the train tilted as it rounded a bend and the paper rolled back to settle once more against his shoe. It lay there for a while as he tried to ignore it, but eventually, unable to stand the tension any longer, he picked it up.

Once more he smoothed the paper out and re-read it, then as his own destination approached, he folded it carefully and placed it in the inside pocket of his jacket.

Chapter 2

London – present day

If it hadn't been so dark, he might have noticed the shadowy figure that lay (hiding?) in the doorway, and the pair of legs flung casually across the pavement, and things could have been very different.

But then…who would there have been to save the world?

But the London night *was* dark. Dark, cold and wet, so the boy hurried along, shrinking miserably into his coat and taking little notice of where he was going. His misery was only partly down to the weather. In truth, he hardly noticed the rain that teemed onto his bare head and trickled inside his coat, or the cold that slowly turned his bones to ice.

In fact, the boy had just been dumped. Well, the last thing Cissy had screamed at him was, "I never want to see you again. Loser!"

I take that to mean I'm definitely dumped, he thought.

So his day was just about complete when he found himself lying face down in a large puddle, water soaking the few pieces of clothing he'd so far managed to keep dry. He sat up quickly and rubbed his nose where he'd banged it.

THE SANCTUARY

What the hell just happened? As the boy looked around, he realized he was surrounded by shadows; he could only vaguely make out a large shape slumped in a shop doorway a few feet away.

The shape didn't move, nor did it speak. In fact, it did precisely nothing.

*   *   *   *

The day had begun so brightly. First day of the school break, the sun shining, meeting Cissy. As he walked (ran) the mile and a half into town, Luke felt like shouting with the excitement of being young and having fun. Sure, she'd dragged him round half the clothes shops in London, but he didn't mind really, because then they'd gone back to hers and spent the rest of the afternoon chatting and listening to music; their favorite thing.

And it had all been going so well. They'd been together almost three months and he'd never had a girlfriend that long. They'd long since passed that awkward first kiss stage of course, and now Cissy's mother, knowing how close they'd become, kept finding reasons to interrupt. Not that Mrs. Hamilton didn't trust her daughter implicitly, but still…*best just to check*. So, every now and then there would be a quiet knock at the bedroom door, and she would appear, make some excuse for interrupting, then just as quickly disappear back downstairs.

Each time the two teenagers would collapse into hysterical laughter until Luke, who began to get a little tired of it and was, as usual, unable to keep his mouth shut, made a sarcastic and rather nasty little comment. Cissy, who could be volatile at the best of

THE SANCTUARY

times, jumped to her feet.

And there'd been an argument.

Which had turned into one hell of an argument.

And that's when it happened. The dumping. And the *loser* thing.

And that's how, instead of getting a lift from Cissy's mum, he'd found himself walking miserably home in the pouring rain, lost in thought, until now…

The boy scrambled to his feet and looked around. He was sure there had been lots of people about earlier.

Only a minute earlier?

In fact, he'd walked down this street hundreds of times and it was never empty.

It was now though.

Now the street was deserted.

Except for me, and the shape, he thought as he peered into the deepening gloom, suddenly feeling nervous without quite knowing why.

And then the boy realized why it was so dark. The streetlights – they were all off. Not a single one was lit; not a single one, that is, except for a solitary orange light far away in the distance, its faint glow a beacon.

This is weird, he thought, wanting to be near that light, wanting it very much indeed. He turned and was about to walk away – *I won't run,* he told himself, *I'm not a coward* – when the shape spoke.

Chapter 3

"It's about time," the shape said. "About bleedin' time!"

The boy didn't know what he'd expected, but this sure wasn't it. He spun round and peered into the shadows.

"Who's that?" he called loudly. Unfortunately, it came out more as a high-pitched squeak, which betrayed the nerves that were making his heart thump frantically.

He cleared his throat and spoke again. "Come out of there." And this time he managed to put on his deepest voice and speak in what he hoped was an unafraid, commanding tone.

The shape spoke again. "Half a mo', dear, I'm coming, can't hurry at my age, you know." The voice sounded breathless, indignant. "And you've kept me waiting so long, I swear my legs have gone to sleep forever." Then, almost under its breath, the shape added, "Three bleedin' weeks is long enough for anyone to have to wait. Bleedin' inconsiderate I call it."

There were sounds of shuffling and grunting, and slowly, from the shadows, a figure emerged. It was a woman, an old woman from what the boy could see. And she was big. *No, she's huge,* he realized as more of her came into view.

"What d'ya think you're doing sitting there in the dark like that?" he began. "I nearly broke my neck tripping over you." Another thought struck him. "And what do you mean I've kept you waiting? I don't even—"

"Be quiet," the old woman interrupted, "there isn't time for that. You the boy they call Luke?"

"Who are you?" the boy demanded. "I'm not going to—"

"Be quiet!" the woman insisted. "There isn't time, I tell you!" She towered over him and her eyes seemed to spark. Despite himself, he took a step backwards. In a softer tone she said, "There isn't time for explanations, I just have to know your name. Now are you the boy they call Luke?"

The boy nodded, unable to trust his voice.

"Luke Simpson?"

He nodded again.

"Good." The woman gave a sigh of relief. "It's about bleedin' time," she repeated. "It's been three weeks."

"What has?" Luke was beginning to feel more than a little dizzy.

The old woman smacked her forehead in exasperation and muttered quietly to herself, "God help us all if this boy really is the one from the ancient prophecy. He seems…stupid. I wonder if Morgan could have made a mistake. But no, that can't be, the resemblance is too great. Those green eyes, quite startling, just like his father's were."

Luke didn't know whether to be annoyed about the 'stupid' comment or curious to know who Morgan was, and he almost missed her last comment. "My father?" he exclaimed, grabbing her arm. "You knew my *father*?"

The old woman glanced down as if seeing him properly for the first time. *Why, he's just a boy,* she thought. *So very young really. And the dangers ahead of him…so many dangers. Can he survive, I wonder; survive what Peter could not, locked away all these years?*

As she had done countless times, the old woman tried to imagine Luke's father in his dark dungeon, fearing death, hoping for a rescue that could never come, and sighed heavily.

We could try, Morgan, at least we could try!

Her gaze softened. "Come on, Luke," she said brightly, "you're soaking wet and freezing cold! Let's get going before you catch your dea…before you catch a cold," she amended quickly. "C'mon, it's not far." And with that she placed a massive arm around his shoulders and hustled him along.

Luke was tall for his age, but the old woman, although not quite as huge as he'd first thought, still towered above him so he had to crane his neck up to speak. "My father, you said you knew him?"

Tears glistened briefly in her eyes and she wiped them away impatiently before sighing. "Yes, yes, Luke, I knew your father very well when he was, well, about your age in fact."

Sensing another barrage of questions, she forestalled him. "Enough now, I can't possibly explain everything, and every minute we spend on this street puts us in danger. Even now, I sense we are being watched. We have to reach the Sanctuary as quickly as we can." She strode down the street even quicker so Luke almost had to run to keep up.

After a minute he looked up again and panted. "What's *your* name anyway?"

The old woman glanced down. "Molly."

He tried again after another pause. "You said you'd been waiting for me?"

Bleedin' 'ell, she thought to herself, *does the lad ever stop asking questions?* Aloud she said, "Come *on*, we must reach the light, not far now."

Luke peered ahead through the gloom and saw that the streetlight was indeed much closer.

Chapter 4

Alone in her bedroom, Cissy looked at the chair so recently vacated by Luke and sighed. *I do like him,* she thought. *A lot, actually.* She knelt on the floor and idly gathered a week's worth of carelessly strewn clutter – bits of clothing, trainers and sheets of unfinished homework – in a halfhearted attempt to tidy up. *But sometimes he's such an…an asshole.*

The word pleased her, summing him up perfectly at the moment. "Asshole," she said, and then more loudly, "Luke Simpson, you are an asshole!"

"Are you alright, dear?" Her mother opened the bedroom door and popped her head round.

"Yeah, Mum, I'm fine," answered Cissy, wondering if her mum had heard. "Dad home yet?"

"No, dear, not yet," replied Mrs. Hamilton. "I just wanted to check that, well, you know, your argument with Luke. Such a nice boy too, such a shame…" Her voice petered out at the look of ferocity on Cissy's face.

"He is *not* a nice boy," she informed her mother in an icy tone.

She stood up and went to lay on her bed, crossed her ankles and cupped her hands behind her head. "He's a moron, like all boys, now I think about it; all boys are such pig-headed, stupid morons and I, for one, am sick of them." She turned her face away, feeling a sense of guilt she couldn't quite explain.

Her mum came in and Cissy moved over so she could perch on the edge of the bed. "The bad news there, darling," she said, "is they don't get much better when they grow up." Lucy Hamilton looked solemnly down at her daughter and winked.

Cissy burst out laughing as her mother lay down beside her and put an arm round her shoulder, drawing her close. "Y'know, Cissy, Luke isn't so bad, far better than a lot of boys his age. I like him a lot and you could do much worse. And think yourself lucky that both your father and I *do* like him. When we were young, just teenagers like you, my parents didn't approve of your father at all. I can hear your grandmother now." She struck a pose and wagged a finger. "Lucy, that boy's no good, you could do much better than him."

She mimicked her gran so perfectly that Cissy had to smile. "That was just because your father's family didn't have money," her mother went on. "She was a terrible snob your grandma; still is in fact."

Cissy had heard this story many times and she found it uncomfortable to picture her parents as teenagers. It seemed impossible that her slim, smart, cultured mum with her expensive clothes and bridge parties could ever have had to put up with things like boyfriend trouble. Surely she'd never had to worry about acne or whether she was fat, and would boys fancy her, and all the other things that made the life of a teenage girl so unbearable at times?

"I know, Mum, don't worry. I'll probably let him suffer for a few days then he can persuade me to get back with him." She sprang up from the bed and resumed her tidying to forestall any more reminiscences about her mother's angst-ridden childhood. And, anyway, she would only get nagged later if she didn't tidy up.

The sound of the front door slamming stopped her.

"Dad!" exclaimed Cissy, tearing out of the room and down the stairs.

"Sweetheart!" exclaimed her father, catching hold of his daughter and swinging her around. He put her down and grinned. "How's my most special lady in the whole world?" he asked, planting a kiss on her cheek but missing and getting her ear instead.

This was their own private joke. For as long as she could remember, right back to when she was a toddler, she'd been her father's 'most special lady.'

"Oh, I'm okay," she replied. She looked at him with concern, for he looked tired; exhausted in fact.

Cissy's father owned a thriving business but never seemed able to take a step back and enjoy his success. It was rare that she saw him in the evenings, for he often didn't get home until long after Cissy had gone to bed. But because it was the school holidays she was allowed to stay up as late as she liked (her mum could be quite cool sometimes, she had to admit).

"Seen Luke today?" he asked.

"Yeah, but I've dumped him," she replied airily.

He grinned. "And how long are you gonna give him, little miss?"

Cissy grinned back; her dad understood her so well.

"Oh, a couple of days, I guess; we'll see." Then, determined to make the most of him being home, she dragged him over to his favorite armchair and sat him down, then pulled off his shoes and grabbed his slippers from under the chair.

She enjoyed making a fuss of him like this, something she rarely had the chance to do. From the corner of her eye she could see her mother trying to find an opportunity to interrupt, and grinned. Her mother was obsessed with being clean and tidy; even now Cissy could imagine the words forming in her mouth to suggest he should take a shower before he got too comfortable.

To forestall this Cissy asked, "Cup of tea, Dad?" before jumping up and heading toward the kitchen, just as the phone rang. "I'll get it," shouted Cissy, changing direction for the phone in the hall. There was a short, one-sided conversation before her parents heard the sound of the receiver being replaced.

Cissy appeared in the doorway of the lounge, her face ashen.

"Darling, what's happened?" exclaimed her mother.

"That was Luke's mum." She glanced at her watch. It was 11:30 pm. "Luke hasn't arrived home yet."

*   *   *   *

"Run, Luke!" shouted Molly. "Run!" They had almost reached the welcome glow of the streetlight when two figures emerged from the gloom. Both were short and their bald heads glistened in the orange lamplight. The left hand of each held a wand, raised and about to strike.

"RUN!" screamed Molly again as bolts of blinding light seared from the wands, almost striking her. But suddenly, and so swiftly that Luke didn't see it appear, there was a wand in Molly's hand, and with a flick of her wrist she deflected the bolts back at the two men, knocking them to the ground.

She grabbed Luke by his collar and literally flung him towards the light. "Morgan," she yelled, "quickly!"

A tiny door, no more than twelve inches high, opened at the base of the lamppost and two hands reached out to take hold of Luke's ankles.

He had only an instant to think *impossible* before he felt his body somehow melt and stretch and, with a faint popping sound, he was pulled through the doorway. He fell heavily onto a hard surface, this time managing not to hit his nose but banging his elbows and knees instead.

There was barely time to yell out in pain, while his brain registered the further impossibility that he was now in a large circular room, when Molly appeared in the doorway above him.

He had the curious impression of her body being *slim* as it oozed into the room and made a rather more graceful entry than he had – well, at least she didn't fall – and then the door clanged shut behind them.

"Come, we must hurry," said a deep voice, and as his eyes became accustomed to the dim light, Luke could make out the figure of a man, Morgan. He was tall – very tall – and he wore a long, dark overcoat. On his head was one of those hats like the ones you saw in those old American gangster movies.

"Who are you? Where are we? What just happened?" Luke's questions came flooding out in a streaming torrent.

THE SANCTUARY

"Sshh," whispered Molly, placing a steadying hand on his arm, "not now." She got to her feet and took hold of Luke's hand to help him up. "Now we must follow."

Morgan was already standing by a door (a normal sized one, Luke noticed with relief) at the other side of the room, looking back at them impatiently. As they approached, he flung the door open and strode through. Molly and Luke hurried to follow.

They were in a passage. Its walls were of rough-hewn stone, but the floor was smooth and polished; *marble,* Luke thought. Embedded into it were what looked like chips of pure silver which glowed as Morgan's feet touched them, then faded as he strode on down the passage.

For the next ten minutes, the three companions walked in silence – or rather Morgan walked while Molly and Luke hurried to keep up. Gradually, Luke's curiosity got the better of him and he caught up with Morgan. The silver light was enough to see that the face of the tall man was lined with deep furrows, his nose long and rather sharp. His features wore a tense, but at the same time determined, expression.

"Where are we?" panted Luke, and Morgan glanced down.

"Nowhere." The reply was terse.

"O…kay…" Luke tried again, "So where are we going?"

"The Sanctuary," Morgan grunted. "Don't talk." And something in his expression warned Luke that it would be unwise to disobey. They continued for a while, Luke trotting to keep up, Molly lagging further behind down the passage which twisted first one way then another. There was no sound apart from their footsteps and Molly's huffing and puffing, and her occasional muttered complaints.

"That's right, you two carry on and leave me behind. It's not as if I'm *old* or anything, I only turned three hundred and… something, last week. Bleedin' inconsiderate, I call it!"

Chapter 5

"Fools!" His breath, fetid and sour, washed over the two men as they shrank away, terrified. He was tall, unnaturally so, and his hair was a thick, oily black that hung onto his shoulders and meandered down his back like the slick from a stricken tanker. It seemed to have a life of its own as his head moved from side to side to look at the two men in turn.

"Tell me again how a boy and an old woman managed to escape two such *powerful wizards*?" His voice dripped with sarcasm.

There was silence for a long moment and then, "We…we're not really wizards," one of them stammered, not daring to look up, "and the wands you gave us, they're not really ours, they're full of demon power. It's agony each time we have to use them."

The man known as the Dark Wizard allowed himself to reminisce how he'd stolen the wands, for no particular reason except they'd been there, from under the very nose of the Demon King when he'd been a boy. Then the servant's words penetrated, and he stared at him in amazement.

"You dare to contradict me?" His eyes were a deep purple but appeared black in the dim candlelight and they flashed dangerously. Without warning he flung out an arm and pointed at the man who had spoken.

Then a curious thing happened. The man was jerked roughly to his feet and he hung there, helpless like a marionette in some bizarre puppet show. As the wizard's arm moved slowly around in an arc, the man began to bend backwards.

Slowly and inexorably, he arched further and further, gasping in agony until it seemed his spine would surely snap. Suddenly, with an impatient gesture, the wizard released him and he fell whimpering to the floor.

"So," he continued as if nothing had happened, "the boy is out of my reach." He glared menacingly at his two servants. "At least for now. No doubt he is being *fussed* over by that do-gooder Morgan even as we speak." He sneered the name.

Then his mood changed abruptly, his tone becoming conversational. "Y'know, there was a time when he – Morgan, I mean – when he and I were the best of friends; inseparable even." The Dark Wizard placed an arm around each of their shoulders, as if they themselves were old friends, and led them around the room. Somehow this display, this charade, was the most terrifying thing he'd done yet. "Of course that was a long time ago, when we were children."

The room was deathly silent for a while, except for the occasional sputtering of candles as they continued to walk, almost in slow motion. When he spoke again, his voice was soft, hypnotic. "But then he turned against me, most unfair of him, I've always thought. I never could understand why he did it." Now he sounded puzzled, almost hurt. The Dark Wizard paused and looked at his two servants as if inviting them to offer an opinion, but they were silent, not daring to speak.

"Mind you," he continued after a moment and the conversational tone was back, "I don't suppose I can blame him for being a little *distant* towards me over the last few hundred years. Morgan was never the same after I killed our father!"

There was a diabolical pause before he burst out laughing, giggling in delight at the open-mouthed shock on the faces of his two servants.

"Now,"—he released them at last and clapped his hands together, the sound shockingly loud after the silence—"to business!" The laughter ceased abruptly and was again replaced by that glinting purple-black gaze. "The boy, as I have said, is lost to me for now, but there is another, a *girl*." He turned away and paced the circular room slowly. "Yes, a girl, a nobody who is without consequence. She has no power, no magic, not like the boy. But he loves her, apparently." He laughed delightedly. "How sweet!"

He faced them again and hissed quietly, "But she will be a means to get to the boy…what's he called?" His fingers snapped impatiently.

"L– Luke, my Lord," stammered the braver of the two men (the one who hadn't a few moments before felt the force of the Dark Wizard's anger). "The boy's name is Luke."

"Yes…" he agreed, drawing out the *s* like the hissing of a snake, "of course. Without you…Luke, Morgan and his group of *sycophants* will be powerless to stop me." He walked across the room to where a candle sat upon a sconce in the wall. He cupped his hand around the flame and caressed it, the room instantly growing dimmer.

"We will use the girl to entice this Luke from his newly-found sanctuary." He smiled and his eyes were filled with malice. "And when he no longer has the protection of my brother, I will take him and snuff out his life." His hand closed around the flame, plunging the room into near-darkness.

"Now, find the girl and bring her to me." His two servants started toward the door, but he stopped them with a gesture. He lifted the chin of each and gazed deeply into their eyes, causing the blood in their veins to freeze.

"This time, do not fail!"

* * * *

In the Hamilton household, Cissy's mother was trying to calm her daughter down. "Darling, I'm sure he's fine," she soothed, "he's probably having a good sulk before he goes home. We'll give it ten minutes, then ring his mother and he'll be back home safe and sound, you'll see."

"Mum, Luke isn't like that," her daughter argued. "Yeah he'll be upset, I know, but he wouldn't just not go home; he wouldn't put everyone through all this worry just because he wanted to sulk! I know him. He wouldn't do that." Her voice rose as panic gripped her.

Her father put a hand on her shoulder. "I agree," he announced. "Luke's a good lad, far too sensible to wander the streets of London at this time of night. Something must have happ—" He broke off at a warning look from his wife. "But I'm sure he's okay," he added hastily, casting a worried glance back at her.

"What are we going to do, Dad?" Cissy looked up at him. "He might be injured or worse. We can't just leave him out there!" Her voice was rising again as she thought of Luke hurt and alone out in the dark somewhere.

Mr. Hamilton squeezed her shoulder and stroked his chin thoughtfully for a moment. "Do you know which way he'd have walked home?"

She nodded. "He'd have gone down towards—"

"Good," he interrupted, "I'll get the car. We're going looking for him."

"Charles!" exclaimed his wife. "You can't, it's nearly midnight!"

"Lucy, look at her," he said quietly. "She's worried sick and Luke *might* be hurt, we have to at least try and find him."

"But the police will be—"

"Lucy, we're going, we have to, don't you see?"

"But—" she tried again, and he took her in his arms and kissed her tenderly.

"We'll be back before you know it and hopefully with good news," he murmured, then he released her and clapped his hands together. "C'mon, Cissy, let's go," and the girl ran to follow him out of the front door, pausing only to grab her coat, then the two of them disappeared into the night.

A short time later, they were in the car heading along the route Cissy knew Luke would have taken. They turned onto the Old Kent Road and slowed so they could peer into every alley and every side street they passed, hoping to catch a glimpse of the boy.

THE SANCTUARY

Suddenly Cissy grabbed her father's arm. "Dad!" He slammed on the brakes just in time to avoid hitting the old man who was shuffling over the crossing in front of them. He was caught in the glare of the headlights as he stood and peered in at them, his head moving from side to side as he looked at each of them in turn.

It seemed to Cissy that the old man's gaze lingered mostly on her and she shivered uncomfortably. *How queer looking he is,* she thought, and shuddered again as she took in the man's strange appearance, his body short and contorted but his head large and oval shaped, seeming much too big. *And he's totally bald, not a single hair on his head.* Not shaved like lots of men had it, but completely hairless so that it shone in the harsh light.

"C'mon, c'mon," muttered her father, his fingers drumming impatiently on the steering wheel. He was about to sound the horn when the old man raised his hand as if in apology and began once more to shuffle across the road.

As the car moved forward again, Cissy craned her neck round to stare back at him. As his eyes met hers, she saw his mouth twist into a leer and one eye droop into a wink. She turned forward abruptly. *What a creep.*

As he watched the car disappear around a bend in the road, the man straightened, instantly transformed from a frail old man into a short but powerful figure. The Dark Wizard's servant watched for another moment, then smiled, displaying yellow, rotting teeth. He turned and walked quickly in the other direction.

Soon he reached a pretty, tree-lined street where the houses were all in darkness; all but one. Here, a light shone in the living room of number 23, and inside sat a pretty, well-groomed woman staring blankly into space, lines of worry creasing her forehead.

Spying on her from his hiding place in the garden was the crouched form of the other of the Dark Wizard's servants, keeping watch to make sure none of the *other* wizard's servants got to the girl first. At a noise behind him, he shrank further into the shadows then relaxed as his companion crept up beside him. Together they watched and awaited the return of the girl and her father.

THE SANCTUARY

Chapter 6

Meanwhile, no longer in London, nor indeed in the 21st century, for the passage-between-the-worlds does not exist in any dimension of place or time, a wizard, a witch and a boy hurried along the silvery passage that descended sharply.

"Hurry," urged Morgan, "we must hurry! It's no coincidence that the Dark Wizard's servants were abroad tonight!" *There must be compelling reasons for them to risk showing themselves so openly,* he thought, then he cast a glance at Luke. *I fear my dear brother has learned of the boy's existence.*

"'Ave an 'eart, Morgan," panted Molly. "I'm just abart all done in." Her cockney accent was always more pronounced when she was stressed. "I ain't twenty anymore, you know."

You haven't been twenty for a long time, he thought sourly, his anxiety making him angry and uncharitable, but he immediately felt guilty as he looked at Molly's red, sweating face. She was exhausted and near the end of her limits, he realized.

"Alright," he relented, "we'll rest here for a few minutes and then take it more slowly. A *little* more slowly," he added with emphasis.

THE SANCTUARY

"Thank Gawd for that." She sank to the floor in a heap. Looking up at the boy, she asked, "How you doin', Luke?"

"Well," he replied, "I'm doing okay considering." His voice was more than a little tinged with sarcasm. "I mean it's not as if anything *unusual* has happened or anything." He turned to Morgan. "But I do have loads of questions, for instance…"

Morgan lifted a hand. "Not now, Luke, save your questions for when we get to the Sanctuary. There are others who will want to talk to you also." *They're only a little bit curious about you,* he thought to himself dryly.

"Now," he added quickly, seeing yet another question forming on Luke's lips, "if we're all rested?" It was an order, not a question. He stood without waiting for an answer and strode once more down the passage, totally forgetting his promise to go more slowly.

Molly heaved herself painfully to her feet. "Well if that's what you call 'avin' a bleedin' *rest.*" She wiped a hand across her forehead, then exclaimed in dismay, "My bracelet! Morgan, stop!"

The wizard turned, frowning.

"My bracelet," she said again, "the one my mother gave me when I graduated into the Sanctuary, it's missing!"

Morgan sighed but kept his voice even as he asked, "Okay, when did you last have it?"

Molly gave him a look that clearly said 'yeah, even wizards can ask stupid questions.' "That bracelet's been on my wrist for more than three centuries," she told him, deliberately misunderstanding. "*That's* how long I've had it."

"Okay, okay," he said soothingly, "I meant how long is it since you last *noticed* it."

THE SANCTUARY

The old woman thought for a moment. "Well, it began to shine when Luke first appeared, and it was dull for the three weeks before that when I was stuck waiting in that doorway." *And thank you very much for that, Morgan,* she thought. *I'm sure you could've found someone else if you'd wanted to.*

Turning to Luke, she explained, "It's a bit tarnished after all this time; I've not polished it for about a hundred and fifty years." Turning to Morgan, she mused, "That was for your two-hundred-and-fiftieth birthday, remember? My, what a night that was, what a party! People still talk, do you remember?"

"Molly, the point?" interrupted Morgan.

"Yeah, sorry. Well, as I was saying, it was just sitting there on my arm as it always does." She sneezed and wrapped her coat more tightly around her. "But when Luke appeared it shone bright gold as if it were brand new!" She sniffed. "Anyway, I *have* to find it."

"Look, I'll send someone—" began Morgan.

"It must've come off when I squeezed through the lamp post!" She jumped up and down in excitement. "That must be it!"

"She's *wobbling*," muttered Luke as he saw Molly's skin undulate like waves on a seashore.

"Anyway, I'm off back for it," she continued, turning away from them. "I'll see you two back at the Sanctuary."

"Molly, wait!" objected Morgan. "You can't go now, we must get the boy to safety!"

She glared at him and answered slowly as if addressing a small, not so bright child, "Morgan, *if* I were to leave it lying there in the street some vagrant or…or…well *somebody* will find it. Then in no time it'll be in a pawn shop down 'Atton Garden and I'll never see it again."

"That's rubbish and you know it! No ordinary mortal will be able to even see it!"

Molly, however, just glared him into silence. She straightened her shoulders and said with dignity, "Now, you *may* be the most powerful wizard on this side of the mortal Earth or any of the parallel ones. More powerful, I dare say, than that *idiot* brother of yours." Aside to Luke she said, "His brother's called Logan and the word idiot doesn't even *begin* to describe him."

Morgan blinked at this description of the Dark Wizard. His brother was far from being an idiot. He was clever, extremely so, and very, very dangerous.

But Molly was well and truly on her soapbox as she continued, hands on hips, "But I remember you as a snotty-nosed little terror in short pants and with dirty knees. Now I'm going to get my bracelet and if you want to *try* and stop me, go ahead, but I'm going!"

This was rather a long speech to make and Molly was even more red-faced when she'd finished. Without another word, she turned and stomped off down the passage.

Morgan looked after her helplessly, feeling a little foolish. *My nose was never snotty, and boys didn't wear short pants in the sixteenth century.* He sighed heavily.

"Molly always was a bit of a law unto herself," he informed Luke, not quite able to meet the boy's eyes. "Does her own thing most of the time, y'know, but I let her get away with it. Don't like to upset her."

Luke smiled to himself; he liked Molly, he realized, and after this small display of human weakness, he found himself liking Morgan too.

"That's okay," he said diplomatically, his face showing no hint of a smile, "we can probably get to this…sanctuary more quickly now we don't have to wait for her to keep up."

There seemed to be nothing else to say and without another word, the two unlikely companions set off once more.

* * * *

The car slowed to a stop.

"What's up, Dad?" Cissy looked at him, taking in the grim set of his features.

"I'm not sure…" her father answered slowly, looking intently at a doorway that was just visible in the darkness over the road. "Just a feeling, as if…as if someone had been here, and recently, someone I know very well."

"What do you mean?" Cissy asked, puzzled. "Someone was here? Who?"

Charles thought for a moment then, with a deep sigh, he released the handbrake and the car moved forward once more.

"Doesn't matter," he told her, "probably just my imagination working overtime. This night is…strange." A minute later, however, he stopped the car again and this time he got out, beckoning Cissy to do the same.

"That." He pointed. "Can you see it?"

She looked down the street. "The lamp post?" She faced him. "Of course I can see it."

Her father glanced at her sharply. "But you shouldn't be able—"

"Dad, what's going on? You're acting weird."

He didn't answer but took her arm and pulled her the short distance to the lamp post.

"Dad!" she cried, rubbing her arm where his fingers had dug in.

He glanced at her absently, his mind intent on the molded iron post, his eyes automatically flicking downward to locate the tiny door at the base, which he knew should be there. He ran his hands over the metal, as if to reassure himself it was real, and as he did so, tiny sparks flew from his fingertips.

"Yes," he breathed, almost inaudible, "someone was definitely here; a woman." He bent to examine the doorway. "I wonder if it was…"

"Dad," Cissy snapped, "now you're scaring me. What *was* that, electricity?"

Her father straightened and looked around nervously. "Cissy, we have to leave quickly, we could be in danger, you especially." His agitation was apparent and it increased her own fear.

"But what about Luke?" she argued. "We can't just abandon him!"

Charles looked up and down the deserted street as fog enveloped the chimney tops of nearby houses. It had begun to drift downwards, as if trying to envelop them in its icy embrace.

"I think," he mused, "yes, I'm certain Molly, and perhaps Morgan too, was here." He was right, he knew it, he could sense their presence. "Cissy, I don't think we need to worry. Luke is okay, he was rescued, I'm sure of it." Charles didn't want to contemplate why Morgan and Molly might be interested in Luke, but the boy *was* Peter's son after all.

Seeing she was about to speak, he placed a finger on her lips. "Not now, there's no time, we have to get out of here." He took her by the arm but, hearing the urgency in his voice, Cissy didn't need telling twice. She was turning toward the car when something caught her eye, nestled in the shadow at the base of the lamppost.

She picked it up and held it out to her father. "Look at this, Dad, it's beautiful."

He took the object from her and turned it around in his fingers. It was a bracelet, solid gold and indeed very beautiful. It was carved with symbols that he recognized as magical runes, and here and there it was encrusted with bright green emeralds. Even if he hadn't already known, it would have been obvious that the bracelet was very old.

"I was right!" he exclaimed. "It *was* her!" He waved the bracelet before Cissy's eyes. "This belongs to Molly; she was here!"

She took it from him and examined it closely. "Who is Molly? This is lovely, we should really try and get it back to her."

Charles Hamilton took a deep breath and forced himself to become calmer. "Cissy, you shouldn't be able to even *see* this," he told her, "and the same with the lamppost; they're both invisible to ordinary people."

Something broke inside Cissy and she yelled, "I don't understand! This is some kind of…of dream. I'll wake up in the morning and…"

"No dream, Cissy." Her father gripped her shoulders gently. "This is all, unfortunately, very real." He pulled her toward him and hugged her briefly. "It also means that you, somehow, are very special, very important in some way I– *we* never expected." He attempted a smile. "Well, I always did say you're my special lady," he joked feebly. Then, becoming serious again, "It also means we have to get out of here, now!"

  *   *   *   *

Logan was worried, more so than he would care to admit. He sat at a table littered with the remains of a long-finished meal and brooded.

For nearly a century now, there had existed an uneasy truce between himself and his brother; both had been severely weakened by the constant battles between them and had needed that time to recover and regroup.

But Morgan had always been the stronger of the two, Logan had to admit. Even as children, it was Morgan who came out on top when they argued and fought, Morgan who was cleverer and more popular, and Morgan, not he, Logan, who had been their father's favorite.

And now Morgan had won again. Impulsively, the Dark Wizard swept an arm across the table. Cups and plates smashed loudly to the floor and wine from a broken flagon trickled across the ground like tiny rivers of blood.

"Why?" he asked, but there was no answer for he was alone. Then louder, "Why?" He slammed a fist on the table and the wood splintered. "Why does he always win?"

Because now Morgan had the boy and if *he* turned out to have the power many predicted, if the boy did indeed fulfill the prophecy, then the next battle might well be the last.

And it had been so close, a matter of a few minutes and he, not that cursed Molly, might have got to the boy first. *Thanks to those two fools who call themselves my servants, the boy is lost to me.* The Dark Wizard had no real confidence they would succeed in kidnapping the girl who could be so useful in luring Luke to him.

Logan thought about his two servants and wondered why he kept them, why he allowed them to live. They had their uses, of course, for small tasks, as spies mostly and the occasional murder of mortals who had unknowingly displeased him. *But set them against anyone with even the tiniest amount of power and they are useless!* At that last thought, Logan slammed his fist down again.

Standing, he paced slowly around the room, thinking about the boy. It was curious, he mused, how power, *great* power, could skip generations so that some were born not knowing or ever finding out they had it, while others were born with such gifts. They could command oceans, the skies, the earth and all the beasts within it.

Morgan had it, as did Logan; he allowed his mind to gloss over the fact that his brother might have more power than him. But since then? Nobody had come close to matching them and he and Morgan had ruled their own realms supreme.

But now there was one who many believed possessed power that would surpass even that of the two brothers. *And Morgan, not I, got to the boy first!* As his anger brewed, Logan took a deep breath and forced himself to think. "What to do, what to do," he muttered to himself.

The boy was out of his reach, he knew that. It would be impossible to even enter Morgan's realm without detection, let alone reach the boy and attempt an abduction.

No, his only chance was the girl; with her in his power, Luke might be tempted to leave his brother's protection and try to reach her.

And it should be a simple enough task to kidnap her, but his servants had already proved themselves adept at failure. *No*, he thought, *I cannot take the risk, I must find someone else for this task. But who?*

He continued to pace and think for a while, then stopped abruptly and smiled. *I wonder…would I really dare?*

Going to a cupboard, he opened a drawer and took out an object: a book, leather-bound and inlaid with silver and gold. He took it to the table and set it down. Opening it at random, he leafed through the ancient pages that rustled between his fingers.

Then he started to read, and as he did so, a plan began to form.

Chapter 7

Fumes from the car's exhaust still hung in the air as the little door swung open and a head peered out cautiously. Seeing the street was deserted, Molly eased herself through and hunted around.

Becoming increasingly anxious as she muttered and cursed, she kept her wand gripped tightly in her hand. She didn't *think* the Dark Wizard's servants would still be about, but she was taking no chances. Eventually though, she was forced to accept the bracelet wasn't there and, returning to the doorway, she passed through once more.

She knew Morgan was right when he'd said it would be invisible to ordinary mortals, those who knew nothing of the parallel world of the Sanctuary. And that must mean someone else had found it, someone with magic.

Molly dropped down into the circular room and closed the door quietly behind her. *And that could be bad news,* she thought to herself. *It could be bleedin' bad news.*

THE SANCTUARY

*   *   *   *

The passageway came to an abrupt end. *Now what?* thought Luke? Aloud, he said, "What happened, did we take a wrong turn?"

"We didn't actually *make* any turns," Morgan pointed out, holding his hands toward the stone. "Wait," he told the boy and, taking out his wand, the wizard slowly traced an outline of a door on the wall before them. As it passed over the stone it left a glittering golden trail and the stone within began to undulate, slowly at first then faster and faster.

Luke stared, entranced as the wall seemed to dissolve into a shimmering, cascading waterfall which splashed silently into the passage and ran away in thin, silver ribbons down the slope. He reached out to touch, but Morgan stopped him with a hand on his arm.

"No, just a few more moments. It is treacherous yet."

The boy watched as the door become paler until it was almost silver and mirror-like; he fancied he could see lights shimmering behind its surface.

"Now,"—Morgan took him by the hand—"step through with me."

Luke hesitated, not relishing a soaking, but the pressure on his hand tightened. As they ducked into the silent torrent, he realized the water, if that's what it was, simply flowed around them, not touching, so they remained completely dry. Then they were through and he looked around in wonder.

He was in a large, oval-shaped room, so big that each end

appeared to recede far into the distance. From the ceiling hung enormous chandeliers, dozens of them, their glass crystals sending prisms of light in all directions, decorating the room with all the colors of the rainbow.

The walls were covered in a rich wallpaper of eggshell blue and the floor was of the same silvery marble as the passageway. Windows reached from floor to ceiling, but these were hidden by curtains of deep blue velvet. Music filled the air and Luke could see musicians with violins and larger stringed instruments. Someone played a small kind of piano – a harpsichord, Luke guessed.

All around him people danced to the music, but how strange they were, Luke thought. The women wore dresses of satin or silk in rich hues of blue, green or red. Some were embroidered with intricately stitched flowers and all had necklines so low that Luke blushed and averted his eyes.

Many of the women had hair styled into short loops that hung to their shoulders, while others favored the older *fontange* style with their hair piled high upon their head and decorated with feathers, jewelry and fruit. Around their necks the women wore precious gems – pearls, rubies and emeralds – and their faces were painted white with vivid streaks of rouge.

The men wore long coats, again of elaborately embroidered silks and velvet, knee length breeches and white stockings. All wore wigs, white, but as with the women, of a multitude of styles; even their faces were heavily made up.

Luke, of course, knew nothing of fashion or hairstyles, but the impression he had was of a riot of color and dazzling extravagance. *It's like some kind of fancy dress ball,* he thought and turned to

Morgan in wonder. "What is this place?" he asked, and Morgan laughed at the boy's wonderment.

"Welcome to the Sanctuary!" he exclaimed. "Or one of them, at least. Come, let me show you around." He took Luke by the arm and led him into the throng of people, introducing him to everyone they passed. There were so many, and the names were so foreign to his ears that Luke forgot them almost instantly, but he noticed that many regarded him with curious stares that lingered long after he had passed.

Then his attention was caught by the figure of a woman across the room who was regarding him with a steady gaze. She was small, yet she appeared to stand out from the others, her hair and dress even more extravagant and her jewels brighter. Everyone else dimmed in comparison. Yet it wasn't this that set her apart, Luke realized. There was a presence about her, so he knew without being told that she was someone of great importance.

"She's beautiful," he breathed softly and, nudging Morgan, he asked, "Who's that?"

Morgan looked to where the boy pointed. "Ah, that," he replied, "is someone you will meet very soon no doubt." Still holding Luke by the arm, he turned him to one side. "Come, let us go out onto the terrace, I want to show you the view."

Luke acquiesced, secretly wondering what kind of view he was going to see in the middle of London in the middle of the night, for he knew it must be well past midnight.

Suddenly he thought of home. "My mum!" he exclaimed, turning to the wizard. "She's gonna be out of her mind, I need to get home!"

"Don't worry," replied the wizard, "I've switched time there." Seeing the boy was about to argue, he said quickly, "All you need to know is that your mother *was* worried when you weren't home by about eleven o'clock,"—his smile was cryptic—"but now in your house it's only eight o'clock and she's washing the dishes and getting ready to watch television." He paused. "After that, well, I'll sort something out." He shrugged but didn't elaborate. "Anyway, come on, let's go outside."

He opened a nearby door and they stepped out. Luke was immediately blinded by sunlight and met with a scene of rolling green countryside and far off mountains. Closer, but still indistinct in the haze, he could see buildings and what looked like a town. *No,* Luke thought, *more like a city.*

"Th– that's…impossible," he stammered. "We're in London, and it's night, and…"

Morgan laughed and placed an affectionate hand on the boy's shoulder. "Welcome to Paris!"

For a moment Luke didn't answer, *couldn't* answer, it was all too much to comprehend and he just stared at the scene before him. Then he was struck by a thought. "That can't be Paris," he said. "Where's the Eiffel Tower?"

Morgan looked at him, impressed. "Well done, Luke, that's sharp, very sharp indeed." He looked at the boy keenly, wanting to gauge his reaction. "There is no Eiffel Tower because…it hasn't been built yet." He turned to the door. "Come back inside, there's a lot of explaining to do and there's someone I'd like you to meet."

*   *   *   *

THE SANCTUARY

As Luke gazed upon Paris, Cissy and her father were arriving back home. Entering the house, Charles shook his head in answer to his wife's questioning look and disappeared upstairs to his study without a word. A moment later, Cissy and her mother heard the door slam and the key turn in the lock.

They sat together for a long time, not speaking, both lost in their own thoughts, until eventually Cissy dozed. Her mother left her like that for a time but then shook her awake and, turning off the lights, they went upstairs to bed.

Outside, the wizard's servants watched the house go dark but remained hidden, silent and watchful, awaiting their master's orders.

Upstairs in his study, Charles Hamilton sat equally silent and still. He was gazing at a small wooden box on the desk in front of him. It was long and narrow, plain and unadorned. On one side was a small keyhole and in it a golden key.

Charles stared at that key for a long time before suddenly coming to a decision. He reached out and muttered several words in a strange language, then turned it.

Slowly, he lifted the lid.

The next day – or rather that same day, for it had been 4:00 am before they'd gone to bed – Cissy awoke to the sound of banging and shouting. She looked at the clock on her wall and saw it was already afternoon.

"Charles," she heard her mother shout, "please at least answer me!"

"What's going on?" Cissy appeared at the door of her bedroom and rubbed her eyes.

"Your bloody father, that's what!" Her mother rounded on her angrily but was immediately contrite. "Sorry, darling, I didn't mean to snap, but it's your dad. He's been in there all night and all day, he's had nothing to eat or drink and he won't even answer me!"

"Do you think he's okay?" asked Cissy. "He might have… collapsed or something."

"Well it is most unlike him to behave this way," admitted her mother, "but I know he's alive at least because I keep hearing him muttering and,"—she hesitated—"chanting."

"Chanting?" replied Cissy, puzzled. "Chanting what?" She bent to peer through the keyhole of the study door but could see nothing. She looked up. "Maybe he's having some kind of breakdown; he was acting really strange last night."

"Strange*ly*," Lucy corrected automatically, then, "I had my ear to the door trying to make it out, but it sounded, I don't know, *foreign.*"

"Dad doesn't speak any foreign languages, does he?"

But her mother shrugged and banged on the door again. "Charles, come out of there!"

This time there was an answer. "What do you want?" came the faint reply.

"A divorce if you don't come out this instant!"

There was silence except for Cissy's shocked, "Mum!"

A few moments later, a chair scraped and the key turned in the lock. When she saw her husband, Lucy Hamilton was sorry she'd been so harsh; he was unshaven and looked haggard and exhausted.

"Oh, Charles," she said putting her arms around him, "what have you been doing?" He didn't answer but held out a hand to Cissy and the three of them embraced for a full minute. Then he stepped away and regarded them.

"Lucy, Cissy, there are…things you don't know about me, things I hoped you'd never need to know." He looked at Cissy. "But now it seems…" He broke off and then, in an attempt at a lighthearted tone, "But first I need a shower!"

An hour later, both he and Cissy had showered and dressed, and a pile of toast and marmalade (a late breakfast, Lucy had explained) had been hastily devoured. Charles Hamilton took his wife and daughter into the living room and sat them down on the settee before pulling up an armchair opposite.

On the table between them sat the narrow wooden box. "What I have to tell you will seem strange, unbelievable." His voice was very serious in a way that Cissy had never heard. "Neither of you have ever seen this box before."

"I have," said Lucy, looking at her husband. "I was in your study, cleaning, and this was on the desk, covered in dust. That was years ago." She turned to her daughter. "Before you were born, dear. I think I was pregnant at the time. Anyway," she spoke again to her husband, "I'd just picked it up to give it a wipe down when your father came into the room and took it from me. He said you shouldn't have left it lying around and that I must never, under any circumstances, open it or even ask what was inside." She smiled. "I thought he was just being silly or trying to be mysterious or something. Or maybe it was the effect of all those drugs he had when he was young."

Cissy interrupted, "Grandad Ben took *drugs*?"

Lucy tutted and tapped Cissy lightly on the arm. "Of course, dear, they all did. Well, it *was* the sixties."

"Anyway," said Charles before his daughter could pursue *that* particular topic, "that's when all this began, in the sixties I mean." He raised both hands to forestall further comment and reached into his pocket, pulling out a piece of crumpled paper, torn and ragged around the edges, but the words, faded with age, were still legible.

Cissy and her mother stared at it curiously. "What is this?" asked Lucy. "The date, 1964, that's a long time ago."

"I know," agreed Charles. "My father was given this around Christmastime that year. Luke's grandfather got one too."

"So, you're telling us that all this…weirdness, Luke disappearing and stuff, is because of some raggedy old leaflet?" Cissy asked.

"Well no, er, yes…well, kind of," Charles stuttered, not quite knowing how to begin his story. "I mean…"

"Charles," Lucy said, putting a soothing hand on his knee, "just start at the beginning and take your time." She nudged Cissy. "We won't interrupt."

He took a deep breath. "Right, well it began on the day before Christmas Eve, 1964." He pointed at the leaflet still in his wife's hands. "My father, Ben, had been working at that clothes shop in Notting Hill; you remember I showed you once, Cissy?"

She nodded. "Yeah, the one that's a McDonald's now. So, Grandad took drugs and sold freaky '60s clothes. What's that got to do with anything?"

"Cissy," her mother chided, "let your dad tell it in his own time, remember?"

Charles gazed sightlessly ahead, remembering. "He told me he was on his way home one night, just before his sixteenth birthday, when a man gave him that leaflet."

"What man? Why?" asked Cissy, forgetting not to interrupt.

With an effort, her father brought himself back to the present. "He was tall, *really* tall, and very thin."

"Yeah, but how does this involve you? I don't get it." Despite herself, Cissy was getting caught up in the story.

He nodded. "Well, your grandad and Luke's were great friends, and remained so all their lives. So Peter and I were often together too; I used to spend a lot of time at their house in Kensington as a child. Sometimes the man would be there." He shuddered involuntarily and lapsed into silence.

By now, the tension in the room was palpable, threatening to engulf them all.

"Then what, Dad?" whispered Cissy. "What happened next?"

"We weren't supposed to notice him, but we did, and to be honest we were a bit scared of him. He was so strange looking. They'd spend hours huddled together behind a locked door; the study, I think. It was as if they were…*plotting*."

Charles reached forward and took the leaflet from his wife. "Nothing happened for years, until Peter and I were sixteen and my father took us both to his study and showed us this leaflet. That's how we met Morgan for the first time. And that's when all this trouble began."

THE SANCTUARY

Chapter 8

Morgan led Luke back inside and into a nearby room. It was small with none of the opulence he had so far observed, containing little more than a simple table and chairs.

"Sit," ordered the wizard, walking over to a cabinet containing bottles of varying sizes and colors. "Drink?"

Luke nodded and sat down; after a moment Morgan joined him, placing the drink on the table.

"Cheers," he toasted, lifting his glass. Luke peered at the liquid in his own then took a sip. He grimaced; it was wine, heavily spiced. He'd been thinking more along the lines of having a Coke.

Morgan smiled, reading his mind almost accurately. "Sorry," he told the boy, "Dr Pepper hasn't been invented yet." Becoming serious he said, "I've a lot to tell you and there may be little time so I would ask that you save your questions until later." He paused and took a long drink then continued, "Alright, Luke, what is the Sanctuary? I'm sure that's what you'd like to know. The more important questions actually should be *where* is it, *when* is it and *why* are you here?"

THE SANCTUARY

He took a deep breath before continuing. "The first thing you have to understand is that you're no longer in your own world." He paused for a reaction but there was none. "There exists a parallel place, well more of a dimension really," he amended. "That's where you are right now." He gestured vaguely around. "And this is the part of that dimension we call the Sanctuary."

He was about to continue when Luke spoke, "Okay, some pretty weird sh…er, stuff has happened tonight and I kinda get the parallel universe idea. Well I *think* I do." He went to a window and drew the curtain to one side, looking out. "But what's it for, this sanctuary? And how come I've never heard of this other dimension? And how have we ended up in Paris when London's, like, a mile down that passageway? And how come we've arrived before the Eiffel Tower is even built?"

"Whoa there." Morgan laughed, holding up his hands in mock surrender. "Which one should I answer first!"

"Perhaps, Luke, I can explain," a soft voice behind him spoke in heavily-accented English. He turned to find the woman he'd seen earlier had slipped into the room so silently he hadn't noticed. "The parallel world Morgan speaks of is a dimension of place and time and there are many entrances to it from your own world." She moved further into the room and stood opposite Luke. Close up she was even more beautiful, thought the boy, her eyes of palest blue mesmerizing as they bored into his.

"Three at least in London, I think." She pronounced it *Lonndern*. "Two that I know of here in Paris, others in Milan, Rome, Moscow, even across the ocean in New York City."

She walked to the cabinet and poured herself a drink. "Most of the big cities have these passageways and they all lead here to the Sanctuary. There are similar ones, although not as many, that lead to the realm of the Dark Wizard, Logan." She paused and raised her glass as if giving a toast. She smiled mischievously and added, "That is, Morgan's brother."

Luke's turned a startled look on the wizard. "Your *brother*? What the hell?"

"Not now, Luke," he said and glanced at the woman. "That was not helpful, Your Majesty," he chided, before speaking rapidly in French, too quickly for Luke to follow.

In English he said, by way of explanation, "Marie has a somewhat playful sense of humor."

Dismissing the subject, Morgan continued, "The passageway we came along and all the others like it are…portals, you might say, between the two worlds. That is to say, between this world inhabited by wizards and witches and other creatures, and your world, Luke, the mortal world."

"And what about all the people here?" Luke gestured. "You and Molly and,"—he looked at the woman—"Marie? Which world are you from? Are you *human*?"

Marie snorted in disgust and Morgan laughed. "Of course we are human!" He rose from the table and opened the door so that music filtered into the room and people could be seen, still dancing.

"Myself, Molly, and a few others are not of your time, Luke, although we are human. But many from the mortal world are born with certain abilities, or powers, if you will. Many live their whole lives without suspecting, while others,"—he swept his arm in a wide gesture—"one way or another find their way here."

He paused to allow the boy time to digest his words, and before he could continue, Marie took up the story.

"There is great evil in the world, Luke," she explained. "Many of the atrocities you hear of on your...televisuals?" She looked at Morgan for confirmation.

He nodded and corrected, "Televisions."

"Yes, of course, your *televisions*." She smiled. "I have never witnessed one myself. Many of those who hold these powers use them for evil, Luke." She turned to the wizard. "Men like your brother, no?"

Seeing the sadness in his eyes, she bent and kissed his cheek, leaving a smear of rouge. "But thank goodness there are people like this man," she told Luke, "and Molly and all those out there who work tirelessly against that evil so that ordinary mortals can live their little lives without ever suspecting the dangers that lurk all around them.

"But *quel imbeciles*!" she exclaimed and nudged Morgan. "Look at the boy, he is dazed with all our prattling!" She laughed delightedly. "He has the look of the, how do you say...the *zombie*?" She took Luke's hand and swung him to his feet. "Come, my friend, you are hungry, no?" She led him back into the large room where there was a table adorned with meat, bread, pastries and a hundred other types of food. Selecting a small cake, she popped it into his mouth.

"Eat," she commanded, "and make yourself at home." With that, she left him and began to mingle with the others; Luke noticed that everyone she passed gave a small bow.

THE SANCTUARY

Looking to the far side of the room, he saw that Molly had returned and was now deep in conversation with Morgan. Selecting another pastry, he took a bite and made his way towards them. Molly looked up at his approach and smiled. "Hello, Luke, how do you like our Sanctuary?" She put an arm around his shoulder. "We've been quite lucky. It seems we've landed smack bang in the 18th century!"

Seeing Luke's puzzled expression, she explained, "The Sanctuary is fluid, it moves around both in time and place. That means when you enter from one of the passages you never quite know where or in what period from history you're gonna land." She winked. "It makes for some great fun, I can tell you!"

"It certainly does," Morgan joined in. "I once arrived and found an enormous Tyrannosaurus Rex!" He took the remaining half of pastry from Luke's fingers and bit into it. "Damn near had my head bitten off!"

Molly tutted and scolded, "Don't be silly, Morgan, the boy has enough to think about without your daft stories."

"Okay." He chuckled. "That wasn't true, but I have met some extraordinarily famous people; the stories I could tell you."

Molly rolled her eyes at Luke in a manner that clearly said 'here we go' as the wizard began to namedrop shamelessly.

"Oscar Wilde – another wizard by the way. Richard the Third, now he was quite a character, nice bloke despite what some people believe. And then there was…" Thankfully he was interrupted by a commotion across the room; there was shouting from outside and people were gathering at the windows, peering out. The three of them hurried over to see what all the fuss was about.

THE SANCTUARY

Outside, trampling across the manicured lawns and approaching rapidly was a large mob, mostly women as far as Luke could see and all armed with weapons of one sort or another. There were shouting "*La mort a la reine!*" – "*Death to the queen!*"

Morgan cursed and raised his voice above the clamor inside the room. "Silence!" The noise subsided instantly. "We must leave, quickly. To the passage, everyone!"

As those around him streamed toward the door, Morgan looked at Marie and raised a questioning eyebrow. "Your Majesty?" he asked softly.

She shook her head sadly. "I cannot, *mon cher*, you know this." For a moment there was a silence between them before he nodded and gave a deep bow.

"Go with God, Your Majesty," he said gravely, then after a further brief pause, he turned and motioned Luke to follow. "Come," he ordered, "quickly."

But Luke hesitated and looked at Marie. "We can't just leave," he objected. "Why aren't you coming with us? That mob, I don't understand why, but if they catch you, they'll kill you! You have to come with us!"

She looked at him and her eyes suddenly brimmed with tears. "Ah, Luke," she whispered softly, "I cannot."

As the boy began to object, she placed a finger to his lips. "Sshh," she said softly, "I cannot, *dare not*, change history." A tear splashed onto her cheek. "If I come with you then yes, I will be safe, but history has ordained a different fate for me."

For a moment Luke didn't respond and Marie saw he still didn't understand. "*Cherie*, think of where you are and when. This is

France, the year 1792, *September* 1792, and think of who I am," she urged. "Think of the history you have learned."

Slowly, comprehension dawned over the boy's face and Marie clapped her hands in delight. "See?" she exclaimed to Morgan. "The penny, it drops at last!"

"Marie Antoinette," Luke breathed. "You're Queen Marie Antoinette!"

"That is correct, Luke, and do not worry, for on this day I escape." She cupped a hand beneath his chin and looked steadily into his eyes. "Today I go to join my family at *Versailles* and then,"—she shrugged and smiled sadly—"history knows our fate."

"But it's wrong! You weren't to blame!" Luke objected, but she shushed him.

"No, Luke, I have not been a good queen to my people, and I learned the folly of my ways too late." She paused as hot, angry tears filled her eyes. She dashed them away. "I have tried in so many small ways to make amends."

"And succeeded, Your Majesty," interrupted Morgan, "but the mob, they are close now."

She nodded and turned to Luke for the last time. "History will record how I failed the people of France, and it is true. But I hope you will think fondly of me once in a while?"

Humbled by her bravery, Luke found he could not answer. Instead he gave a low bow and, taking her hand, placed it to his lips in a clumsy attempt at gallantry. She bent forward to kiss his cheek and the scent of her perfume filled the air around them.

"Now go." She stepped backwards. "You must keep safe; you in particular, Luke." Her voice was urgent. "Your life is more important than any other; the fate of the world, the *entire* world, may rest upon your shoulders."

Then she whirled abruptly and was gone. The boy stared after her for a long moment.

"Luke." Morgan's voice shook him from his reverie and the boy turned and followed him from the room, back out into the passage-between-the-worlds. Luke assumed they would need to retrace their steps, back the way they'd come, but now he saw their way was no longer blocked and the passage stretched onwards and upwards into the gloom.

*   *   *   *

In another place inside that same parallel world, but in the present day and not over two centuries in the past, the Dark Wizard was summoning a demon.

If this were just a story, a tale to frighten young children then this would be a simple matter of throwing some kind of magical powder into a flame, chanting a few words and – Hey Presto! – the demon would appear.

The reality, the Dark Wizard knew, was very different. The incantation was difficult and fraught with risk. One wrong word or one spoken out of sequence and all his efforts might be in vain and no demon would appear. Or worse, you might fetch up the wrong one and there were some that even he, powerful as he was, might fear to bargain with.

But now, after many hours of standing dead still in the cold, dark chamber, he sensed a change in the air, and the room, if it were possible, became even colder. Imperceptibly at first, the darkness receded and slowly a figure materialized before him.

"Welcome, esteemed one," intoned the Dark Wizard gravely, and he sketched an ironic bow. "My thanks for answering my summons so…swiftly." His eyes couldn't quite hide his anger and there were traces of it in his voice. "I began the ritual at dawn, and it is now nearly midnight."

"You are welcome," the demon sneered in reply. "I was tempted, *mighty wizard,* to make your wait even more painful." The demon approached Logan until its face was only inches from his. "It amused me to observe your penance, unable to move, knowing that if you did so your efforts might fail." It grinned evilly. "Your need must be great indeed!"

Logan frowned and he fought to keep his temper. "You owe me, demon!" he snarled. "Have you forgotten your war against my brother in which you begged for my aid?" He gave a derisory snort. "Your memory of that particular debacle must be short!"

The demon seethed. "Be careful, wizard," it warned with a hiss, "I allow you some latitude but do not think you can taunt me thus."

Logan laughed and held up his hands placatingly. "Relax, demon, relax," he said merrily, his voice still containing a hint of mockery. He knew exactly how much latitude he could take with this particular demon. "I didn't waste a whole day in bringing you here in order to argue. I have a task for you, a small favor." He paused dramatically. "Something that will hardly be a problem for a *mighty* being such as yourself."

After a long pause, the demon accepted the peace offering

grudgingly. "Come then, make haste." He looked around the dim chamber with distaste. "I hate this place, this *mortal world*. Tell me what you require so I can grant this favor and return to my own domain."

Logan clapped his hands together. "Excellent!" he exclaimed. "To business then!" From the wooden table he picked up a flagon and poured himself a generous measure then held it toward the demon.

It shook its head impatiently. *He knows a demon cannot consume human drinks,* he thought sourly. *One day, wizard, you will go too far and then I will take great pleasure in bending you to my will.*

The wizard interpreted the smile accurately and grinned. "Sorry," he said, not sounding at all apologetic, "I forgot." He shrugged. "Now let me tell you why I summoned you." *It doesn't do any harm to remind you that you are here at my bidding,* he thought and allowed himself a secret, satisfied smile.

He sat down without inviting his companion to do likewise and swung his feet onto the table. He placed his hands behind his head and looked up at him.

"Now," he said, all mockery and amusement gone from his voice, "there is a girl."

*   *   *   *

It was getting late as Charles Hamilton described to his wife and daughter how his father had taken him and his friend Peter Simpson to Soho Square late one night and left them there. How they'd been met by a tall man, wearing a cloak and a black hat, and how they'd somehow found themselves transported to another time and place. How the man, Morgan, had turned out to be an old and powerful wizard.

It should have sounded ridiculous, a pack of lies, but somehow, to Cissy and Lucy it all sounded very real.

"That was the first of many visits," Charles told them. "Once, twice, often many times each month for the next three years, we would be summoned to the Sanctuary to continue our training."

"You'd get another leaflet, like this one?" Lucy asked, picking up the ragged piece of paper.

"No," replied Charles, "somehow we just knew when we had to be there. We weren't actually told, we could just kind of sense it. Peter and I were always there together, although I always suspected there were times he was summoned when I was not. It quickly became obvious he had more power than me and so he got extra training."

"Power? Training?" Cissy was a little skeptical; this was her dad they were talking about. She adored him but he didn't exactly fit the profile of your average superhero.

"Yeah," Charles continued, "it was exhausting, painful and never-ending." He shuddered at the memory. "In fact, it was absolute hell."

He spent the next two hours describing those difficult times and the rigorous training he and Peter had undergone. He told them how Morgan had worked patiently but in the end, fruitlessly, to teach him the deep and mysterious arts of wizardry. With a hint of embarrassment, he told them how, unlike himself, Peter had taken to it as if he'd been born with a wand in his hand.

"So, I turned out to be quite rubbish at it really." Charles smiled ruefully. "Even Morgan had to admit in the end that he'd made a mistake with me. But Peter showed real talent, right from the start," he reminisced. "He was soon an integral part of a select band of wizards; him, Morgan, Molly and a few others."

"Doing what?" Cissy asked as the image of a bunch of Harry Potters going around waving their wands popped into her head. "Turning people into frogs and stuff?"

"Hardly!" Her father's voice was sharp. "Cissy, this is no joke; there is evil out there that you, most people, cannot…well, you've no idea!"

"Okay, *okay*!" Cissy hadn't really meant to make fun of him, but she was having trouble taking it all in. Twenty-four hours ago, she'd been an ordinary teenage girl who'd just dumped her boyfriend. Now, apparently, she lived in a world inhabited by wizards and witches and magic and goodness knew what else! Eager to make amends, she asked, "What did you and Peter do then?"

"Do?" he echoed. "Well I didn't do anything. In the end, Morgan told me I hadn't made the grade, so to speak. I was told to go home and never to speak of what I'd seen."

"And Peter?" It was Lucy who spoke for the first time in ages; like her daughter she was having difficulty taking it all in.

"Oh, he went from strength to strength and became a very good wizard indeed. He used to tell me things, even though he wasn't supposed to." Charles rose from his seat and went to the window, looking out into the darkness. With his back to them, he went on, "And then one day, about five years after we first met Morgan, he simply disappeared."

THE SANCTUARY

He turned to look at Cissy. "That would be a week, maybe two, after Luke was born." He smiled gently, knowing how worried she was about the lad.

"So that's how Luke's father died," she breathed, taking hold of her mother's hand and gripping it tightly.

Charles Hamilton stared intently at his daughter for a long moment, deciding what to say next. *Morgan won't be happy,* he thought, and then shrugged inwardly, *but I don't care anymore.* He returned to his chair and hung his head for a moment. He looked first at his wife and then his daughter once more.

"Oh no," he replied at last, "Peter isn't dead." His eyes seemed to bore into hers. "He's a prisoner of the Dark Wizard."

Chapter 9

Once again Morgan led Luke and Molly along the passage-between-the-worlds, followed this time by about a dozen others. But not everyone had accompanied them, and many had gone in the opposite direction.

"Where are they going?" Luke whispered to Molly.

"They will take refuge in another time and place until it is safe for them to return again to their own homes. Now hush, don't talk."

Ignoring her, he asked, "But where are their homes?"

She turned to him irritably. "Seventeenth century France; Paris. You've just *been* there! Now be quiet!"

He was silent for a while, digesting her words, and as they traveled quickly along the passage, Luke noticed that every once in a while, faint outlines of doorways appeared then disappeared as they passed.

"What are those?" He nudged Molly, more to annoy her than anything.

She didn't rise to the bait. "Doors."

"Where do they lead?" He persisted, somewhat dangerously. Molly's lips set in a grim line.

She's so moody, he thought, grinning in the dark.

Surprisingly, it was Morgan who answered; there were just the three of them now, the others having silently slipped away, unnoticed by Luke.

"Each door leads to a place where the Sanctuary has given aid at one time or another. That could be anywhere on Earth, perhaps a year ago or one thousand. As you can see by the number of doors, your world has needed our aid many times."

"What kind of aid?"

"The Sanctuary exists to preserve the world of humans, the mortal world if you like, from evil," he explained simply.

"I don't get it. I mean, take that mob back there; they were angry yes, but not exactly evil."

Molly gave a heavy, eloquent sigh, but Morgan placed a hand on her arm.

"Calm yourself, Molly, the boy is new to this." Despite his previous urgency he stopped and faced Luke. "No," he agreed, "not all of them; many are merely dissatisfied with their king and queen. They resent the wealth and opulence in which they live, while they themselves starve. But some," he said, peering intently at the boy, seeking to gauge his reaction, "some were demons."

"Demons!" Luke exclaimed, wondering if he was being made fun of. "You're joking, right?" But another sigh from Molly, and the expression on Morgan's face, told him otherwise. "You're telling me that wars are not caused by people?" The incredulity in his voice was plain.

"Oh, some are, certainly," the wizard admitted, "but not all. The evil in your world doesn't come *entirely* from the human race."

"Right..." Luke was at a loss for what to say next.

"Anyway, it's not just wars," Molly joined in. "There are many forms of evil, Luke. Without the Sanctuary, the human race would have become extinct long ago."

"But, Marie—" He blushed. "I mean the queen, she said she had tried to make amends. Surely, she isn't – or is it *wasn't?* This is so confusing – a demon?"

He heard Morgan snort, then stifle a curse as Molly kicked him in the shin.

"She did make amends, Luke, she performed many acts of kindness, saved many people before she..." Molly stopped abruptly, unwilling to continue.

"Before she was killed," Luke finished for her. And there was silence.

Deciding they had wasted enough time, Morgan hurried them along the passage once more and stopped at a small door similar to the one in the lamppost that Luke had first encountered back in his own world.

"Come on," he ordered, "get through quickly. You first, Molly."

The witch gave him a dark look and sank painfully to her knees. "Can't you make these doors any bleedin' bigger?" she complained, and her head disappeared into the hole. "It's..." She paused as she struggled to squeeze her shoulders through.

She's going to say it's bleeding inconsiderate, thought Luke with a smile.

"Bleedin' inconsiderate!" came the muffled shout from the

other side.

"Serves you right for getting fat," Morgan called back tersely and motioned impatiently for Luke to follow. When they were all through, Morgan closed the door behind him and looked around. "Home," he announced with satisfaction.

Luke looked around and saw they were in a large room filled with modern furniture and lots of paintings on the walls. Some were clearly valuable, but these were mixed up with large black and white photos of famous people and prints of movie posters for films like *Pulp Fiction* and *Casablanca*. Spotlights in the ceiling filled the room with a glow that reflected off the highly-polished wooden floor. On a chrome and glass stand along one wall stood an expensive-looking sound system while on another was a large plasma TV.

"Well, at least we're back in the twenty-first century," said Luke with some relief, "but where are we?"

Morgan smiled at the boy. "Let's have a look, shall we?" He led him toward a perfectly ordinary looking front door which he flung open then stood aside, allowing Luke to pass. "Recognize it?"

Stepping outside, Luke looked around and caught his breath. "We're back in London, aren't we? Isn't this Soho?"

"That's correct," confirmed Morgan. "All the safe places we use throughout the world tend to be known as the Sanctuary because that's exactly what they are; a sanctuary from evil and from our enemies." He looked upwards and pointed at the magnificent Gothic architecture of the building. "But this is the original and the biggest!" He turned proudly to Luke. "This has been my home, all of our homes, for…well, for a very long time. It's where we live,

THE SANCTUARY

eat, sleep. It's where we study and learn and where we train to make ourselves stronger and more powerful against our enemies." Dramatically, he threw his arms into the air in an expansive gesture and cried loudly, "This is the Sanctuary!"

Panting slightly, Morgan lowered his arms and gave the boy a sidelong glance. In a deliberately conversational voice, he said quietly, "It's also where your father came to train; before you were born."

* * * *

Charles's announcement was met with a stunned silence that was eventually broken by Lucy.

"Peter is *alive*?" she exclaimed. "But I don't understand. All these years I thought…I was told!" She looked at him accusingly.

His eyes couldn't quite meet hers. "I was instructed to tell you he was dead," he said, "by Morgan!" He jumped up and paced the room, but quickly sank wearily back into his chair. "Even Peter's wife doesn't know! Morgan said that nobody knew for certain where Peter was being held, and that even if they did, a rescue attempt would be too dangerous!" He shrugged. "Morgan said it would be better for everyone to think Peter was dead, rather than waiting years for a rescue that might never happen."

"And you just accepted that?" Cissy shouted. "You didn't try to do something?" The stress of the last twenty-four hours finally hit her and she was suddenly incandescent with rage. "You just let Luke and his mum think he was dead?"

The look her father gave her was one she'd never seen before, devoid of warmth, and it did more than words could ever have done to quell her rage.

"What could I have done?" he asked sharply. "I didn't– I *don't* have any power, remember? I've no way of finding out where Peter is, let alone trying to rescue him. I can't manage anything beyond a few party tricks at Christmas," he added bitterly. He placed his hand on the box that lay in front of him on the table. "In my hands, this thing is useless."

Cissy's anger diminished as quickly as it had come, and curiosity took over. "What's in there?"

Charles smiled at his beautiful, volatile daughter who now looked like an excited child waiting to open a birthday present.

"Why, it's my old wand," he replied as if it were the most obvious and natural thing in the world. "I thought I'd have to leave it behind, but Morgan insisted I take it; said it might be needed one day." He lifted the lid and added nonchalantly, "Wanna see?"

He laughed at her eager nod and took out the wand, laying it across the palm of his hand. "Don't touch it," he warned, "it might be dangerous in the wrong hands." The wand was about the length of a school ruler and tapered to a point at one end. It was made of a hard, dark, shiny material and the handle was inlaid with intricate patterns of silver and gold.

"It's beautiful." Lucy looked at it in wonder. "Why have you never shown me this?"

He shrugged. "Like I told you, I wasn't allowed to. And anyway, can you imagine the explanations and the lies I'd have had to tell you if I had?"

The wand felt hot in his hand and he moved to put it back into its box, but the air in between felt strangely resistant. Puzzled, he pressed down harder but it wouldn't move.

"What's up?" Cissy had noticed his struggle. "What's it doing?"

"I don't know, it won't seem to let me put it back." As he said this, the wand suddenly rolled – jumped? – from his hand, but before it landed on the table it stopped in mid-air. The three of them stared, open mouthed, as it hovered there for a moment then slowly, like the needle of a compass, began to rotate, first one way then the other.

"What's it doing?" repeated Cissy, and at the sound of her voice the wand spun quickly then stopped with its pointed end facing her. She moved back but almost immediately it rotated again, this time going full circle, pausing slightly as it passed each of them.

"Make it stop, Charles," Lucy pleaded. "I don't like it. It's as if,"—she shuddered—"it's as if it's searching."

"No," argued Cissy excitedly, "don't stop it, I think it *is* searching!" Her face was eager as she leaned forward and stretched out a hand. "I wonder…"

Instantly, the wand shot toward her and she jumped back, startled. Then she looked down as she felt it nestling into her hand and, involuntarily, her fingers closed around it. Cissy immediately had the strange sensation that the wand fitted her hand perfectly and that somehow it had always been her own.

Charles and Lucy Hamilton looked at Cissy in astonishment as she sat rigid and unmoving, the wand gripped so tightly her knuckles were white. Her parents glanced at each other, unaware that within a few short hours their daughter would be lost to them, perhaps forever.

But even if they had known, what could they have done except sacrifice their own lives in a futile attempt to save her? No, better that they didn't know. And anyway, fate had taken a hand.

The future could not be changed.

*   *   *   *

It so happened that as her father was removing the wand from its box, the supposedly ceaseless watch being kept by the Dark Wizard's servants had faltered. For hours they had taken turns peeping through a chink in the curtains, their eyes never leaving the girl. They both knew the terrible price they would pay should she somehow slip through their fingers.

So far, however, nothing out of the ordinary had happened as far as they could tell, and the two men were cold, hungry and bored. Although they couldn't hear a word through the closed window, all the inhabitants had seemed to do all night was talk. So, gradually their vigilance relaxed until it was no more than a cursory glance through the window every minute or two. If the two men could have heard what was being said they'd have been instantly on their guard.

*   *   *   *

"It wanted to find me, I'm sure of it," Cissy said.

Her father thought about this for a moment then nodded. "I think you're right." He leaned forward and took Lucy's hand. "Morgan once told me that mine is an old and powerful family but that the power we have can skip generations. My grandfather had a measure of it, I know that, my father only a little, and I inherited none at all." He looked intently at his daughter. "I think it's been saved for you, Cissy, judging by how that wand sought you out."

"No!" his wife exclaimed. "I won't have it!" She was nearly sobbing with agitation. "If what you told me about Peter is true then she could be in real danger!" She gripped his hand painfully. "We have to protect her!"

Charles prised his fingers gently from her grip. "I agree," he said, "we have to think, work out what's best for her."

"Hel-looo," Cissy interrupted, "I am still here, you know. Don't I get to have an opinion?"

They both looked at her in surprise. "Of course you do, darling," said her father, "but you have to realize the danger you might be in. I believe Morgan will sense the wand has come into your possession and I think he will make contact soon. In the meantime, it might be safer if we all get out of town for a while, make it harder for our enemies to find you."

Lucy objected immediately. "But won't that make it harder for Morgan to find her too?"

He shook his head. "You can't possibly imagine how clever and powerful Morgan really is," he told them. "If he wants to find us, he will." Charles Hamilton didn't add that the same could be said for the Dark Wizard. Suddenly noticing how exhausted they were, he added, "Anyway we can discuss arrangements in the morning." He gestured toward the wand. "Cissy, put that away now, we all need some sleep."

She did so and the wand immediately sank into its velvet cushion inside the box without any hint of resistance. She closed the lid and made to give the box to her father, but he shook his head. "It's yours now, you must keep it close and never let it out of your sight." She nodded and placed the box deep into the pocket of her jeans. Then, in silent accord, the three of them stood, the light was turned off and they went to bed.

*   *   *   *

Neither of the two men outside had seen the box on the table, for it was shielded from view by Charles who had sat opposite his wife and daughter, his back to the window. And they missed the moment when he took out the wand because just as he leaned forward to do so they'd heard a noise and decided to investigate.

"You go around the back that way," one of them had said, "I'll go the other."

They'd each crept silently away to search the large garden at the back of the house. But they never did see what had made the noise, for the demon didn't want them to. By the time the two luckless, some might say hapless, servants returned to the window, their quarry had left the room and the house was in darkness.

*   *   *   *

Tired though she was, Cissy lay on her bed without undressing and let the evening's events run through her mind. She thought about the wand and how it seemed to have a life of its own, how

THE SANCTUARY

it had hovered and spun, then chosen her. She reached down and felt the box through the material of her jeans and wondered if she dared take it out again. But the excitement of the day suddenly caught up with her and she yawned widely, her eyes heavy.

As she drifted off, she was awakened by a noise outside and groggily went to the window to investigate, cupping her hands against the glass and peering out into the night. A giggle sounded behind her. She spun around and her mouth dropped open in shock.

Facing her was a figure, a monster that wasn't human, so huge it had to stoop beneath the ceiling. Its skin was peeling from its body in great suppurating patches, and huge gobs of drool poured from its mouth. Cissy's shocked brain managed to absorb all this in the instant before she let out a long, piercing scream.

Within moments, her parents, who'd been unable to sleep, had dashed across the landing and flung open her bedroom door. But they were too late as, with a maniacal laugh, the demon sprang forward and enveloped Cissy in one putrid, rotting wing before leaping through the window, shattering it into a thousand pieces.

*   *   *   *

At the derelict mansion in Southwark that he called home, the Dark Wizard paced moodily around the garden, lost in thought.

In truth, he might call it home, but only a few of the rooms were livable, the rest having long ago fallen into ruin. But these he maintained in their original Victorian splendor, and they were more than sufficient for his needs.

THE SANCTUARY

The garden was a large jungle of weeds and stunted bushes and trees, for nothing flourished long in this evil place. Logan was oblivious to it as he waited impatiently for news of the girl, and his thoughts turned to his servants.

Maybe I should have them killed, he mused. *They've long outlived their usefulness.* He picked a long-dead rose from a nearby stem and idly plucked off the petals. Aloud he said, "The problem is that good help,"—the word 'good' seemed something of an exaggeration so he amended—"*any* help is so difficult to find these days."

As he picked off each petal in turn, he chanted, "To live, to die." More petals fell to the floor. "Let them live, let them die." Before he could finish, he heard a noise, thus perhaps extending their lives for at least a little longer. There was a pause, then over the crumbling walls leapt the demon. It dropped the girl at the Dark Wizard's feet and gave an ironic bow.

His bad mood gone, Logan dropped the rose and strode toward the house. "Bring her inside," he ordered.

THE SANCTUARY

Chapter 10

His hair was streaked with gray and hung almost to his waist; it looked silver in the moonlight that shone through the barred window of his cell. Despite his long captivity, the man looked younger than his forty-two years, for his spirit still burned brightly and his belief that one day he would be free had never completely faded, even on his darkest days.

Now he sat brooding, sleep eluding him as it often did. *Morgan will come,* the man thought, as he'd done a hundred thousand times before. *One day he will come for me.*

Just then, he heard the key to his cell being turned. He stepped forward, puzzled, wondering who it could be in the middle of the night, for he saw only one soul, his jailer, each evening when his single, meager meal was brought to him. In sixteen years, that pattern had never varied.

The door opened and he stepped back involuntarily. Peter Simpson was no coward but the man before him emanated a palpable aura of evil.

"Well now," crooned the Dark Wizard, "it *has* been a long time, hasn't it? I must say you're looking very well, all things considered." He grinned, displaying a mouth full of unnaturally white teeth. "And you've lost weight, I think. Have you been dieting?"

"What do you want, Logan?" Peter asked sharply, wondering if the wizard had at last grown tired of keeping him alive. "What brings you here after all these years?"

"Tut, tut." Logan wagged a long bony finger in mock admonishment. "So unfriendly!" He laughed and it wasn't a pleasant sound. "I've been concerned about you, Peter. You've been here so long." His eyes shone with malice. "So I've brought you a companion!"

For the first time ,Peter saw the figure of the girl who cowered behind Logan, her arm held tightly in the wizard's grip. She cried out in pain as she was flung roughly into the cell to sprawl on the floor at Peter's feet. He bent to help her, but she shrank away from him in terror.

"Now you can keep each other company," sneered Logan. "You can rot here until you die!" The door slammed shut and the room dimmed as the light from the passage was extinguished. Once again there was only the glow of the moon shining through the tiny barred window to cast dark, vertical shadows across the damp, cold walls.

* * * *

Charles and Lucy Hamilton walked quickly along the deserted streets of central London, their footsteps echoing in the otherwise silent city. It was three in the morning and an hour had passed since they'd stared in horror as the demon smashed through the window, their daughter's screams fading into the distance.

At his wife's hysterical entreaties to do something, Charles had wracked his brains to come up with a plan, discarding one after another as crazy or unmanageable. In reality he knew there was only one thing they could do: they had to find Morgan.

Despite the years since he'd first gone there, Charles knew exactly where to find the Sanctuary for he'd gazed at the ornate, Gothic stonework of its exterior, blackened with London pollution, many times since.

He'd even been inside on a few occasions, for in this world it served as a well-known high street bank. The cubicles, behind which sat expectant cashiers, were made of wood and glass designed to complement the building's ornate plaster walls and ceilings.

It's just a damned bank, thought Charles hopelessly. *It looks a lot different in the other world, in Morgan's world. I don't know if he is even here, let alone whether he'd be able to see me.*

Charles couldn't possibly have known that Morgan was most certainly there, as oblivious to Charles and Lucy's presence as they were to his. By some curious chance, they had arrived at exactly the same time as Morgan had stepped outside the Sanctuary with Luke. There they stood, only a few meters, yet a world, a universe, a *dimension* apart.

So, as Luke stood in bright sunshine, full of delight and wonder at the magical world he now inhabited, Charles and Lucy could see only black, silent windows. Somehow, they knew that shouting for Morgan would do no good and it might attract unwelcome attention. Eventually, defeated and with heavy hearts, they returned home.

* * * *

Smiling to himself in satisfaction, the Dark Wizard returned to his chamber, where the demon awaited him.

"I trust you have no further need for me. I would like to return to my own realm." The demon forced itself to keep his tone respectful for, having been his summoner, only the Dark Wizard could release him. "As I've told you, I dislike your world. I cannot think why you would waste my time on such a simple task."

Logan regarded the demon for a moment and considered finding another reason for keeping it here longer, but then realized he couldn't be bothered. Anyway, he knew this one could be quite unpredictable, and he wasn't entirely certain how dangerous it might be. No, best not to antagonize it too much, and anyway, one never knew when he might need it again. So he thanked the demon solemnly and managed to keep any trace of mockery from his voice. Then he said the words that would release it and slowly the demon faded from view.

As soon as the foul creature had gone, the smile faded from Logan's face as he thought about the girl. He'd expected to feel triumphant at her capture, and at first he had. But there was something about her, something he couldn't quite fathom. She should have been prostrated with fear, ready to bend to his will as he pleased, but he'd felt it might not be that simple.

Oh yes, she'd been terrified, no doubt about that, but he'd also sensed a determination and something else; power? The Dark

Wizard couldn't tell and that worried him.

He'd intended to question the girl, find out as much as he could about the boy Luke. But he'd had the odd feeling that she might not give him the answers he expected. And he'd suddenly been uncomfortably aware of the demon's presence, watching and judging, alert for any sign of weakness. The deeper he dwelt on the problem, the more Logan felt something he hadn't in a very long time: uncertainty.

*   *   *   *

"Keep away from me!" Cissy warned as Peter again moved forward to help her.

Instantly he stopped, holding up his hands to placate her. "It's okay, I just wanted to make sure you weren't hurt," he reassured her gently. "Who are you and how did you manage to land yourself in this God forsaken place?"

She hesitated and looked up at him warily, but there was a kindness in his face that was reassuring, she thought. Abruptly making her decision, she got to her feet and held out a hand.

"Cissy," she announced, "short for Cecelia. Please don't ever call me that, by the way."

He smiled and shook her outstretched hand. "I'm Peter," he replied, "Peter Simpson."

Cissy's jaw dropped.

"Oh my God," she gasped. "Luke's father?" For the first time she noticed his eyes, which were a vivid green – *just like Luke's,* she thought.

THE SANCTUARY

This time it was his turn to gasp. "You know my son?" Despite himself, he gripped her shoulders tightly. "Tell me," he said, "you must *tell* me!"

"Hey," yelled Cissy, "pack it in, that hurts!"

He released her and stepped back, once more holding up his hands.

"Sorry," he said, "I'm really sorry, but you must understand. My son, I've not seen him, not had word of him, in sixteen years, not since he was a newborn baby!" Peter heard the rawness of his voice and turned away for a moment, the pain almost unbearable.

"I…I know," stammered Cissy, tears filling her eyes at the emotion in his voice. "He…he's fine really, but he misses you." She wiped the tears from her cheek. "And he talks about you all the time." She looked at him with sympathy. "But you must understand, he doesn't remember you, doesn't even *know* you."

When he turned back to her, she saw his own eyes were wet.

"My one dream, the only thing that's kept me sane all these years, is the hope, the certainty, that I will see my family again one day." He took a deep breath. "But now, tell me how you know Luke and how you managed to get on the wrong side of that monster out there."

So, Cissy told him all about her and Luke, how he'd gone missing and how she and her father had gone to look for him only to discover he'd been rescued by Morgan and Molly. This prompted lots of exclamations and Peter's hopes soared, now he knew Morgan was involved and had taken Luke under his wing.

Finally, she described how her father had told her and her mother all about his and Peter's youth and about the Sanctuary and how she'd been captured by the demon and brought here to this cold, damp cell.

Cissy didn't mention the wand and how it had chosen her. Although she thought she liked him, and she certainly felt sorry for him, she didn't know Peter yet and some instinct, some inbuilt caution, told her to keep quiet, at least for the moment, and so she said nothing.

Chapter 11

Inside the Sanctuary, Luke was exploring. There seemed to be an enormous number of rooms and he said as much to Molly who'd volunteered to show him round.

"Bedrooms, most of 'em," she explained. "There was a time when a lot of people lived here, though we're a bit thin on the ground right now." A frown clouded her features for a moment. "Many were lost in the last great battle between Morgan and that evil..." She stopped herself just in time and lapsed into a brooding silence.

But she could rarely stay sad or angry for very long and soon her natural good humor returned and they walked on. Molly opened doors as they went, revealing dining rooms and lounges, libraries and rooms with lots of desks that looked to Luke uncomfortably like those at his school.

"Classrooms," Molly confirmed with a smirk. "And this," she announced, flinging open yet another door and standing aside so he could enter, "is your room."

He stepped curiously into a large room dominated by a big

four-poster bed and a huge bookcase on one wall filled with books of all colors and sizes. Some were modern with clean, shiny dust jackets, but others were clearly ancient, their spines cracked and crumbling.

There were two doors at either end of the room. One led to a bathroom, which contained a huge tub with taps and a shower made of that intricate silver colored pipework that was so fashionable a few years ago. Luke's mum had had it installed when she'd had the bathroom at home refurbished last year and she thought it was marvelous, although Luke found it a bit fussy.

He had the feeling though that these pipes were original. *Probably about a hundred years old,* he thought. *Noisy as hell and don't work half the time.* Thinking about his mother had soured his mood for he couldn't help worrying about her, despite Morgan's assurances that she was okay. Pushing his fears to the back of his mind, he entered the other room and found a small study containing more books and a desk upon which sat, Luke was pleased to see, a very modern and up-to-date-looking computer.

I wonder if it has internet, he thought. He turned to ask Molly but stopped as he reflected she might not know what internet was.

"You'll be spending a lot of time in 'ere, Luke," she informed him, "but maybe you've seen enough for now?" He nodded. "Come on then, let's go and find Morgan." She led him back along the corridor and down a narrow staircase he'd not yet seen.

"Shortcut," she explained, "past the kitchens."

They reached the bottom and Luke was about to remark that he'd never be able to find his way around this huge place with all its nooks and crannies when he heard angry shouting. He jumped back, startled, as a small, fat man wearing kitchen whites came charging past, closely followed by a tall, stick-like figure, similarly dressed, brandishing a large, very sharp meat cleaver.

"Come here and face me, you miserable little coward!" he roared as he swept past, pausing slightly to give a breathless *ciao* to the startled boy before continuing his pursuit.

"*Attendere fino a quando non ho le mani su di voi!*" he yelled. "*Stupido idiota!*"

"That's Alessandro, our chef," sighed Molly not looking at all startled. "He's the kindest man in the world, but he's Italian," she said, as if that explained everything.

"Why was he chasing that guy?" asked Luke. "He looked like he was gonna kill him." He glanced worriedly down the corridor. "Shouldn't we, I don't know, warn someone?"

"It's okay." She laughed. "It's a daily occurrence. Hans probably put too much salt in the soufflé or something."

Luke thought for a moment as they continued on their way to find Morgan. "So, there's Alessandro, that's Italian, Hans, that's… German?"

She nodded.

"Okay, then you're from London and Morgan told me he was born in Wales. It seems like there's people here from all over the place." Another thought occurred to him. "And are you all wizards?"

"Well, you've seen how doorways into the Sanctuary exist all around the world, the queen *told* you that, so it stands to reason we'd have quite a mix of people living here." She gave the impression he'd just asked a really stupid question. "And yes, of course we're all wizards; no point in being here otherwise." She glanced sideways at him. "Although I'm a witch, obviously."

Luke ignored the sarcasm and presently they came to the large room where he had first entered the Sanctuary. Morgan was relaxing on a sofa, chatting to a man Luke didn't know. As Luke entered, the man got up and left without introducing himself.

"Ah, Luke!" exclaimed the wizard. "Pizza?" He gestured to a large table where there were half a dozen delicious looking pizzas of all varieties. Luke nodded, took a slice and munched hungrily. His eyes went wide with delight; this had to be the best pizza he'd ever tasted! Morgan gestured for him to sit beside him.

"Now," he said, "what do you think of your room? D'ya like it?"

"It's fine." Luke nodded. "Lots of books." He didn't sound very enthusiastic. "And the computer looks fab. Does it have internet?"

"Of course it does," Morgan replied and he looked quizzically at the boy, "but only for your studies, not for playing games!" He smiled at Luke's look of disappointment. "You'll have plenty of leisure time in the evenings," he said reassuringly. "There's TV, music, lots of records to choose from." He gestured across the room. "You won't be bored."

Records? thought Luke. "Can't I download stuff? You know, like…" He paused, realizing that was probably too much to hope for. "Are there any CDs at least? Any modern music?"

"Er, I think so, somewhere." Morgan gestured vaguely again. "And there's one of those game thingies somewhere. Nexbox or something, I think it's called."

The boy smiled at the wizard's mistake. *He's so living in the seventeenth century or something,* he thought.

Morgan caught the smile but misunderstood it. "That doesn't mean you'll be spending all your time playing games," he warned. "During the day from eight till five you'll be in the classroom, or weapons training when you're not studying. That never varies, seven days a week."

Luke stared at him in horror. "You're joking! That's worse than school!"

"Well, that's how it is," replied the wizard firmly. "You've an awful lot to learn and very little time to do it in." He realized he'd spoken a little harshly. *I must remember how difficult and strange all this must be for him.* He lightened his tone. "And talking of training, did Molly show you the training room? She didn't? Come on then!" He jumped up and strode toward the door, Luke running to keep up.

*   *   *   *

"So why are you still alive?" Cissy could be tactful when she wished but, quite honestly, she didn't think this was the time to be pussyfooting around. "Why does he keep you prisoner? Why hasn't he just *killed* you?"

Peter shrugged and smiled. "You don't think I haven't asked myself that, like a zillion times? The truth is I just don't know; maybe he thinks he might have a use for me one day." His tone was tinged with irony. "Actually, I think it amuses him to keep me alive knowing how desperate Morgan must be to set me free. The sensible thing would be to kill me, of course, but he hasn't. Not yet."

Something else occurred to Cissy. "Why is this Morgan so keen to set you free? I mean, I know he was your friend and everything but, well, sixteen years is a long time." Peter made as if to answer but she went on. "The other thing is that if he's really determined to rescue you, well, why hasn't he? Are you sure he's gonna come?"

"He'll come because he's my friend and because I'm good at what I do." There was no pretense at false modesty. "Very good." Ignoring Cissy's amused look, he continued, "Before I was captured, I was on my way to becoming a very powerful wizard. Oh, not nearly as powerful as Morgan of course, or Logan either, that's why he was able to capture me." He gave a rueful laugh. "But still pretty damn good."

Peter got to his feet and paced around the four walls of the tiny cell. "As for why Morgan hasn't rescued me, the simple answer is that he can't. Powerful though he is, Morgan cannot risk battling the Dark Wizard alone." He ceased his pacing and faced her. "Look, some of the other wizards are very good. There's a woman called Molly, for example; she's a witch not a wizard, and she's very dangerous, though you wouldn't think it to look at her."

Peter let his mind drift back to the early days of his training, when it was all strange and new. He recalled how Molly had looked after him and Charles; how she'd prevented Morgan from getting too impatient when he thought they weren't progressing quickly enough. *Poor Charles had borne the brunt of that of course.* Cissy cleared her throat and brought him back to the present.

"Sorry," he said, "daydreaming, I'm afraid." He sank down beside her. "Anyway, as I was saying, good as some of them are, they're not powerful enough to stand against Logan, so essentially Morgan would be fighting alone. And if he were to be killed, the consequences, for the world I mean, are just too great." As if to contemplate such a thing was simply too much, Peter once again sprang to his feet.

He's very edgy at the moment, she thought. *What's wrong with him?* She watched as he stood under the tiny, barred window set high up in the wall. Abruptly, he bent his knees and, with arms outstretched, he sprang upwards, grasped the bars and pulled himself up. Looking across London, Peter could just make out the tall Gothic towers of the Sanctuary in the middle distance.

So close, so very close, he thought as he'd done many times before. *Soon, Morgan, please, I can't go on much longer.* Dropping down, he turned to Cissy with a sigh.

"And so," he said simply, "I wait."

* * * *

Before Morgan could take Luke to the training room, he was stopped by a man who waited for him by the door, the same one who'd been talking to him earlier. "Morgan, a word, if I may?"

"Sure," he replied and turned to the boy. "Luke, this is Wallace, he will be responsible for much of your training."

Luke regarded the man curiously as they shook hands. His first impression was of the left side of the man's face which was horribly disfigured. The second was how old he looked.

As if to confirm this, Morgan said, "Wallace is one of my oldest, most trusted friends. We spent much of our childhood together.

He's been with me from the start and he has more reason than most to hate my brother." He didn't elaborate further, and the man merely nodded to Luke.

"Wallace is a man of few words, as you will come to realize." Morgan smiled at the boy then turned to the man. "What is it, Wallace?"

"In private, Morgan, if you please."

And, seeing his serious expression, the wizard nodded. Looking across the room he called, "Molly! Would you show Luke the training room while I deal with this?"

As he left, Luke and Molly wound their way along corridors, round corners and up staircases. When they stopped outside two large double doors, Molly pushed them open and motioned him to enter.

It was a large room with windows on all sides so that bright sunshine bathed it with golden streamers and countless millions of dust motes danced within their beams of light. They were at the top of the building and there were skylights made of stained glass so the entire floor was carpeted in a riot of color. There were the usual mats and training equipment; weights, treadmills and rowing machines etc., so it could have been any ordinary gym, anywhere in the world.

What made this one unique, however, were the racks upon each wall, filled with weapons of all descriptions. Fearsome looking swords and spears, chains with spiked iron balls on the end, and myriad others that Luke couldn't even begin to name.

He stepped forward in wonder and lifted one of the swords from its rack, holding it high above his head. As he was about to *swish* it around, Molly removed the sword from his grasp.

"Careful with that," she advised, "it's very sharp and extremely dangerous. Plenty of time to use these when you've had some basic training."

"I wish people would stop treating me like a kid," he grumbled, and Molly smiled.

"Nobody thinks that," she soothed, "but you need to understand that in terms of becoming a wizard, that's very much what you are. You haven't even got going yet!"

"Well, when do I start?" he asked, still a little grumpy, then brightened as he looked at the rows of weapons. "I'm really keen to begin!"

"Tomorrow, I should think," she answered. "Spend today finding your way around, meeting a few people, relaxing, that sort of thing. Then bright and early tomorrow we'll make a start. Not in here though, I'm afraid, you won't be doing any weapons training in the first week. There's lots to learn before that." Seeing his crestfallen look, she winked and added, "The Xbox is in the cabinet beneath the CD player, second drawer down."

When they arrived back downstairs, they were met by a grim-faced Morgan. "Molly, Luke," he said shortly, "a word." There was no one else in the room and once they were seated, he wasted no time. "Luke, do you know a couple called Charles and Lucy Hamilton?"

Luke nodded, surprised. "Yes, their daughter Cissy is my girlfriend." It didn't seem relevant to add that this was no longer technically true. "Why? Has something happened to them?"

"No, but they were here." He waved an arm impatiently. "Not

THE SANCTUARY

here, exactly, but outside the building in their own world, in the middle of the night." He frowned at Luke's puzzled look. "In their own dimension, Luke. Queen Marie *explained* it to you." He looked at the boy and fought to keep the exasperation from his voice. "We always have people in the other world, keeping watch," he explained, "and they were seen. We don't know what they were doing there but it must be serious for Charles to come looking for me, as I suspect he was. I haven't seen or heard from him in, oh, it must be about twenty years."

"You know Mr. Hamilton?" Luke exclaimed.

Morgan held up a hand and Molly took the chance to correct him.

"It's sixteen years, Morgan. Luke was just a baby, remember?"

"Yes, of course," replied the wizard. "Anyway, as I was saying, we don't know why they were here." He glanced at his old friend who understood what he was about to do. She took a deep breath and held it as Morgan continued, "But I rather think it has something to do with your father."

There was a long silence as Luke gaped at him; it was eventually broken by the sound of Molly's breath escaping.

"My father?" Luke managed to say eventually. "But I never knew him, he died when I was a baby!"

Morgan shook his head uncomfortably, finding this very difficult indeed. He'd planned for Molly to be the one to tell the boy.

"No, Luke," he said at last, "your father is very much alive."

Chapter 12

After two days of constant fear, as well as utter boredom, Cissy had decided she'd no choice but to trust Peter. The cell was unbearably hot during the day, but the nights were freezing, and she'd been forced to huddle against him for warmth. *I can't take much more of this,* she thought. *How on earth has he stood it for so long?*

Aloud she asked, "What keeps you going?" Her parched voice croaked. "Apart from seeing Luke again, I mean."

He smiled. "Well that's mostly it really, but I do other things to pass the time as well."

Cissy looked around the bare cell; there wasn't anything *to* do in here. "Like what?"

"Well, every day I count all the bricks, starting on a different wall each time." Seeing her eyes flick automatically to the walls he laughed. "Don't bother, there are 3492."

"Okay." She also laughed. "That's pretty geeky, what else?"

He thought for a moment. "I do exercises, push-ups and sit ups and stuff, different exercises depending on what day of the week it is. And I jog."

"Noooo." She laughed. "You don't really."

"It's true! Although I can't do it for long; I get dizzy."

"No wonder you're thin then," she remarked, "and I thought it was the lack of food." Her voice became serious. "I've got something I need to show you." She reached into her pocket and took out the box. When he saw it, Peter drew a sharp breath for he recognized it immediately; he'd once owned one exactly the same.

"Come over here." He motioned her into the corner, and they crouched, backs to the door. "Open it," he whispered, and Cissy obeyed. When he saw the wand, Peter hissed. "Where the hell did you get this and how'd you get it past Logan without him discovering it? Didn't he search you?"

"No, he didn't," she whispered back. "I don't think he regards me as any kind of threat at all." She picked up the wand and once more felt the sensation of it snuggling into her hand. "As for how I got it, that's easy, my father gave it to me. Well, to be honest it chose me."

He looked surprised at that but then realization dawned. "Of course!" he exclaimed. "Your dad was never, er…that good at being a wizard." He looked apologetic.

"It's okay," she reassured him, "he told me he was rubbish at it."

"Yeah, well…" He shrugged uncomfortably but then looked at her sharply as he registered her words. "You said the wand chose you?" He looked thoughtful. "Judging by how perfectly that wand seems to fit in your hand, I'd say you were right and that means you must be the one in your family that holds the power, not your dad!"

"Yeah, and a fat lot of good that is," she said gloomily. "I haven't a clue how to use it." She looked down at the beautiful object that lay there, inert and useless, then a thought struck her. "But you could," she whispered, grabbing his arm excitedly. "Dad said you'd become a powerful wizard. You could use my wand to get us out of here!"

He smiled sadly and gently removed her hand. "If only it were that simple." He hesitated. "May I hold your wand for a moment?"

She held it out to him. "Go ahead!"

Slowly he reached out and, taking a deep breath, closed his hand around the wand. Instantly there was a shower of sparks and it clattered to the floor as he dropped it, grimacing in pain. Across the palm of his hand there was a long, angry burn.

"See?" he said. "Not that simple. A wand chooses its wizard or witch and from then on it remains loyal to that person. Nobody else can use it and if they try…" He pressed his hand to the cold stone floor in an effort to ease the pain.

"Sorry," she muttered, upset, "you didn't have to show me, you could've just *told* me."

"I needed you to believe me," he explained, "so you can't blame me later on if…if…"

"If Logan comes to kill us," she finished for him. "It's okay, I understand."

There didn't seem to be much to say after that and they remained silent for a while. "What happened to your wand anyway?" she said at last. "Did Logan take it when you were captured?"

"I don't think so," he replied. "I think I'd know if he had it. No, when I knew capture was inevitable, I managed to drop it without being seen. My hope is that Morgan found it and has it safe."

"Well that doesn't help us now, does it? We have a wand-less wizard and a wizard-less wand. Just great."

He smiled and patted her shoulder. "Don't worry, we're not beaten yet, we'll think of something." He moved away from her and started to exercise, grunting and panting. She listened for a while until the noise got on her nerves. Then she put her hands over her ears to block out the sound and lay in a fetal position on the floor, feeling alone and suddenly without hope.

After a while, Peter noticed her and immediately felt guilty. *She's just a girl*, he thought, *a bewildered, frightened girl who's lost her parents, lost everything, and doesn't even know if she'll be alive this time tomorrow.*

He sat down beside her and drew her into his arms. Cissy didn't resist; it felt comforting to have him there. She missed her mum and dad so much. Determined not to cry, she muttered, "Thanks, Peter."

"That's okay," he replied, feeling awkward. "I know this is hard for you, but don't worry, we'll sort this out."

"How?" she asked, moving away slightly. "Got any ideas on how we're gonna get out of here?"

He grinned. "I have actually. I was thinking about it while I was exercising, and I've come up with a bit of a plan."

She grinned back, cheered by his enthusiasm. "We're gonna need more than a bit of a plan, I think, but fire away!"

He punched her arm lightly. "That's better," he said, "got to keep your spirits up. Now, we're going to need that wand of yours."

"Why? I don't have a clue how to use it."

"Because I'm gonna give you a crash course on *how* to use it," he replied, "and then we're going to get the hell out of here."

Cissy regarded him doubtfully but did as he'd asked and removed the wand from its box.

"Good," he applauded. "Now here's the plan."

*   *   *   *

Not too far away, Morgan was also making plans. After his startling disclosure, he had left hurriedly, leaving Molly with the job of explaining everything to Luke, muttering something about 'things to sort out'. He'd spent the rest of that day trying to decide what to do next.

Eventually he'd come up with a rough plan where he, Morgan, would sneak into the mortal world and see Charles Hamilton. He must find out why he and Lucy had tried to seek him out, but it was a plan fraught with danger. One did not go lightly into the mortal world where so many of the Dark Wizard's spies lurked.

Later, he and Molly were just adding the final touches to the plan when Wallace arrived with news that revealed exactly why Charles had come. The Dark Wizard wasn't the only one with a network of spies, and reports had filtered through of the kidnapping of the Hamiltons' daughter.

Wallace was of the opinion that they should do nothing. The time wasn't yet upon them when they could attempt Peter's rescue, he argued, and without his help there was little chance of defeating the Dark Wizard and finding out what he'd done with the girl. Harsh reality though this was, Morgan was inclined to agree, but

THE SANCTUARY

Molly was furious.

"You're a set of bleedin' cowards!" she shouted. "And yes, you, Morgan, are the biggest coward of all!" They were speechless at the force of her anger; she really was magnificent when in full flow and they knew from experience there was no point in arguing back.

"That man did his best to learn how to be a wizard!" she thundered. "It was hardly his fault he turned out to be so…well, so crap at it!" Being angry didn't do anything to make her more tactful either. "Can you imagine how worried sick those people are about their daughter?" She didn't wait for a reply but simply left the room, not even slamming the door behind her. As she left, she turned and looked at each of the wizards in turn. "Shame on you, Morgan," she said, quietly. "Shame on you both."

Luke was so far unaware of these latest developments and the next day he began his training in the classroom as planned. But after Molly's tirade, Morgan decided it was time to seek the boy's opinion.

He is one of us now after all, the wizard reasoned, although once again it would fall to Molly to break the news to the boy. And so Luke found himself sitting, once more, in a room with Morgan, Molly and Wallace, each seeking his opinion on what should be done next. He felt pleased, if a little nervous; he'd never really had adults take him seriously before. He'd taken the news about his father remarkably well and Molly was proud of him. Even so, he was unable to prevent tears forming and he dashed them away angrily.

"Try and leave your emotions out of it," Molly advised. "I know it's hard, love,"—she patted his arm—"but we have to think about the risks involved for everyone if we move against the Dark Wizard just yet."

"And there are rumors he is using demons now. If it's true, that risk is doubled, tripled even," added Wallace glumly, his face set with its usual dour expression.

Luke tried to think logically and without emotion, but all he could see was Cissy being tortured by the Dark Wizard.

"It *is* difficult," he admitted. "I…I love Cissy, you see." His cheeks burned as he said it. "But I do understand when you say it's risky and if you decide to,"—he gulped—"to do nothing, I would understand, truly I would." This admission cost Luke a lot, but to his surprise he realized he meant it. He was already learning to consider the welfare of his companions as a group, rather than individuals.

"But there's one thing you haven't considered," he continued. "What if Cissy is being kept in the same place as my dad? Doesn't it seem logical that Logan might do that?"

The other's looked thoughtful as he continued. "And if he has done that and we attempt a rescue we not only find Cissy, but I get to meet my dad for pretty much the first time!" The emotion in his voice was plain now and Molly had to turn away to hide the tears in her own eyes. "You haven't thought of that, have you?"

Morgan had, in fact, thought of exactly that and knew it could indeed be the case, but he also knew his brother might have killed the girl right away. Peter Simpson was one thing; one didn't waste a valuable wizard on a whim. But the girl was different, she had no power, was no use to Logan at all as far as he could see. He sighed. *But then why kidnap her at all?* he wondered. Frustrated, he scraped his chair back and rose to his feet.

"This is no good," he announced. "I need to think, make a decision. We'll meet here again when I've worked it out.

And with that, Luke had to be satisfied. What would Morgan decide? Luke asked himself the question repeatedly. Would he play safe and protect those within the Sanctuary but leave Cissy in the hands of the Dark Wizard? Or would he go and see her parents, find out what had happened and attempt a rescue? Luke desperately hoped it would be the latter. They could do it; he knew they could!

* * * *

Logan was wondering what to do with the girl. It had seemed such a good idea at the time, but now he wondered if kidnapping her had been wise. The girl's defiant attitude troubled him. He could sense she had power but couldn't see how that was possible. *Oh, not enough to be a danger of course, but even so…*

And then there was the problem of how to let Morgan know he had the girl, because it would all have been pointless unless he could do so, and he could hardly parade her through the streets of London as bait. He stopped suddenly. *Now there was an idea! I could send her out with those two servants, entice Morgan from his lair and if they were killed at the same time…well it would save me a job!*

But then his excitement subsided as quickly as it had risen when he realized that if Morgan managed to get the girl there would be no reason for Luke to leave the Sanctuary and come looking for her. He sighed, as frustrated as his brother was, only a few miles away.

In truth, the Dark Wizard wanted a war. He was tired of coming second to his brother, sick of being the *second* most powerful wizard and, worse, everybody knowing it. He'd been in negotiations with the demons for some time now and everything was nearly in place. Soon he would travel into their realm, a journey not without its own dangers, to make the final arrangements. There would be a war to surpass all others, one that Morgan could not possibly win.

"With the demon army behind me there is no chance my brother will prevail!" Logan spoke aloud as if doing so might make it true. *This Luke might turn out to be powerful,* he thought, *but he's a novice. Morgan cannot possibly get him trained and ready in time.* He grinned in satisfaction, his good humor fully restored. "Ten days," he said, "that's all I need to convince the demons they should side with me, and then…"

Logan allowed himself a few moments to daydream about the time when he would rule this world of humans – sometimes he forgot that he himself was human – without the need to skulk in the shadows, hiding from his saintly brother. He felt his mood becoming sour again as he thought of Morgan and he quickly put him from his mind.

"Servants!" he shouted, and the two men, who never dared be far away, came scurrying in to stand before their master, heads bowed respectfully. "You did well," he told them, "in not allowing the girl to escape." The Dark Wizard would have had a different viewpoint had he known that Cissy possessed a wand and that the two men had missed it entirely. But they didn't know, so neither did Logan, and he was prepared to be benevolent. "But I find I'm tired of her already, so I've decided to grant you a reward."

The two servants looked up in surprise, for not once in all the years they'd served him had he praised them, let alone rewarded them. They waited for the catch, for they knew there must be one.

Logan noticed their doubt and laughed with delight. "Ah," he said jovially, "you suspect I trick you." He rubbed his hands together in a gesture that made him seem even more menacing. "Not at all," he assured them, "I'm pleased, I tell you!"

They simpered and giggled pathetically as they waited to find out what their reward would be.

"I'm going away for a short time, a week or so, and when I return…"—he paused and once again his eyes became hard—"you will kill the girl."

Their eyes widened, first with shock and then dawning delight.

"Actually, you will kill the girl and the wizard," he corrected himself. "I don't care how you do it, your choice entirely, but I want them dead." He wagged a finger at them. "Not until I return, you understand? I don't want any mistakes."

As the full import of his words sank in, the two men grinned, the prospect of murder clearly pleasing to them. As their mouths widened, the Dark Wizard could see into the rotting caverns and he turned away in disgust.

"Now go!" he commanded. "You both bore me." As the two servants hustled quickly from the room, he called after them, "And clean your teeth, they're disgusting!" Logan summoned his spy, a crow, huge with sleek purple feathers, its beady eyes black

THE SANCTUARY

and cruel. "Take a message to my brother," he whispered softly. "Tell him the girl has ten days to live, unless he delivers the boy in return. Tell him an exchange can be made. Immediately, with a loud screech, the crow soared high into the room, then swept out of the window.

Chapter 13

"It's no use!" Cissy threw the wand to the floor in frustration and Peter looked at her in horror.

"Don't *ever* treat your wand like that," he told her sternly. "It won't thank you for it."

"What, like it's alive or something?" she answered back, giving him a look full of hostility. They'd spent most of the last few days sitting in the corner of the cell with Peter trying to show her how to get some kind of response from the wand, without success.

"That's exactly what it is," he replied. "Well, not alive exactly, but it knows what's happening, it knows what you're trying to do." He sighed heavily. "And I keep telling you, it won't respond until you feel at one with it. There has to be harmony between the two of you and treating it like that certainly isn't going to help you achieve it!" He glared back at her with a look that matched her own hostility. "Now pick it up and stop behaving like a spoiled brat!"

That stung but she picked up the wand all the same.

"Sorry," she muttered, unsure whether she was saying it to Peter or to the wand. She knew he was right, that she was behaving badly, but she couldn't help it. At any given time during the last few days she'd been too hot, too cold, scared, bored or frustrated. At the moment it was the latter because try as she might, she could not get the tip of the wand to glow as Peter was trying to teach her to do.

"Now remember, you must clear your mind and allow your command, your desire, to flow through your body." His voice had lost its anger and was once more soft and soothing. "It must flow into your wand without effort or even conscious thought."

"A bit like the Force?" she tried to joke, feeling quickly ashamed of her childish behavior. At his blank look, she explained, "You know, Star Wars, Jedi Knights and all that?" She stretched out her arms in parody, closed her eyes and put on a frown of pretend concentration. In a deep voice meant to sound like Obi-Wan Kenobi, she intoned, "The Force, use the Force, Luke."

The instant the words left her mouth she wanted to bite them back, but it was too late. Her eyes snapped open and she looked at him in alarm.

"I– I'm sorry," she stammered.

The angry look he gave her was now tinged with hurt. "Not only were your parents unable to teach you how to use that," he snapped, jabbing a finger toward the wand, "but it seems they weren't able to teach you any manners either." His voice was heavy with sarcasm as he spat, "What a pity you couldn't just be a *nice* person."

He jumped up abruptly and pulled himself up at the window to look out. Cissy had seen him do this a dozen times over the last few days, but now she ached for him to come back down and talk to her and like her again.

Peter Simpson was angry, but a part of him knew she hadn't really meant to upset him, that it had been just a slip of the tongue, and his anger was at least partially fueled by his fears for her. Cissy's capture had changed everything; he didn't know what the Dark Wizard had in store, but Peter doubted it would be pleasant. He had the feeling neither of them were destined to live much longer and he felt impotent. Cissy had to master her wand, she simply had to! *It's our only chance!* His breathing returned to normal as his anger subsided, then, sighing loudly, he dropped down and went over to her.

"I'm sorry, Peter," she said, standing up to meet him.

"It's okay," he replied. "Now hold out your arm and concentrate, but not too much. Remember, you can't make it happen, you must will it."

She did as he asked, trying to clear her mind and imagine the command flowing through her. For a long moment nothing happened, but then the faintest of glows appeared at the tip of the wand. Cissy was so surprised that her concentration almost broke and the light flickered.

But she regained her composure, trying to remember everything he'd taught her, and the light steadied then became brighter. She glanced at Peter in excitement, then there was a faint popping sound and the wand shone with such intensity it was impossible to look at.

*   *   *   *

THE SANCTUARY

When they met again, Morgan was troubled, wondering how he could repeat the message he had received only that morning. He leaned forward and regarded Luke with his dark, keen eyes.

"You have ten days at most," he said, the words coming out more abruptly than he'd intended; even to his own ears they sounded shocking.

"Ten days!" exclaimed Molly. "You've got to be 'avin a bleedin' laugh, Morgan. Luke can't possibly be ready! And suppose we do manage to rescue the girl. What then? What if Logan really is seeking help from the demons as we suspect?" She paused and gathered her courage. "You need to speak to the warrior queen, Aeryn. Ask her forgiveness."

"No!" The word ripped harshly from Morgan's lips and hung in the air for a moment.

"Yes! Morgan you have to, it's our only chance. Even the demon king would hesitate to join Logan in his war if she were on our side."

"I will not seek her aid! She banished me from her world, remember? The days when we were close are long past!" His face was flushed with anger, but the old regret at his estrangement with Aeryn showed briefly in his eyes.

Centuries ago, a curse had been put on Aeryn's land, in the time when her mother had been queen. The curse had killed her father and decreed that no woman would bear children unless the queen of the land did so. The curse was to last a thousand years.

Soon after, Aeryn had become queen, and as she'd had no husband since then, she'd borne no children. So neither had any other woman in the land, and although they were a long-lived people, the menfolk had gradually dwindled and her proud army, once tens of thousands strong, now numbered fewer than a thousand.

Many from that army had died fighting with Morgan in his old battles with the demons, something Aeryn couldn't forgive him for. Finally, she'd banished him from her world and sealed its borders to all.

Morgan thrust his memories firmly aside and turned once more to the boy. "Luke, there is news, bad news I'm afraid." He repeated the words of the Dark Wizard's spy. There were gasps of horror, but he ignored them. "There is no question of an exchange, so, as I said, you don't have long to be ready."

Molly tried to interrupt again but she was stilled by the pressure of Luke's hand on her arm. He did his best to put aside his shock and fixed his gaze on the wizard's face.

"Ten days for what exactly?"

Morgan shifted uncomfortably in his chair for he knew he was asking the impossible.

"We'll forget all classroom lessons for now," he said, avoiding Molly's angry glare. "The theory of wizardry will just have to wait awhile." He looked at the boy. *So young, so very young.* "You will go straight into the training room where you'll work from dawn till dusk to learn skills that others have months to acquire." He took a deep breath then almost blurted out, "Soon, we move against the Dark Wizard."

"Morgan, no!" cried Molly. "You can't do this," she tried again. "You know it's not possible!"

The old wizard looked at her and she saw his eyes were haunted. "I know," he said bleakly, "but what other choice is there?"

Luke was puzzled. "I don't understand; why me?" There was no reply and he went on, "I mean, you are a great wizard, then there's Molly, Wallace, all the others round the world." He waved a hand vaguely. "Why am I so important? What difference can I make?"

It was Wallace who answered. "There is a prophecy, Luke, that a wizard of unsurpassed power will come one day." His voice had the tone of a teacher giving a lesson. "You are descended from a long line of wizards going back many centuries." He paced the room, hands behind his back. "Your grandfather showed great promise, your father even more so, but sadly…" His voice trailed away as he remembered two of his most promising students and it was Molly who finished.

"It's our hope, Luke, that you may be that one." She looked at Morgan. "But even so, it's not long enough!" Then to Wallace, "Can it be done?"

"Honestly?" He shrugged. "I don't know, but I do agree with Morgan, I think we have to try." He turned to the boy. "Will you do it, Luke?"

The boy nodded emphatically. "To save Cissy? You bet I will!" But then he sobered. "And anyway," he said quietly, "it's not like I have much choice."

"I must warn you now," Morgan told him seriously, "your body will shriek with pain and exhaustion till you beg for it to stop. Wallace is a hard taskmaster and he must be doubly hard on you." He smiled to take the sting from his words. "I also have to mention that you do have a choice, nobody can, and no one would want to, force you to do this." He glanced at Molly who looked at him approvingly. "Luke, you can refuse, walk away, go home and forget all this ever happened. We can attempt the rescue without you."

"Except he'd be in mortal danger from the Dark Wizard," Wallace pointed out bluntly and Morgan was forced to concede.

"Well, yes there is that, but there are protections—"

"I'm not going to refuse, but what are you gonna be doing while I'm enduring all this…torture?"

"I have a few errands to run, lots of preparations to make," Morgan replied. "For a start I have to pay a rather difficult call to Charles and Lucy Hamilton, see what information I can get, and tell them we're doing everything we can to rescue their daughter."

"And my mum!" exclaimed the boy. "Can you visit her? She must be worried by now!"

Morgan laughed. "Your mother is fine, Luke, she knows by now that you are here. She understands the reason, even if she doesn't like it."

"Okay then," said Luke doubtfully. "When do we start?"

"No time like the present," Morgan answered. "Wallace?"

The old man stood and motioned for Luke to do likewise and together they left the room.

There followed days of what Luke would later describe as sheer misery. He rose every day at six am and returned to collapse, exhausted, into his bed after ten pm, only to be shaken roughly awake again after what seemed only minutes. Then he would wash, eat a hasty breakfast and stumble bleary-eyed into the training room, a place he soon learned to detest with a passion.

Wallace was a hard, stern teacher who had little sympathy for weakness or mistakes. He knew he was pushing the boy too hard, but he also knew time was running out. After three days of brutal punishment, Luke was making progress, more than the old wizard would have believed possible. His skill, particularly with the sword, had proved surprising; Wallace could already tell this would be Luke's specialty weapon and that one day he would make a fearsome opponent.

But his abilities were still raw, untested. *Not enough, not nearly enough, and there's just not the time.* Wallace wasn't given to panic but even he was beginning to feel the pressure. He watched the boy practicing his swordplay. *He's good*, he thought, *very good*, but he knew that at his first meeting with an experienced opponent, Luke's defenses would be pierced as easily as opening a tin can.

On the fourth day, Luke was allowed to stay in bed a little longer and, as a result, he rose feeling refreshed and ready to face the day. He ate his usual hurried breakfast then entered the training room with more enthusiasm than he'd had for some time.

However, he soon learned why he'd been allowed a little more sleep, for he found Wallace waiting for him wearing full body armor and holding two swords: his own and Luke's. The safety guards, placed on the blades to avoid nasty injuries, had been removed.

"I hope you've made the most of your extra rest," Wallace told him and there was no hint of friendliness in his voice, only a steely coldness. "Because today we fight for real, and I warn you, allow me inside your guard and I will cut you." He hesitated, not wanting to frighten the boy and affect his ability to fight. *But soon he will be fighting far more difficult opponents than me. The time for play-acting is done.* "The only thing I won't do today is kill you, but soon you'll be meeting enemies who will try to do just that!"

Luke put on his body armor and, as he did, he thought about his opponent. Wallace was a skilled sword master, *no doubt about that*, he mused. He was predominantly right-handed but had the ability to switch hands in the blink of an eye and could fight almost as well with his left. But he didn't move as freely as Luke did; an old wound given to him many years ago caused Wallace's left leg to drag slightly and Luke knew he could use this to his advantage.

Soon he was clad from head to foot in the lightweight but tough body armor, strong enough to turn most blades, yet flexible enough to allow perfect ease of movement. He nodded to Wallace and the wizard threw him his sword. Before long they were circling, testing each other, and then trading blows with an intensity that was new and frightening to the boy.

A dozen times Wallace almost had him backed into a corner, but each time he managed to fight his way free. Another dozen times he found himself on the floor and only his youth and agility saved him from what would have been, had this been a real fight, the killing blow.

But now Wallace was tiring, Luke's confidence surged. *I can win this*, he thought, *I can really do it*, and he launched a ferocious attack of his own that had Wallace backing away and panting heavily.

He's good! The old wizard felt a wave of pride, but soon there was no room in his mind for anything but survival. Now it was

THE SANCTUARY

Luke who held the upper hand and only the experience gained from a hundred fights saved the old man.

And so it went on, the advantage switching from one to the other, but eventually it was his old wound that let Wallace down. Seeing his opponent begin to falter, Luke watched for the drag of his bad leg and when it came, he hooked his foot around it and tripped him to the ground. Instantly Luke was astride him, his sword held a few centimeters from Wallace's throat, his knee pinning his right arm, the one that held his sword.

"I win!" Luke grinned, but Wallace didn't answer directly.

Instead he smiled and panted, "That was well done, my boy." Luke felt proud until Wallace continued, "But look down."

He did so and saw that Wallace held a small but wickedly sharp knife to his groin.

"Get off me, boy," he panted. "Yes, yes, you win. But we would have both died," he said. "You must be ever mindful of treachery from your enemy." He got to his feet and held out a hand to help the boy up. "But that was a good fight and you beat me fair and square."

They were interrupted by the sound of a slow hand-clap and they turned to see Morgan striding into the room. "I trust there'll be none of that *I win* business with a real opponent, Luke." The wizard beamed at him in delight. "When you get the chance to kill your opponent, just kill him!"

Luke grinned, pleased at their praise. "Do you think I'm ready then? To help rescue Cissy, I mean?"

"Hey, slow down." Morgan held up his hands and laughed at the boy's eager look. "We said ten days, remember?" Seeing Luke's

THE SANCTUARY

disappointment, he added, "You're doing really well, better than anyone could have expected but your training isn't yet finished. Go have some lunch now and meet me in the lounge afterwards; I have a gift for you."

Chapter 14

The moment Luke left, Morgan went on an errand. He walked hurriedly along the passage-between-the-worlds, popped his head out of the lamp post door and looked around, alert for any sign of the Dark Wizard's servants.

Seeing none, he squeezed himself through and looked at the busy scene before him. The Old Kent Road was crowded with cars and buses, people hurrying and scurrying at great speed. The noise was deafening after the hushed atmosphere of the Sanctuary. He was an unusual figure as he weaved along the crowded pavement, unnaturally tall, his black hat adding to his height and his long, black coat swirling in the wind that gusted strongly from the west.

But to mortals he was invisible unless he wanted them to see him. Only those who served Logan would be aware of his presence and he kept a wary eye out for any hint of danger. The door he had chosen, the same one Molly and Luke had escaped into a few days before, was not too far from where Charles and Lucy Hamilton lived. Nevertheless, he wouldn't relax until he'd returned to it and was once again in the safety of his own world.

When he reached the garden of 23 Magnolia Avenue, Morgan slipped inside and surveyed the house cautiously. His acute hearing could clearly make out the voices of a man and a woman inside. They were arguing, as they had for most of the last few days, their worry for Cissy making them fractious. Lucy blamed her husband for not doing something to find their daughter and Charles blamed her for not understanding there was nothing he could do.

Shaking his head sadly, Morgan cast a last look around and, seeing no sign of danger, he left his hiding place, strode boldly up the path and rang the doorbell. The voices inside fell silent, footsteps sounded, then the door opened. Ignoring the look of amazement on the face of Charles Hamilton, he brushed past and brusquely told him to shut the door. Striding into the kitchen, Morgan held out a hand to an equally surprised Lucy, who just stood there.

"Hi, I'm Morgan. We have met, long time ago, but you won't, er…remember me." There was no reply from Lucy who continued to stand there, open mouthed, as Morgan sat at the kitchen table. "A cup of tea would be lovely, Charles; you remember how I like it?" The wizard smiled at him reassuringly.

As her husband proceeded dumbly to switch on the kettle and ready the cups, Lucy's mind cleared and she said in a rather halting voice, "You…you're Morgan, the wizard, the one Charles told me about."

He nodded. "Yes, I know!" He grinned but then realized perhaps now wasn't the time to be flippant. "How do you do?" Again, he stuck out a hand and this time she shook it weakly. Meanwhile,

Charles had finished making the drinks and he put them on the table.

"Cissy," he said warily, "you wouldn't be here if you didn't have news of Cissy." Charles Hamilton looked bravely into the eyes of the wizard and said the hardest thing he'd ever had to say in his life. "Is she, you know, is she…dead?" He leaned forward and clutched at Morgan's sleeve. "We have to know."

Morgan looked at him in horror as the magnitude of their anguish dawned on him. He should have come sooner, much sooner.

"No," he said gently, taking a sip of his drink and managing not to grimace because Charles had put both tea and coffee into the cup. "There's no reason to think that." *Not yet,* his mind quailed at the thought. "But I do know where she is." He looked at them both. "And that's why I've come."

The news that he thought she was still alive sent waves of relief flooding through them.

"Where is she? Who took her?" asked Lucy almost inaudibly, and he steeled himself to reply, to tell them the one thing that would once again fill them with terror.

"She," he began, not wanting to say the words, "She's the prisoner of…"

"The Dark Wizard," finished Charles tonelessly.

Morgan nodded. "Yes, and that's why I need you to tell me everything that happened."

"Who is this…this Dark Wizard?" asked Lucy. "Is all this connected to that wand of yours?"

Morgan looked at her sharply, then at Charles who said, "He's called Logan, a very bad wizard indeed. In fact, the evilest son of a bitch you could ever wish to meet." The words sounded incongruous coming from his lips, for he didn't often swear. "Or not wish to meet, I should say."

But Morgan wasn't listening. "You told her about your wand?" he asked, and despite the sympathy he felt for them, his voice was cold. "She *knows*?"

Charles shrugged defiantly. "There was no choice, Morgan," and he related how he and Cissy had gone looking for Luke and found the doorway in the lamp post and how Cissy had been able to see it.

The wizard nodded slowly. "Go on," he said quietly, and Charles described how he'd finally shown them the wand and how it had rejected him and chose her.

"I see," said the wizard as his mind swirled with a dozen possibilities.

"Oh, I nearly forgot!" Charles jumped up and opened a kitchen drawer. "We found this, and Cissy could see it too. It's Molly's, isn't it?"

Morgan took the bracelet and nodded. "Yes, it's Molly's. You say Cissy was able to see this and the door to the other world?"

Charles nodded. "What does it all mean, Morgan? What's going on? Why would Logan want to take our daughter?"

The wizard hesitated. "I don't know," he lied at last, "but if you're right about the wand choosing her it means she must have some kind of power, and that's something no one suspected."

"No one except perhaps this Dark Wizard," said Lucy shrewdly, and they both looked at her in silence for really, what was there to say?

Cissy's mother, ever the practical sort, stood and threw the contents of their cups down the sink and made fresh drinks, this time containing only tea.

"So, what do we do next?" she demanded. "You're the one with the most power, Charles told me that, so if this Logan does have Cissy, you can go get her back, right?"

"I'm afraid it's not that simple," he began, holding up a hand as she tried to interrupt. "Tell me what happened when your daughter was kidnapped."

Lucy shuddered. "It was horrible. Its skin was…it was so…" She lapsed into silence.

"It was a demon, Morgan," her husband went on, "a goddamn *demon*!"

The wizard nodded and somehow it didn't come as a surprise. "I see," he said quietly. "There have been rumors that he is using demons." He looked at the distressed woman. "That's why it isn't so simple."

He stood abruptly and made toward the door. "I'll be in touch," he declared, the door already open before he realized that maybe this wasn't quite the way to leave things. He crossed the room and gripped Lucy's shoulders with his big bony hands. "I'm going to do everything, and I mean *everything*, in my power to bring Cissy back safely." His reassuring gaze seemed to reach right into her, and she read the honesty there. Charles Hamilton was already putting on his coat and Morgan turned to him. "What are you doing, Charles?"

"I'm coming with you," he replied fiercely. "This is my daughter we're talking about!"

"And leave your wife here alone?" The wizard's voice was still quiet. "And what, truthfully, could you do?" Morgan shrugged. "To put it bluntly, Charles, you were never any great shakes as a wizard, now take off your coat."

Shoulders slumped, Charles Hamilton did as he was told, and Morgan felt very sorry for him. "This isn't some macho thing, Charles. Some of us are born to be wizards and some are not; we have no choice in the matter." He turned to Lucy. "Your husband is a fine man," he told her. "He's a wonderful father and has an integrity and honesty that's rare these days." He smiled. "But then I'm sure I don't need to tell you that."

"You don't," she replied simply as she moved to her husband's side, "and I'm very proud of him. I know he'd do anything, *anything at all*, to protect us."

Morgan nodded but didn't reply. He gripped Charles's hand briefly and then he was gone.

THE SANCTUARY

Chapter 15

After wolfing down his lunch in record time, Luke was disappointed to find Morgan had gone out somewhere. He waited impatiently for his return until, at last, he rejoined the wizard, along with Molly and Wallace, eager to find out what the mysterious gift would be. A small narrow box had been placed on the table and without delay Morgan ordered him to open it.

When he saw what the box contained, Luke realized immediately what it was, and he reached forward eagerly.

"Slowly," cautioned Morgan, "the wand has to accept you. Just place your hand over it, but don't touch until I tell you."

The boy did as he was asked. Morgan held his breath and, glancing at the others, saw they were doing the same. The wand should accept Luke for it had been crafted with wood from the same centuries old tree as that of his father's. But if it rejected him the boy would receive one hell of a painful shock and, worse than that, their hopes that he was the one who fulfilled the prophecy, the wizard who surpassed all others, would be dashed.

Morgan could put off the moment no longer and he nodded

THE SANCTUARY

at Luke who hesitated only a little before he lifted the wand and allowed his fingers to close around it. Three breaths sighed heavily with relief as it nestled into his hand, in the same manner that Cissy's own wand had a few nights ago.

"Well done, Luke." Molly beamed at him and slapped him on the back. "You're truly one of us now!"

Luke grinned. "When do I learn how to use it?"

"Tomorrow," Morgan answered. "Back to the training room for today; some of those moves of yours are still a bit rusty." He smiled at the boy. "Molly will begin her instruction in the morning."

So now Luke's day was now split into two. In the afternoon, his training with Wallace continued and since his 'victory' over the old wizard he found himself looking forward to it. Wallace was right, Luke would soon be a fearsome opponent. But the mornings spent with Molly didn't go nearly so well because, never the most patient of people, she became increasingly frustrated at his lack of progress. No matter how hard he tried, he couldn't get a spark of life from his wand. It lay inert in his hand, beautiful but useless. Unknown to him, only a few miles distant, Cissy had recently been having the same problem.

"Come on, Luke!" Molly exclaimed for the dozenth time that morning. "Try harder!"

"I *am* trying and losing your temper isn't gonna help!"

"Well you're not trying bleedin' hard enough and if you think this is me losing my temper, you wait till I really lose it!"

And so the angry exchanges continued until finally she stormed out of the room, slamming the door violently behind her. A short time later, Morgan found her in her rooms, pacing around, lifting objects and putting them down again and muttering irritably to herself.

"What are you doing?" he inquired mildly and received a cold glare in return.

"These bleedin' things," she said, pointing to a long row of ornaments that decorated the windowsill. "I can't seem to get 'em lined up properly." She lifted another then banged it down in exactly the same position. "It bothers me when they aren't lined up properly."

Morgan smiled and sat down. "Well calm down, I've something that should cheer you up."

"Oh yeah, what is it?" Her tone was still unfriendly, but she sat anyway.

Morgan took an object from his pocket and handed it to her.

"My bracelet!" she exclaimed, her annoyance completely forgotten and a beaming smile on her face. "Where did you get it?"

"From Charles Hamilton." He hesitated, "His daughter Cissy found it." The wizard paused to let his words sink in.

"That's great!" she began, but then her brain caught up. "But she shouldn't…"

"Have been able to see it?" Morgan finished for her and she looked at him with a troubled expression. "You're having difficulty with Luke, aren't you?" he side-tracked, and she nodded soberly.

"He just can't seem to get the hang of his wand." She hesitated, knowing he wouldn't want to hear her next words. "It should be easy for him if he really is the one." She shrugged helplessly. "Look how well he's taken to the fighting. He's as good if not better than Wallace already." She took a deep breath. "Morgan, I'm not convinced Luke's gonna be the one who fulfills the prophecy."

There, she'd said it at last, and she felt relieved for she'd been dreading this moment. She knew Morgan had been pinning his hopes on the boy. If Logan were to form an alliance with the demons as was rumored, they'd have no chance, not without the power they'd hoped the boy would bring.

But to her surprise, Morgan nodded. "I agree, but we have to give him a chance. Anyway, there are things I have to tell you." He told her of his visit to the Hamilton's, about Cissy and how her father's wand had chosen her and how she'd been abducted. Molly sucked in a sharp breath.

"So, it's true!" she exclaimed. "Logan is using demons!"

Morgan nodded irritably. "But that's not the point right now, Molly, you're not concentrating!" Before she could answer he went on, "All this time we've been assuming that because Peter was such a talented wizard, his son would turn out even better and be the one who fulfills the prophecy, right?"

"Yeah, go on." Molly still didn't understand what he was trying to say. "Luke might still be the one, maybe he just needs time. As you say, Peter was a very good wizard himself."

Morgan gave a snort of irritation. "But we've completely discounted Charles, haven't we? Because he showed no talent as a wizard himself, we've totally overlooked his family!"

Comprehension dawned over the old witch. "But Charles's *father* had power. Him and Peter's father were a formidable team in their day." She looked at Morgan excitedly. "And power can skip generations."

"What if it isn't Luke?" His eyes were shining. "What if *Cissy* has inherited the prophecy?"

"But Luke is such a good fighter, it must be him," argued Molly.

But Morgan countered, "I agree it's unusual, but anyone can become adept with weapons given time. Only a few can ever master a wand, and Luke has showed no aptitude at all so far."

"Yeah, but we only have her father's word for the wand choosing Cissy! I'm not suggesting he was lying or anything, but proud parents are not always the best judge."

And so it went on until Morgan finally held up a hand in frustration.

"This is no good, we need action not arguments. We have to rescue Cissy in the next few days anyway."

She nodded her assent.

"Good, round everyone up, Molly, and let's get this mess sorted."

Chapter 16

A few miles away across London, Cissy was getting to grips with her wand. She was already able to perform small feats of magic with increasing confidence and Peter was pleased with her progress.

"I think you realize now what I meant by being at one with your wand," he said, and she nodded. Already it was like a part of her arm, an extension almost, and she found she liked the feeling of power it gave her.

Now Cissy and Peter waited with a mixture of excitement and trepidation for the cell door to open. They hadn't planned to make their move yet because Peter felt she needed more time to master her wand and, eager as she was to leave that damp, dark place, she knew he was right. They were both confident that soon she would be able to deal with the Dark Wizard's two servants and, as far as Peter could tell, they were the only two in the building. He'd never seen any others, not in all the years he'd been there. Nobody except for the Dark Wizard himself of course, and that was the problem, for they would have to overcome the servants and escape before Logan could intervene. If he became aware of the attempt, it would surely fail.

Eventually, they were handed the most incredible piece of luck, quite literally a lifeline. An hour earlier, they'd heard horses' hooves on the cobbles of the yard outside and, pulling himself up at the window, Peter had been just in time to see a gleaming black carriage, pulled by two magnificent black stallions, sweep out of the gate.

He had witnessed this scene many times and knew exactly whom that carriage contained. He dropped down and whispered, "That's Logan, he's gone out!" His excitement was infectious, and they hugged each other gleefully. "We have to act quickly, tonight," Peter continued. "We don't know when he'll return."

In fact, the Dark Wizard would be gone for many days, for he went to meet with the Demon King, a journey fraught with dangers, and he did not know when he would return. But the two prisoners could not know this, and Peter looked through the window anxiously to check the position of the moon.

"One of the servants will bring our meal anytime now; it's almost six o'clock." He glanced at her. "Are you ready?"

She nodded. "As ready as I'll ever…"

"Sshh," Peter cautioned suddenly, "someone's coming." And sure enough there was the sound of approaching footsteps then a key turning in the lock. They stood tense and alert as the door swung open.

Cissy concentrated harder than she'd ever done before and as soon as the servant appeared, she sent a lightning bolt flying toward him. It should have taken his head off, but with the reactions of a cat he moved in the nick of time. But the bolt did just enough, and he gave a shriek of pain, clutching the side of his head where his ear had been a moment earlier, blood seeping through his fingers.

He gave a howl of protest, but they were already running for the door. Peter shoved him roughly aside and in moments they were up the passageway and out of sight round the bend. They found themselves in a small, circular lobby with six closed doors. Cissy hesitated, unsure which one she'd been brought through after her capture.

"I don't know which one," she hissed. "It was dark, and I was scared." She looked helplessly at Peter. "I can't remember!"

"Think," he urged, "and quickly!" Already the servant had picked himself up and was stumbling along the passageway in pursuit. Suddenly Cissy had an inspiration; she held her wand pointed loosely forward and forced an image of an open door into her mind. The wand turned in her hand and pointed at the door immediately to her right.

"Come on!" She grabbed his arm and pulled him through just as the servant, his face now a bloody mask, appeared round the bend. She slammed the door in his face, but their troubles weren't over for they were immediately confronted by the other of Logan's servants.

"Quickly!" This time it was Peter who pulled them through yet another door and, by a stroke of good fortune, they found themselves in the large, black-and-white-floored entrance hall of the old mansion. Mercifully, the big wooden doors were unlocked and within moments they were in the yard outside.

"The gates!" yelled Cissy. "We never thought about the gates!"

She could have cried in frustration.

"Blast them!" Peter yelled back. Cissy raised her wand and in no time, the gates were a tangled heap of wrought iron and rubble. Seconds later, the two companions were into the street beyond and running for their lives.

As they ran, they were watched by a hundred wary eyes from behind the dark windows of the houses that lined the street, but nobody tried to stop them. From a nearby rooftop they were observed by the Dark Wizard's spy, returning from delivering its message to Morgan. Seeing the two fugitives pass below, it gave a loud squawk and rose gracefully into the sky until the whole of London lay beneath. Then it soared and wheeled for a few moments, searching.

When it spied what it was looking for, it swooped downward, picking up speed as its wings brushed rooftops and chimneys before it swept into the open window of the black carriage, alighting onto the Dark Wizard's shoulder. At the news, the carriage swung around, so violently that it teetered on two wheels for a long moment, its side almost brushing the ground. Then it righted itself and hurtled back in the direction it had come, towards the old mansion where his two fearful servants waited.

"Where are we going?" panted Cissy as she ran at full speed to keep up with Peter's long strides. "This sanctuary you've told me about?"

"Yes, but not from this world. Now stop talking and run."

But she could go no further and she tugged at his sleeve. As they stood taking great gulps of air she gasped, "What do you mean not from this world? Why not?"

"It's too far, about five miles," he grunted in reply, "the other side of London nearly. We can't possibly run all that way without being caught." He looked fearfully behind as if he expected hordes of their enemies to bear down upon them. "But there's a shortcut, a doorway into the mortal world. It's only about a mile away, at the end of an old alley. If we can reach it and get through, I know where there's an entry into the Sanctuary. We can reach in no time."

"Won't we be followed?"

"I don't know, we might be, but we have to try. Now, are you ready to go on?"

She wasn't but she made no reply and was about to set off again when he put a warning hand on her shoulder.

"Listen," he cautioned.

Faintly to start with but rapidly getting louder there was the unmistakable sound of hooves and the clatter of carriage wheels.

"It's Logan!" he cried. "Someone must have warned him of our escape. Hurry!" Spurred on by their terror, they ran even faster than before. Twisting and turning, Peter led them through the back streets of the city while the sound of the Dark Wizard's pursuit became louder with every second.

At last they turned into a narrow alleyway and Cissy stared in dismay.

"Peter, it's a dead end!" And sure enough, only a few dozen meters away, they were faced with a high brick wall blocking their way. But he kept on running, half dragging her now. She was so exhausted.

"Come on!" he urged. "Keep going!" And as he spoke the

THE SANCTUARY

gleaming black carriage careered into the alley behind them, gaining rapidly.

But now she saw that in the very middle of the wall was a shuttered window, and as they approached it the shutters opened wide, welcoming them.

"Jump!" cried Peter, and as the hot breath of the horses washed over them, they leaped upwards, hand in hand, with all their strength. It was as if something magical aided them and they just managed to clear the window ledge and disappear into the world beyond. But still they weren't safe as moments later the two black horses crouched back on their haunches and sprang forward in pursuit.

As the horses landed inside the mortal world, one of them stumbled and fell, dragging its companion down in a tangle of legs and hooves and harnesses. It gave Cissy and Peter the chance they needed, and by the time Logan could continue the chase, they'd already reached the lamp post that led to the passage-between-the-worlds.

Frantically, Peter shouted hurried instructions into Cissy's ear. She waved her wand at the tiny doorway then he bundled her through. As soon as she was out of sight, he turned to find the Dark Wizard approaching, wand held aloft, his servants close behind.

Chapter 17

In the lounge of the Sanctuary, Luke, Wallace and Alessandro, who as usual had supplied them with too much food, listened as Morgan and Molly explained their plan for rescuing Cissy.

Morgan cleared his throat. "It's almost a week since we last met and, in that time, Luke has made more progress than any of us expected." He smiled at the boy who blushed. Molly winked to show him they were friends again, their argument forgotten.

"It's true you haven't done as well with your wand as we might have hoped, but as a fighter you've excelled." This time it was Wallace who nodded proudly.

Morgan looked at their expectant faces, knowing what they hoped to hear.

"We can delay no longer," his said, his voice low and hushed. "It is my intention to announce a call to arms across the entire wizard world. I am not hopeful that any will be in a position to answer and we must prepare to fight alone. Either way, a few nights from now we will attempt the rescue, as soon as darkness descends."

He studied the faces of his companions. Wallace, solid

and reliable, clearly approving; Molly wearing a broad smile; Alessandro, his face troubled but trying valiantly to hide it. And as for Luke, the boy's eyes were shining at the thought of battle, of finally doing something.

"Whether aid arrives or not, we must act fast. We can be sure that when the call goes out, the Dark Wizard's spies will quickly hear of it. The less time Logan has to prepare, the bigger our advantage will be."

The small group stirred, already thinking about their preparations. "Alessandro, we will need provisions and lots of them." The young chef nodded and stood up. "Wallace, weapons and body armor must be prepared for any who arrive to aid us." He needn't have spoken, for the old wizard gave him a look that clearly said he'd done this a hundred times before. "And, Luke, I think it might be best..."

He was interrupted by a loud, frantic hammering from across the room. Someone was in the passage-between-the-worlds. Wand ready, Morgan strode over and flung it open.

To their amazement, someone fell headlong into the room and sprawled onto the floor at Morgan's feet. Three wands were immediately drawn against this stranger who had invaded their world, but Luke lay a warning hand on each of their arms in turn for he knew who the stranger was.

He stared in shock at the newcomer. "Cissy," he breathed.

"Come on!" Cissy screamed. "Peter is outside with the Dark Wizard and he needs your help!"

Without delay, Morgan rushed out of the room, followed by Molly and Wallace. Luke followed, throwing a last, astonished glance at Cissy as he rushed past her.

"Stay here, you'll be safe!" he called to her before he disappeared out of sight.

Joining the others, Luke quickly donned his body armor, grateful for the hours of practice that meant it took only seconds. He quickly lifted his sword from the rack and saw that Wallace had done the same. Morgan and Molly selected no weapon though, armed with only their wands.

Luke noticed Morgan take something from a drawer and quickly secret it within the folds of his robe, but there was no time to wonder what it might be.

"This way," ordered the wizard, pointing his wand at the only piece of completely bare wall in the entire room. He chanted words in the same language Luke had heard him use before, outside in the passage-between-the-worlds, and instantly the wall parted like a pair of curtains, leaving a narrow gap through which they could pass.

On the other side was a staircase that, to Luke's surprise, led upwards. *We're already on the top floor,* he thought. *This must lead to the roof.* Morgan had already charged up to yet another door which swung outward at his command and he passed quickly through. As Luke and the others appeared beside him, the boy had only a moment to realize that they weren't on the roof at all but back on the street in his own world. But his surprise was fleeting and replaced immediately with absolute horror as he was confronted by the nightmarish, apocalyptic scene before him.

There were ruined cars everywhere, some overturned, many burning fiercely, shop windows smashed, and the street awash with a sea of broken glass. Nearby, a bus lay on its side, its passengers trying desperately to climb out. Some had managed to do so and were staggering aimlessly around, dazed and bleeding. Many others were still inside but they didn't move. Overriding everything was the acrid stink of petrol and burning rubber.

And amidst it all, there was a solitary figure just visible through the smoke, whirling frantically as he fought to dodge the storm of lightning bolts that rained down from the three men who surrounded him.

"Peter," breathed Morgan. "Help him!"

The Dark Wizard gave a satisfied smirk when he saw his brother. He sent a bolt of lightning hurtling towards him, but Morgan deflected it with ease then took out the object he'd hidden minutes earlier.

"Peter, catch!" He sent it sailing through the air and Peter caught it deftly. For the first time in many years, wand and wizard were reunited.

Logan's servants were dismayed as three against one in their favor suddenly became five against three, and they paused to look to their master for instruction. The brief distraction gave Peter the time he needed to send a bolt of his own and one of the servants sat down suddenly, staring with a look of comical surprise at the gaping hole in his chest. A moment later he toppled over, dead.

The remaining servant gave a howl of anguish and redoubled his attack against Peter who, despite being the far more skilled of the two, was weakened by years of captivity and hunger.

"Help your father!" Morgan shouted to Luke as he and the others faced the Dark Wizard.

Luke needed no further encouragement, although his brain only half registered that this *was* his father. Grasping his sword even more firmly, he charged forward and was soon standing side by side with Peter, using his sword to deflect bolts that came so fast he could only defend himself and was unable to strike a blow of his own.

As he fought, there was a commotion further down the street and there appeared about twenty more of Logan's servants. These were misbegotten beings, the homeless, drug addicts, people who had been abandoned by the society that should have helped them. They had been easily swayed toward evil by the Dark Wizard's false promises of riches and power.

None of them were wizards and no more than a few had anything other than rudimentary magic, but they could fight, and all were armed with vicious spikes and swords. Even so, they would be no match for Morgan and his companions, Logan knew, but they would be a diversion while he planned his escape. Oh, they would all die, of course, but what did that matter when these *lost souls* could be replaced easily, a hundred times over from the dirty, hidden side of London that most people never saw or wanted to admit existed?

As Morgan and his companions defended themselves against this new threat, Logan took the opportunity and there was a sudden, loud whinnying from the two terrified horses as they reared, hooves pawing at the empty air before the carriage hurtled away.

"No!" It was Morgan's angry, anguished howl, but even this was drowned by the even louder shout from the remaining, abandoned servant.

"Master!"

He flung a final poisoned bolt towards Peter then ran after the carriage in a vain gesture; the carriage was already lost from sight. But the blow had been a lucky one, or perhaps the wand's demon power had directed its aim, for Peter now lay among the broken glass, blood pumping in huge, sticky gouts from the wound high in his chest.

"Dad!" sobbed Luke, flinging his sword aside and kneeling beside him. "No!"

But to Peter the cries were already faint as he began to lose consciousness.

"Luke," he whispered, his breathing already labored. "My son, my dear son." A gob of blood spilled from his mouth. "If you only knew how I've prayed for this day, to see you once more." Peter's vision blurred as the poison from the demon bolt invaded his body and he struggled to make out Luke's sobbing form. His eye's flickered in the direction the Dark Wizard's servant had run. "Stop him," he breathed hoarsely.

The last thing Luke wanted was to leave his father, fearful these precious moments were the only ones he might ever have. But he couldn't refuse him, and without a word he stood, picked up his sword, though its weight now seemed intolerable, and ran after the receding figure. Without warning, a cloak of anger enveloped him and he forget everything, even Peter, as he was consumed with the desire, the absolute need, for revenge. It gave life to his feet and he hurtled down the street, quickly gaining on his quarry.

"Fight me, you dirty, stinking bastard!" he roared, and the

servant's head whipped round in shock. Realizing that fleeing was pointless, he turned and raised his wand, flinging a long stream of bolts, staccato-like at the boy.

But Luke kept running, deflecting them and only subconsciously noting how very *easily* he was suddenly able to do so. He held his sword high as he ran, then it came flashing down in a vicious arc and the man's head flew from his body, bouncing down the street before rolling to a stop. It faced Luke, its eyes wide with surprise as the light inside them dimmed.

Only then did Luke's anger abate as quickly as it had arisen, and he trudged slowly back to his father, exhausted and frightened at what he would find. As he did so, the last vestiges of the battle ended; a half-dozen of the Dark Wizard's *lost souls* lay dead or dying, the rest fled with dismayed howls.

Morgan looked sadly at the dead around him and wished it could have been otherwise, for he knew it hadn't been their fault, that they were victims of a society, of a *world,* that had failed them.

Sighing deeply, he turned his attention towards Peter, grimacing at what he saw. "Bring him," he ordered curtly before disappearing through the door, back toward the Sanctuary. He was followed by Wallace, who carried Peter gently in his arms, and Luke who trailed miserably after them.

Only Molly remained behind. There was a task to be done that should have fallen to Morgan, but she knew he would forget, that he would be wracked with guilt at the deaths of innocent mortals that day, even though the blame lay not with him. Nevertheless, she would do this small service for her friend. She surveyed the chaos, looking at the walking wounded, most of whom didn't seem too badly hurt, and at the others who were beyond help.

Already there were sirens in the distance and she thought she saw the flicker of blue lights. Sightseers were gathering, some just watching but some getting involved, trying to help.

Molly was beginning to attract curious glances and she quickly raised her wand, swinging it in a wide semi-circle over the scene before her. Instantly she was invisible as the glamour, which had slipped in the heat of battle, was fully restored and those few mortals who'd witnessed the conflict now forgot it. Later it would be reported as some kind of terrorist attack.

Her task completed, Molly turned and was about to follow her companions when she noticed a small figure sitting on the pile of rubble that had half buried her mother. It was a young girl, no more than nine or ten years old, pretty in an elfin kind of way, despite her tattered clothes and the tears that coursed down her face, leaving bright pink tracks.

"Oh my," breathed Molly, "you poor little mite." She knelt cautiously, so as not to frighten her. "What's your name, love?" she asked gently, but got no response as the girl just stared blankly ahead. Realizing the glamour was hiding her, she adjusted it slightly and spoke again, but still she received no reply. *Shock*, she thought, momentarily unsure what to do. Then, knowing she couldn't just leave the girl, Molly made a decision, one that would prove to be momentous.

"Come on, love, I'll get you to safety," she told her. "We can always come back and find your family later." She hoisted the girl into her arms, not without difficulty for she clung stubbornly to her mother's outstretched hand, then without a backward glance

THE SANCTUARY

she followed her companions into the Sanctuary.

THE SANCTUARY

Part Two

THE SANCTUARY

Chapter 18

Luke Simpson used to be just like any other teenager, occasionally sulky, often self-opinionated, and at times a real pain in the ass. But most of the time he was friendly and even tempered, easy going and good-natured. That was before the events of two weeks ago, in that other lifetime before he'd seen his father struck down in front of him. Now Luke was a boy filled with anger.

Anger at Morgan and Molly who'd got him involved in all this, and at Wallace who'd not trained him well enough to protect his father. Then there was anger at Cissy's mother who'd not insisted on driving him safely home on that fateful night, and at Mr. Hamilton who'd not arrived home in time to somehow sort things out.

And he was angry at his own father for not being around to see him grow up, and then for being stupid enough to get himself hurt. Although Peter Simpson still clung stubbornly to life, death hung above him like a shroud. Luke could sense it hovering, awaiting its chance every time he sat beside his bed, as he did for many hours each day, praying for a miracle he knew would never come.

He was mad at Cissy, although he wasn't sure for what exactly, he just knew he wanted to blame her. Maybe it was because her parents were safe at home, while his own father suffered.

But most of all Luke Simpson was angry at himself. Guilt gnawed at his very soul for he'd had the chance to fight beside his father, protect him, *save him!* But he'd failed and his father had been wounded, struck down by the Dark Wizard's servant. Now he was going to die a vile and horrible death as the poison crept inexorably through his veins. Even as he watched, Luke could see them turning black like the tributaries of an oil-soaked river. Soon the poison would reach his father's heart.

And with this guilt came a deep, burning anger, more than any boy his age should ever have to feel. The more that people were nice to him and tried to offer comfort, the angrier he became, and although everyone tried, nobody could reach him.

Molly and Morgan attempted to rekindle his interest in wizardry, describing the exploits of famous wizards and witches down the centuries, but he just turned away from them.

Wallace tried to persuade and even goad the boy into another training bout, each day bringing Luke's sword and laying it on the bed beside him, but it lay there untouched, ignored.

Alessandro and his cooks competed to make the choicest and most succulent treats, but Luke would pick at them before pushing them aside.

And then there was Cissy, and for her it was worst of all. She seemed to excite in him an anger out of all proportion to any harm she could possibly have caused. Not that she *had* done anything and that made it all the more inexplicable. But the fact was, the sight of her enraged him. Nevertheless, she was determined, refusing to give up on this boy who, she'd come to realize, meant so much to her.

So, every day she steeled herself to knock on his door and enter, only to be met with a torrent of abuse that sent her reeling back out the door. Then her eyes would fill with tears, some for herself but mostly for Luke. Only her pride prevented the tears from falling until the door was firmly shut behind her. Then Molly would just happen to be walking down the corridor and she'd gather the girl into her arms and hold her close, whispering endearments.

"It's okay, love," she would say, "he'll soon come to his senses. It's not the real Luke in there, so don't let it upset you." Then Cissy, grateful to the old woman, would pretend to be comforted and wipe away her tears.

If it wasn't Molly keeping an eye on her, Alessandro could always be relied upon to have something delicious waiting for her in the kitchen. To the kindhearted, rather crazy chef, food was the answer to all the world's problems. And before she followed him to the kitchen, Cissy would take a few moments to find the girl – and this wasn't difficult, for the timid little thing was never far away from Cissy, her hero worship a source of delight and embarrassment to the older girl.

Penelope was a quiet, withdrawn child who'd said very little since Molly rescued her from the battle that had killed her mother, and the old witch's conscience had troubled her greatly. Had she done the right thing in bringing the girl into the Sanctuary? Perhaps she should have left her for others to find and look after, allowed her to grieve for her mother in the normal way.

Taking Morgan's advice, she'd gone back out into the mortal world to make inquiries and these had revealed the girl had no other family. And so it had been decided she should come to live with them rather than abandoning her to the lottery of the English social services. When she was older, she'd have the choice of staying with them or going back into her own world.

Meanwhile, Luke became unhappier, angrier and more withdrawn, and those around him felt increasingly helpless. It went on like this day after day, and might have done so indefinitely if not for Penelope who eventually saved them.

Although Morgan, Molly and the others were kind to her and she liked them immensely, they were simply too old to have anything in common with a nine-year-old girl. But with Cissy it was different. The teenager was young enough to connect with her and she treated the girl with a patience and kindness that helped her overcome the loss of her mother.

Many times in the last two weeks, Cissy had been awakened by the sound of weeping and she would go into the girl's room and pick her up, then take her into her own bed and cuddle her till she slept. Or if Penelope's crying didn't disturb her during the night, she would often wake the next morning to find the girl snuggled beside her.

Then one night, Penelope suffered a particularly vicious nightmare and stumbled sleepy-eyed and shivering with fright into the corridor. In her exhaustion she turned the wrong way and entered what she thought was Cissy's room. The next morning, Luke awoke and the first thing he saw was the sleeping form of the little girl beside him.

As he sat up in surprise, the movement awoke her, and Luke felt a new emotion that left a bitter taste in his mouth before it slid like an oily, bitter medicine into his guts. That emotion was shame, for in the eyes of the little girl there was a look of abject terror.

If this is the effect I have on her, how horrible must I have been to everyone lately? he thought. *She doesn't even know me and she's scared stiff!*

He reached out a tentative hand. "It…it's okay," he stammered, "I won't hurt you." But the girl shrank away from him. "I'm Luke," he tried again, "you must be Penelope?"

Recently, Luke had taken to refusing to eat in the kitchen with the others and Morgan had reluctantly given permission for meals to be served in his room. So an hour later, when Alessandro knocked on the door and entered with breakfast, he almost dropped the tray in surprise. He was met with the sight of Luke holding one of the dolls Molly had found for the girl, pretending to walk it up her arm to sit on her shoulder.

Penelope scolded him. "No, Luke, she can't sit up there. She'll fall off, silly!"

Alessandro stared open mouthed at the sight. *Luke, sixteen-year-old, angry Luke, playing with dolls?* He cleared his throat and Luke turned and gave him a radiant smile.

"Hi, Alessandro! Is that breakfast? I'm starving, is there any for Pen?"

* * * *

THE SANCTUARY

Ever since the battle, Logan had been in a foul mood, angry that his servants were gone and only now realizing how useful they'd been.

"Damn them for being so useless as to get themselves killed!" he raged. "And damn that boy!" An image of Luke appeared in his mind's eye but was quickly replaced by that of his own brother. "And damn you too, Morgan!"

He stormed the corridors of the old mansion, brandishing his wand so furiously in his temper that lightning bolts flew in all directions, knocking vases from shelves and paintings from walls. In no time at all there were holes in the floor, cracks in the ceilings and tiny fires burning everywhere.

The whole place was beginning to resemble the aftermath of a war zone. It was only when the huge chandelier that had hung in the entrance hall for more than a century came crashing to the floor that he sobered. Logan didn't take much pleasure in material possessions, but that thing had been worth a fortune.

Breathing heavily, he forced himself to think, to still the turmoil in his mind and stem the rising tide of panic, and presently he went outside, confident he could still find some who were willing to serve him. But the street was deserted and strangely silent, no frightened eyes observing from behind curtains, nobody peering furtively around corners. No dogs scavenged in bins; no cats slunk silently in the shadows; even the rats had gone. Looking upwards, Logan realized the sky was empty of life.

Angrily, he went in search of some of his *lost souls* to replace those killed in the battle, but since the vast Cardboard City near

Waterloo station had been demolished a few years before, these had become increasingly hard to find. He'd been certain there were still a few willing or desperate enough if one went down to the South Bank around Lambeth, but when he made the journey, he discovered even those had heard of his coming and either moved away or were hiding. Logan was finding out that the inhabitants of London, be they human or animal, would rather run and hide than serve him, knowing that to do so offered no great promise or reward except that of despair and death.

So, he sat in his lonely old mansion, cold and hungry for there were no longer servants to light a fire or cook. Slowly it dawned on him that he was truly alone, without friend or ally, and as he sat there in near darkness, his mood was indeed black and foul.

But the Dark Wizard was no weakling and he would not succumb to self-pity for long. He rose and gathered the things he needed to undertake a difficult and dangerous venture. It was late morning and the pale November sun held no warmth as he went outside to see the only two creatures who'd remained loyal.

He whispered softly in their ears and they nickered their understanding. Logan worked busily for a time attaching halters and harnesses and soon all was ready. The horses neighed with excitement, the sound so high pitched it could have been mistaken for screams. Then they reared onto their hind legs and the gleaming black carriage thundered through the gateway of the old mansion and resumed its interrupted journey.

*   *   *   *

THE SANCTUARY

After he'd made friends with Penelope, it would be nice to say that everything was okay for Luke, but that would be too easy and it wasn't, although things had certainly improved. He'd been subjected to merciless teasing from Cissy about the doll incident, which was already being referred to as *Barbiegate,* but he'd taken it in good humor. The realization of how badly he'd been behaving had come as a shock and he was determined to make amends, although he found it was easier said than done.

Nevertheless, Luke was able to push his troubles to the back of his mind at least a little and he found he was happier for it, and at least that look of wariness was beginning to disappear from the eyes of his companions. For much of the time he was able to adopt a façade of happiness, particularly when Penelope was around, and although everyone else knew it was a pretense, they were grateful.

But nothing could alter the fact that his father was going to die, and he suffered periods of suffocating despair when he would lapse into long silences. And although they became less frequent, he was still plagued with sudden, unreasonable fits of anger, and when that happened it was best to keep out of his way and let him get on with it. He still spent much of his time sitting by his father's bed, praying for a miracle. But deep in his heart he knew that miracles didn't exist and that there was no hope.

It was a curious fact that although Cissy was the person Luke was closest to, it was Molly who was most affected by the boy's unhappiness. After all, it was she who had first introduced Luke to the Sanctuary and she felt responsible, guilty even. It wouldn't have been so bad if she didn't like him so much, but the old witch had a fondness for Luke that bordered on love and she saw in him something of the son she'd always longed for but never had.

"It wasn't just your decision to bring him here, you know, it was mine too," Morgan had tried to soothe his old friend, but she'd rounded on him furiously.

"Then we're both to bleedin' blame, aren't we!"

And Morgan could only nod helplessly. "If only there were something we could give Peter, some…I don't know, some *magic potion* to make him well again." Then he'd left the room abruptly, angry with himself, for rarely in his life had he felt so impotent.

Molly hadn't answered or tried to call him back. She'd simply stared after him thoughtfully.

Chapter 19

As a healer for her kind, Molly had learned her craft many years ago as a young girl under the tutelage of the legendary witch Siwaraksa, and she'd inherited a vast store of knowledge about potions and spells for just about anything. So, while Luke sat at his father's side, Molly spent most of her time in her chamber surrounded by dozens of books, some so old they crumbled slightly at her touch. She was searching for something, anything that would cure or at least slow down the effects of the poison in Peter's veins.

But she said nothing to Luke for she dared not raise the boy's hopes and, truthfully, Molly had little herself. She'd never heard of a spell that could counter demon poison and now she'd scoured every book in the library without success. All except one, which she'd left until last simply because it was the oldest and by far the most fragile.

Bleedin' hell, it was ancient when Siwaraksa owned it, she thought wryly as she placed it carefully on the table before her. With the utmost gentleness, Molly opened the front cover, but it immediately crumbled to dust in her fingers. Cursing to herself, she blew away the fragments of ancient paper and turned the first page only for that to disintegrate too.

The witch sat there and stared at it for a few minutes, thinking. Then she selected another, much newer book – newer in the sense it was only a couple, rather than a score of centuries old. Flicking rapidly through its pages, she found the spell she needed, written in an ancient, long-defunct language by the hand of some unknown scribe many years ago. Then she took out her wand and began to chant.

For a long time, nothing happened, but then very slowly two tiny creatures appeared before her. They seemed to form from the very fabric of the page, each no bigger than a child's finger, wings thin as gossamer, fluttering so quickly they were a blur. Glad to be freed from the confines of the page, they buzzed excitedly round her head, giggling and chattering in their squeaky high-pitched voices, one girl and one boy, as was always the way with faeries.

Molly let them play for a while as they enjoyed their newfound freedom. Faeries could be tricky little creatures, she knew, and it was always best to keep them happy. Eventually she was able to calm them down and tell them what she needed.

At once they flew to the ancient book and gripped the edge of the first page in their tiny hands. Together they flew upwards and turned it, then the second and the third. Their touch was so light and delicate that not even a fragment of the pages crumbled. On and on it went, Molly reading and re-reading carefully so as not to miss any vital clue. Mealtimes came and went, people knocked at the door and were ignored, night came then a new day dawned until, at last, the faeries turned the final page.

Disheartened and exhausted, Molly scanned it quickly. Her tired eyes looked at the words without seeing and when she reached the bottom, she motioned for the faeries to close the book. But instead of doing so they fluttered around her for a moment then zoomed over the page back and forth, all the while chattering with excitement. *Look again,* they seemed to be telling her, *look again!*

Mindful of the old maxim 'ignore a faerie at your peril', Molly did as they asked but even then, she almost missed it for the words were written in a language that was all but forgotten.

But there it was, in the very last spell written in the final paragraph of the book, the words *Daemono Diablo*. The old witch sat back with a sigh and allowed herself a tired smile.

"Demon Poison," she breathed and began to read.

*   *   *   *

When she looked up from the book at last, Molly rubbed her tired eyes and regarded the two faeries who lay curled up together on the table fast asleep. She thought about the spell she had just read; she had everything she needed – almost. Molly thought for a moment about where to find the last ingredient. She needed Cissy's help, she decided at last, and quietly, so as not to disturb the sleeping faeries, she left the room and went in search of the girl.

An hour later she found the faeries still hadn't moved. She blew very gently in their direction and the slight breeze startled them awake.

"Thank you," she said, her voice formal and polite, as one must sometimes be with the faerie folk. "We of the Sanctuary are most grateful."

Their eyes twinkled brightly back at her, full of mischief.

"Would you like us to close the book now?" they inquired, their laughter tinkling like tiny bells, and without awaiting an answer they closed the pages of the ancient book with great care. But then, instead of disappearing, they simply sat with chins resting on their knees and regarded her.

Molly looked back expectantly. "Erm, don't you have somewhere you need to be?" She tried to keep the politeness in her voice but was unable to prevent a trace of that 'Molly' impatience creeping through.

"Not really," replied one of them merrily.

"We like it here," said the other, "we thought we'd stick around!"

"But you can't!" Molly was appalled and already wondering what Morgan would say when he discovered she was responsible for two mischievous faeries wandering the place, no doubt creating mayhem. "I mean, why bother? It's really boring here, nothing to do at all!"

The girl flew up suddenly to perch on the end of Molly's nose, then bit it.

"Oy! That bleedin' hurt!" She swatted a hand at the girl, but she wasn't quick enough and the faerie flew away laughing. Then the boy landed on her ear and leaned right in.

"No use arguing!" he shouted, making her jump. "We told you, we like it here!" The vibration made her ear itch and she lifted a finger to poke it. The boy jumped to the other side and shouted again, "And, more importantly, we like you!" As another finger approached, he flew to the tip of her nose and tapped it sternly. "Luckily for you!" he added darkly.

"Yes!" The girl was back. "Even though you're a fat, bad tempered old witch, we still like you!" As well as being mischievous, faeries could be extremely rude.

Molly was speechless as she stared indignantly at the grinning pair, then she marched out of the room to find Morgan. Fortunately, he was alone, and he looked at her in surprise.

"If it's not a stupid question, why do you have a faerie sitting on each shoulder?" he inquired mildly.

"Never mind *why*," she snapped, "I've just been called a fat, bad tempered old witch!" She flopped into a chair and glared at him defiantly as her chins wobbled from side to side.

"Well," he started, trying to be diplomatic, "sometimes you can be a bit… irritable, and,"—he smiled disarmingly—"you are a witch."

It would probably be unwise, he reflected, to point out that as well as being extremely old she was also more than a little on the plump side. To change the subject, he turned his attention to the Faer Folk. "What are your names?"

"They won't be staying much longer so they don't need names." Molly was still annoyed and was quite unaware of just how rude and ungrateful she sounded.

The wizard merely waved her to silence and raised a questioning eyebrow. The boy bowed respectfully.

"We do have names, of course, oh Great One, but they would not translate well into your human tongue." He took a deep breath and recited his name, then nudged the girl to do the same. When they'd both finished nearly a full minute had passed and Morgan was forced to agree that they're names were impractical for everyday use.

"Come now," he said, smiling easily, careful not to antagonize them, "you can play your faerie games if you want, but I know something of your ancient lore, enough to know you will have been given more…*manageable* names before you deigned to enter our world."

The statement was delivered pleasantly, yet it was a command, and the faeries recognized it as such.

"You are right, of course," the boy acknowledged with a slight bow. "I'm Moth and this is Velveteena." The girl, in turn, bowed.

"Thank you. And perhaps you will tell me why you have entered this place?"

The boy's smile was replaced by a mutinous expression and the girl would not meet his eyes.

"You were summoned?" the wizard guessed; they nodded, cautiously. "By Molly, I presume." He gave her a dark look.

"Yes, the fat one summoned us," acknowledged Moth, while Velveteena grinned at Molly's stifled splutter of outrage.

"Or at least, she thinks she did," she added.

"We do not lightly allow strangers into the Sanctuary," Morgan pointed out, stern but without heat.

"Yet we will stay, for our purpose is beyond even you, oh Great One, and we will not, cannot, say what that purpose is."

And now Morgan had a quandary. It would be unwise to pick an argument with these two. He closed his eyes and thought, allowing instinct to take over, an instinct which told him they held no threat to the Sanctuary, although the purpose they spoke of was hidden to him. He opened his eyes at last.

"Then be welcome in our home," he said, and now it was he who bowed to them, the age-old acknowledgment of respect, not of subservience, in the faerie world.

"Do you like our names, Molly?" Velveteena asked, a little shyly.

Molly shrugged huffily. "That's a totally pointless question. If I had my way, you wouldn't be around here much longer." But even to Molly's ears her argument was starting to sound weak. There was something attractive and likable about the Faer Folk and she didn't really want them to leave, she just didn't know how to back down. She realized she was being unkind and that just made her more annoyed; with herself, mostly.

But faeries only ever took offense at people they didn't like, and Velveteena nibbled Molly's ear affectionately.

"We're staying and there's nothing you can do about it."

"And you did summon them," added the wizard, wickedly rubbing salt into the wound.

"Well, she didn't really, I'm not gonna lie," Moth put in.

"And you'll need our help getting all the stuff together for that spell," added Velveteena, giving him a look of caution.

Morgan opened his mouth to ask what she was talking about, but he didn't get the chance.

"Oh my! The spell!" yelled Molly, her annoyance forgotten. "I almost bleedin' forgot!" She clutched the wizard's sleeve urgently. "I have to show you something, quickly!" Then she was gone, leaving Morgan gaping after her in astonishment; it was a very long time since he'd seen her move that fast.

Back in her chambers, Molly showed him what she'd discovered. He rubbed his chin thoughtfully as the faeries turned the pages of the ancient book once more. When he'd finished reading, Morgan stared at it for a long time.

"Some of these ingredients are common, but others are not and one or two are extremely rare," he said at last. "I take it you don't have them all?"

"All but one," she replied and pointed to an illustration of a thin, straggling plant with tiny leaves and long, cruel looking thorns tipped with red. As they watched, the illustration swayed gently, as if touched by an invisible breeze, and red liquid dripped from the tips and splashed to the foot of the page.

"Blood thorn," said Molly. "The book says it's incredibly rare and only grows in about three places in the entire world. Unfortunately, it doesn't say where those places are. She looked expectantly at the wizard but he made no comment so she went on, "I can't find anything about it in my books. I've even tried that interweb thingy on the computing device but found nothing."

Morgan looked at her skeptically, knowing she was a total… what was it Cissy called her? A *technophobe*? He and most of the others at the Sanctuary had managed at least a rudimentary grasp of this mortal technology, but Molly had remained completely baffled by it all, unable or unwilling to have anything to do with what she called *unnatural magic*.

He looked at her, doubtfully. "You know how to use the internet?" She smiled ruefully.

"Okay, I got Cissy to do it for me; didn't tell her what it was for of course." She sighed heavily. "But she found no mention of blood thorn anywhere."

"I've never come across it either," came Morgan's unwelcome reply, "and if neither of us have heard of it in four centuries I've no idea where to even begin to try and find it."

Molly's shoulders slumped. "I was so sure you would…" She lapsed into silence. She'd been so full of hope and the despair she felt now was almost too much to bear.

The faeries had been silent so far, but now they looked at each other and in that almost telepathic way common to the Faer Folk they made their decision.

They hovered in front of Morgan and Molly and said in unison. "We know."

"Know what?" The wizard's voice was sharp and wary. Faeries were not always a trustworthy race.

"We know where to find blood thorn," said Moth. "It only grows in three places."

"The book did say so," Velveteena reminded them cheekily.

"Where?" Morgan asked, no less suspicious.

"Well, the first place is in the continent you call Asia, in a ravine high on a mountain," Moth continued.

"But the ravine is protected by a dragon," Velveteena went on, "and you'd have no chance of getting past it."

"Wizard magic doesn't work on them," Moth explained.

"And anyway, it's much too far to walk," finished Velveteena.

Morgan wondered if they were having fun at his expense; one could never tell.

Molly's temper was starting to rise. "Okay, where's the second place?"

"At the bottom of the sea," replied Moth. "The Pacific, or the Atlantic. Probably."

"It's in the Caribbean actually," said Velveteena, "right at the bottom where humans can't go."

"It is not!" he said, crossly.

"It is!" she yelled. "You think you know everything!"

"I do know everything, I'm a faerie, you idiot!"

They were up in the air shouting at each other, their tiny wands raised and firing streams of silvery light. One ricocheted from the lampshade and singed Morgan's eyebrow.

"Enough!" he roared. "If you can't behave, I'll send you back to your own realm!"

They sobered instantly, for although they could make his life difficult for a while in a hundred mischievous ways, they knew Morgan had the power to carry out his threat.

"Sorry," they muttered, eyes downcast, but almost immediately they winked at each other and giggled. "Don't you want to know where the third place is?" They jumped onto his shoulder. "It's in Wales," they continued, not waiting for an answer. "That's not too far at all!" They grinned at each other. "Practically around the corner!"

"How do you know?" Despite her growing liking for the pair, Molly still didn't entirely trust them. "How can you be so sure?" She didn't notice that Morgan was now staring intently at the faeries.

"We're faeries," said Velveteena simply, "we know everything."

"For goodness sake, stop boasting," snapped Morgan, his anxiety

THE SANCTUARY

for Peter making him short-tempered. "Our friend is dying while you play your silly games. If you know where to find it just tell us, please."

Faeries didn't often feel shame, but the suffering in his voice made them flush a deep red and they bowed in apology.

"We intended no offense," said Moth gravely. "A single plant can be found in Wales, in one place only."

"In an area to the North known as *Gwynedd*," Velveteena went on and the wizard's head turned sharply toward her.

"Where?" His stomach churned into a tight knot as he waited with a sense of inevitability for her answer.

The faeries hesitated only for a second then looked at each other again and nodded.

"One plant only can be found."

"Just one, and only at certain times of the year."

"Only when there's a blood moon."

"I know about the blood moon." Morgan looked at them in surprise. "It was very important to our village and many others when I was a boy, but I've never heard of this blood thorn."

"Then you'll know the altering of the moon doesn't happen very often," said Velveteena, "and this thorn is invisible at any other time."

"Which kind of explains why not many have even heard of it let alone seen it," Moth added, trying to be helpful. "Only once more this year will it occur, the blood moon, I mean. It will happen at the next full moon." He paused. "That's only two days from now."

"Okay, okay we get it." Molly's patience was wearing thin. "Where is it?"

"One plant," Moth said again, "can be found at the entrance to a cave."

"Go on," ordered Morgan in a whisper, "where is this cave?"

"It lies near to the village of your birth, Lord Morgan." The faerie used his hereditary title and the old wizard nodded, already knowing what they would say next.

"The plant grows in the entrance to the realm of the Demon King."

THE SANCTUARY

Chapter 20

The carriage left London behind and headed west. As dusk approached, the Dark Wizard thought of his destination and the time he'd spent there as a boy, centuries ago…

Two brothers, twins. Morgan the eldest by five minutes – only five! Logan the second born, always second in everything.

As children they were close, sharing a special bond only found in twins. But they'd grown, become teenagers and Logan's jealousy, long kept dormant, began to take hold. Morgan would inherit their father's land, his titles. Morgan was the stronger, more handsome. Morgan was luckier, braver. Morgan was their father's favorite.

There was a cave, high in the hills above the village, and inside was a crack in the wall so narrow one had to squeeze tightly to get through. As children they'd not done so, for it was forbidden; all in the village knew this to be a way into the demon world. The place emanated a sense of evil that kept even the foolhardiest away, evil so palpable it could almost be tasted.

But Logan had grown older and his jealousy ate at him like a cancer, insidious and unrelenting. The way to the demon world tugged at him, a magnet, until at last his chance came when for once he was separated from his brother who lay ill in bed. It was the first of many visits, but as he became more secretive, his brother grew suspicious and followed him one day. So, his secret was discovered and when his brother tried to stop him they'd fought. But Morgan had the ill fortune to slip on a loose stone and fall, smashing his head on the rough stone floor.

As he lay there dazed, Logan was already squeezing through the crack. Morgan cried out, causing him to turn and look back with something like regret in his eyes. And Morgan had held out an imploring hand, so tempting! How Logan had wanted to take that hand! But he'd shaken his head slowly and turned toward the demon world knowing he could never return, that home no longer existed...

The carriage yawed violently as one wheel hit a large rock and Logan was shaken from his reverie. He looked out but saw only dark fields and hedgerows flashing silently by. Far away he could make out the dawn breaking over distant mountains and he knew they would soon cross the border into Wales.

Just then he noticed a faint black speck in the sky, tiny but rapidly growing as it sped toward him. The Dark Wizard smiled, and a few moments later the black crow once again swooped into the carriage.

As it perched in its usual place on his shoulder it cawed its news softly into his ear and his good mood evaporated.

So, Peter Simpson still lives, he brooded. *I should have murdered him while I had the chance.* But on hearing that Luke was proving most adept – with a sword, if not yet his wand – he felt a frisson of fear. The Dark Wizard also knew of the prophecy. Even the crow hesitated before imparting its last piece of news, that the girl, who wasn't supposed to have any sort of power, had surpassed the boy and was now by far his superior with a wand.

Logan clenched a fist. *I'd had her in my power and let her escape!* More than ever he needed the aid of the demons. *Kanzser must help me, I must win him over.*

It was many years since he'd laid eyes on the king of the demons, but the memory still made him shudder, and the Dark Wizard's mood was as black as his soul as the carriage thundered on.

But its swaying, rocking motion soothed him, and he was lulled once again into a half-trance…

He'd been tolerated among the demons, no more than that. But when they learned he could no longer return home, he was suddenly welcomed as one of their own and the boy was too naive to question why that might be. So, he basked in the glow of their friendship, for the first time in his life enjoying the sensation of being popular. And he learned magic even his own father didn't know, a darker, more sinister magic intended for harm, not good. Even the Demon King himself took time to speak to him, now and then offering a smile or a word of praise. To the young Logan these were heady heights indeed. He felt flattered, important, for Kanzser rarely deigned to speak to the likes of him! He never even suspected he was being manipulated.

But the Demon King bore a grudge, one that festered within his already poisonous heart. For once there'd been a woman, one so fair her beauty was known far and wide, and men plotted and schemed for her hand in marriage. The Demon King had pined for her, lusted after her, and he'd plied her with gifts for a whole year, confident of winning his prize in the end.

Yet she'd chosen another, and the Demon King had been consumed with rage, love instantly congealing into cold hatred. Whore! But before he could exact his revenge, the woman was dead, her lifeblood draining away as she gave life to her twins. So his hatred turned to the man she'd spurned him for, the village elder Owain, a man of no consequence in the demon's eyes. Yet no opportunity had arisen, for he was well guarded, and he was a wizard, too clever and powerful to be caught unawares. But now his chance had come at last and how fitting that this boy, this twin, child of the whore herself, should be the one to provide it!

As Kanzser scrutinized the boy, lids hooded to hide the cunning in his eyes, Logan looked around the chamber, both nervous and excited to be summoned by the Demon King himself. If he wanted food, Kanzser served it to him personally. More wine? Kanzser was insistent. Comfortable? Kanzser was most solicitous. And as he ate and drank, firelight flickered over the walls and formed strange caricatures of men and beasts, each one twisted and deformed. Then, as the figures danced, the Demon King and the boy made their plans…

The carriage slowed at last and Logan realized they'd arrived. He stepped out, immediately engulfed in yet more memories as he looked upon the village of his birth. In the mortal world, this place had grown bigger over the past few centuries and was now a popular tourist spot. But in this parallel world it remained almost unchanged. A little larger perhaps, but with the same circular houses made from the trees which covered the hillsides all around, smoke curling upwards through their thatched roofs. And despite the distance, the pungent smell of the cattle pens at each end of the village and the pigs that roamed freely reached his nostrils and they wrinkled with distaste. Over it all, there hung the haze from a score or more cooking fires.

Logan's eyes moved slowly to the center of the village where a larger, more substantial building stood. This one was rectangular, timber framed, its roof made of slate; even its windows were glazed. Logan wondered idly who the village elder was these days. He knew there was no longer a wizard in the place; he and Morgan had been the last ones.

Surely not the same decrepit old man I'd encountered on my last visit a year ago? he wondered. On that occasion he'd been unsuccessful in gaining entry into the demon world and he'd taken his anger out on the inhabitants of the village. Through the haze, he could see the villagers going about their business. *Little people,* he thought scornfully, as he remembered how they'd borne the brunt of his anger that day.

He laughed harshly and said out loud, "If they knew that I, Logan, was in their midst again they'd cower in terror!"

For a moment he considered testing his theory by going down to the village, but decided there wasn't time for such indulgences. He turned and made his way up the hillside, the crow as ever perched on his shoulder. It was a steep climb and he was panting when he finally approached the entrance to the cave. He took a last look at his own world and wondered when he would see it again, then he mustered his courage and continued toward the

THE SANCTUARY

entrance to the demon world.

But one didn't just walk into this realm unannounced and before he'd gone a dozen meters he was met, as had been arranged, by one of the Demon King's personal bodyguards. To his consternation, Logan realized the face was familiar. He bowed slightly to show respect, always a wise policy; it had been a long time.

Chapter 21

There'd been a long silence following the faeries' startling news and Morgan had cut off any attempt at interruption, but at last he raised his head and spoke. "I will make my preparations and set off tonight, after everyone has gone to bed," he announced, but Molly gave an outraged splutter.

"You will not!" she exclaimed, getting hurriedly to her feet and standing before him, arms akimbo. "Who was it that spent days looking for that spell? Me!" Now she leaned over the desk until her face was inches from his. "Who was it that summoned these two?" She gestured vaguely toward the faeries. "Me!"

Morgan leaned back slightly and wiped spittle from his cheeks. "Yes but—"

"Never mind *yes but*, Morgan," she growled, "it's them who told us how to get the one ingredient we don't have, it's me who got them here and it's me who's going!" The last word was accompanied by a mighty thump on the table that sent the faeries scuttling into Molly's pocket. She stood upright, panting slightly, and gave the wizard a smile full of charm and feminine wiles. Cocking her head cheekily to one side, she played her trump card.

"And anyway, you're needed here. What if the Dark Wizard attacks?"

Morgan had been about to argue but that stopped him. She was right, he realized; for him to leave the Sanctuary now was unthinkable.

"Okay, you win," he acknowledged, "but we must make plans quickly. It might not be a long journey, but it could and probably will be dangerous, you realize that?"

She nodded and now the decision had been made, Molly suddenly felt a little uncertain at what she had let herself in for. But no way was she going to let anyone know her fears. "Never mind making plans, there ain't time for that, just tell me how to get there."

"Oh, that's easy." He smiled. "You take a train."

There were times, Molly had to admit, when her best friend was pretty amazing. They'd sat in complete silence for nearly two hours since Morgan had cautioned her not to speak and she'd watched him stare at the wall for all that time while absolutely nothing happened.

She'd been about to remark that he might like to get on with it because she was getting bleedin' cold when she felt a vibration beneath her feet, faint at first but rapidly becoming stronger. She glanced at her friend and was alarmed to see his face was a deep crimson and there was what appeared to be steam coming from his ears.

By now the passage was shaking and bits of wall were starting to fall off; in no time the air was cloudy with dust. The noise was deafening, and the vibrations made her teeth chatter uncontrollably, and her flesh undulated and shook like a wobbly jelly. Presently though, Morgan's color returned to normal, his ears stopped steaming and the vibrations faded then ceased. As the dust cleared, Molly saw that a brick wall had been revealed, one that looked to have been built many years ago.

"Okay, terrific, it's a wall. Two hours and all you come up with is a wall." She gave him a sarcastic look. "That's impressive, even by your standards." She got to her feet and trudged back down the passage.

"Oh no, my cantankerous old friend, that wasn't impressive at all," Morgan replied, his voice heavy with irony, "but this is." He pointed his wand and considered the bricks for a moment, then chose one near the bottom where the mortar was particularly rotten and crumbly. He muttered softly and pushed it with an outstretched finger. It moved easily backward then dropped into the void beyond to reveal a black, rectangular hole.

Quickly he pushed another, then another. The bricks above sagged slightly then they too collapsed into the void and within seconds the whole lot had fallen. Lighting his wand, Morgan stepped through and was joined almost immediately by Molly who'd come hurrying back up the passage as the bricks began to fall.

"See? An entry into the mortal world!" Morgan tried and failed to look modest. "Easy!"

She ignored him and looked around in wonder at the tunnel, the railway track and the station platform beyond, the whole thing

THE SANCTUARY

made from tiles that had once been pristine white but were now blackened and grimy. She could just make out the faded London Underground logo and the words *St Mary's*.

"Okay,"—she turned to face him—"it's official, you're amazing. Is this where I catch the train?"

"No, this is *St Mary's* station in Whitechapel, abandoned years ago before that war the mortals had with each other."

"Which one?" she said laconically. "They've had a few."

"The big one, involved most of the world," he said vaguely, "the *second* one." He gave her a small push. "Anyway, get going, you're wasting time. The station you're going to will close soon; that's when the Conductor will come. Across the track and climb onto the platform. Then I'll tell you what to do next."

"Cross the track. Climb the…" She turned to him furiously. "You've got to be bleedin' joking," she started, but Morgan was already stepping back into the passage-between-the-worlds.

"Get on with it, it's for Peter, remember."

Molly put her tongue out at him and jumped heavily down onto the track, muttering darkly about it being a 'bleedin' liberty' and 'people who lay on guilt trips'. She cursed loudly as a sharp stone got into her shoe.

"Don't step on the live rail!" Morgan called after her and she jerked to a halt, foot raised.

"Which one is it?" she called back nervously as she stood wobbling.

"Absolutely no idea, just avoid them all!"

Molly swore she could *hear* him smirking. Gingerly stepping over the rusted, metal rails, she managed to get to the other side and haul herself up onto the platform. Morgan averted his eyes as her dress rucked up around her waist to reveal enormous pink knickers.

"Now what do I do?" she panted, looking across the tracks and wishing she was back in the passage-between-the-worlds. "How do I get out of here?"

"The war-slogan, slide it to one side." There was urgency in his voice now.

She looked to where he pointed and saw a large, red board, rectangular in shape, screwed onto the tiled wall of the station. Painted in white near the top was a crown and beneath it the words, *Keep Calm and Carry On.* She slid it across as he'd instructed, not bothering to wonder how this was possible, and saw there was an opening behind. She was about to investigate further when he called to her again.

"Molly, when you reach the cave, don't hang around."

She peered back through the gloom of the tunnel to where he stood silhouetted in the golden glow of the torchlight from the passage-between-the-worlds. His features were indiscernible but there was no mistaking the worry in his tone.

"Get what you need and leave," he warned. "I've arranged it with the Conductor, the train will return for you the next day and you must be there; it will not return again. He is doing all of this only as a favor to me and it is not one to be taken lightly.

She nodded distractedly, not really hearing his words and forgetting he probably wouldn't be able to see her properly. Then she stepped through the opening into a room beyond.

"This is the way into the station?" she called softly back to him.

THE SANCTUARY

"A toilet cubicle?" And when he didn't answer, "Is it the Men's or the Ladies?"

The wizard shrugged, never one to be concerned with insignificant details. "How would I know?"

Beyond the cubicle door, she heard a young child say, "Mummy, the lady in the toilet is talking to herself," and her mother's terse whisper, "Hush, child, she might hear you!"

The Ladies, thank goodness for small mercies, Molly thought to herself and, remembering just in time to slide back the board and flush the toilet, she unfastened the lock on the cubicle door and stepped out. She gave the child a brief smile and hurried out, just catching the child's high-pitched:

"Mummy she didn't even wash her hands!" before the door slammed shut behind her.

Gazing round, she found herself in the ultra-modern surroundings of Canary Wharf station with its gleaming chrome and huge escalators that seemed to reach toward the sky. There were fewer people around now as the last of the day's trains arrived or departed.

Ignoring the curious stares of passers-by, she sat on a vacant seat and picked up a magazine that lay beside her and began to read. It occurred to her that when the station did close, she would have to leave also. Surreptitiously glancing round to check no one was watching, she took out her wand and waved it discreetly. The glamour instantly hid her from the view of mortals and, abandoning the magazine, she lay her head against the back of the seat, closed her eyes and was soon asleep, soft snores escaping from her nose.

THE SANCTUARY

*   *   *   *

As Morgan stepped back into the lounge of the Sanctuary, the first thing he saw was the curled-up figure of Penelope fast asleep on one of the settees. The wizard sat next to her and softly stroked her forehead until she stirred. The little girl prised one eye open and looked up at him.

"Where did Molly go?" she murmured sleepily.

"Oh, she went on a journey, but she'll be back soon." He crossed his fingers as he said it, hoping fervently it was true. He hated sending his friend into danger and was still not entirely convinced he shouldn't have gone himself. Outside in the passage he'd kept up the banter and teasing, which they often used to disguise just how fond they were of each other. But both had known it was a feeble attempt to hide just how worried he was; how worried they both were.

"Molly won't be gone long," he repeated, but the girl was already fast asleep again. The wizard gathered her gently into his arms and carried her upstairs, back into her bed. He arranged the sheets and blankets around her shoulders and smiled tenderly as she instinctively curled into the fetal position. Morgan brushed her forehead with his lips, turned off her bedside lamp and quietly closed the door behind him.

When she awoke the next morning, Penelope remembered the adventures of the night before. She got out of bed and pulled on her dressing gown and slippers, determined to find Morgan and see where Molly had gone. She was about to knock on his door

THE SANCTUARY

when she heard voices from within; it was Morgan and Wallace. Then she heard Molly's name mentioned and paused to listen, pushing to the back of her mind the fact that she was actually eavesdropping.

Although she couldn't hear everything and much of what she heard she didn't understand, she learned enough to know Molly had gone on a journey to a cave and it was something to do with a 'blood moon', whatever *that* was. And it seemed that the recovery of Luke's father depended on the success of Molly's journey and whether she could find a cure.

The first instinct of most nine-year-olds would have been to run and find Luke so she could tell him what she'd overheard. But now the caution she'd learned since the death of her mother and her own natural reticence served the girl well. Young as she was, she understood the danger of raising Luke's hopes unnecessarily, so instead of seeking him out, her feet quite naturally took her to the room she'd come to regard as her own private sanctuary. It was a place where she could retreat from the sometimes tumultuous world around her and forget about her own grief for a while; the library.

Always a studious child, she loved the room's hushed, almost dream-like atmosphere, particularly when the sun streamed through the windows on sunny days, catching thousands of dust motes in its rays. Today was such a day but for once Penelope didn't notice the warmth of the room or that smell of old leather and paper peculiar to libraries that she normally loved so much.

Today she was on a mission, a quest of her own to find something out. She would look through every single book if she had to until she found some information about blood moons. Much easier to look on the internet of course, and like all children of her generation she was even more comfortable with computers than with books. But that would mean asking someone for their password which in turn would invite awkward questions. In any case, the girl had a sneaking feeling the information she wanted might not be found on the internet, which after all was a mortal invention. Although she'd only been a resident of the Sanctuary for a short while, there were times when Penelope forgot she herself was a mortal. When Alessandro came to fetch her for lunch, she was sitting on the floor surrounded by books.

"*Cara Mia!*" he exclaimed. "There you are!" He looked in puzzlement at the scene before him, for it was unusual for the child to be so untidy, particularly with books. "What are you doing, *Cara*? Are you looking for something in particular?"

For an instant the girl was tempted to share her secret; she'd become very fond of the extravagant young Italian and her task would certainly be easier with two. But that innate caution prevented her, and she just shook her head.

"Oh nothing!" she lied brightly. "Just killing time."

Alessandro nodded doubtfully; something here didn't add up. Seeing he was about to ask more awkward questions, Penelope sought hurriedly to distract him.

"By the way, Alessandro, please may I borrow your internet password?"

Chapter 22

Molly awoke to the sound of footsteps click-clacking on the concrete platform as a man dressed in a dark blue uniform came striding toward her.

On his head he wore a matching cap with the letters 'AT&SF' stitched on the front in gold thread. She surmised that he was the Conductor.

"You want this train?" he called out, his voice deep and rich. "Y'all better hurry if you do!" The broad Texan accent was straight out of an old cowboy movie, the image enhanced by his side whiskers and the drooping handlebar mustache that curled round magnificently before ending in finely waxed points. She stared up at him, bleary eyed, unable for a moment to recollect where she was but then she spotted the huge, gleaming machine beyond him.

"Is that the, erm, the magic train?"

The man turned and followed her gaze for a moment, hooking his thumbs inside the old-fashioned braces that held up his trousers. The train was beautiful, a poem of shining black metal, polished wood and burnished steel. The enormous pistons that drove the huge iron wheels were painted bright gold and the oversized funnel on top of the engine belched great clouds of steam. At the very front was a huge lantern that shone with the intensity of a thousand light bulbs.

"Well now, let me see." The man stroked his mustache thoughtfully. "It sure 'ain't the train to Tooting Broadway now, is it?"

It took Molly a moment to work that out because what the man, with his heavy Southern American drawl, actually said was: 'itshoewainthetrayntootootnbrordwhynowayseet?'

But the sarcasm was unmistakable, and Molly flushed. "Oh, right, I see. Stupid question, sorry."

"Although if you did want to go to Tooting Broadway," the man was already saying, "it would be the Jubilee line, which is over… there." He pointed down the track. "Till you come to London Bridge, then onto the Northern Line for Tooting." He smiled helpfully. "You, er, don't want to go there, do you?"

Molly shook her head impatiently. "Of course not, I need this one." She stood and marched past him, thinking the man was much too big for his boots.

She was about to climb up into one of the carriages when he asked softly, "You *do* have a ticket, of course?"

Molly turned and gave him a steely look.

"Nope." She didn't need to add, 'and what are you going to do about it?' Her tone was quite clear.

The Conductor sighed. "You're supposed to have a ticket, didn't Morgan tell you?"

"No, he didn't. Can we get going now?"

He sighed again and took out a large fob watch, then a horrified look came over his face.

"Late! No time to lose! Quickly, onto the train!" He hustled Molly up the steps and only just managed to stop himself placing both hands on her ample buttocks to give her a push. He replaced the watch, took out a shiny silver whistle, placed it in his mouth and gave a long, shrill blast. Almost immediately the enormous pistons moved, the wheels turned, and the train glided slowly down the track. It picked up speed as it entered the long, dark tunnel where it would remain until it reached the next station.

Except this train wasn't going to the next station. It thundered along in the darkness and quickly approached a large gap in the tunnel wall, invisible from inside due to the glare from the windows. At the last moment, a set of points clicked and the track shifted, sending the train hurtling through the opening, which closed as soon as it was through. The train continued in darkness for a few seconds then it was out into open countryside, already free of the confines of the city. As she settled into her seat, Molly looked with interest at the other passengers, mostly children, very excitable in that end-of-school-going-on-holiday kind of way.

Then there was the balding, middle-aged man fast asleep in his seat, clearly some highly-paid executive in his dark, beautifully tailored, pin-stripe suit. An aroma of expensive aftershave hung about him and his shoes were handmade from the best leather. Yet the shoes were unpolished and scuffed, the suit creased and his shirt grubby around the collar. He looked like he hadn't shaved for at least a week.

Across the aisle from him was a much younger man, immaculate in clothes even more expensive than the middle-aged man's. He spent the entire time marching up and down the gangway talking loudly and annoyingly into the mobile phone glued to his ear.

"I've been wondering," said Molly when the Conductor appeared in the carriage a short time later, "what do the letters stand for?" She pointed to his cap.

"Stands for the 'Atchison, Topeka and Santa Fe'," he said proudly, "but most folks call it the Santa Fe Railroad for short."

"Santa Fe?" Molly was puzzled. "But that's in Mexico!"

He muttered something under his breath which she couldn't quite hear; out loud he just said, rather sarcastically, "That's right."

"But we're only going to Wales." Molly attempted to return his earlier sarcasm, but the man was clearly a master of that particular art and he gave her a withering look.

"No, *you're* only going to Wales, the rest of us are going much further. He didn't actually say 'stupid' but his tone implied it. Molly couldn't think of a comeback, so she changed the subject and motioned him to come closer.

"What's the story with these two?" she whispered, indicating her fellow passengers.

"Ah!" He became secretive and gave a sidelong glance up and down the carriage. Like many conductors on any public transport the world over, he liked nothing more than to chat and gossip. Sitting on the seat beside her, he covered his mouth and spoke in a loud whisper, "You see the rumply-suit guy?"

Molly nodded.

"Well, he's not what he seems..."

Just then, the lights of the carriage dimmed in readiness for the night journey and through the window there appeared a vision of absolute horror. Taken unawares, Molly let out a small scream, quickly stifled as she reached instinctively for her wand. The Conductor placed a gentle hand on her shoulder.

"Relax, they cannot see us," he murmured, his mouth close to her ear.

"Easy for you to say," she snapped, her voice shaking. She tapped the window. "This is glass; it breaks."

The Conductor was pleased to hear some of her natural abrasiveness reassert itself. "Nevertheless, they cannot harm us. They exist in between dimensions. They are there, yet not there."

"What are those bleedin' things? They're hideous."

"They are the deformed; the unwanted. Demons mostly. Experiments of the Demon King, probably; experiments that did not…succeed."

"You're certain they can't get in?" Molly was by no means certain she shared the Conductor's confidence.

"I told you, they cannot see us, and anyway, even if they could, I and this train are not without power." He reached across and drew down the blind then moved along the carriage, doing the same at each window. "Sleep now," he called softly, "all of you. You may each rest without fear tonight."

With that, the Conductor went to do…whatever it is that conductors do, and Molly closed her eyes and tried not to imagine the apparitions outside.

They're only six inches away, she thought unhappily, *I don't care what he says. There's no way I'm gonna get any sleep tonight.* She peeped inside her pocket to find the two faeries sleeping soundly and gave them a sour look. But secretly, she was relieved they'd not been awake to witness her earlier weakness. Presently, she slipped into a fitful doze which eventually turned into sleep.

It was mid-morning when she awoke to find the blinds had been raised once more. Outside, she saw the English meadows and hedgerows had given way to the more rugged beauty of the Welsh mountains. She could see the distinctive shape of Cader Idris in the distance, unmistakable because Morgan had described it to her so many times over the years.

It had been his favorite childhood haunt; he'd loved to climb the mountain as a boy, often with his brother in happier times. He'd often told the story of how Llywelyn ap Gruffydd, possibly the greatest of all the legendary Welsh princes, had supposedly found peace and rest within the shelter of the mountain, a brief respite from his battles against the English King Edward I.

Molly smiled. Her old friend was such a romantic at heart and she knew the tales of the Welsh people's struggles for independence had greatly appealed to his chivalrous heart. For a time, she lost herself in these reminiscences until, at last, the train slowed with a great hissing and squealing of brakes. Molly peered through the window but could make nothing out through the great clouds of steam. Gradually though the outline of a building began to emerge. Above the door was a sign, freshly painted with a bright red dragon on a green and white background. A pair of brass coach lamps shone with a harsh, electric light giving the curious effect that the dragon was coming toward her through the billowing cloud.

As the steam cleared further, Molly saw that in the doorway

of the gray stone building stood a tall, stick-thin man holding a pewter tankard that foamed with a thick, black beer. Beside him was a small dog, a Yorkshire terrier, that barked furiously at the train as if trying to scare it away. The train finally halted, and the man strode forward, flung open the door and popped his head into the carriage. The dog continued its shrill, high pitched barking.

"Hello! Hello!" he greeted her. "Just yourself getting off?" She nodded and he exclaimed, "Well come on in then, I'm the Landlord. Sorry about the dog, he's very excitable. Welcome to *The Red Dragon*! Be *quiet,* Oscar!"

Moments later, Molly was standing on the platform. She reached down to the dog who instantly stopped its noise and licked her hand. From behind she heard the sound of the train moving again and turned to find it was already some distance down the track.

The Conductor raised a hand in farewell and she just caught the faint, "Goodbye, y'all take care now!" She waved back, then the train was gone, out of sight around the bend, and she followed the Landlord into the pub, Oscar trotting happily at her side. The place was empty and looked as if it had been for a very long time judging by the cobwebs that hung everywhere.

This place could do with a right old scrubbing. Molly gave a disapproving sniff which turned into a sneeze as the dust got up her nose.

"Bless you." The Landlord patted each of his pockets, searching in vain for a handkerchief to give her.

"Thanks," she replied somewhat absently, thinking, *no wonder he ain't got no customers, I bet it's ages since anyone came in 'ere.* And this was indeed the case, although not for the reason she surmised.

The fact was people simply had no reason to visit the place these days; after all, nobody needs to cross a portal into seventeenth century Wales anymore, do they?

Except that now, someone did.

And this was the reason the Landlord had dutifully kept the portal open for all these years, in preparation for such a need as this.

"Drink?" he was saying as he indicated an array of bottles on a shelf behind the bar.

"It's still morning," Molly told him primly.

"Cup of tea then?"

She nodded gratefully. As she waited, she looked around curiously at her modern surroundings; the glass, the chrome and the blue neon lighting seemed incongruous given the bleakness of the pub's location. The only thing that didn't look brand new was the jukebox, clearly an original from the 1950s. As she looked, a black circular disc dropped into place and the machine began to belt an old rock 'n' roll tune.

She commented on it as she sipped her steaming mug of tea and the music changed to something she'd heard Cissy and Luke blasting out in the lounge of the Sanctuary. To her it was just noise and the Landlord caught her grimace.

"Ah yes, the jukebox." He hurriedly skipped the song. "Probably some pimply kid sent it to the wrong collection point when we ordered it. Got the right address but the wrong time."

At her puzzled expression he explained, "In years, I mean, not minutes. That thing was delivered here in 1850 or thereabouts, then it stood gathering dust for decades until records were invented." Then, just in case she might not know what records were, he added, "They're flat discs that have music in them. Black, usually. They go around and round."

Molly was fast losing interest as the man rambled on with an air of importance as if he expected Molly to be impressed at his knowledge.

"Don't see them much nowadays since CDs came along, and now even they…"

She drained the last of her tea and stood. "Fascinating," she said politely, "can we get on now?" She beckoned him closer. "I have to get to…"

He frowned and placed a hand on her arm. "Morgan already sent me a message; I don't need to know more." He took the cup from her and washed it at a sink behind the bar, dried it and folded the dish cloth neatly and a little fastidiously.

"Never did get around to buying a dishwasher," he explained with a smile. "The whole jukebox thing rather put me off. Now, if you're ready?" He lowered his voice, "Nice and quiet now, it's not everyone who's seen what you're about to." He looked nervously from side to side and Molly, tactfully for once, decided not to point out that there was nobody actually in the place to see anything anyway.

"Quickly now," he repeated, this time in a whisper and led her through a doorway behind the bar and along a narrow corridor. Oscar trotted behind them, his paws pattering softly on the tiled floor; it seemed he never strayed very far from his owner. It went on for some distance, far longer than it should have, considering the size of the place, which wasn't *that* big. But eventually they arrived at a stout, very old looking door set with iron studs and a large iron knob. The Landlord grasped it in both hands and used all his strength, but nothing happened.

"Give us a hand," he grunted and together they managed to turn it and pull the door inwards. Molly stepped over the threshold and into a land bathed in the last rays of the setting sun.

"What the bleedin'—" She caught herself and looked at him in puzzlement. "It was morning a minute ago!"

"We can't have everyone knowing our secrets now, can we? We're in the same place, different time. The door you've just come through is like the ones in your passage-between-the-worlds."

It took a second for Molly to register his words then she looked at him curiously.

"Yes, yes," he said impatiently, "I know all about that. I'm not as stupid as I may look, see?"

Molly had the grace to look guilty; she had been thinking the man seemed rather dense.

"Morgan's an old friend," he went on. "Matter of fact, I used to live in the Sanctuary myself."

Once again Molly was surprised, and it must have shown on her face for he winked.

"Of course, that was long before you were born, my dear." He scratched his nose reflectively. "Or Morgan for that matter."

"So, where and when are we now?" she asked.

"Well now, let me see, when you were on the other side of the pub it was…well I suppose it was your own time in a manner of speaking, wasn't it? Though it definitely depends what year you were in when you set off…probably." He scratched the side of his nose again and tried to concentrate. "Now when you're *inside* the pub it's...well to be honest, it's anybody's guess what year it is, changes so often, it does."

By now Molly suspected that, not for the first time in her life, someone was having a laugh at her expense. "And this side of the pub?"

"Wales, North Wales, 1684," he said. "Always 1684. Until next year," he added helpfully. He stopped suddenly. "Or is it 1864?" He scratched his head and looked perturbed. "One forgets these things so easily around here you know," he explained apologetically. "Last week it was 1979 for a bit, we had a party of holiday makers with spiky green hair and metal pins." He stopped as Molly's eyes narrowed.

"Yes, well,"—he cleared his throat hastily—"you should probably be on your way, it will be dark in a few hours and the moon rise is some time off yet." He wondered briefly if he should tell her about tonight's blood moon but, unsure of how much she already knew, he decided against it. Morgan hadn't seen fit to mention why his friend was coming and it really wasn't any of his business.

Let the witch find out about the blood moon for herself, he thought. The Landlord liked a quiet life and meddling in the doings of wizards and witches was something he had given up a very long time ago.

"Up there to the sign-post at the top." He pointed to a long flight of stone steps. "Then it's up to you which way you go. Bye!" Oscar gave a single, sharp bark of farewell and before she could reply to either of them the door slammed and they were gone.

THE SANCTUARY

Molly sighed with resignation, but the faeries didn't mind, they were just glad to leave the confines of her pocket where they'd been hiding. They chattered excitedly and flew in circles around her head, seeing how close they could get their wands to her nose without actually hitting it. Molly took a last look at the door to the inn which remained closed. "Looks like we're on our own then," she announced.

As she huffed and puffed up the long, steep flight of stairs, she was unaware that the door had opened once more, just a crack, and that from the shadows two eyes watched her. When at last she had disappeared from sight, it closed again with finality.

The Landlord sighed and returned to the interior of the old railway station, his face grim and the joking, idiotic act he often adopted as a disguise completely erased. Oscar trotted beside him, occasionally jumping and trying to nose into his pocket.

"Okay, okay," he agreed, and took out a small piece of cheese, smiling as it was instantly swallowed in one. He bent and ruffled the dog's fur fondly. "Think she'll survive, Oscar?"

The dog answered with a series of sharp, high-pitched barks. The Landlord sighed again, and his smile was replaced by a worried frown.

"I hope so too, boy," he replied. "I hope so too."

THE SANCTUARY

Chapter 23

It had indeed been a long time. Nearly four centuries had passed since Logan and the demon had last stood on this hillside and cautiously approached the high wooden fence that surrounded the village…

They'd remained hidden as the night watchman made yet another circuit, and as he moved out of sight, they quickly scaled the fence and were enveloped by the shadows once more. All had gone well, for the hour was late and the village slept. Soon they approached the house of his father and brother, a house Logan no longer thought of as home. The place was in darkness but as Logan took out a key and inserted it into the lock, a torch flared in an upstairs room and they quickly returned to the shadows. A figure appeared at the window, peering out into the darkness. It was Daffyd, their father's manservant – some instinct or premonition of danger had awakened him.

Logan cautioned the demon to remain still, then stepped out into the pool of light cast by the flickering torch, calling to the old soldier to come down and open the door. After a few minutes, bolts were drawn and a key turned. The door swung open and Dafydd stepped out, hand upon his sword hilt, suspicion etched onto his face.

The twins' father had been a loving but also an oft absent one, and this old man had done as much as anybody to raise them. He had taught them, played with them, comforted them and tended to their boyhood cuts and grazes. More than anything, he had given the twins his love, and indeed he loved them still. But for some time there'd been a reserve between Dafydd and Logan, something the old man couldn't quite put his finger on. But he had heard the talk about Logan and the Demon King, rumors to be sure, but enough to make him wary.

Now his fears were stilled by the boy's outstretched arms and his excited cry of "Dafydd!" All thoughts of caution were forgotten as he moved forward into Logan's embrace. For a moment, they stood locked together, the old man's eyes tight shut to stem the tears that threatened to spill. But an instant later, those same eyes snapped open and, as well as tears, there was a flash of pain followed by utter shock as the knife slid silently into his heart.

As Dafydd stumbled backwards, there was time for only a brief, accusing look before he fell lifeless to the ground. Logan gave him a momentary, dispassionate glance then motioned for his companion to follow. Together they made their way through the darkened rooms until they reached the staircase that led to where his father and brother slept. At the bottom of the stairs, the boy remained still for a long time as he pondered the Demon King's promises. He was suddenly unsure he'd be able to carry out the plan to its very end and so he hesitated. Somehow, he sensed that once he took the first step up that staircase, there'd be no turning back.

The demon made no attempt to hurry him; he'd been warned there was to be no persuasion or coercion, the boy must do it of his own free will, for only then would the Demon King own him completely. And if he didn't... The creature ran a scaly finger along the edge of his own dagger, then placed the finger into his mouth and sucked greedily at the blood that welled from the cut.

His master's orders had been clear and the demon found himself hoping the boy's nerve would fail. He glanced at him furtively, his eyes almost drooling with malice and for a moment he allowed himself the luxury of imagining his knife against that soft, white throat. It had been a long time since he'd had the opportunity to kill a human, perhaps tonight would be his chance. His lips curled back to reveal razor sharp teeth and he grinned to himself; surely his master wouldn't begrudge him the pleasure of killing the brother too? He was shaken from his daydream as Logan abruptly made his decision and headed upstairs, stretching his long legs over the sixth and ninth steps, knowing they creaked.

As they neared the top, they heard heavy snoring; his father's bedroom lay just along the passage. Moments later he was looking down at the familiar face. Familiar but also changed, for there were streaks of gray, even white in his beard where before there had been none, and new, deeper lines around the eyes and mouth.

The old man is becoming frail, thought Logan, and he noted with distaste the slack lips and the drops of spittle that flew from them as his father snored. But as he looked at the once-loved face, his resolve faltered. The twins had never known their mother and this man had been both to them, despite the demands on his time that came with being leader of the village.

But it was his duties as a powerful wizard that had made the greater *demands and taken him from them for long periods, for their father was leader of a mysterious band of wizards called the 'Sanctuary.'* At fifteen years old that was as much as Logan knew, but both he and his brother had been promised an introduction to a new and exciting world once they came of age at sixteen.

Now *you'll never have the chance to show me*, the boy thought sadly as, with trembling hands, he took out his knife and held it high above the heaving chest. "Goodbye, Father," he whispered, his voice tremulous as he tensed, ready to strike – but suddenly unwilling or unable to do so.

"Go on," the demon hissed, "do it!"

But still the boy hesitated until his arms began to shake. Their father had raised them alone without support of a wife to help share the burden. It had been this man who'd offered praise or punishment, who'd given them love. And when he couldn't be there, he'd made certain Dafydd was.

Dear Dafydd, *the boy thought*. Dear, dead Dafydd.

"What are you waiting for?" The demon licked his lips in anticipation. *The boy isn't going to do it! Gleefully he moved silently behind Logan and the hand that held his own knife drew slowly backward.* "Remember the plan!"

And the words steadied the boy, giving him renewed resolve as he thought of the riches and power he'd been promised.

"He loves your brother more," the Demon King had said, "he will give him everything, leave you with nothing!"

And suddenly, with utter clarity, Logan knew it to be true. His grip on the knife tightened as he held it high above his head. At last some instinct or sense of danger caused the eyes of the sleeping man to snap *open.*

And Logan plunged the knife deep into his father's chest...

Logan thrust his memories aside as the demon bowed in return and motioned for him to follow. The crow hissed in warning; it didn't like this creature of the underworld.

"Hurry," urged the demon, and he looked anxiously up at the sky. "We must enter the cave quickly for the night is clear and there is no cloud to hide the moon when it rises."

"But surely nobody will see us right up here, even if the moon is bright? And even if we were seen,"—Logan shrugged—"what does it matter? What could they do? They are mere mortals," he spat contemptuously.

"Tonight will be a full moon," came the reply, and now it was not anxiety the Dark Wizard heard but rising panic. "But it is not the brightness I fear, it is the blood moon," the demon continued and gestured toward the horizon. "See?"

Logan looked to where the sky was turning into a blazing collage of reds and oranges. "The sunset?" He was puzzled by the demon's behavior and obvious unease. "What's wrong with it?"

"It is not the sunset!" The creature was now almost frantic. "It is the rising of the blood moon!" He hastened toward the cave entrance, almost running now. "It is fatal to we demons," he called over his shoulder. "Should its evil light touch me, I will not survive." His voice became fainter as he at last passed into the safety of the cave.

Logan found he had to duck his head beneath the low entrance as he himself entered. He looked thoughtfully at his companion;

THE SANCTUARY

that little snippet of information was certainly interesting. He stood in the entrance and watched as the moon, a deep crimson, began to peep above the horizon.

"The moon's light is fatal, you say?" He turned to face his companion. "To all demons?"

It nodded. "If we even look at the moon we are blinded, and should its light touch us, the very flesh is blasted from our bones." The demon shuddered and it was pleasing for Logan to see the normally arrogant creature so discomfited. "No one is exempt; not even the Demon King himself can withstand its evil."

Logan looked at the reddening sky and gave a secret smile of satisfaction. *Very interesting indeed,* he thought. Abruptly he swung toward his companion; the time for idle chatter had passed, there was work to be done. As he stepped forward, he gave an exclamation of annoyance as his robe caught on an old, dead thorn bush that clung to a crack in the rock by the cave's entrance. Impatiently, he tugged it free leaving a scrap of black silk fluttering in the breeze as it hung from one of the wicked barbs.

"Come on," he ordered, "let's get this over with." And together they eased into the passageway that led down to the world of the demons.

* * * *

Hidden behind a large boulder outside the cave, Molly had also found the demon's words interesting, although she'd only caught a fraction of what had been said.

Earlier, red-faced and panting, she'd at last reached the top of the steps to find herself on a wide, neatly cobbled road that stretched, dead straight, to the north and south. Looking down at *The Red Dragon*, now far away in the distance, she'd noted that from this side of the old inn, there was no sign of the train track, just fields and hedgerows as far as the eye could see.

Mindful of the Landlord's warning about time, she turned her attention to the signpost. It was painted white and the signs pointed in all directions, their destinations, along with a cautionary warning painted neatly in black.

Two of them pointed up and down the cobbled road, one proclaiming 'Scotland (eventually),' the other 'London Town (a long, long way).'

The third sign, rather uselessly Molly thought, was angled to point down the steps and announced 'The Red Dragon (finest ale in all Wales)' and the fourth pointed in the opposite direction not along a road or path but toward a distant gap between the mountains. Beyond them the sea could just be seen glinting brightly in the evening sun, and the sign said 'The Americas (probably).'

But the fifth and final sign was different. It pointed along a narrow dirt track that was overgrown with nettles and brambles. While the others were handsomely painted and well cared for, the wood of this one was rotten, the letters barely legible. Peering shortsightedly in the disappearing light, Molly could just make out a single word: 'Seriously?'

Molly spent no little time pondering and grumbling to no one in particular. "Morgan didn't tell me what to do when I got to this part." She allowed the faeries to alight onto her outstretched arm.

THE SANCTUARY

"What do you two think we should do?" Eventually they decided to risk the overgrown trail and it had taken almost four hours to reach the edge of the valley. Her legs were scratched, the skin torn and bleeding from the brambles.

In the last hour she'd walked in near darkness as the sun set and she'd needed the light from her wand to aid her.

Nevertheless, she'd twice twisted her ankle painfully on the uneven ground and her shoes were soaked from stepping in puddles. Then, after finally spotting the location of the cave at the far side of the valley, it had taken another hour to scramble around the steep slopes and approach the entrance.

Morgan must've known it'd be like this, she thought crossly. *Bleedin' inconsiderate, I call it.* She'd just finished resting and was about to climb the last part of the hill when Moth had given a warning hiss. As she froze and peered into the gloom, she could just make out two figures reaching the cave entrance ahead of her.

"Who is it?" she whispered and ducked hurriedly down behind a large boulder while he went to investigate. In a few moments, he returned and whispered in her ear.

"The Dark Wizard?" Her voice was incredulous. "What's he doing here?" Getting no reply, she went on, "And who was that with him?" This time Moth did answer, and Molly felt her entire body go cold. "So soon? We knew he was negotiating with the demons, but *so soon?*"

When the coast was clear, she stepped cautiously out and made her way toward the cave. The faeries had none of their usual jauntiness however, and were huddled together half hidden beneath the collar of her robe, shivering uncontrollably. Winter was approaching and faeries do not feel the cold, but they do fear demons. Very much.

The sky in the distance was aflame as the full moon was revealed and the countryside to the east was awash with blood. As the moon rose higher the effect was that of a raging forest fire creeping inexorably toward them. Molly hurried; there was something unnerving about that vast, red cloak.

"Slow down!" It was Moth who hissed in her ear. "The blood moon is not evil!" The faeries wanted to give the demon and his companion time to get as far away as possible. "Look, see what's happening in the village!"

So intent had Molly been on reaching the cave that she'd paid scant attention to the village of Morgan's birth. But now she paused and looked back down the hill to where the outer buildings were already bathed in the light of the moon. As she watched, people began to pour from their homes and congregate in the streets and the fields beyond.

"What are they doing?" she asked, as more people appeared. Some hobbled out on crutches, others were aided by friends and family, and yet more were carried out on makeshift stretchers. Clearly these were the injured and sick of the village.

"That is the wonder of the blood moon, it has the power to heal," Moth answered. "Only the gravely ill, those beyond all hope, will remain in their homes this night."

"And before you ask,"—Velveteena saw the old woman was about to speak—"it cannot reverse the effects of demon poison, that's why we need the blood thorn."

Molly's face fell; for an instant hope had surged within her.

Seeing this, the faerie sought to distract her. "And that's not all it does," she went on, "it's also a fertile moon, Molly, just look!" They pointed to where there was frantic activity in the fields. Some people were digging and sowing great armfuls of seed while others drove horses that pulled great wooden plows.

"By morning these fields will be fully grown and ready to harvest. There will be enough wheat, fruit and vegetables to see the village through the winter." Moth spoke in a hushed tone as if even he couldn't quite take in the wonder of it.

Molly too was enthralled but she realized the night was passing them by. "Come on, the moonlight is already halfway up the hillside."

She marched resolutely once more toward the cave entrance, the red light of the moon almost nibbling at her heels as it followed. She was panting with effort by the time she stooped and entered the cave's dim interior. Then she lit her wand, an action she'd performed without conscious thought a million times, one that used a minuscule amount of magic.

But far down the tunnel the Dark Wizard sensed it and stopped abruptly. Slowly he turned and peered back up the passage, alert for danger. His companion, the demon, was about to speak but Logan stopped him with a raised hand. He wondered if he could have been mistaken but no, now he could smell it, the faint but unmistakable ozone stink of recent magic!

Logan muttered to the crow on his shoulder and it hopped onto his arm, listening intently to his instructions. Then, with a sweep of its big purple and black wings, it went soaring back up the passage.

THE SANCTUARY

In the cave, Molly looked around in despair for apart from a few sparse tufts of grass poking up through the sandy floor and an old, clearly dead thorn bush clinging to a small crack in the wall, there was no sign of life.

Moth and Velveteena were deep inside one of her pockets, almost prostrate with terror. Their ears were so sensitive they could hear far off demons laughing, a coarse, horrible sound that set their teeth on edge and made their ears hurt. There was the harsh, clanging sound of hammers on metal as the worker-demons toiled at the furnaces and forges deep below the ground. The terrified faeries could clearly hear the screams of slaves as their masters beat them in an effort to exact every ounce of work before they fell down dead with exhaustion.

Then there were the sounds of fighting, for demons will fall out over even the tiniest thing. These fights would usually end suddenly with chokes and gurgles as the weakest was strangled to death. Apart from a knife between the ribs in the darkness, this was the demons' favorite method of killing. Any minute now the faeries expected one to appear and so they held each other close, deep in Molly's pocket.

Nevertheless, when Moth heard Molly curse with disappointment and begin to make her way from the cave, he gathered up every ounce of his courage. Then out of her pocket he flew, chattering frantically and pointing.

Sure enough, the light from the blood moon was seeping inside and creeping up the cave wall. Seconds later it touched the thorn bush and the transformation was astounding. The bush seemed to burst into flames and Molly took an involuntary step backward.

THE SANCTUARY

When she looked again its stems had turned a vibrant green, exuding health and vitality. Its wicked, razor sharp thorns were a bright orange and sap, its very life force dripped, from their tips, a viscous, crimson liquid. It was suddenly very apparent how it had got its name.

"Quickly!" Moth urged the witch. "Choose one and let's get out of here. Be careful not to prick your finger. The consequences would be… unfortunate."

Molly did as she was bid and snapped off a thorn. Working on the principle that biggest is best, she chose the largest one she could see, wrapped it in her handkerchief then reached out again. "I'll take another just in case, can't do any bleedin' harm."

But now Velveteena's head popped up in alarm. "Don't!" she whispered loudly. "It most certainly can do harm!" She perched on Molly's outstretched hand as if attempting to stop it reaching further. "You cannot take more than you need, you mustn't abuse the magic you've been offered!"

Molly withdrew her arm hurriedly. Faeries possessed knowledge that went back millennia, far surpassing that of witches and wizards, goblins and even demons. She wasn't about to take any chances.

"I get it," she said, already ducking out of the cave, much to the relief of the faeries, "let's go." And having got what she'd come for, she made her way quickly down the slope, Moth and Velveteena balancing on her shoulder.

But even though she was suddenly in a hurry to get home, she took a moment to pause and look at the stunning panorama laid out before them. The entire countryside all around was lit with a

THE SANCTUARY

hundred, no a thousand shades of orange and red. Faraway forests looked as if they were burning, rivers flowed like crimson ribbons and lakes were huge pools of molten lava. She took in the awesome sight knowing she might never see the like again, until eventually she felt Velveteena nibbling her ear.

"Okay you've seen enough, let's go," the faerie whispered softly but urgently. They were still far too close to the demons' lair and the faeries wouldn't rest till they were far away and safely back behind the walls of the Sanctuary.

Molly jerked back to reality and suddenly she too wanted very much to get home. She hurried but still it wasn't quick enough for the faeries.

"Shouldn't you have a broomstick or something?" complained Moth, adding for good measure, "And one of those black, pointy hats?"

Molly was all at once very disheartened at the thought of the trek to the railway station and the long wait till morning and the arrival of the Conductor and his train. His words irked her, and she snapped back, "This isn't a bleedin' kid's story, y'know! In real life witches don't have broomsticks!" She shrugged him from her shoulder angrily. "Nor do we have black, pointy hats! This isn't *The Wizard of* bleedin' *Oz!*"

So, with Molly dispirited and angry and the faeries' fear making them argumentative, there was the perfect recipe for falling out and they did just that. In no time at all things were so heated that the crow was almost upon them before Molly sensed it and began to turn. But she was far too late, and she could only watch aghast as the great black bird swooped down and grabbed one of the faeries in its claws. It was already rising high into the air before Moth's anguished "Velveteena!" roused her into action.

Now, there is no doubt that in appearance Molly resembled a fat, old woman with a bright red face and wobbling triple chins, and she was all of those. But she was also a very powerful witch.

Instinctively she raised her wand, took a brief but careful aim, then let fly with a single, white-hot bolt. As it hurtled upward, the crow was already a distant black dot, but her aim was true and, fast though it was, the Dark Wizard's servant could not outdistance it. The lightning bolt struck the bird squarely in the center of its back and it screamed in agony. Its claws opened and Velveteena's unconscious body plummeted toward the ground.

Chapter 24

"Where's Molly?" The question was an idle one for the witch had not yet been gone long enough to cause concern and Luke was unprepared for Morgan's reaction.

"Mind your own business," he snapped with unnecessary force, causing the boy to stare at him in surprise. "Sorry," Morgan muttered, immediately contrite, "she, erm, she had to go somewhere. Suddenly."

Luke was intrigued. *Why was Morgan being so evasive? What was going on?*

But Morgan remained tight-lipped and refused to be drawn. "Not now, Luke, please," and there was that edge to his voice again that warned the boy not to persist. They were in one of the classrooms where Morgan was trying to instruct him in the use of his wand. He had taken over in Molly's absence because of the urgency and lack of time. But now he was beginning to understand why she had so often flounced into his chamber to complain indignantly and let off steam after her sessions with Luke.

THE SANCTUARY

The boy shows no aptitude at all. Surely we couldn't have been so wrong about the prophecy? Morgan excused Luke before the allotted time had passed; they were getting nowhere and the wizard knew he was not being fair to the boy, for his own heart wasn't in it either. It should have been Molly here, trying to each the boy. *I should never have let her go!*

So, Luke escaped the tedium of the lesson, and to him it was tedious. He couldn't understand Cissy's fascination with her wand. Give him a sword any day!

At that moment, his friend was undergoing similar emotions upstairs in the training room where Wallace was attempting to instruct her in the art of weaponry, and he was having the same lack of success as Morgan. Cissy simply couldn't see the attraction in running around with a sword. Most of them were too big and cumbersome for her anyway and they made her arms ache in no time. *No, swords were for boys*, she decided. Her wand required subtlety and concentration whereas swords just needed brute strength and no brains.

She knew this wasn't really true and she secretly admired Luke for how good he'd got in so short a time. She'd heard Wallace tell Morgan that Luke was becoming a match for anyone and it had filled her with pride for him. But now, as she held a short sword in her right hand, one more suited to her strength, and tried to summon some enthusiasm, her left hand fingered her wand in the pocket of her jeans.

Cissy thought back to when Peter had told her she must be as one with her wand, that it should become almost a part of her. He had been right; she kept it with her always and missed the feel of it when she wasn't practicing, missed the way it molded into her hand and how it almost seemed to talk to her. Already she could hardly remember a time when she'd not had it. *Thank goodness Dad was a rubbish wizard so his wand passed to me,* she thought.

But now she had to practice with the sword and although she could see the need to do so, the weapon felt alien to her, and she knew she would never master it. When the lesson was finally over, she was about to leave when Luke burst into the training room in the hope she was still there. Thinking Wallace had gone, they spent the next thirty minutes play acting with the weapons and pretending to fight in single combat on the gym mats.

But Wallace hadn't left and was watching from the shadows. He was half-amused at their antics but, like Morgan, he was also concerned they wouldn't be anywhere near ready for the war that would surely begin soon.

*   *   *   *

"No!" screamed Moth, his mind unable to accept that fate would allow his friend to be rescued from the clutches of the Dark Wizard only to fall to her death. "Do something!" The emotion in his voice was raw at the realization he was about to lose the one person that mattered; the very reason for his existence.

His anguish galvanized Molly into action. She raised her arms skyward, screwed her eyes tightly shut and concentrated as hard as she could.

"*Exaudi nos deus caelum et auxilium!*" Beads of sweat immediately covered her face, so great was the effort. But nothing happened.

THE SANCTUARY

"Try again!" Moth begged, utterly distraught as Velveteena's descent continued, it seemed to him, even more quickly than before.

Molly nodded. "*Exaudi nos deus caelum et auxilium!*" This time she fell to her knees, groaning. And still nothing happened.

"Again," he screamed, "again!" His tiny fists pummeled the old woman's back and shoulders but she hardly felt them.

"I'm sorry," she gasped, barely able to speak she was so exhausted, "I'm truly sorry. I...I cannot."

There followed a string of insults so foul that Molly blinked in surprise, and as the filth poured from his mouth, she was stung into action. Later she would never know how she found the strength but now she hauled herself to her feet for one final effort.

"*Exaudi nos deus caelum et auxilium!*"

As the words were caught up by the breeze, Velveteena plummeted beyond the tops of the tallest trees and as she did so she finally regained consciousness.

"Moth!" She gave a terrified scream and at that moment a powerful gust of wind arose at Molly's command. It flattened the grass around her feet and whipped her hair painfully across her cheeks. She staggered at the force of it, arms still outstretched as she focused her entire will to bring it under her control.

"*Exaudi nos deus caelum et auxilium!*"

She quickly directed the wind toward Velveteena and at the last moment the faerie plunged not into the earth but into the whirling maelstrom and her descent was halted, abruptly, scant centimeters from the ground. Molly had just about enough strength left to lay her gently down onto the grass before she pitched forward and fainted.

The sun was high in the sky when she awoke to find Velveteena trying to trickle water into her mouth from an acorn cup. She raised her head slightly to make it easier and was touched to find the faeries had covered her with leaves to keep her warm during the night.

"Thank you," the words came out hoarsely for her throat was dry. "I can't believe I've slept so late; I must have been asleep nearly twenty-four hours!"

"Thirty-six actually," Moth told her, "you've slept right through, it was the day before yesterday when you fainted."

"What?" Molly tried to get up, but the faeries protested so vehemently that she lay back onto the pillow they had made for her from dried leaves and moss.

She yawned widely. "You shouldn't have let me sleep so long." She yawned again. "Morgan will be worried." She lifted a tired hand and stroked the head of each faerie gently. "It's most... *inconsiderate*." Then her eyes closed and within moments she was asleep again.

*   *   *   *

It is well known that demons delighted in humiliation and in the three hundred or so years since they'd last met, the Demon King's soul had become, if it were possible, even blacker.

For nearly two days now, Logan had stood in this bare cell, neither moving nor speaking, while through the open door he watched the Demon King gorge himself on food and drink. Not once was sustenance offered and neither could he ask – even now, as weak as he was with hunger, barely able to keep upright.

But the Dark Wizard was no prisoner; no chains held him. He was free at any time to leave the cell and join the Demon King at his table, or indeed to leave his realm entirely. But he knew the rules of the game, that this was a test designed to remind him just who was doing the asking. Logan needed the Demon King's aid, and both knew it. So the Dark Wizard suppressed his anger and his hunger and he remained silent.

Even so, his body and his pride could only take so much, and he was on the point of telling the Demon King to go to hell when he felt something nudge against his leg. He was relieved to see the crow, for it had been gone for two days and he'd thought it lost. But he was concerned, as much as he was capable of such emotions, to see the bedraggled state it was in. Quickly he took in the scorch marks along its back and the bald patches where the feathers had been burned away altogether.

After being hit by Molly's lightning bolt, it had plunged toward the ground only for a sudden, strong wind to rise. The helpless bird had been blown across the valley to be eventually deposited violently onto a patch of rocky ground miles away. Sick and weak it had lain there for a long time until it could stagger to its feet. Finding itself unable to fly, it had been forced to walk back to its master, stopping frequently as waves of nausea and dizziness washed over it. Only the minute traces of magic inside the bird, a legacy of its long association with the Dark Wizard, kept it alive. Nevertheless, two days had elapsed before it eventually found its master.

Now Logan bent, allowing the bird to hop onto his arm. Then he listened and his expression became serious as it related the events of the last few days. When it finished, the Dark Wizard was silent for a long time while he made his decision. At last he straightened and looked across at the Demon King and cleared his throat.

"Kanzser, I would speak with you, if I may." The subservience in his voice was enough to make him want to vomit. "A matter of the utmost urgency has arisen." For several minutes the Demon King did not acknowledge him but continued to eat. It was a calculated act, for he knew Logan was seething inside and that only a huge effort prevented him losing his self-control.

Kanzser savored the moment a little longer, his cruelly sharp teeth tearing at the hunk of meat he held in his hand as he watched the wizard from beneath hooded lids. Thick, yellow grease oozed from the meat and ran down his chin to drip like weeping suppurations onto the table. But at last he raised the silver goblet to his lips and slurped greedily, spilling more of the wine than he drank. Then he set it down on the table, wiped his sleeve across his mouth and turned to look at him.

"Join me." It was a command not a request.

Nonchalantly, trying not to show just how hungry he was, but fooling no one, Logan sat at the table and ate while he related all he had learned from the crow.

"What do you think that old witch was doing here?" he finished. "Spying?"

"To what end?" Kanzser scoffed. "Morgan wouldn't dare attack me in the heart of my own realm."

Logan remained silent but shrugged eloquently, managing to convey the suggestion that the Demon King might want to reconsider.

Kanzser was thoughtful as he scrutinized the Dark Wizard. "Perhaps you are right," he conceded at last, his voice sour. "Morgan probably would dare. In fact I know he would, it's happened before, after all." The Demon King didn't want to dwell on the details of that particular encounter, many years past. "However, there would be no purpose in such an attack right now. But still…" He turned to the guard who stood respectfully behind his shoulder and spoke softly. The creature nodded and left the room hurriedly. Moments later, he could be heard barking orders. The Demon King turned to Logan. "Now, wizard, why are you here?"

*   *   *   *

To command the elements was no small thing, even for a witch who was young and strong. Molly was more than four hundred years old, hardly in her prime, and it took another day until she felt strong enough to travel. The first thing she noticed was how hungry she was, for she'd eaten nothing since the night of the blood moon apart from the few berries the faeries had scavenged. Knowing a long journey home lay ahead of her, she decided to go into the village to find food and perhaps somewhere warm to spend the night.

It was still early evening and the ten o'clock curfew was not yet in force. Molly, who was looking somewhat bedraggled, attracted

THE SANCTUARY

curious stares as she walked through the open gates. Accustomed though they were to weird and wonderful sights, this large, odd-looking woman with her strange clothes was unlike anything they'd ever seen. Deciding to err on the side of caution, they gradually melted away until the street, busy only moments before, was totally deserted.

"And that's how to clear a crowd in record time," she muttered to the faeries, who were again hidden from sight inside one of her pockets. "I don't think they liked the look of me."

Actually, that wasn't the reason the villagers had disappeared. Odd as she undoubtedly appeared, Molly didn't realize she emanated a sense of magic that was quite impossible for her to conceal. Now, the people of this village knew all about magic, for they'd lived with it for many generations stretching back to the times of Morgan's father, grandfather and beyond. So they could recognize a witch when they saw one, but the trouble was they didn't know if she was a good one or bad one; a *Glinda* or *Elphaba*, so to speak. Good witch, they thought, but they'd not survived so long by being careless.

Presently, Molly came to the ancient stone cross in the middle of the market square and, having nowhere else to go, she sat down on its rough stone steps, grateful to rest again.

Then she waited.

It seemed to take an age, but eventually a single figure appeared far down the street and approached slowly.

As it got closer, Molly realized what was taking so long. The man was old, no he was ancient, with stick thin legs that seemed hardly able to carry the weight of his body, slight though it was.

THE SANCTUARY

His eyes were big and round as they stared fearfully at her, and the hand that grasped his walking cane shook so violently that it tapped rapidly, rat-a-tat-tat, on the ground.

Molly guessed he'd been chosen on the grounds that he would be the least loss to the village should she turn out to be a bad witch, but in this she was mistaken. Although the man was undoubtedly old and frail, he was also the village elder, its spokesperson, and he would let no one else take on the dangerous task of confronting the witch.

She let him get closer. Then smiled.

There was a brief pause while he made up his mind whether this was some kind of trick, then decided it wasn't. His face split into a great, gap-toothed grin, then he turned and gave a whoop of triumph and punched his fist into the air. From nearby houses, from their hiding places in bushes and trees, from workshops and from behind market stalls, from the shadows, they came, the entire population of the village. Young and old now jostled to be among the first to welcome this stranger, no ordinary visitor but a *witch* no less. Many of the younger inhabitants had never seen one before.

What was she doing here? How had she got there? There'd been no coaches pass through recently. Had she come by horse or had she used magic? Those were all important questions, but the most important of all was what news was there from the Big City? There were other cities round about, the villagers knew, or at least large towns, even some in Wales. But 'Big City' referred to London, a place of legend where none of them had ever been – indeed most of them had never been further than the edge of their valley.

THE SANCTUARY

And when they asked what news, what they really meant was who was winning? Even the youngest knew the legend of how Logan had murdered his father and tried to murder his twin brother so many years ago, and of the resulting feud between them. Molly fended off their questions as tactfully as she could.

"Just passing through," was all she would say. But she didn't tell them of the faeries who hid in her pocket, for she knew they would be suspicious of the Faer Folk. Eventually she managed to quiet them down enough to ask for food and immediately a few of the children were dispatched to see what they could find. They could find a lot. Bread, cheese, meat, wine. Too much; she knew someone would go hungry tonight because of these gifts.

"No," she objected, "I can't take all this, I'll not have the village go short just to feed me."

"Nobody," the old man reassured her, "will go hungry tonight." He smiled. "The blood moon was bountiful and there is food to spare."

"Thank you," Molly said, touched by the generosity of these people, "but you must let me pay." She swung the big cloth bag from her shoulder and delved inside, ignoring the protests of the old man, whose name she had learned was Ffranc.

Disorganized as usual, there were a handful of coins thrown carelessly into the bottom of the bag, but as she was about to take some out, she saw the silver head of Queen Elizabeth II shining up at her. She glanced at Ffranc. "What year is this?" Perhaps the Landlord had been joking.

"1684." He looked at her curiously. With her hand still hidden, she rubbed the coins between her fingers and the face of the queen disappeared, replaced by that of Charles II. She took them out and handed them to him.

"Thank you!" he exclaimed delightedly, "it's too generous!" But the coins were already disappearing into his pocket. Molly smiled but said nothing; she'd paid at least ten times what the food was worth, but she didn't mind.

"Is there somewhere we could spend the night? There are no trains." She stopped as she realized trains hadn't been invented yet; the first passenger stream trains were still forty years in the future. "Er, we don't want to be traveling through the night," she amended quickly.

"We?" asked Ffranc and looked pointedly beyond her as if expecting to see more strangers coming up the street.

"I!" Molly corrected herself, flustered. "I meant *I* don't want to be traveling at night." He was looking at her strangely again. "All alone," she finished lamely.

"Very well." He tactfully avoided pursuing it further. "You are a strange one and no mistake, but keep your secrets if you will." He couldn't help glancing at her pocket where he'd spotted movement a moment ago; the faeries were bored and becoming restless. But he said nothing, after all it was none of his business, and anyway, witches could be notoriously volatile, although this one seemed friendly enough.

"Catrin!" he called, and a pretty, red-haired girl of about fourteen appeared. "My granddaughter," he said proudly. "Catrin, would you show…?" He looked at her questioningly.

"Molly."

"Show Molly to our home and make up a bed for her, she'll be our guest this night." The girl nodded and beckoned to Molly, but didn't speak.

"Catrin is mute," Ffranc explained, "but she…" He broke off at the sounds of shouting and at the sight of the man running up the street toward them. One of the guards from the gate, Molly realized.

"Demons!" the man yelled, gesticulating wildly. "Demons are coming!"

And even as he shouted, a dozen of the vile creatures could be seen running down the hillside toward the village.

Chapter 25

"Why are you here?" the Demon King repeated and this time his words cut through the Dark Wizard's reverie and he forced himself to concentrate.

"You know why I'm here." He tried without success to keep the anger from his voice but Kanzser merely smiled faintly.

"Humor me, wizard." And now he was grinning. "Please," he added mockingly.

Logan wisely kept his eyes downcast lest the Demon King see the hatred there. "I seek your aid in killing my brother." *There, I'd said it, now let this demon decide quickly so we can end this charade.*

"Hmm." Kanzser made a show of stroking his chin as if deep in thought. "Shouldn't be too difficult." His cruel eyes swept over the Dark Wizard. "But it's my understanding you had the chance years ago?"

When Logan remained silent he went on and now his tone was playful, "You know, the same night you murdered your daddy – nice piece of work that, by the way, saved me a job." The Demon King broke into a long, rasping laugh that set him coughing.

Hilarious, thought Logan sourly, *I long for the day when I no longer have to humor this fool.*

"Be careful, wizard, I can almost read your thoughts." There was no hint of playfulness now. "You don't like me much, do you?" he continued. "But you need me." Now there was anger. "You need me to do the thing you've never been man enough to do! So, I ask you, wizard, what's in it for me?"

Struggling to curb his own anger, Logan kept his voice even. "The sure and certain knowledge that Morgan is finally dead. That has to be worth something; have you forgotten the time you faced him in single combat?"

Probably shouldn't have mentioned that, he thought, *but this foul creature really is such an insufferable bighead.*

The demon looked at him sharply and Logan plowed on recklessly. "Anyway, with Morgan gone, I will rule the world of mortals and with you as my second in command there will be none to stand against us! In time we might even move against Aeryn herself!"

Kanzser genuinely didn't know whether to be angry or amused; he chose the latter and his laughter rang out, echoing up the passageways and out onto the hillside so that the villagers heard it and wondered.

"No, no, wizard, your offer does not tempt me." The Demon King's laughter subsided and he observed Logan closely from beneath hooded lids, his small, piggy eyes gleaming maliciously. "I have no liking for mortal affairs, no interest in your petty squabbles. The feud between you and your brother is of little consequence to me or my kind." He shrugged contemptuously. "And if you think

I am fool enough to try and defeat Aeryn, with or without your help, particularly inside her own world then,"—he jabbed a long, bony finger at the Dark Wizard—"*you* are the fool!"

Logan felt panic rising. *He isn't going to help me,* he thought desperately, but he fought the sensation and wrestled it back into the pit of his stomach. *I must not show weakness before this creature.* He managed to keep his voice steady although he was unable to prevent a note of pleading.

"What will it take?" he asked. "I have gold, jewels."

The Demon King made no answer and the silence lengthened. At last Logan made his decision and breathed deeply before uttering his next words, aware that once said, they could not be unsaid.

"I will do anything, *anything.*" He hesitated. "Name your price." It was foolhardy, an incredibly dangerous offer to make to a demon and the Dark Wizard knew it.

Kanzser knew it too and he grinned spitefully. He regarded his companion for a long time before he spoke.

"Desperate indeed, my friend," he said softly. "I hadn't realized just how much you require my aid." The creature hawked a big, green gob of phlegm into the back of his throat then spat it into the fire. Logan watched, transfixed with disgust as it sizzled in the flames. Somehow the act made the Demon King seem petty, a little less intimidating, and Logan found he was able to look him in the eye.

"Name your price," he repeated.

Kanzser nodded. "No more games," he agreed, "let us do business." He poked a long, dirty fingernail into his ear and scooped out a big ball of brown, foul-smelling wax. He rolled it between his fingers and regarded it for a moment before looking at Logan once more.

"As I say, I have no interest in your mortal affairs. Oh yes! You offer me gold and jewels but look around you, wizard! I have more than I could possibly need! I have no use for your trinkets!"

Before Logan could reply, Kanzser stopped him with a casual gesture. "But there is one thing you can do, one thing only that will suffice!"

Logan breathed a sigh of relief. *At last we get to the point and soon I can leave this place forever.*

"Name it," he said.

"I would have you acknowledge me as your lord and master." The Demon King grinned evilly and thick, viscous saliva oozed from between his teeth. "I would have you *kneel* before me!"

Logan stumbled from the room in horror, peals of maniacal laughter ringing in his ears.

*   *   *   *

All at once there was chaos as the streets emptied, and in seconds they were as deserted as they'd been moments earlier. Catrin tugged at the witch's sleeve and led her down a narrow path between buildings and into a small courtyard paved with rough, stone slabs. In one corner stood a collection of tall earthenware jars and behind these was a small iron ring set into the floor. Ffranc was already pulling on it and there must have been some kind of pivot mechanism for the stone slab tipped easily to reveal stairs that led underground.

Moments later, Molly found herself in a cellar, its walls made of stone, the floor bare earth. There were no comforts as far as she could see, no tables or chairs even, but at least it was dry and warm. They found a vacant spot among those already gathered and sat down.

"We will be safe here." Ffranc tried to offer reassurance but Molly wasn't convinced.

"That iron ring isn't so well hidden," she said doubtfully but he only smiled.

"These hiding places, there are three of them in the village, were built many years ago by one of the old magicians, a distant descendant of Morgan and his accursed brother." Molly looked up sharply at the mention of her friend and Ffranc noticed. "You've heard of Morgan?" he asked slyly.

"Er…" Molly hesitated, momentarily caught on the hop, "hasn't everyone?" She was blushing again, unable to meet his keen gaze and she changed the subject hurriedly. "So you believe the demons won't find us here?"

He smiled. "I know they won't." He took a stub of candle and some flint and tinder from his pocket and attempted, without success, to create a spark.

She watched him struggle for a few moments then, as ever prepared for anything, delved into her bag and took out a Zippo.

"Here," she said and spun the wheel, instantly creating a flame.

Ffranc drew back in surprise. "A wondrous thing," he said, "the ability to create fire in such a way." He held the candle to the flame and in the dim, flickering light she saw he was staring intently at her again. "One might almost suspect you to be a witch."

Was there the slightest trace of irony in his voice? she wondered. *Or perhaps I imagined it.* She dismissed it from her mind and examined her surroundings. Molly saw that the room contained shelves on which candles had been melted onto the wood; clearly this wasn't the first time the room had been used as a hideaway. More to avoid having to answer than anything else, she busied herself with the candles until light danced around the walls and she could make out the room and those gathered there more clearly.

"Wanna try it?" She held out the lighter and after a moment's hesitation he took it. "Spin the wheel with your thumb," she instructed, "like this," and she mimicked the action with her own thumb.

Ffranc attempted it but nothing happened.

"A little more firmly," she encouraged and this time a jet of flame leaped upward, almost singeing his eyebrows. Molly burst out laughing as the old man cried out and dropped the Zippo. He rubbed ruefully at his eyebrows, but after a moment he also saw the funny side and smiled, which quickly turned into a grin followed by laughter.

It was more a release of tension than that the incident had been that funny, but soon the two of them had tears of mirth rolling down their cheeks. The other villagers watched them, some wary and more than a little puzzled, some uncomfortable at the display of magic but most of them amused at their merriment.

Sat a little apart from them, Catrin was laughing too, silently, and the sight of her sobered Molly at once. "Why can't she speak?" There was something unutterably sad about this lovely girl who was unable to properly express her joy. "Was she born that way?"

Ffranc's laughter also dried and he stared at the floor between his feet. Seeing his grim expression, she feared the question had been a massive faux pas, but she saw no anger in his eyes, just a pool of sadness that seemed bottomless.

"Not from birth," he said, and now anger could be plainly heard in his voice, "but these last twelve months, since that *wizard*,"—the word dripped with venom—"came here."

Molly was unable to hide her surprise that her friend had been here recently or at the hatred this old man held for him. "M… Morgan?" she stammered tentatively but the old man shook his head.

"His *brother*!" The word ripped from his mouth as corrosive as acid.

"Logan was here?" Molly thought it wise not to upset the old man further by telling him the Dark Wizard was nearby even as they spoke, or of his negotiations with the Demon King. "Why? When?"

Ffranc didn't answer directly but continued, "It is said that after he murdered his father, Logan fled and did not return for many years. Nobody knows for sure where he spent those years, although there are rumors of dealings with the Necromancer." He gave an involuntary shiver. "What is known is that he spent many years, decades probably, transforming himself into the powerful wizard he is today."

"No match for Morgan!" she interrupted fiercely, her pretense of not knowing him quite forgotten.

"Just so." Ffranc inclined his head, smiling slightly at her vehemence. "We know of the battles between the two brothers. It is our belief Morgan will prevail in the end and this is why we do not complain of his absence these many long years. We know he will return to see us one day; we trust him, you see." The old man's eyes bored into her again, full of dignity and strength. "And you can tell him that from me."

Molly was unable to meet his eyes any longer and dropped her gaze. *If you only knew the struggle between Morgan and his brother will continue for centuries yet,* she thought. But she found she couldn't lie to him.

"I will tell him," she promised, and he nodded, satisfied.

"But you were telling me about Catrin?" She smiled at the girl and touched her arm a little shyly. "You said it had something to do with Logan?"

"His evil knows no bounds!" There was rage in his voice now and they were beginning to attract attention. "He did this to her and one day he will pay!" The old man coughed violently, such was his passion, but there were murmurs of assent from those around them. "Yes, he will pay!" His voice was quieter as he regained control. "That poor girl didn't deserve what he did to her." He looked at Molly and his expression was bleak. "He is evil!"

"What happened?" The question emerged in a whisper, for Molly was scared she might cause another bout of coughing, but the old man had regained his composure.

"A year has passed since he was here, trying and failing to solicit aid from the Demon King!" Molly's eyes widened. "Oh yes! Another evil bastard!"

She was speechless. *He has been negotiating with the demons for so long?* But Ffranc hadn't finished and all around, conversations stopped as people moved closer to listen.

"We were caught unawares when the Dark Wizard came and so great was his anger at the Demon King's refusal to meet with him that he burnt our crops, killed our livestock for no other reason than that he could." There was a low muttering as they remembered the horror of that day. "Pure malice drives his every act. He condemned us to months of hardship, for it was winter. Many died, the old and the sick."

"There's not hardly a one of us gathered here didn't lose someone close. My husband was one of the first to go." It was an old, gray-haired woman who spoke, her face lined with hardship and grief, her eyes flat and without hope.

"And my wife, God bless her soul," this from a rheumy-eyed old man who struggled to his feet with the aid of his stick.

"And my grandmother!" this time it was a teenage boy, strong looking and fierce. He gave the impression of wanting to go out and face the Dark Wizard that very instant.

"Peace, Gruffydd," Ffranc chided quietly, "it may be you'll get your chance soon enough." And to the old man, "Sit yourself down there, Davey boy, get near to the fire lest you catch a chill." Then as the noise in the room quietened once more, he continued, "My granddaughter was thirteen at the time, she was, nothing but a thin waif of a girl." He stroked the girl's cheek with a calloused finger, and she grasped his hand and kissed it. "This girl was the only one who had the courage to stand up to him." He looked around at the silent faces, pale in the flickering candlelight. "Myself included." He bowed his head in shame.

THE SANCTUARY

"Go on," Molly encouraged softly, "what happened then?"

"That girl, my granddaughter,"—tears glistened in his eyes but they shone with pride—"stood in the middle of the street while everyone else ran to hide."

By now Catrin's face was red with embarrassment and she made urgent signs for him to stop. He drew her close and continued.

"She held up those stick-thin arms and shouted at the Dark Wizard to stay where he was or else!"

There were smiles among the faces now as they remembered the young girl's courage.

"And he did!" Ffranc chortled. "That great and powerful wizard actually stopped at this little girl's command!" Ffranc was still smiling proudly, but now the tears poured down his face. "But then he punished her, because she dared challenge him. He did this to her, made it so she can never speak again!" He wiped away his tears savagely. "But one day he will pay!"

Catrin flung her arms around his neck in an effort to still his agitation, and the old man became calmer as he continued.

"There was a rumor, only a few months ago, that he would again attempt to see the Demon King. The way into the world of the demons lies in a cave on yonder hillside, and we had people watching secretly. This time we were armed and ready, but he did not come. I don't suppose we scared him off really, but whatever his reasons, he chose to leave us alone." There were murmurs among the others now and Ffranc nodded. "It is our belief he will return again soon and so we live in fear." He took a firm grip of her arm. "Promise me you'll tell Morgan of our plight!"

Molly nodded, unable to look at him and witness the anguish

in his face. She could not tell him Logan was already here and she was ashamed that tomorrow she would leave these people to their fate, yet she knew she must. Morgan had to be warned as soon as possible and, in any case, she alone, just one witch, was no match for the Dark Wizard.

The old man misunderstood her hesitation.

"Swear it!" he urged. "*I* need you to swear it, my granddaughter needs you to!"

This time Molly looked him in the eye and took his frail, wrinkled hands in hers. "I swear," she promised, "truly I will make sure he knows what's happening." She looked round at the expectant faces. "Morgan will win, I guarantee it and he – all of us – will prevail!"

There was a cheer at that, but muted so as not to attract attention from above. Embarrassed, Molly said, "I must leave for London as soon as possible, particularly after what you've said about Logan and the Demon King." A hint of uncertainty crept into her voice, "And would you mind telling me just how you can be so sure they,"—she jabbed a finger at the ceiling—"aren't gonna find us?"

"Calm yourself." Ffranc smiled reassuringly. "Visits from the demons are not uncommon." And now he was filled with contempt, "Not once in a thousand years have our hiding places been found." He laughed scornfully. "Those bastards are very short-sighted and, more to the point, extremely stupid!"

"I hope you're right," she grumbled, "we must get word to Morgan." There seemed little point in continuing to hide her association with the wizard.

"It will be safe at dawn for you and your friends to leave." He gave a smile and gestured at her pocket. "Won't you ask them to come out? My granddaughter always had a yearning to see the Faer Folk."

Molly blinked in surprise. "How did you know?"

"Oh, an educated guess," he said vaguely. "I have a few minor abilities, I'm a distant cousin of…" He stopped as a dramatic change came over Catrin, her cheeks flushed bright red with pleasure and a wide smile split her face.

Velveteena and Moth didn't need asking twice and as soon as they heard Ffranc's invitation they flew from Molly's pocket and fluttered in front of Catrin, so close their gossamer wings tickled her nose and lips. Then, as the girl's eyes shone with delighted tears, they flew in figures-of-eight before her, their wands leaving trails of silver and gold faerie dust that clung to her hair and eyelashes so that she glistened in the candlelight. Faster and faster they flew, twisting and turning this way and that in an impossibly intricate aeronautical display.

Tears flowed down Catrin's face, so overcome with joy was she, and her grandfather's eyes were moist too; it was a long, long time since he'd seen her so happy. As for Molly, she made no attempt to maintain her usual, brusque exterior and she sniffed and blew her nose with a loud, trumpeting sound. Tired at last, the faeries slowed and came to a stop. They each cupped their tiny hands and blew faerie dust into Catrin's face. The girl yawned widely and suddenly she could hardly keep her eyes open. She lay down on her mattress and the faeries snuggled into the nape of her neck. Within seconds all three of them were asleep.

Molly and Ffranc chatted softly for a while but weariness

overtook them also and it wasn't long before the room was quiet.

Chapter 26

Standing there, his hands still gripped around the knife's hilt so that Owain's blood, still warm, ran over his fingers, Logan allowed himself to daydream. It was a dream very much to his liking, a fantasy of how he would transform himself from mere village elder as his father had been. Although a very talented wizard from a distinguished line of ancestors, Owain had never sought the prestige his talents warranted. But he, Logan, would be different. He would rule the entire world of mortals! No one would stand against him, not even Morgan! But thoughts of his brother soured the fantasy and...

"It is still unfinished!" the demon hissed, jerking him from his thoughts. And Logan nodded, attempting to pull out the knife. Except it was stuck! The boy colored slightly, hoping the demon hadn't noticed. He tried again but still nothing, suction keeping the knife firmly in place, deep inside his father's heart. It took all his strength, but at last, it came free with a loud sucking noise. A glance at the demon, at the faint sneer around its mouth, told Logan the creature had indeed noticed his struggle.

Without a word, he wiped the knife on his sleeve and made as if to *leave the room, then paused as he spotted his father's sword inside its scabbard, hanging from the bed post. He took it and quickly buckled it around his waist, then motioned for the demon to follow. He moved silently along the corridor but quiet though he was, Morgan awoke, cat-like, and sprang out of bed, his senses screaming danger! With trepidation at what he would find, he stepped into the corridor. The air was thick with the stench of blood and, with a feeling of having entered a nightmare, Morgan took in the scene. His brother, drenched in it, his face a scarlet mask.*

Whose blood was it?! And a demon? How dare he bring that vile creature into this house!

"What have you done?" There was no reply. "For pity's sake, Logan, what have you done?" Morgan fought down the urge to panic and rush to his father, for only now was his brain able to process the sight of bloody footprints leading from the bedroom.

"What have you done?" he repeated and now his voice was low and dangerous. Instinctively, his hand felt inside his robe and closed around the weapon concealed there.

Logan ignored the question and looked at him coldly.

Savor these moments, dear brother, he thought, *for they'll be your last!*

Aloud he said simply, "I've come to kill you," and took a step forward. Instantly the wand was in Morgan's hand and a white-hot bolt of light left its tip. knocking the sword from Logan's grasp. It was more luck than judgment that it took only the sword and not his hand as well, for Morgan did not yet have the skill that would eventually make him the most powerful, most feared wizard in the land.

Nevertheless, Logan gaped in astonishment. "You can't do that! I mean, we can't have our wands until we're sixteen! Until we've been introduced into the Sanctuary. It's illegal!" He didn't hear the petulant, childish whine in his voice, nor did he realize the utter ridiculousness of his words.

But Morgan did and he laughed without mirth.

"Poor, Logan," his voice was almost soothing. "You fear the wand, I see. As ever, I'm ahead of you in the game. You prefer swords? Well never let it be said I seek to gain unfair advantage." Now his eyes were like granite, cold and unyielding, and by the time Logan could retrieve his weapon Morgan had stepped swiftly into his chamber, taken hold of his own sword, and was striding down the passage with unbelievable speed, the blade held high above his head.

Logan was dimly aware of the demon running away down the wooden staircase, but he had no time to resent the creature's desertion. Fear dulled his reflexes and it seemed to take an age for his hand to close around the hilt of his sword and for it to lift and meet his brother's blade, which was already arcing down toward his head.

Morgan's anger lent unnatural power to the blow and it would have cleaved Logan's entire body in two had he not turned the sword at the last instant so that it bit deep into the wood-paneled wall instead. It took long seconds to free the blade, long enough to give Logan the respite he needed, and they came together in a harsh clashing of metal, each straining against the other, each trying to gain the advantage.

Five, ten, twenty times they clashed, trading blows with increasing ferocity until the sweat poured from their bodies and exhaustion set in. Now Morgan's superior strength gave him an advantage as Logan left gaps, holes in his defenses that could have been exploited. Time and again Morgan could have ended it, yet he found he was unable *to do so.*

He's my brother! No matter what he's done, I cannot kill him!

Logan noticed his reticence but misunderstood it. "You think you can toy with me like this? Your arrogance will be your undoing, Morgan. You should kill me now for I swear that if you do not then one day, if it takes a hundred or even a thousand years, I will revenge myself upon you!"

"Revenge?" *There was surprise in Morgan's voice.* "What ill did I ever do to you that would make you seek revenge?"

Logan faltered for a moment, for how to explain the jealousy that was eating him up inside? And the knowledge that his brother could not truly be blamed for being the first born only served to fuel his anger.

"Don't try to trick me with your honeyed words, brother," *he snarled and resumed the attack with renewed vigor.*

And so it went on until finally their strength was gone. Panting heavily and momentarily unable to speak, they regarded each other and the gulf between them was a chasm.

At last Morgan straightened. "Even now we could be reconciled, if only..."

"Never!" *The single word was filled with venom and Morgan nodded.*

"Then we are enemies." *The look he gave his brother held a wealth of sadness.* "And we will remain so until one of us kills the other."

Logan stared at him for a moment, then sketched a mocking bow. Without speaking, he turned and was gone...

As darkness fell outside, Logan stirred uncomfortably, the scene so vivid in his mind it might have happened days or weeks ago instead of centuries. There was one memory he didn't possess however, for he hadn't been there to see Morgan sink to the floor, to see how his limbs shook violently as reaction set in. How, after a while, they had stilled and the boy had stood, steeling himself for what he must do next.

How it had taken every ounce of courage he had, more even than he knew he possessed. How eventually he had squared his shoulders and entered their father's room.

By the time that happened, Logan had already passed through the cave, back into the demon world, too far away to hear his brother's cry of anguish. But the boy had served his purpose and Kanzser had no further use for him. Logan was allowed to leave with his life. No more than that.

So now, homeless and without friend or ally, he had undertaken a journey that would take many months and involve many dangers. Eventually he reached the home of the Necromancer, but in reality he had only exchanged one monster for another. Logan would never tell another living soul what depths of depravity he had descended to as servant to the Necromancer; even the Dark Wizard was capable of shame. But in return he had been instructed in the dark arts and over many decades he had been transformed into a wizard so renowned the very name Logan was a byword for evil.

And then the day had come at last when the Necromancer believed him ready, and together they had challenged the might of the Sanctuary. In his arrogance, Logan could not conceive of defeat and yet it had happened. His brother had not been idle either and if he, Logan, had gained immense power, then Morgan's was greater still. Morgan and the witch Molly had stood against them and had prevailed; the Necromancer had been destroyed and he himself had been forced to flee, running away like a thief in the night.

He had found the old mansion, chosen it perversely because from it he could look upon that accursed place where his brother dwelt. And since then he had brooded, schemed and plotted. He had built his army of lost souls and had sporadically moved against Morgan, only to be repulsed every time. Over the centuries there had built an uneasy kind of stalemate, neither side able to achieve that ultimate victory; Logan because he did not quite possess the power he thought he did and Morgan because he had one, single weakness – he was unable take that final, irrevocable step of killing his twin, and deep down he still hoped they could be reconciled.

And so, thoughts of the past, the present and what the future might hold chased around the Dark Wizard's tortured mind. *So here I am again,* he thought, *seeking the Demon King's aid and tomorrow...* He shied away from the thought of what tomorrow would bring. Eventually he gave up on trying to sleep and sat quietly brooding as he watched the dawn appear.

THE SANCTUARY

Chapter 27

The night wore on and shooting stars streaked across the cloudless expanse above. Inside the cellar, the low hum of conversation gradually stilled as one by one they slept. Soon there were few sounds other than those from the guttering candles and the occasional snore. Molly lay flat on her back, arms outstretched, fast asleep.

A small spider ventured over one plump, rosy cheek, paused briefly to peer into the wide, open mouth, but thankfully decided to continue on its way. Her nose twitched as one of its tiny, hairy legs brushed against a nostril, and as her hand moved to automatically scratch it the spider scuttled to safety. When it reached the cavern of her ear it was sorely tempted to explore the warm, inviting tunnel. But just then, fortunately for both ,spider and witch, a cataclysmic snore thundered from the sleeping woman and in a flash the spider was gone.

And outside, the Big Dipper sat high in the clear northern sky as it pursued the majestic figure of Orion across the heavens. Molly slept on and not even when a mouse, emboldened by the stillness of the room and unable to resist the delicious aroma of discarded crumbs, ran over her foot did she stir. Nor when a child, troubled by dreams of monsters and other nameless terrors, called out; her mother gathered her sleepily to her breast and whispered words of comfort. In no time at all, mother and child had slipped into an easy slumber and still Molly did not stir.

And the super-giant Betelgeuse, shining bright and red at the shoulder of Orion, prepared to disappear over the horizon, its task accomplished for another night.

And then there was a noise. Only the *slightest* of noises, the faint scrape of a scaly, horned foot against stone. Instantly, Molly was wide awake. She got quietly to her feet and tip-toed silently up the short flight of steps, glued her ear to the trapdoor and listened intently. Scant centimeters above her, two demons searched the deserted courtyard, bodies bent nearly double, heads swaying from side to side as they peered shortsightedly, their vision severely restricted in the darkness.

As the loathsome creatures searched, globules of snot fell from their noses and gathered in little fluorescent-green puddles. Demons liked to be hot and surrounded by fires whenever possible and they weren't enjoying their work on this cold, winter night. But despite the cold and the snot that clogged their noses, their sense of smell, which as with all demons was excellent, was not affected.

Luckily for those hidden below, however, and this may have been mentioned before, most demons were mind-numbingly dim-witted. So, although they knew their quarry was nearby, for they could smell it, nothing in their pea-sized intellect suggested to them that those they sought might be hidden below. The demons couldn't see their quarry so, simply put, it wasn't there. Soon they left the courtyard to look elsewhere and as Molly heard their footsteps recede, she breathed a sigh of relief.

At a noise from behind, she turned to see Catrin staring up at her, wide-eyed. She put a finger to her lips and made a *sshh* noise and immediately felt stupid as she remembered the girl couldn't speak. She gave an apologetic shrug, but Catrin, good-natured as ever, just smiled and patted the floor for Molly to lay beside her. The girl looked so young and vulnerable at that moment and the old woman was gripped with a fierce feeling of protectiveness.

"Morgan, my friend the wizard," she added in case there was any doubt, "is gonna help you!" She gripped Catrin's slim hand in her own pudgy one. "He will fix whatever evil that…that man has done." The word *man* dripped with contempt. "I'm going to make sure you can talk again one day," she promised urgently. "Soon!"

Now the girl's clear blue eyes filled with tears as she gave Molly a slight smile. Within them was an inexorable sadness and the old woman realized the girl didn't believe her, didn't believe she would ever speak again, despite the promises of Molly and her grandfather. Catrin hugged the old woman then turned the other way. After a few minutes, her breathing deepened and Molly knew she was asleep. She stared at the back of Catrin's head for a long time until her own eyes began to droop and she slept too.

*   *   *   *

The terrified demon stammered out its excuses for failing to locate the intruders, terrified because those who delivered news not to their master's liking rarely survived long.

Kanzser listened in silence and nodded thoughtfully. "It is of little importance," he said and smiled reassuringly. "Now leave us." The demon bowed low, its nose nearly scraping the ground, and it almost cried with relief as it turned hurriedly away.

"Actually, it's not going to be that easy." Kanzser's voice was low and menacing. The demon halted in its tracks and closed its eyes tight because it was better that way, better not to see its death coming. Almost at once, the Demon King's huge hand clamped around the top its head and squeezed. The muscles of his forearm bunched together as he applied more pressure until the skull cracked. Then he twisted slightly and, with a curious sucking noise, the top of the demon's skull came apart revealing the glistening pinkish-gray mass beneath.

Kanzser looked at Logan and shrugged dispassionately.

"I can't bear it when people *snivel!*" He scooped out a handful of the creature's brains and ate. When he'd finished, he wiped his mouth in satisfaction with the back of his hand. "Now, wizard, I believe you were deciding whether we have a deal?"

Fighting the urge to vomit, Logan nodded, but still he hesitated before taking that final, irrevocable step. Kanzser regarded him sardonically but remained silent. Then, slowly, as if it was the most difficult act he'd ever made, which indeed it was, the Dark Wizard sank to his knees and bowed his head.

Kanzser felt a surge of triumph but he kept his voice low and cold. "Lower."

Startled, Logan almost looked up at the demon but stopped himself just in time. Instead he hunched his shoulders closer to the ground.

"Lower." This time the word was a hiss, dangerous and filled with malice. "I would have you prostrate yourself before me!"

I can't do this! Logan's mind screamed silently. *But I have no choice!* And all at once he knew it to be true, knew this was no longer about the Demon King and his aid, no longer about Morgan or even about Logan himself. No, this was about power and who had the most. And suddenly the Dark Wizard wanted out, wanted to be anywhere but this dark, evil place. He no longer cared about the Demon King's help.

It wasn't worth it!

But it was also too late; far, far too late. Logan knew if he refused, he would not leave this room alive. Slowly he let himself fall forward until he lay full length on his elbows. Moments later he felt a huge, scaly foot placed squarely between his shoulder blades.

Then the foot pushed down viciously, and he had no choice but to lay there in total submission, face crushed against the rough stone floor. Kanzser stooped until his face was only centimeters from the Dark Wizard's; Logan tried not to flinch from the vile stink of his breath.

"I will raise your army, wizard," he hissed. His drool fell onto Logan's cheek and ran down into the corner of his mouth. "But now the sight of you sickens me. Call yourself a wizard?" he sneered. "I may detest your brother, possibly even more than I despise you, but at least he is a worthy opponent! Curious, is it not, how twins can be so different?"

What followed would live long in Logan's memory as a stream of foul, disgusting vitriol poured from the Demon King's mouth. Eventually it ceased when he paused for breath, panting heavily. "I will tolerate you in my realm no longer, wizard! You bring a foulness to my home that I cannot abide."

A bit harsh, thought Logan, somewhat illogically, given the danger of his current situation.

"You will receive word when my army is complete, but until then be gone! If you are still here when dawn comes, I will have you strangled." Logan felt the pressure between his shoulders ease and when he raised his head again, the Demon King was gone.

THE SANCTUARY

Chapter 28

The next morning, Molly awoke to find Catrin busy over a small fire and most of the cellars' inhabitants already awake, sipping cups of hot, steaming tea. Looking around for Ffranc, she saw he was perched on the stairs exactly as she herself had the night before.

The boy Gruffydd approached and sat beside her. "He's been like that for at least two hours, just sat there, listening." His voice grated on her nerves a little as he complained, "I don't see the point actually, we're all sick of being down here by now." His moans were halted as Catrin thrust a hot cup into his hands and he blushed and smiled at her gratefully. The rather sulky mouth was transformed when he smiled, and his features became handsome.

Molly looked at him thoughtfully, then at the girl. *Why, the boy is besotted with her,* she realized suddenly, *he's absolutely crazy about her!* Under her scrutiny, Gruffydd blushed even more hotly and to cover his embarrassment he called out loudly, "Hey, come on, Ffranc, the demons are long gone by now!"

Instantly the old man rounded on the boy furiously. "Be quiet!"

he hissed. "They might be out there still!" He knew the boy was right though, it was unlikely that demons would still be about in broad daylight and he was sorry he'd snapped. But years had made him wise and he wasn't about to take any foolish chances.

The sun was high in the sky when Ffranc was at last satisfied it was safe to open the trapdoor. As they blinked painfully in the harsh light, most of the villagers dispersed immediately. Some muttered about getting some proper sleep while others had sheep to tend to, cows to milk, chickens to feed. Gruffydd muttered something about needing to be somewhere, glanced at Catrin, and hurried quickly away. Soon only Ffranc, Catrin and Molly remained and the old man rubbed his hands together briskly, for despite the sunshine, the day was cold.

"Come, let's have breakfast." He looked upwards. "Or should I say lunch?" Shortly after, they were sitting around a rough, oak table in the simple dwelling shared by the old man and his granddaughter. The single-story house was basic but spotless and consisted of just two rooms. One contained a primitive stove for cooking and a large, stone sink used for bathing and cleaning their clothes. The other, larger room in which they now sat, had a large, open fireplace, two oddly matched armchairs and the table. On opposite sides of the room were two small cots, shielded by curtains for privacy.

After a simple meal consisting mostly of bread, cheese and olives – Molly didn't even bother to ask how the latter had found their way to a tiny Welsh village in the middle of the seventeenth century – the three of them settled around the fire to talk. Molly would have liked to explore the village more fully and meet more of its inhabitants, but she reluctantly agreed with Ffranc's assertion that it would be unwise to risk being seen by prying eyes.

They chatted for the next few hours, deliberately keeping the conversation light and not dwelling on thoughts of the looming conflict. Instead, Ffranc entertained her with legends and stories of village life and how times had changed since he was a boy, a very long time ago. He described happier, more carefree days when Catrin's parents had been alive and the mischievous antics his granddaughter had got up to as a girl.

Molly noticed her expression become wistful and a little sad at the mention of her parents. She wanted to ask what had happened to them but didn't dare for fear of causing unnecessary pain. Then Ffranc spoke of a time long before his own birth and of legends handed down through the generations. Molly learned with fascination of Morgan's boyhood, and with sadness about the murder of his father. This was something her friend had never really talked about although she knew that afterwards he'd fought with his brother and that Logan had been forced to flee into exile, not returning until many years later.

Velveteena and Moth soon grew bored with all the human talk and went off to see what mischief they could create. Having spotted a spider high up in one of the beams which supported the roof of the cottage, they each grabbed one of its legs and flew with it at great speed, in and out of the rafters. With its other six legs waving frantically but helplessly, the spider could do nothing but submit and think about the revenge it would have on the faeries if it ever had the chance.

Then Moth saw something even more interesting poking from

its abdomen; spider silk! He called out to Velveteena and each simultaneously released the leg they held whilst also grabbing the tiny silver thread so that as the spider fell it left a long, shimmering string behind it. Only just managing to stop its descent before it crashed into the floor, the spider hung there for a moment, swinging like a pendulum and silently pronouncing double damnation upon them.

Then as it lowered itself to the ground and scuttled away, they zoomed down and wrapped the silky thread around Molly's ankles until her feet were well and truly tied together. The material was so light and delicate she was quite unaware of what they'd done, and they waited, hugging each other delightedly, to see what the outcome would be.

When she didn't oblige them by attempting to stand, they went off in search of more mischief and soon found it in the shape of the chimney. Dodging the dancing flames, they flew up inside the narrow brick opening and were instantly drenched in thick, black soot. Flying back into the room, it fell off them in tiny black puffs of cloud. Thinking it would be a shame to waste it, the faeries proceeded to walk all over the pristinely whitewashed ceiling leaving long trails of tiny, sooty footprints all over. This time Molly did notice and jumped up in horror. Only to trip and go crashing to the ground as the faeries hugged themselves with glee.

"Why you bleedin…" Mindful of Catrin's presence she stopped herself just in time, but the girl hadn't heard for she herself was doubled up in silent laughter at the faerie's antics.

Smiling a little forcedly, for he didn't entirely trust the faerie race and it had taken him ages to whitewash that ceiling, Ffranc excused himself by saying he had things to organize if Molly wished to leave in the morning. After he'd gone, Molly untangled herself then sat by the fire and watched as Catrin played with the faeries, enjoying the girl's obvious pleasure.

It was warm in the little cottage and as the sky outside darkened, the shadows inside deepened. Catrin didn't bother to light candles, content to let the flames from the fire illuminate the room. Presently the warmth and the silence, apart from the occasional giggles from the faeries and the faint swishing noise of their wings, made the atmosphere soporific and Molly was lulled into sleep.

Much later, when Ffranc returned, Catrin put a finger hurriedly to her lips, warning him to tread quietly, and she did not awaken. He found an old, threadbare blanket and gently covered the sleeping witch. They sat together for a time while he described to her the preparations he had made and she spoke to him with her own, made up brand of signs and gestures. After a time though she yawned widely, barely able to keep her eyes open, and she needed no persuasion to climb into her bed.

Ffranc sat for a long time after, gazing out of the window into the night, and wondered what the coming weeks would bring. He sensed the approaching conflict would be the last, in his lifetime at any rate, and he wondered if he would end his days as a free man or slave. Eventually, with his mind still troubled, he went to his own bed and closed his eyes. But sleep was a long time coming.

The next morning, after a hurried breakfast, they left the tiny house and made their way to where the pony was stabled. It

THE SANCTUARY

seemed to take an age until they were ready to go. Ffranc was full of last-minute instructions and there were many people wanting to give them gifts, mostly of food or hurriedly-made trinkets, but often simply good wishes and prayers to speed them on their way.

It had been decided that Gruffydd would accompany Molly and drive the carriage, and he'd also been tasked with protecting her. She had smiled wryly on hearing this, but when she saw how proud the boy was, she quelled her natural desire to tease. Now he sat on the carriage seat, reins held loosely in his hands and adopting a nonchalant air, as if this was an everyday occurrence, but fooled no one. Molly noticed he kept stealing glances at Catrin and that the girl blushed and looked away each time. Again, she kept quiet and hoped desperately that there would be a happy ending for these two.

At last they'd said all their goodbyes and it was a relief when Gruffydd clicked his tongue and the pony was spurred into action. It seemed the whole village had turned out to wave and cheer as the little carriage swept along the village road and out of the gate. Soon the village was far behind and Molly sank back into her seat with a sigh of relief. The pony settled into a rhythmic canter and less than an hour later they turned a sharp right onto the cobbled road that ran south past *The Red Dragon*.

"I wish I'd know about that bleedin' shortcut earlier," she remarked, remembering the scratches and nettle stings she'd received on the overgrown trail a few days before. *Nearly a week ago already* she mused, *Morgan will be worrying*.

"You wouldn't have seen it though, would you?" Gruffydd interrupted her thoughts and she looked at him, startled. It came as a pleasant surprise to find he could manage complete sentences. So far he'd rebuffed all her attempts at conversation and all she'd had from the rather taciturn young man had been grunts and single word answers.

"Why's that?" she asked cautiously, not want to risk breaking this newly found friendship. But she needn't have worried; it seemed that once he got going, he couldn't stop.

He took a deep breath and continued, "Because of the glamour Ffranc has put on the land hereabouts, protects us from prying eyes, see? Oh, I'm not sure if he's a wizard in the technical sense, you understand, but he's learned a few tricks of the trade, you might say, over the years, if you get my meaning?"

Gruffydd's face was looking a little flushed and there was a sheen of sweat across his forehead as he took another breath. "Rumor has it that Ffranc is more'n six hundred years old, though I don't know if it's true." He looked at Molly, trying to gauge her reaction to that particular bit of news; it was generally accepted that Morgan and his brother were the oldest wizards around. "Could be, though if you think about it there's definitely wizard magic on his side of the family that I do know, but he didn't inherit much magic himself, you see." He shrugged. "Luckily for him. Or unluckily I suppose, depending on your point of view."

Gruffydd lapsed into silence once more, seemingly exhausted by such a long speech. He didn't appear to expect an answer anyway, so she didn't bother. Just then she spotted something familiar far ahead.

"Look," she exclaimed, "isn't that the signpost? We must be near *The Red Dragon*!"

"Yes," he replied shortly; it seemed he had resumed his habit of speaking in monosyllables, "and there's smoke."

Molly peered ahead but could make nothing out at first. But every moment brought them closer and soon she saw it too. In the valley where *The Red Dragon* stood, tendrils of smoke curled lazily into the air.

"Hurry, Gruffydd," she urged the boy, "we must hurry!"

He nodded and the carriage surged forward as he flicked the reins, sending it clattering noisily over the stony ground. In no time, they reached the signpost and now the acrid stink of smoke was very strong.

As soon as the carriage halted, Molly leaped out, probably more quickly than was wise for a woman of her age and size. She ran to the top of the steps and let out a dismayed cry. Far below her, *The Red Dragon* was a smoking ruin. She ran down the steps and approached the building, Gruffydd close behind. Wincing at the touch, for it was still hot, she pushed open the door through which the Landlord had so recently brought her. There was the crunch of broken glass beneath her feet as she stepped inside, as well as that of burnt wood, and there was now a strong smell of alcohol. She stepped into the main bar area and saw that every single bottle had been smashed in an act of sheer vandalism by whoever had destroyed the ancient building.

Looking through the window, she saw its glass had survived but was now buckled and distorted, so fierce had been the heat. The bright, shiny jukebox was a tangled heap of metal and melted plastic. Sadly, she wondered what had happened to the Landlord and who had done this. Logan perhaps? But why? Just then, she heard a scuffling noise that seemed to come from behind the ruined bar. She peered cautiously round and saw two big, brown eyes peering at her from the shadows.

Poor bleedin' thing, she thought, and beckoned to the dog. He hesitated only a second then came running to her.

"Hey, Oscar." She scooped him up into her arms and stroked him gently. "What happened here?" The dog licked her face madly for a moment before struggling to be let down again. He ran across the room, somehow managing to avoid the shards of broken glass that lay everywhere. He paused just once to turn and look at her, then he was gone. It was useless to try and follow and she could only hope he would be alright. Then another thought occurred to her and she went quickly to the front door, which now hung partly off its hinges. She stepped carefully past and onto the station platform...

Which was no longer there. Neither was the railway track, and Molly nodded for she'd half expected this. It seemed that now the building was gone, or perhaps it was the absence of the Landlord, the magic of the place had been destroyed also.

"I won't be catching any train back to London," she mused, forgetting the boy's presence for a moment.

"Train?" he said in a puzzled voice. "Why do you need to catch it? Is it some kind of animal?"

Molly smiled at the boy and found herself warming to him now he was a bit more talkative; she really couldn't do with sulky teenagers. "It would take far too long to explain." She smiled but almost at once became serious as the implications of her situation sank in. "Morgan will be getting worried; I wish I hadn't forgotten my cell phone."

Molly had been watching a lot of U.S. television recently and had fallen into the habit of Americanizing a lot of her words. Mobile phones had become cell phones, pavements were now sidewalks and the bonnet of Morgan's valuable *Duesenberg Model J* convertible had become the hood, its boot the trunk, and so on.

The habit had amused her friends in the Sanctuary to begin with, but this had swiftly turned to irritation.

"What's a *selffone*?" Gruffydd wanted to know. "Selffone, train, I've never heard these words." He hesitated and smiled shyly. "You are a strange one, Molly."

She patted his arm and smiled back. "That I am, my boy, that I certainly am," and she hurried past him back into the ruined shell. "It's no surprise you've not heard of them seeing as they haven't been invented yet!"

"What do you mean?" he called after her.

"Doesn't matter!" She was already through the rear of the building and on her way up the steps. "I need to get to London Town; can you take me?" The question stopped him in his tracks; he'd never been anywhere like as far in his entire life.

"Er, yes... no. I don't know."

Molly paused, allowing him to catch up, then waited patiently, no mean task for her, while he gathered his thoughts.

"I suppose I could ask Ffranc," he decided at last.

"Excellent!" She patted his arm again and once more ascended the steps with surprising agility. "Let's do that then!"

*   *   *   *

THE SANCTUARY

The black carriage hurtled through the night on its long journey back to London and it was a pensive, slightly unsettled Logan who lay sprawled on the leather seat of its richly decorated interior.

Why did I not foresee this? he asked himself. *How could I not know that Kanzser would exact so high a price?* He stared blankly into the darkness, chewing unconsciously at his lower lip as he worried. This should have been a time for celebration, now that he'd finally persuaded the Demon King to aid him, and soon, when the demon army was assembled, Morgan would at last be defeated and he, Logan, would rule supreme.

The Dark Wizard let himself fall into a dream where all of the mortal world bowed down and did his bidding. Where men and women competed to bring him the most expensive gifts, the most delicious and succulent foods. A world where he had the power of life or death over every one of his subjects. But then reality returned to ruin his dream and one reality in particular loomed the largest; *the Demon King!* Kanzser could demand payment for his promise for years or decades, even centuries, Logan knew. He shook his head angrily, as if trying to banish the thought from his mind. *I can't let that happen! I won't let it happen!* But to defy the Demon King was not something to consider lightly.

His thoughts turned to Molly and he felt a sudden flash of anger. *The witch had spied for Morgan! How else to explain her presence at the cave? Now Morgan will know of my plans involving the Demon King.* But then he dismissed the thought as unimportant. *The knowledge won't save him. It is only a matter of time before my brother meets his fate!*

THE SANCTUARY

Logan's gaze moved idly outside the carriage to the figure tied spread-eagled between the two galloping horses. *The price for helping my enemies.* He smiled as he envisaged the punishments he would inflict on his unfortunate prisoner. *If he survives the journey!*

And it did seem impossible that the figure could do so.

His body was being cruelly pulled first one way then another, arms and legs wrenched almost from their sockets with every stride the horses took. His muscles screamed in protest at the pain and the noise was so deafening it was an assault on his senses. Soon his world, his entire *universe,* had shrunk until all that mattered was that small rectangular patch of ground which was all he could see. As it flashed beneath him, the horses' hooves kicked mud and stones up into his face leaving it cut and bloodied; almost unrecognizable as human. But the Landlord would survive, *had to survive!* He had lived too long for it to end like this! So, he retreated within himself, to a place deep inside his inner consciousness where the nightmare he was going through could barely penetrate. And so, battered and bruised as his body was, his spirit remained undimmed. And he endured.

* * * *

Meanwhile, back in his lair, the Demon King kept to his promise and began to build his army, issuing a call to arms far and wide. The tunnels that reached out in all directions from his underground kingdom were beyond counting and wound this way and that for many hundreds of kilometers, like a vast arterial web far below the Earth's surface. Eventually they lead to the

THE SANCTUARY

Plains of Desolation, a bleak, terrifying place where nothing grew, where the landscape was pure rock and the heat was tremendous. Everywhere were pools of acid and sulfur that belched and boiled so that the atmosphere was smoky and foul smelling. This was where the demons lived in their tens, hundreds of thousands – or perhaps *existed* would be a more fitting description.

Demons are solitary creatures who do not live in communities or families. Nor are there children; their offspring are born fully adult and able to fend for themselves immediately. And so they must, for demons are cannibal in nature and practically the only food they eat is each other. As soon as the creature escapes the womb, it eats its own umbilical cord, for it is born ravenously hungry. This is the only respite it is allowed throughout its long life, often a thousand years or more, if it can survive. From then on it abandons its sires – or is perhaps abandoned by them, who knows? Now it must fight and win and continue to do so or die in the attempt.

Only those chosen by the Demon King are exempt. These lucky few are his servants and personal bodyguards and they live alongside him in his kingdom, close to the world of men. They have even adopted certain human habits, such as a liking for eating *vegetables,* something their cousins far below would not stomach. And a love of fine wines and beer, although spirits, curiously, were corrosive to them.

And strangest of all, these privileged few abandoned their nakedness and copied the human penchant for wearing clothes. Some even adorned themselves with jewelry or painted their faces in an effort to copy; unwittingly becoming grotesque caricatures of the humans they so despised.

And all this because they were envious. Envious of the race of men, who can live above ground so naturally, as demons cannot. Sunlight, unless it is of that pale, nondescript sort found on the bleakest of winter days, is painful to them, although not fatal. Rain is like a mild acid against their skin; again not fatal but unpleasant nonetheless. And the very daylight itself becomes intolerable after a time because eons of living underground in semi-darkness made their eyes weak and unable to abide bright light.

Now the Demon King sent his fastest runners down these tunnels to the Plains of Desolation with the task of delivering his message into that vast expanse of spite and misery. Not that those he sent would survive the task. Years of easy living had made them weak and those who lived in that unforgiving place had long regarded them with jealousy.

But they served their purpose and their message got through. Demons made their way along the tunnels, gradually at first, a mere trickle, but rapidly becoming a steady stream. Finally, a thronging mass of demon flesh crowded the tunnels, cursing and falling over each other in their eagerness to be part of their king's war. Who the enemy was they did not know, nor did they care. Each of them hoped to stand out, to be noticed by Kanzser. Perhaps then they might escape the purgatory in which they existed and become one of the chosen few.

Within days of the call to arms, an enormous army was encamped on the far side of the hillside, out of sight of the village. Kanzser wasn't ready just yet to reveal the extent of his army to prying eyes, and the less warning Morgan received the happier he would be. Every hour saw their numbers swell and the activity in his slave pits doubled, tripled and quadrupled as the need for more weapons became ever greater. And with it came the need for more slaves to manufacture them and many of those migrating upward from the bowels of the earth found themselves snatched suddenly and delivered into the Demon King's slave pits where they merely exchanged one form of purgatory for another.

* * * *

It was only another three hours before Molly, complete with food and spare blankets for warmth, was ready to set off again. The faeries hadn't liked the derelict inn, were frightened at the destruction and the aura of evil which emanated from the place. They'd stayed buried deep in Molly's pocket, only emerging once she'd left and the carriage was on its way back to the village. Now though, they buzzed around excitedly, eager to leave this strange, disconcerting land and return to the Sanctuary. But by now, on this short winter's day, dusk was already falling and Molly had no choice but to reluctantly accept she'd have to spend another night in the village.

Bright and early the next morning though they were finally ready. The pony, lent by the village blacksmith Dai, was again harnessed and impatient to leave, hooves pawing at the ground and steam blowing from its nostrils in the cold of the morning. Dai also had a gift for Molly; he had been up all night making a simple but beautifully crafted dagger especially for her. When he presented it, blushing warmly, she curbed the instinct to protest that her wand was the only weapon she needed, far greater than any knife, and accepted his gift graciously.

Lastly, he had a gift for Gruffydd, who accepted it eagerly and examined its shining, silver blade proudly. He'd never held a sword before and the blade of this one was carved with runes that would help to protect him in battle. "It is my own," Dai told the boy in his low, gruff tones, "handed down through many generations." He grinned. "But I've never used it, see? Just a simple blacksmith I am, so I never had the chance." He punched him lightly on the arm in embarrassment. "May it serve you well, Gruffydd."

Ffranc was taking an age to give last-minute instructions on where it was safe to stay the night and where they could get stabling for the pony. Molly kept trying to interrupt, her mouth opening and closing like a goldfish, but the old man was having none of it. It was Moth who finally took matters into his own hands when he flew to the pony's hindquarters, drew out his sword and jabbed. Although in comparison to the pony's rump it was only the size of a needle, it was also very sharp.

And it stung! The pony gave a shriek of protest and reared onto its hind legs, throwing Molly backward into her seat. Then they were off down the street in a cloud of dust, leaving Ffranc and the entire village staring after them, open mouthed. Soon the pony settled into the same easy canter as the previous day and presently they turned once more onto the cobbled road and headed south.

The day was unusually hot for November and the heat, as well as the rhythmic swaying of the carriage, soon caused Molly's eyes to become heavy, and before long she dozed. Her soft snores drifted into the still air as Gruffydd guided the carriage while Velveteena and Moth kept guard.

It was a well-known fact that faeries weren't always welcome in the mortal world. If they did enter that realm it was within the power of any witch or wizard with sufficient power to send them right back again. Velveteena and Moth knew this of course, and that was why they felt a love and loyalty for the old witch that was rare indeed between faeries and humans. For not only had she summoned them into the mortal world, but she had also let them stay there.

Not that there was anything particularly wrong with the faerie realm. It was just that the mortal world was so much more exciting! So their feelings for the witch went way beyond mere liking and, since she'd saved Velveteena's life, bordered on adoration. The faeries owed Molly a debt they knew could never be repaid, but if the chance did come, they would be ready. So while they rode along, perched between the pony's ears, which was a lot like being on a merry-go-round, they kept a sharp eye out for danger, determined to keep her safe at all costs. But the day passed without incident and it was with relief later that evening when Molly could climb stiffly from the carriage. While Gruffydd removed the pony's harness and took her to the stables, Molly entered the old coaching inn where hot food and a soft bed awaited.

Chapter 29

It was four days since Molly had disappeared on a mysterious errand. Only Morgan and Wallace knew where she'd gone, and they weren't saying. The only information Luke and Cissy had been able to glean was that it was some kind of secret mission, but what that mission might be they couldn't begin to imagine. To think of dear, irascible but kind Molly as some sort of secret agent was too much to envisage. Like most everyone who came into contact with the witch, the teenagers tended to underestimate her, and they certainly had no clue as to her true power.

Meanwhile, the wizards were becoming increasingly worried for their old friend. *Surely she should have sent word by now?* As time went on, Morgan's anxiety made him ever more irritable and Luke complained to Cissy how the wizard had nearly bitten his head off over something quite trivial that morning.

"Well he does have a lot on his mind right now," Cissy tried to defend him, but Luke flared up in temper.

"What, and you think I haven't?" And he stormed from the room, slamming the door so violently the windows shook.

Cissy sighed and considered going after him, then gave up on the idea; there was really no point. Although Luke's mood had improved since the incident with Penelope, he could still be so bloody tetchy! And so an air of gloom settled over the Sanctuary. Morgan knew he was being unfair, but he couldn't tell the two of them how worried he was because that would mean telling them where Molly had gone and why.

"I should never have let her go," he confessed to Wallace. "If anything has happened to her…well, you know."

"It's only been four days," his old friend reasoned, "she may not have had time yet to send a message." And honesty forced him to add, "Or she might have forgotten; this is Molly we're talking about."

But when four days became a week, even Wallace had no more words of comfort to offer and the atmosphere of tension in the Sanctuary worsened. Even the eternally optimistic Alessandro was struggling to keep cheerful. Morgan was almost unapproachable and by now he'd convinced himself that Molly was dead, and he took his guilt out on others, finding fault with every little thing. He snapped at people when they made even the most innocent of comments, and he'd reduced one of the cooks to tears the other evening simply because the soup had been too salty. Then the normally placid and cheerful Alessandro had told Morgan exactly what he thought of the way he was behaving and Morgan, knowing he was in the wrong, had been forced to seek the poor man out and apologize.

Wallace was more pragmatic, but he was miserable because he had no role to perform right now. Luke and Cissy spent their days practicing swordplay and were too wrapped up in each other to include him and he was worried.

"Luke is getting very expert, better than myself in some ways," he admitted to Morgan, "and Cissy is okay, kind of. But I can't help feeling they're playing, not taking it seriously somehow."

Morgan agreed. "And Luke has made some progress with his wand, I admit, he can use it quite effectively as a weapon now. But he is totally unable to cast a spell with it; he doesn't even try and just gets mad when I suggest it." In fact, Morgan had again tried that very morning to teach Luke, but had been met with even less success than last time. They were both too volatile in their moods right now for it to have any chance of working.

"There's a confrontation coming and we are not prepared," he told Wallace. "Peter is out of action, Molly is missing, and those two kids are acting just like that; *kids*."

Wallace opened his mouth to protest that this was a bit harsh, but Morgan interrupted.

"We have to accept that Molly may be lost to us and that Peter is going to die." The words sounded shocking when spoken aloud, but Wallace could only nod in sober agreement. He remained silent as Morgan went on. "Luke and Cissy might be the future hope of the Sanctuary or they might not. I don't know if either of them will fulfill the prophecy, but right now they're all we have; they must take it seriously. The Dark Wizard and his demons could be upon us at any time!"

Wallace sat down wearily and regarded his old friend. "You have a plan, Morgan?" He smiled. "You always have a plan." But he wasn't smiling a few minutes later when Morgan told him what he intended. "That's too dangerous, it could go wrong in so many ways. At best you'll destroy their belief in you forever and at worst someone could get killed."

The wizard nodded and his expression was bleak. But he didn't speak; he knew his friend was right and, after all, what more was there to say?

*   *   *   *

Despite her fears that the Dark Wizard might still be close by, exhaustion served to ensure Molly had an unbroken night's sleep at the inn. The next morning dawned in bright sunshine and it promised to be another unseasonably warm day. Before she would allow Gruffydd to venture outside, she sent the faeries scouting far and wide for danger, and while they were gone, Molly and the boy ate a hurried breakfast. When Velveteena and Moth returned and reported no sign of either Dark Wizard or demon, Molly and Gruffydd heaved a sigh of relief.

In truth they needn't have worried, for eager as she was to return to the Sanctuary, Molly recognized they couldn't push the aging pony too hard. Its strength had to be preserved, for the way was long and there was no provision for fresh animals. But while they trotted along at whatever speed could be managed, stopping frequently for rests, the Dark Wizard was already nearing London. His magnificent stallions were touched with dark magic which lent wings to their hooves. Logan wanted to put as much distance as possible between himself and the Demon King and he couldn't help thinking he'd been lucky to leave that accursed place unscathed. Not only that, he was eager to interrogate his captive and he drove his horses mercilessly, allowing only brief stops for food and water.

As for the Demon King, he was far too engrossed in building his new army to be concerned about the whereabouts of one solitary witch. Kanzser simply could not perceive Molly as a threat; nor did he believe in the prophecy. No, the only one who mattered was Morgan. The Demon King looked forward to the coming war, relished the thought of pitting himself, or rather his army, against the might of the wizard. So inflated was his ego, so convinced of his own omnipotence was he, that he craved the day when Morgan was dead. Or even better, captured and forced to toil out the remainder of his life in the Demon King's slave pits.

The thought made Kanzser drool with anticipation. *Morgan might live for centuries, each day a living hell from which there would be no surcease!*

But Molly and her companions were unaware of any of this and they kept a wary, nervous watch for trouble. Increasingly anxious to get back to London, they traveled late into the night and were ready to begin again with the dawn. Nevertheless, their journey took several days, but at last, still far away in the distance, the unmistakable shape of Ludgate Hill, London's highest point, could be seen. Upon it stood the partly built structure of Wren's Cathedral, although it would be another twenty-five years or more before it was finished.

As it came closer, Gruffydd stared, open-mouthed at the already magnificent building, the likes of which he'd never seen. To the boy, it seemed impossible that something could stretch so high without falling down, and Molly smiled indulgently at his innocence. She cast her mind back to the old, wooden church that had stood on the same spot for so many years, since long before she herself had been born. Until that fateful night when it had burned to the ground; that terrible night when much of the city had been devastated, so many lives lost.

She, Morgan and others from the Sanctuary had stood side by side with the people of London battling the flames that raged all about them. It was the first and only time in history that the one cardinal rule had been broken: *a wizard or witch shall never use magic in the presence of a mortal.* Together they had been able to prevent even greater loss of life but still, *the heat! The dense, stinging smoke! The smell of burning flesh!*

The chattering of the faeries roused her from her thoughts and she saw with surprise that they'd left the cathedral behind and were close to the center of the city. And now there was another problem. This London was very different to the London of the 21st century, so where was the Sanctuary? She couldn't remember! This London was more than three hundred years in the past and unrecognizable from when she'd left it ten days before to search for the blood thorn. *Only ten days!*

The rebuilding of the city following the great fire meant that most of the wooden buildings had been replaced with stone. But these had definitely not included four-story Gothic edifices like the one the Sanctuary had adopted during the nineteenth century.

Millennia had passed since a council of wizards had gathered, the most powerful of their kind ever assembled, and plans were made to counter the growing threat of the demons, the Necromancer and the witches of the Banished Land. The result had been the creation of the Sanctuary, which crossed dimensions so that it existed both in the mortal world and the magical one. It was a place where they could live and work in secret to uphold the pledge made at that council, now so many years in the past.

And the pledge was a simple one; to protect the mortal world from whence most of them had originally come. But their existence must remain secret for it was a human failing to destroy what it didn't understand. If humans knew of the existence of wizards they would first be frightened, then they would try to eliminate the threat; this was the basis of most of their wars. To maintain that secrecy, the Sanctuary needed to blend in with its surroundings and its appearance had altered many times in three thousand years.

And for the life of her, Molly couldn't remember what it had looked like in the late seventeenth century!

"How can you not know?" Moth hissed in her ear. "You *lived* there!"

"Yeah, three hundred bleedin' years ago!" She countered angrily but he merely shrugged; to a faerie that didn't seem a very long time at all.

And then she smelt it, that ozone smell. *Magic!*

Chapter 30

Cissy and Luke were practicing hurling lightning bolts at each other when Morgan entered the training room, but neither took their attention from the wand in the other's hand. They ignored his presence and continued to circle each other warily, the strength of the bolts kept purposely at a low level. The intention was to train, not to maim or kill, but they still hurt like hell.

"Have either of you even noticed I'm here?" drawled Morgan. "It's rather rude to ignore people, you know."

Luke glanced at him and held up a hand in irritation. "I'm concentrating!" Without warning, he was hurled to the ground as a powerful bolt slammed into his back. He was dazed and winded and it was a minute before he could look up to see that Morgan stood facing him, wand in hand and a strange, unfathomable look upon his face.

"What the hell? You did that just because I ignored you?" Luke was incredulous. "That really hurt, Morgan!" He had just enough time to gasp the words before another bolt hurtled toward

THE SANCTUARY

him. This time he was able to fend it off, but only just; if it had connected it would have taken his head off.

"Hey, stop!" exclaimed Cissy. "What are—" Another bolt left Morgan's wand and struck her squarely in the chest, knocking her onto her back.

What is this? wondered Luke. He moved cautiously forward, not taking his eyes off the wizard for a single second as he helped Cissy to her feet. They glanced at each other and a flash of understanding passed between them. They circled Morgan and he retreated a little, seeing what they were planning.

"Ah! You want to play?" he asked mildly, but there was nothing remotely friendly in his voice or in the expression on his face.

"What's going on, Morgan, what is this?" Cissy's voice was full of caution.

"I said," he repeated, "do-you-want-to-play?"

Cissy sighed; men really, really could be such assholes! "Go for it," she invited.

He smiled and raised his wand again. "As you wish." He bowed slightly and suddenly there were bolts of lightning everywhere. The two friends frantically returned bolts of their own, but the wizard deflected them with ease.

"Is that the best you've got, wizardlings?" he mocked. "C'mon, show me what you can do!" And he attacked even more ferociously.

Now it was Luke and Cissy who were retreating; soon they'd both been hit a half dozen times. Hard stinging blows that left scorch marks on their clothes. Cissy had a nasty burn on her arm where a lightning bolt had touched her bare skin; she'd be lucky if it didn't leave a scar.

THE SANCTUARY

What's going on? Luke thought again. *Those aren't killing bolts he's throwing at us. They hurt like hell, but they won't kill us. Why doesn't he just finish us off?* And suddenly he knew the answer. Why or how, he didn't know. But Morgan had betrayed the Sanctuary!

"He's toying with us," he yelled at Cissy. "The bastard, he's playing with us before he kills us!" In fury he faced the wizard and gathered his strength for one last effort and began hurling bolts of his own, so swiftly that his arm was a blur, and beside him Cissy did the same.

Now Morgan had difficulty in defending himself against their combined attack and was gradually forced to his knees. Luke knew he should be delivering killing blows, but he couldn't bring himself to do so. A small part of him still refused to believe that Morgan could betray them, betray the Sanctuary like this.

But suddenly the wizard, who should have been begging for mercy, laughed. He actually *laughed.*

It was too much for Luke and a red mist descended in front of his eyes as he completely lost his temper. "You bastard!" he yelled, tears of anger and disappointment spilling from his eyes at the wizard's betrayal. "I hate you!"

His barrage of blows became even more intense and now they were killing blows; if any had found their mark the wizard would have been dead for sure. But Luke's anger clouded his judgment and they went astray. Before long there were more lightning bolts hitting the wall behind the wizard than were actually going near him. And worse, he was getting in Cissy's way so that she could no longer join in the attack for fear of injuring Luke.

Suddenly Morgan rose to his feet and flung his wand to the

floor.

"No, no, NO, LUKE!" he yelled. His voice had completely lost its mocking tone and was now full of exasperation. "How many times must I tell you to keep your temper?"

Luke's arm paused mid-strike and he glared at the wizard in amazement. *What was this, some kind of trick?* He lowered his wand cautiously but remained tensed and ready.

"What's going on?" His voice was flat and unemotional. "What the hell was that all about?"

The wizard heard the mistrust in Luke's voice and sighed; he hadn't liked doing what he'd just done, but it had been necessary. The time for friendly training bouts was over, it was time for Luke and Cissy to realize what fighting real enemies was like. Still, he hadn't liked it and he reflected sadly that he'd have quite a lot of bridge building to do before either of them trusted him again.

He kept any note of apology from his voice however and said harshly, "Both of you, ten minutes, in my chambers, don't be late." And without another word he marched quickly from the room.

A half hour later, they left Morgan's chamber not quite knowing what to think. They'd not realized just how much hope he was pinning on them and the responsibility weighed heavily. They both knew they'd mastered their respective weapons very quickly and it came as a shock to realize it might not be enough. Then the news that Molly might be lost was too much to bear and both of them had to fight to hold back tears. Now they felt chastened and determined to try even harder.

Over the next few days, Wallace coached them in swordplay, both individually and together, while Morgan did the same with their wands. There was no doubt they were making progress now they were trying harder, but it wasn't enough; not nearly enough.

Actually, both of them did better when left to teach each other. Cissy's innate patience did more to help Luke than Morgan's heavy-handed, rather impatient manner of teaching, and although he was never likely to master his wand fully, he could at least use it as a second weapon with reasonable accuracy if he really concentrated.

As for Cissy, she found the sword a heavy, cumbersome weapon in comparison to the delicacy of her wand. But she'd taken quite a liking to a thin, rapier-like weapon, although if she was honest it was its beauty she liked as much as anything.

Its blade was delicately engraved with swirling runes and the hand guard intricately wrought in silver and set with rubies that flashed and sparkled as she swung the sword. She couldn't exactly say she enjoyed the lessons, but she much preferred Luke's company than the repetitive, monotonous drills favored by Wallace.

Luke still found the time to sit for long periods with his father and could only watch as the poison moved inexorably toward his heart. Now though, Cissy often accompanied him, and they would sit together, sometimes for hours, in companionable silence, both simply watching and hoping. Whereas before he'd found her presence unbearable and only wanted to vent his anger upon her, now he found her company a source of enormous comfort. Luke knew his father would die soon; nothing could prevent that. But he felt he might be able to bear it somehow if she were by his side.

Meanwhile, Penelope was left to her own devices. But she didn't mind; she'd always been a solitary child, not particularly bothered about a lack of close friends. In any case, Cissy and Luke always

THE SANCTUARY

had time to spend with her in the evenings before she had to go to bed. And during the day she had her library; nobody else but her spent any real time there, so it was hers. Mostly she read, all day, every day, her quick intellect soaking up information like a sponge and, more importantly, retaining it, ready to be retrieved from the index of her mind when needed.

Chapter 31

"OMG!"

Wallace looked at him skeptically, one eyebrow raised in an expression that conveyed more than words ever could. Morgan had the grace to blush.

"Sorry, I, erm…I picked it up from Cissy; thought I'd try it out." He turned away from his old friend and busied himself tidying the mass of paper on his desk (something he never did) to hide his embarrassment.

"Well I'd leave it to the younger ones if I were you." Wallace grinned, enjoying his friend's discomfort; it wasn't often one had the chance to get one up on the wizard. "What are you 'OMG'ing about anyway?"

Morgan looked at him thoughtfully for a moment. "Molly's been gone…a week now?" Wallace nodded and the wizard continued, "What if she simply missed the train?"

"Missed the train? Morgan, we know she got on the train, the Conductor sent word, remember? What are you—"

"Not going," the wizard interrupted, "I'm talking about coming back." He sighed at Wallace's baffled expression. "What if she just didn't get to the station in time? There could be any number of reasons why that might happen, knowing her!" His voice was rising in his excitement. "But she might be okay!"

"Right." Wallace spoke slowly, thinking. "And the Conductor wouldn't be able to wait for her, so…"

"Yes! Yes!" Morgan was almost jumping up and down in his agitation. "And if that's the case it would take her days to get back to London and…" An expression of horror entered his features. "OM…"

"Morgan, stop it, it really doesn't suit you." Wallace paused as he saw the look on the wizard's face. "What?"

"It's the seventeenth century."

"No…I'm pretty certain it's the twenty-first century, Morgan." He sometimes wondered where he got these ideas from.

"No!" Morgan was irritated. "Molly is in the seventeenth century, probably in or about the 1680s I should think!"

"So?"

"*So* London was totally different back then, the Sanctuary looked totally different, the city, the countryside, everything!" Wallace was still shaking his head and Morgan could have cried with frustration. "Wallace, what if she missed the train and just can't find her way back?"

Comprehension dawned at last over his old friend's face.

"O… M… G," he said.

*   *   *   *

THE SANCTUARY

As dusk descended over London, a cloaked figure appeared at the door in the base of the lamppost, climbed out onto the street, and immediately scuttled into the shadows. His movements were furtive for he had no wish to be seen. Not that any mortal could perceive his presence with the glamour he had placed over himself.

But he would be using magic this night and to do so outside of the protective walls of the Sanctuary meant he may as well place a flashing neon sign above his head, to be seen by his enemies, reading, 'I AM HERE'.

Looking around and seeing no one, Morgan took out his wand and quickly drew a pattern in the air. Then he walked briskly down the road for about twenty meters or so and did the same again. He kept walking, every so often pausing to draw his pattern, until he reached his destination and the great, soaring dome of St Paul's Cathedral towered above him. He hurried around its circumference, wand still weaving its magic above his head, until he'd gone all the way round. Then he stopped, panting slightly, and wondered if he'd miscalculated.

She will have entered London by this road, will have to pass by St Paul's, he thought, hoping he was right. He pondered for a few moments longer then, satisfied at last, or as satisfied as he could be, Morgan raised his wand once more and headed southeast toward Tower Hill. His destination was only a mile away and soon he was looking down on the imposing fortress of the Tower of London.

He sat and pondered once more. *Where to put it,* he mused. *Where can I place the door?* Then he smiled; he knew the very place. The wizard approached the wall in a few long strides and drew yet another sign with his wand, this time on the stones themselves. Then he stepped back a few paces, ran toward the wall again and skipped nimbly over.

He dropped down the other side and looked around to get his bearings, noting with satisfaction that he was exactly where he wanted to be. He walked quickly along the narrow cobblestone road, underneath the archway, and there it was, the impressive, but terrifying, Traitors' Gate.

Not forgetting to place a sign on each one, he went down the broad steps until the water lapped over his boots. He pondered whether he should put the doorway above the waterline or below, but there was no option really. Hundreds of tourists passed by here every day, even at this time of the year, and he couldn't risk the door being seen, unlikely though that was. Anyway, the presence of his kind hadn't remained concealed for so long by being careless.

No, it had to go below the water, and he grinned. *Molly will be furious,* he thought, imagining his friend's reaction when she arrived. He immediately sobered. *If she arrives.* His fists clenched involuntarily. *If she's still alive.* The wizard dismissed these gloomy thoughts and without further hesitation, for he wasn't really looking forward to the next bit, walked into the water, gasping at the cold, until he was in up to his chest. Then he took a deep breath and sank below the surface.

For the first hour he simply sat, suspended beneath the water while he acclimatized to the cold. He scrutinized the huge stones of the ancient gateway, black and green from the accumulated dirt and slime of a thousand years. The only trace of his presence was the occasional tiny bubble of air that escaped from the corner of his mouth and rose to the surface where it burst with an almost inaudible plop. At last, he felt his body gradually warm and he was ready to begin.

With his wand he traced a single, horizontal line about half a meter in length. He nodded, pleased when the line glowed a bright, vibrant purple color for a few seconds before it faded and became invisible. Then swiftly but carefully he drew impossibly complex patterns, his wand flicking delicately over the stones, weaving an intricate web of glowing lines.

The sun rose over London and still Morgan cast his spell. The entrance to the fortress was opened and visitors from every continent began to spill inside. Most were armed with cameras to capture memories of what, for many, was a lifetime's ambition. On and on they came, up into the main part of the Tower, pausing in wonder to look at the huge wooden gate through which so many unfortunate individuals had passed over the centuries, on their way to imprisonment and sometimes death.

The sound of clicking cameras mingled with excited chattering and drifted away in the still London air, but Morgan was oblivious to them all, safe in the knowledge that his glamour concealed him.

At last the spell was finished and he allowed himself a few modest – actually not so modest – congratulations, although truthfully he'd just worked a spell which no other wizard would have had the skill to do. For there in front of him was a door, only small but perfect in every detail. A door and, more importantly, a door *with a handle.*

But now his entire body ached from crouching for so many hours and he allowed himself to drift to the surface, then he stood and stretched his limbs gratefully. Many of those who happened to be there at that moment would later wonder at the strange apparition that appeared in their photos. In turn this would give rise to various magazine articles relating to the ghost of Traitors' Gate, yet another one to add to its already impressive collection. But for now, they continued to snap away, completely unaware of the wizard's presence.

Except for one young boy who stared at him with frank curiosity.

One for the future, thought Morgan, as he knelt down to speak to him. "How old are you?" he whispered conspiratorially into his ear.

"I'm eight," replied the boy, and his mother, who stood beside him, gave an embarrassed frown. *This habit of talking to himself is becoming much too frequent,* she thought to herself. *Perhaps he needs to see a doctor…*

"Well when you're sixteen…" Morgan fished into one of his many pockets and pulled out a small card. It was a little damp and the ink was slightly smudged, but the words 'Be there' next to the image of a black hat could clearly be seen.

Morgan winked and slipped the card into the boy's pocket.

"Keep it hidden and don't forget!" And with that he turned, held his nose and jumped back into the water. His hand grasped the handle of the door and opened it. Seconds later he was in the circular room which led to the passage-between-the-worlds.

* * * *

"Are you ready to talk or shall we continue what we started

earlier?"

The Landlord didn't reply at once but regarded his tormentor through eyes that were bruised and swollen from the beatings he'd received. "I've already told you I know nothing."

The Dark Wizard sighed and looked at him for a long moment before saying conversationally, "You do know I'm going to kill you, of course?" He didn't wait for a reply. "In fact, the only way I won't kill you is if you give me the information I want," he lied.

The Landlord stared at him for a long moment, then laughed.

Afterwards he would be unable to say how he managed it, but his laughter soon rang around the cell and tears poured down his face. The sound echoed and bounced from the walls and through the small barred window into the street far below.

The few passers-by who dared to come close to the Dark Wizard's home looked fearfully up to the cell so recently occupied, it was rumored, by that wizard protégé of Morgan. And they listened in wonder at the sound; laughter was something rarely heard in these parts.

"Kill me? You threaten to kill me?" His voice was incredulous as he wiped the tears from his eyes. He took his time and when he'd finished his eyes were quite dry. "Wizard, listen to me," he said, his voice now scornful, "I was put on this earth many centuries before you were born, and I will occupy it long after you are gone."

Logan was surprised, first at the laughter then at being spoken to in this way. *He should be terrified and begging for his life, dammit!* He was rendered momentarily speechless.

Taking advantage of this brief silence, the Landlord continued. "You think me a bumbling fool of an innkeeper, but trust me, you have no idea who and what you are dealing with." He grinned at Logan's evident discomfiture. "And anyway, it is you who will die, when Morgan gets his hands on you."

Now Logan's face twisted with rage but still he could not speak. "Because you've never beaten him, have you?" The Landlord was openly jeering and now his voice taunted. "Morgan has always been better than you!"

At last the Dark Wizard found his voice and he bellowed with anger, giving the Landlord a vicious backhand that sent him sprawling to the floor. Blood poured from his lip where Logan's ring had cut him, but there was no fear in his expression. The Landlord, ever the optimist, wasn't overly worried. He knew something would turn up; it always did.

All at once his eyes shone with triumph for he suddenly knew that despite the odds, despite the immense army that was no doubt being amassed at this very moment, the Dark Wizard was doomed; had always been doomed.

Logan saw the triumph in his eyes and an involuntary shiver of fear passed through him. It was enough to still the impulse to extinguish the life of the man before him, and instead he turned away, closing the door softly behind. He turned the key and walked slowly back up the passage. So lost in thought was he that he only vaguely heard the Landlord's parting taunt. "Do your worst, loser."

Surely Morgan couldn't win again? Not this time! he mused as he passed through the passage door and into the room beyond. *For sure, those at the Sanctuary are powerful, but so few! And the demon army will be many!* He was halfway up before he remembered he'd left the key to the cell door in the lock. He turned to go back then stopped and shrugged. It didn't matter, his prisoner couldn't reach it the from inside and he was no wizard, couldn't use magic to get it.

But what if someone… He dismissed the thought from his mind angrily. *Where has this sudden indecision come from?!*

Logan went to the window and peered out, but could see nothing in the darkness. He could smell magic though, and it came from the direction of the Sanctuary.

It's you, Morgan, he thought, *I know it's you.* He turned worriedly way from the window. *What are you up to now?* He considered for a moment, then whistled softly and the crow, never very far away, came flying through the open window and alighted on his shoulder. It cocked its head, listening as Logan murmured into its ear, then off it flew again out into the stormy London sky. Its progress was slow, for the wind was high and the crow had still not fully recovered from its wounds.

But eventually the tall, Gothic exterior of the Sanctuary came into view and with a loud, defiant *caw* the crow descended.

Back in his cell, the Landlord forced his skinny arm through the narrow bars and attempted to reach the key. Even with his arm out up to the shoulder, so that his cheek was pressed against the bars, his fingers fell agonizingly short. Eventually he gave in and sat down, suddenly exhausted but not too discouraged, and awaited developments.

* * * *

THE SANCTUARY

The instant Molly caught that faint tang of magic she lost it again as it was borne away on the gentle breeze. She spent the next hour searching fruitlessly for it and becoming increasingly angry and frustrated. It was the faeries who eventually found it by simply working out which way the breeze was traveling.

"Simple really," Moth boasted, and received an irritated look in return. But now the smell was stronger and easier to follow, until the wind suddenly changed direction and carried it away again.

"This is no bleedin' good!" exclaimed Molly. "We'll never find out where it's coming from at this rate!" She sat down by the roadside, fed-up. "There must be an easier way!"

Velveteena and Moth looked at each other thoughtfully, then flew up into the air, touching wands as they went, much in the manner of a high-five. They each took a handful of faerie dust from their pocket, counted '1, 2, 3' and blew. Instantly the dust was carried on the wind and there, about ten meters or so down the street, a bright green arrow was revealed, hanging in the air.

"Come on!" Molly exclaimed excitedly. "Let's go see!" She got to her feet and hurried down the road to where the sign hung, and examined it minutely. "Looks okay," she muttered, "and the magic *smells* okay. But there should be…" She stood on tiptoe to get an even closer look. "I can't quite… Yes! There!" She jabbed a finger. "There, look!"

The faeries flew closer to the sign, careful not to touch, and sure enough there it was, tiny but clearly visible if you looked hard enough; the letter 'M'.

"Morgan!" They chimed in unison. "It's Morgan!"

"I think it is!" agreed Molly. "Quick! Blow some more!"

This time, with the breeze becoming stronger, the dust was carried further so that two signs were revealed, and in this way, they were soon back at Ludgate Hill.

Why has Morgan led us back here? Surely, we don't have to go all the bleedin' way we've just come?

It took some time because they had to follow the arrows nearly all the way around the newly emerging cathedral, but eventually they picked up the trail again. An hour later, Molly stood near the entrance to the Tower, trying to appear inconspicuous and looking at an arrow which clearly indicated she should go inside.

"I wonder why it's pointing in there," she said. "If this is Morgan's idea of a bleedin' joke…" But for once, the faeries had nothing at all to say, and with a sigh Molly glanced around to make sure no one was looking, then quickly placed a glamour around herself. She slipped easily past the guards and followed the arrows for a while, then stopped in shock.

"You've got to be joking." She couldn't believe what she was seeing.

The faeries looked at each other and grinned.

"You have got to be bleedin' joking," she repeated as shock turned to outrage. "Morgan, I'm gonna bleedin' kill you." She could imagine the wizard's face, laughing at her. "Morgan, you utter, utter…" There followed a string of expletives far stronger than the one she normally used.

The faeries simply covered their ears.

Chapter 32

One evening, while Cissy and Luke were playing on the Xbox (a fighting game, naturally), the door that led to the passage-between-the-worlds burst open and someone came tumbling into the room.

"Molly!" they cried in delight, then stopped and looked at her in astonishment, for although she was always a bit scruffy, right now she looked a total mess.

She'd used a spell to dry her clothes after ducking in the filthy water of the Thames – *I'll be having words with Morgan about that* – and now they were rumpled and creased. Her hair, never tidy at the best of times, hung lank down past her shoulders, and she smelled alarmingly; goodness knows what was in that river. Cissy and Luke took all this in at a glance and wrinkled their noses at the stink, but they really didn't care and ran to her in delight, throwing their arms around her.

Before they could speak, however, there was a loud exclamation. "Molly, welcome home!" Morgan swept into the room and enveloped her in a massive hug. To her surprise, tears filled her eyes when she saw her old friend and she completely forgot to be angry with him.

The relief on his face was evident. "We were beginning to worry!"

That has to be the understatement of the century, thought Wallace who followed close behind. He added his own congratulations at her safe return, then Alessandro arrived and promptly burst into tears.

"*Benvenuto a casa!*" He beamed. "Welcome home!"

Morgan used the cacophony of noise as cover to whisper to Molly, "Did you get it?"

"Get what?" asked Cissy, who had extremely sharp hearing, but Molly raised her hands in protest.

"It's lovely to see all of you again, but you'd think I'd been gone a year instead of just over a week. Alessandro, do stop bleedin' crying, for goodness sake." Just then she remembered something. "Oh my!" she exclaimed and hurried across the room to where Gruffydd stood shyly, half in and out of the doorway. He'd gone unnoticed in all the excitement and Molly rather guiltily realized she'd forgotten all about him. "This is Gruffydd, everyone."

She smiled encouragingly at the boy, beckoning him into the room. She introduced them all individually, but unfortunately he'd once more lost the power of speech and could only manage a nod to each of them.

Molly sighed and tried to quell her impatience, for on the long journey he'd come right out of his shell and revealed himself to have wit and a dry sense of humor which she liked immensely. Now though, faced with a crowd of strangers, he retreated back into his shell and stood there awkwardly, shuffling his feet from one to the other. Seeing his embarrassment and ready as always to take waifs and strays under her wing, Cissy moved over on the settee and patted the cushion.

"Come and sit here, Gruffydd. Did I say it right? We were going to play on the Xbox later if you fancy a turn?"

Gruffydd of course had no idea what she meant but he was grateful to be included and nodded eagerly. His face burned an even deeper shade of red as he squeezed himself between her and Luke.

Molly yawned widely and suddenly looked exhausted. "Well I'm glad that's bleedin' sorted." She winked gratefully at Cissy then raised an arm and sniffed at her armpit. She wrinkled her nose in distaste. "Anyway, before you lot start pestering me I must 'ave—"

"A bath!" interrupted Cissy and Luke together, laughing.

She was about to stand when two tiny heads popped up sleepily from the pocket of her coat and the two faeries came flying out. Cissy squealed and clapped her hands in excitement as they landed on the arm of the settee.

"Oh, you're faeries! How cute!"

Moth frowned at her. "We know what we are and we're definitely not cute!" He wagged a tiny finger at them both. "Don't underestimate us," he warned.

"No, don't," Morgan echoed and Cissy's face fell.

"Sorry," she muttered, worried she'd caused offense.

"That's okay!" Velveteena hopped onto her shoulder and kissed her on the cheek. "Just ignore my friend, he's always grumpy. Who are you two children anyway?"

THE SANCTUARY

Cissy took an instant liking to her, though she wasn't too sure yet about the boy. She decided to ignore the 'children' comment and introduced herself and Luke, then waited for the faeries to do the same.

When they didn't, Luke prompted, "And your names are?"

Velveteena flew down and bowed to the teenagers. "He's Moth and I'm Velveteena."

"Pleased to meet you." Cissy smiled politely and, in the silence that followed, nudged Luke painfully in the ribs.

"Oh, me too." Luke looked at Moth doubtfully.

"How did you all meet?" Cissy asked.

But Molly developed a hearing problem at that moment and got to her feet. "Okay, you lot," she announced, "I'm off for that much needed bath!" She fled from the room before anyone could ask more awkward questions. She wasn't going to be the one to tell Luke about the possible cure for his father, not until they knew it would work.

While Molly went to get cleaned up, Cissy and Luke did their best to find out where she'd been on her mysterious errand, but neither the faeries nor Morgan were giving anything away.

"She'll tell you about it later," the wizard said firmly. "It's not my place to tell her secrets." And, of course, the knowledge that there were secrets only piqued their interest more.

"It's not fair to keep things from us!" complained Cissy, sounding unusually petulant.

Morgan laughed. "I honestly don't know any more than you do!" The wizard was just as anxious to find out what had happened to Molly. He was also desperate to know whether she'd managed to find the one ingredient that might save Peter.

He said nothing about this of course; he didn't want to raise the boy's hopes just yet, and he cast a warning glance toward Velveteena and Moth, who understood perfectly and bowed solemnly.

Cissy would have argued further, but at that moment she saw a small figure peeping out from behind the curtain. Seeing she'd been spotted, Penelope ducked hurriedly out of sight.

Cissy smiled and called out gently, "It's okay, Pen, you can come out!" The little girl stepped out hesitantly and crawled up into Cissy's lap. Luke leaned over and ruffled the girl's hair fondly.

"What were you up to?" he asked. "Playing hide and seek?"

In her short life, Penelope had already come to realize that grown-ups didn't really take kids her age seriously; didn't even notice they were there half the time. Oh, they were often kind and pretended to listen and take notice, but they didn't really, their heads were too full of grown-up things. Even her mother, who had loved her very much, Penelope knew, had been like that sometimes.

But Cissy and Luke were different, they spent time with her and made her feel important, and in return the little girl adored them. Although she was far too young to understand or articulate these feelings, she saw in the teenagers a mixture of older brother and sister, replacements for her lost mother. Now, however, she had absolutely no time for either of them for her gaze was transfixed on the table, or rather at what was on it.

As a very young child she'd enjoyed nothing more than snuggling up with her mother at bedtime, being read to until she fell asleep. Her favorite story had been about the *Misery Witch*, a horrible old woman who wouldn't let anyone into her beautiful garden and who chased away the faeries who loved to sneak in and play. Until one day she'd chased them down her garden path and fallen badly and the faeries had cared for her until she was well. After that the faeries were always welcome, and the old woman was no longer the *Misery Witch* but the *Good Witch*.

At nine years old, Penelope knew she was far too old for such baby stories and had even begun to suspect that faeries didn't really exist, despite her mother's insistence that they did.

But now here was proof, right there in front of her, on the table!

"Hi!" Velveteena grinned. "We're Velveteena and Moth." She hovered so close to the girl's face that her wing tips tickled her nose. "Might we have the honor of knowing your name?"

She couldn't answer for a moment, her mouth just opened and closed silently until she was able to stammer, "I…it…it's Pen…el…ope."

"Well hello, Pen…el…ope," they mocked, but not unkindly, for most faeries are fond of children, tending to tolerate them in a way they didn't always with adult humans. Penelope smiled uncertainly, not knowing what to say.

"Come on!" Velveteena laughed. "Bet you can't catch us!" And soon the child was chasing the faeries along corridors and up and down staircases all around the Sanctuary. Penelope thought she'd not had so much fun in her entire life; she was in a dream from which she never wanted to awaken.

Meanwhile, Cissy, with much patience, had managed to get Gruffydd talking. He was a little in awe of this pretty, confident teenager who was quite unlike anyone he'd ever met before, but gradually, with her coaxing, he began to talk. He told them about the night they'd had to hide from the demons, and they listened to his story in wonder. He told them about Ffranc and about Catrin; tears filled Cissy's eyes when she heard how she'd been made mute by the Dark Wizard, tears just as quickly turning to anger.

He's going to pay for it big time, she thought, unconsciously echoing Molly's sentiments when she'd first met Catrin. *I'm gonna make sure…*

But Gruffydd was speaking again, describing the scene at the inn and how the dog, Oscar, had been left all alone in the wreckage of the building. This time it was Luke's turn to be angry, for he loved dogs and now it was he who promised vengeance upon the Dark Wizard.

Gruffydd was quite enjoying being the center of attention and finished up by telling them about the journey through Wales and the English countryside, how they'd reached London and not known the way back to the Sanctuary, and how Morgan had placed magic arrows to guide them.

When they heard how Molly had been forced to get soaking wet in order to reach home, Cissy and Luke howled with laughter.

"I bet she was furious!" Luke nudged her with delight.

"Yeah and you can bet Morgan did it on purpose!" She grinned back at him.

Gruffydd looked at them both, a little bemused as he finished telling his story. One thing he didn't tell them, because he didn't know, was the reason Molly had gone to the village in the first place. She had remained tight-lipped whilst in the village itself and on the journey back to London, despite the boy's numerous attempts to find out. On one occasion he'd plucked up his courage and asked Moth, only to receive a painful bite on the nose and told to mind his own business.

Now Cissy and Luke were determined to find out for themselves, but when they reached Morgan's chamber the door, very unusually, was closed. They knew this meant 'do not disturb under any circumstance,' and although they could clearly hear Molly's voice through the door, the words were too indistinct to make anything out and they dared not interrupt.

Disappointed but suddenly very tired, they decided to call it a night and go to bed. They found an old duvet and a pillow for Gruffydd to sleep on the sofa, for in all the excitement no one had remembered to sort him out a room, then yawning, they said goodnight.

Soon, apart from the low hum of voices in the wizard's chamber, the house was quiet.

THE SANCTUARY

Chapter 33

Luke wasn't sure what woke him but as he sat bolt upright in bed, he suddenly became aware of a stinging sensation in his left ear. Before he could reach up to investigate, something sharp pricked his neck and he heard Moth's voice hiss, "Wake up, human!"

"Hey!" Luke gave the faerie an indignant look. "I am awake, you idiot, couldn't you just shake me or something?" He looked at the clock on his bedside table. "It's one o'clock in the morning, for goodness sake!"

"Idiot am I, human child?" Moth lifted his sword threateningly. "You should be more careful where you aim your insults, we faeries are not a people to take lightly!"

"Oh, stop it you two." Velveteena glared at them. "Luke, you are needed; get dressed quickly."

"What's going on?" he asked as she turned away to give him modesty, but it was Moth who answered, evasively.

"We don't know exactly," he lied, "but I think it's something to do with your father."

"Moth," exclaimed Velveteena, "we aren't supposed to…"

But Luke had turned drip white and sat down suddenly on the edge of the bed. "My father?" His voice was low and oddly defenseless. "Is he…?"

Moth cursed softly to himself and sheathed his sword.

"I'm sorry. *Very* sorry," he said earnestly. "I didn't mean for you to think that!" He grasped Luke's finger in both hands. "It's quite the opposite, Molly has found a cure!"

"Moth!" Velveteena was appalled. "We don't know that. It's not a complete cure!" But she was talking to an empty room for they'd already hurried into the hall.

As she followed them, she was unaware of two shiny black eyes watching her from the window ledge outside. Moments later, the crow hopped through the open window and into the room.

To Luke's surprise, the faeries led him not to Molly's chambers as he expected, but along a narrow corridor that ran between his own room and the one next door, a passage he could swear hadn't been there earlier.

How can that be? he wondered and stared round at his dim surroundings, lit not by electric light but gas lamps from a bygone era that Luke had only ever seen in museums or on TV. The walls were of the same elegant wallpaper and wooden panels that decorated the rest of the house, yet the paper was faded and grubby, its edges peeling away from the wall. The wooden panels, instead of being burnished over time to a rich luster, were dull and faded, covered in scratches.

For several minutes the passage continued and never wavered either right or left nor up or down, but continued straight as an arrow. Luke looked behind to see how far they'd come. *The house wasn't that big, for goodness sake.* But now there was only an inky blackness; he hadn't noticed the gas lamps extinguishing as he passed beneath. Abruptly, the corridor ended at a staircase that circled down and down. When he leaned over the banister, Luke realized he couldn't see its end and he knew it must lead deep underground.

He hesitated and looked at the faeries with mistrust. "How do I know this isn't some kind of trap?" And he was suddenly uncomfortably aware that he didn't really know these strange creatures at all. "How do I know you're not servants of the Dark Wizard sent to harm me or capture me or something?" He looked at their faces, half shrouded in darkness, their eyes sharp and clever, and they seemed to take on an aspect of menace and danger. So he was surprised when they burst into a fit of giggles, and the atmosphere seemed to lift a little.

"If we wanted to harm you or capture you or *something*," said Velveteena, and Luke flushed hotly at the sarcasm in her voice, "we could have done *something* while you slept." And Luke had no choice but to acknowledge the truth of this.

"Sorry," he muttered, feeling foolish, and Velveteena kissed him on the cheek.

"That's okay, human, it's very wise of you to be cautious. Now come, we need to go down."

*   *   *   *

Penelope was awakened by the noise of Luke's protests as he

and the faeries passed near her room, but by the time she'd got out of bed and run into the corridor there was no sign of anyone. She climbed back into bed and lay there for the next hour willing sleep to come. But now she was wide awake and at last she gave in and decided to go to the library. Suddenly excited, she dressed quickly, in a hurry to return to the book she'd found the previous afternoon. She went into the corridor and up the staircase opposite, and soon she was once again lost in tales of dragons and unicorns and other mythical beasts.

For the next hour, Penelope sat alone, happy in her own world, until she gradually became aware of her stomach rumbling. *Just a few more pages,* she promised herself, *then I'll see if Alessandro is about.* But just then there was a knock at the door and Alessandro came in.

"There you are, *Cara*!" he exclaimed, throwing his hands up in mock horror. "I've searched all over London for you!" He grinned at the thought, for these days everyone knew exactly where they would find the girl. "I imagined you'd been eaten by one of those dragons you're always reading about!"

She grinned back at him. "You're crazy, you know that?" She stood and placed the book back on the shelf. "Is breakfast ready?"

"Of course not, it's still only four in the morning, but I was on my way to check something in the kitchen and I saw your bedroom door was open." And then, as she reached for the door handle, he exclaimed, "Stop! Don't move!"

She froze, alarmed. "What's wrong?" Her voice was fearful, breathless.

He looked at her, his face deadly serious. "I am very much afraid, *carissima*," he said slowly, "that you have spent so much time in this room,"—he reached out and gently touched her forehead—"that you are beginning to turn into…"—his voice dropped to a whisper and he glanced theatrically from side to side—"a book!" He traced imaginary words across her forehead and pretended to read aloud. "Once upon a time, there was a little girl…"

Penelope giggled and smacked his hand away. "You're so silly, Alessandro. Race you to the kitchen!" She ran from the room and sped down the stairs, and Alessandro grinned, pretending to chase after her for a second, then following at a slower pace, finding her waiting impatiently outside the locked kitchen.

"It's far too early for breakfast, but I can make something quickly if you're hungry." He grinned and ruffled her already tousled hair. "But seeing as you're up and about instead of in bed where you're meant to be,"—he winked—"there's an urgent meeting going on up in the living room so you may as well…"

But he was talking to thin air, for the girl was already running excitedly up the stairs, eager to find out what was happening. Alessandro watched her, smiling, until she disappeared from view.

*   *   *   *

Round and around went the staircase as the three of them descended into the bowels of the Sanctuary. And there was a fourth who descended with them, for the crow had not abandoned its pursuit and was keeping its secret watch. The air was getting colder the deeper they went and the darkness beyond the staircase was sinister and filled with foreboding. Luke realized he was shivering, and not entirely from the cold. Beneath his feet, the steps descended into the gloom while high above him they curled round and round until they disappeared into nothingness like a wisp of smoke.

These are going on forever, he grumbled to himself, *doesn't this place believe in elevators?* But at last the gloom started to fade and he was able to make out the outline of a door frame. As they got closer, he saw that the bottom half of the door was made of wood, but the top half was frosted glass across which, in black letters, was written 'Laboratory.'

Through it, Luke could make out the distorted figure of someone moving about but, curiously, the space around the doorway was simply that; space, a vast world of emptiness as far as the eye could see.

"Open it," whispered Velveteena.

"Yes, open it," Moth echoed.

Luke gripped the door handle but didn't turn it. *What will we find inside?* he wondered. He tried to peer through the glass but couldn't make anything out.

"Open it!" insisted the faeries, and Luke nodded, then resolutely turned the doorknob.

*   *   *   *

There had never been an army like this one. Such was its size it could no longer be contained on the hillside and had spilled out into the valley below. The noise was tremendous as a hundred different sounds rent the air. Armor clanged and scraped, the noise harsh and frightening, as was the high-pitched scream of swords being sharpened on grindstones. Demons laughed maniacally as excitement grew at the prospect of the coming war. But more often than not they argued, snarling and fighting over the pettiest of things, so that hundreds died before the army even began its long march.

Above it all, the sky was thick and hazy from the smoke of many cooking fires, and the stink of it was foul; the disgusting stench of raw excrement and rotting demon flesh would pervade this place for years to come. Nothing would ever grow upon this hillside again and no wildlife remained, having long since fled.

From his vantage point high upon the hillside, Kanzser surveyed it all with satisfaction. *My army is ready,* he thought, *it is time.* He motioned for one of his guard captains to approach and the creature scurried forward and knelt before him.

Irritably, he motioned for it to rise and it did so, giggling nervously, bowing and scraping subserviently and hopping from one foot to another in its fear and agitation.

Kanzser regarded it sourly. *How can I be expected to win this war with idiots like this one?* Impulsively, he gave a vicious backhand, which shattered the creature's jawbone and drove one of its elongated molars up into its brain, killing it instantly. By the time it had crumpled at his feet, he was already beckoning to another of his captains. This one was more confident and stood before its master, head bowed respectfully, awaiting its orders.

"Sound the drums."

The demon nodded and hurried away. Moments later, a dull, rhythmic throbbing noise reverberated across the hillside.

THE SANCTUARY

Gradually, the Demon King's army organized itself into some kind of order, then with infinitesimal slowness the long march began. The army was huge and unwieldy and took an age to get going. Eventually though, the ground shook from the tramping of thousands upon thousands of feet.

The villagers had abandoned their homes when their lookouts had first reported the beginnings of the demon army. Now they watched fearfully from their hideouts in the forest across the valley, and for the hundredth time Ffranc bemoaned his inability to send warning to Morgan. But there was nobody he could send; most had never even traveled beyond the next valley, how could he expect them to travel the great distance to London? And even if, by some miracle, someone did get there, they'd never be able to find the Sanctuary, let alone a way inside.

Only he himself knew the way and he cursed bitterly, cursed his frailty, his failing body. Standing beside him, Catrin sensed the old man's mood and felt for his hand. He glanced down to see her face smiling up at him and his spirits lifted for her uncomplicated trust and love always gave him strength.

It didn't matter about sending a warning. Morgan would find a way, Morgan would win. And the thought crept into his mind unbidden and unwanted, *he must win, for all our sakes.*

The demon army had almost cleared the valley, but Ffranc would not abandon his post until it had done so. When the last of the creatures had passed out of sight, he turned and joined his companions who waited below. It would be many days, Ffranc knew, before it reached London, but the final chapter of the centuries-old war between good and evil had begun at last.

THE SANCTUARY

Soon, there would be a reckoning.

THE SANCTUARY

Chapter 34

Luke's first impression was of noise and heat, as well as light and vibrant color. And the most disgusting smell.

The place was just like any high school chemistry lab anywhere on the planet. There were beakers and test tubes everywhere, each filled with colored liquids which threw shafts of light around the room as they bubbled and hissed over the naked flames of a score or more Bunsen burners. The noise of popping and hissing as they boiled was tremendous and the heat caused beads of sweat to form across his forehead and on the back of his neck, to run in tiny rivulets down his back.

In the center of the room was a large figure wearing a white coat, gloves, an NYC baseball cap and, rather incongruously, a pair of Wellington boots at least three sizes too big. It was bent over a bowl of foaming liquid and as he cautiously approached, Luke saw that the head, which looked rather like a boiled beetroot, wore a pair of swimming goggles.

Molly?" he wondered. "What on Earth…?"

"Hi, Luke, you got here quick." Molly pulled back her sleeve and looked at her watch. "Bleedin' 'ell!" she exclaimed and grabbed a bubbling jar of green liquid, seemingly unaware that it was scalding hot. "Quick," she ordered, "somebody grab that red one!"

In an instant Velveteena and Moth were beside a red test tube that was taller than they were. They wrapped their arms around it and flew it over to Molly, all traces of their earlier mischief now gone. She took it from them and poured it hurriedly into the green liquid.

"Luke, put a light under that." She pointed to a large beaker containing a thick black sludge. "We have to get it boiling hot." And as his eyes searched round for matches she snapped, "Use your wand dammit!"

"I don't have it with me," he objected. "I got dragged from my bed in the middle of the night!"

"A good wizard always has his wand," she told him sternly as she flicked her own and a jet of flame whooshed beneath the beaker. "Remember that in the future!"

Seeing the mutinous look on his face, Velveteena flew over to the boy. "Don't sulk," she whispered in his ear then kissed his cheek, "everything will be fine, but you must do exactly as Molly tells you."

He sensed the urgency in her voice and forced his bad mood away. "What's next?" he asked brightly, and Molly patted his arm.

"Good lad," she said, and took a long glass thermometer from her pocket. She gave it a quick polish on her sleeve and tossed it into the sludge. "I need you to watch that closely," she told him, "it mustn't go above ten thousand."

"Ten thousand what?"

"Degrees," she said, absently. "Do concentrate, Luke."

"But that's impossible! Thermometers don't go above about a hundred, do they?"

"Well not usually," she admitted, "but that's far too cold for this kind of spell so we need a proper one, in other words, a magic thermometer. Now watch out, ten thousand remember, not a degree more."

He suddenly remembered what Moth had said to him back in his bedroom; *how long ago that seemed.* The excitement surged within him again as he realized what the witch was making.

"Will this cure my father?" His voice was almost an entreaty, but Molly rounded furiously on Moth and Velveteena.

"You couldn't just keep *bleedin' quiet,* could you?" In a gentler tone she said, "I hope so, Luke, but the odds aren't great, you mustn't build up your hopes too much."

The boy nodded but he was suddenly filled with excitement and he grinned at Molly.

She sighed again. "Just watch the thermometer, Luke."

He looked curiously at the glass tube sitting in the sludge that now bubbled fiercely and was no longer black, but bright orange. It was marked with little black lines just like any ordinary thermometer but was numbered in hundreds of degrees rather than tens. And along its center, tiny quicksilver horses galloped back and forth, their hooves leaving minute silver prints on the glass. Already they had reached the three-thousand-degree mark.

As he stared transfixed, the temperature rose to four thousand degrees, then five.

"It's going up quickly," he called, "already on five… no, five and a half!"

"Keep watching!" Molly was busy throwing powders and leaves, what looked like flower seeds, petals and goodness knew what else into a bowl and shaking it vigorously. The faeries were helping although they seemed to be getting more on themselves than anywhere else; Moth's face was bright blue while Velveteena's hair had turned an interesting shade of pink.

The tiny horses continued to gallop ever more furiously along the tube as minuscule droplets of silver sweat flew from their flanks.

"Seven thousand!" called Luke.

"Quickly, you two, there's not much time," panted Molly.

"Eight!"

Molly's arms were a blur as she worked, frantically racing the silver horses that were galloping with increasing speed toward their goal.

"Nine thousand!" Luke almost screamed as Molly poured the jars of red and green liquid into the bowl. "Nine and a half!"

Molly was by his side now, poised and ready; the faeries held their breath anxiously, their tiny hearts beating furiously, and Molly sweated with exertion and nerves. Would it work or would it all be in vain?

Luke could almost taste the tension in the air even though he didn't fully understand what Molly was attempting.

"Nine and three quarters." He held his breath. "Ten thousand, it's at ten thousand!" he yelled as Molly blew out the flame and simultaneously poured the contents of the bowl into the beaker, which had once more turned a cloudy black color. As the two liquids collided there was a loud bang that shook the room and rattled the windows and, directly above in Morgan's room, a faint cloud of plaster floated down onto the wizard's head.

I wonder if she's been successful? He thought as he got to his feet at once and hastened toward the stairs.

Inside the lab there hung a cloud of acrid smoke that made them cough and set their eyes watering. As it gradually cleared, Molly stared anxiously at the beaker. Velveteena and Moth were sitting on her shoulder with their hands over their faces, not daring to look. Luke tried to stare through the smoke despite his watering eyes.

Was this it? Would it work? *Please let it work, please, please let it work.*

With infinitesimal slowness, the beaker emerged into view and at last its contents were revealed. A small amount of liquid, about half a mug full, as transparent as a fine wine except instead of being golden in color, this was a beautiful, vibrant purple.

"Is this it? Is it okay?" Luke panted excitedly, picking up the beaker and examining it curiously. "What exactly is in this?"

"Careful," Molly warned and took it from him, "that's the most important, most valuable liquid in the world right now." She put it down carefully. "And it's not quite finished." From her pocket she took the blood thorn. "This is the ingredient that will determine success or failure!"

Luke looked curiously at the curved thorn with its bright red tip.

"Is that why you went away?" he asked with a flash of intuition. "To find this?"

"Yes." She tossed the thorn into the beaker. Instantly the whole room was bathed in crimson light and the liquid once more hissed and frothed violently. As it began to slop over the rim, Molly feared there'd be none left. Gradually though it settled into stillness and the redness of the room faded.

And there, much reduced but still about a quarter of a mug full, was the finished result. Now the liquid was infused with tiny bubbles as if it were the finest champagne, except it was the color of blood.

"We must hurry," urged the witch, "if it's not used within about twelve hours it will lose its power!" She stroked her chin worriedly for a moment. "Although it might be six or even two." She stopped at Luke's horrified look. "But it's more than two, definitely, without a doubt." She gave him a reassuring pat on the arm that did nothing at all to reassure him. "Absolutely sure of it, no need to worry." She shrugged. "Actually the book wasn't that clear and the language kept changing. I don't think whoever wrote the spell was too sure either."

"Then we have to hurry!" Luke was suddenly frantic. "It might only be an hour or even ten minutes or something!" He tugged at her sleeve with one hand while simultaneously making a grab for the beaker with the other.

Quick as a flash the faeries swooped down, took hold of it between them and placed it high on a shelf out of reach.

"Careful!" Molly told him. "Break that and there's no hope at all!" Seeing Luke's face fall, she relented, "I'm sure we have enough time, Luke." Her hand moved slowly behind her back and she crossed her fingers as she said it. "But I must speak with Morgan, tell him the potion is ready."

A short time later they were gathered in the living room waiting for Morgan to speak. Hidden behind one of the thick curtains that held the night at bay, the crow listened attentively, ready to report back to the Dark Wizard.

"Well now," began Morgan when they were all settled. "All of you know by now of Molly's quest to find the vital ingredient, blood thorn, which might provide a cure for Peter."

Cissy opened her mouth to speak but Morgan held up a hand.

"I'm sure Molly can fill you in with all the details of her adventures later, but right now there is no time to waste. All you need to know is that her quest was successful, and she was, with the help of our friends the Faer Folk, able to obtain the necessary ingredient. Not, I understand, without considerable danger."

Molly grinned, pleased at the acknowledgment, while Moth and Velveteena tried and failed to look nonchalant about the whole thing.

"Tonight, Molly has made the potion, which I have here." They all looked intently at the small glass jar that contained all their hopes. "She was assisted by Luke, which I think is fitting. Well done, Luke."

The boy blushed brightly, embarrassed to be the focus of attention as everyone looked at him approvingly. Cissy leaned over and hugged him tightly. "You're amazing," she whispered and kissed his cheek.

"Alright then," Morgan rose to his feet. The potion is made and there's no point delaying." He looked at Luke sympathetically;

this was the moment of truth for him. "Are you ready, Luke?"

"Let's do it." The words croaked from his mouth, and they all rose together and made their way to the door.

"No! You can't give it yet!" Penelope emerged from behind the armchair where she'd been hiding after sneaking into the room behind Molly, hidden in the voluminous folds of the witch's dress.

"What the...?" Morgan exclaimed in surprise and the faeries grinned; they'd been the only ones who'd noticed her sneak in. "How did you get in here? You should be in bed!"

Deciding attack was the best form of defense, she retaliated, "And just how am I supposed to sleep with all this noise going on?" Desperate to keep talking so he wouldn't send her back, she went on quickly, "And I *know* you have to give the potion at midnight!"

Morgan looked at her, half amused now. "And just how do you know that? You're *nine*."

That's just typical of an adult, she thought indignantly as she prepared to do battle with the most powerful wizard on Earth. "Just because you're like a...a *thousand* years old or something," she told him sassily, hands on hips, "does not mean you know everything." She took a step forward, legs shaking like jelly but determined to win. "And what's more, I'm nearly ten!"

"Don't push your luck, kid." Luke nudged her but Morgan was now trying without much success to hold back a grin.

"Okay, Penelope, we're listening, tell us what you think you know."

The girl took a deep breath. "Okay, well first I looked through all the books in the place but didn't find anything."

"Wait," Luke broke in suddenly, "how did you even know

Molly was looking for a cure?"

Penelope shrugged and avoided his eyes. "I'm small and people don't notice me because I'm *nine*." She looked pointedly at Morgan. "And I have ears." Penelope neatly glossed over the fact she'd been using those ears to listen at doors to conversations not meant for her. "Anyway, like I said," she went on quickly, "I looked at lots of books but I couldn't find anything. So then I went on the internet."

"The internet!" Luke was aghast. "Have you any idea how unreliable that is? Penelope, I know you're trying to help…"

"Stop interrupting!" the girl exclaimed, exasperated. "Please just listen! I know the internet can't always be trusted, but this article mentioned the Great Wizard, Owain the Original!"

Morgan looked at her sharply. "But mortals wouldn't know that name," he said, "it is only ever mentioned in books that lay within the Sanctuary."

"Exactly!" She gave him a grateful look. "Which makes me think the article I read was somehow put onto the internet by magic so I would find it!"

"Could you log in and show us, Pen?" Cissy asked.

"I printed it off." She fished inside her pocket and handed Morgan a crumpled sheet. "But it wouldn't print in English for some reason. It's some foreign language, probably a long dead one."

The wizard began to read but then looked at Penelope suspiciously. "Hang on. If you couldn't read this, how do you know what it says?"

She looked at him, just managing not to roll her eyes. "I used a translation app." *Obviously*, she thought.

"Of course you did. Well this language is far from dead, Penelope," he told her and his mouth quirked. "Actually, it's Welsh."

"Then you're the only one who can understand it, so go on." Wallace grunted. "What does it say?"

The room fell silent while Morgan read until he looked up, his face grave.

"Penelope's right. Thank goodness you found it, Pen. If we'd just given the potion at any time, in the normal way, it would not have worked. In fact, could have done more harm than good."

She beamed, pleased at the praise, as Morgan continued.

"It seems this potion, because of the blood thorn, has to be given in two halves. At the first then the last chimes of midnight. Something to do with mimicking the rise and fall of the moon. That part's a bit unclear. But the instruction itself is not."

"We can trust this, Morgan?" Wallace asked, ever the pragmatist.

"Yes, I'm sure we can. The style is Owain's and the signature certainly genuine. So, we should get some sleep now. We will gather again in Peter's room just before midnight."

As Luke filed out with the others, he knew this would be the longest wait of his life.

Chapter 35

Peter's skin was gray and sallow, waxy in the pale moonlight coming through the window. A sheen of sweat bathed his face and his breathing was barely discernible. He'd thrown off the blankets and the black veins in his chest were stark against the pale skin. The creeping tendrils looked like fingers reaching for his heart.

"Dad," Luke whispered, and when there was no response, "Dad!"

Peter's eyelids fluttered then opened. It took him a moment to focus, but then he smiled slightly.

"My boy," he whispered, the words faint so that the others gathered in the room moved closer to hear. As he noticed them crowded into the small bedchamber, Peter heaved himself onto one elbow, panting with the effort. "What's going on?" he croaked then sank back, exhausted, onto his pillow. Peter's skin looked even grayer now, the beads of sweat more pronounced. Luke could swear the black, spidery tentacles that sought to end his father's life had spread even further in those few moments.

"Hurry," said Morgan, "it's almost midnight." He and Wallace moved quickly to Peter's bedside and together they heaved him into a sitting position, an easy task, for he had lost so much weight.

"Peter." Morgan shook his shoulders gently, but now there was no response. "Peter," he said, louder this time, a little less gentle on the shoulders followed by a tap on the cheek. Still no response. "Peter!" This time the slap was shockingly loud in the stillness of the room and his eyes flew open. Morgan saw a flash of anger in them and welcomed it. Peter's spirit still burned inside that wasted body; he could still fight!

"What the hell?" he rasped.

"Peter, you must drink this." He reached for the cup of precious liquid and held it near so Peter could see and smell its contents.

"What's that? Are you trying to kill me?" Peter laughed at his own joke but no one else joined in. Aware that the potion was his only hope, he looked at each of them in turn and nodded slightly. "Thank you, my friends."

Then he looked at Luke and, with a great effort, lifted a hand to stroke his cheek and ruffle his hair. "I love you, son." His voice rang out bright and clear.

"I love you too, Dad." The words came out equally strong, without the hint of a tremor, even though he felt he was dying inside. Peter nodded proudly, squeezed Luke's shoulder,

Just then the old Grandfather clock in the hall began to chime.

"Drink," ordered Morgan and held the cup to Peter's lips. Taken by surprise, he gulped it down so quickly that Morgan had to remove it quickly before he drank it all.

The chimes continued; it seemed to Luke they took an age.

Then, as the final bell sounded, Morgan spoke again.

"Drink." He held the cup once more for Peter.

Instantly Peter's body spasmed and went rigid, his lips drawing back into a rictus grin.

"Dad!" The anguish in Luke's voice was terrible to hear. He looked at Molly, the accusation clear in his eyes. "Do something!"

"Oh my God! What have I done?" She hurried to Peter's side, but Morgan caught her arm.

"Wait! Look!" And sure enough, although the veins on Peter's chest were still prominent, still evil, they'd stopped moving! Hadn't they?

Yes! Now it became obvious, they'd definitely stopped. And some of the thinner ones, surely they were going backwards? A minute later there could be no doubt. The poison was definitely receding. Then, gradually, Peter's muscles relaxed, and his head fell back onto the pillow. His features softened, and it seemed that the corners of his mouth lifted into the faintest glimmer of a smile.

Molly warned Luke it would take some time for his father to fully recover but at last there was hope and Luke was finally able to start living again. He felt curiously nervous when, a day or so later, he walked cautiously into the training room where Cissy was practicing with Wallace.

They didn't see him enter and he watched quietly for a while as she struggled to get to grips with the difficult art of swordplay. Eventually he sauntered casually forward and nonchalantly took down his own sword from the rack, pretending to examine its edge closely; he wanted desperately to join in but was suddenly shy and unsure of his welcome.

"Come on, Luke, look lively." Wallace kept his voice casual; he'd noticed the boy's reticence and understood it, but he didn't want to make a fuss and embarrass him.

But Cissy had no such concerns and she grinned at him. "It's about time you turned up!" She swung her sword and it clashed with a loud, ringing clang against his. "Been too scared to fight me?"

In no time at all they were fighting playfully, having fun until they ended up in a giggling heap on the training room floor. Wallace smiled and let them play, pleased to see Luke looking so relaxed for once. He knew they both needed this time to get to know each other properly again and to enjoy themselves for once.

Now they trained together every day, and Luke became so skillful that Wallace could no longer match him. Cissy resumed her training with Molly, much to Morgan's relief, and was as good with her wand as Luke was with his sword.

And they were happy, despite the threat of war that hung over the Sanctuary. Cissy, in particular, had reason to celebrate when, one night, Morgan took her along the passage-between-the-worlds and out into the mortal world where she was reunited with her parents. It was an emotional visit and Lucy had objected strongly when her daughter revealed her intention to return to the Sanctuary. Charles, though, was immensely proud – if a little envious – when he learned just how formidable she'd become with her wand. It was he who was able to persuade Lucy that Cissy must return, that it was her destiny to do so, despite the danger she would soon face.

Luke was less fortunate for he was unable to visit his own mother. As Morgan had explained, how could he tell her that the husband she'd thought dead these last sixteen years was actually alive? That he'd been dangerously ill and close to death? Bitterly disappointed though he was, Luke consoled himself with the thought that soon, with luck, he would be accompanied by his father the next time he returned home.

It was two weeks before the last of the blackness left Peter's veins and his skin returned to normal. Only then did he awaken from the semi-coma in which he had lain whilst his body healed and the first person he saw was his son. For the next couple of days the other occupants of the Sanctuary kept a respectful distance, but it wasn't long before Peter himself was impatient to be up and about. He spoke excitedly to Morgan of playing a part in the battle against the Dark Wizard, and one of his first acts was to enter the training room where he'd spent so many hours as a young man.

To his chagrin he found he barely had the strength to lift anything but the smallest of swords from the rack. Even then he could only manage five minutes of gentle practice before his legs and arms felt so weak, he was forced to rest. He tried again the next day and the next, testing himself to the limits of his strength. At last, worried he would relapse totally, Morgan ordered him to cease and Peter had to accept the unwelcome fact that he would be unable to take part in the battle. He would have to leave the Sanctuary and it was of absolutely no consolation that he would be given the task of taking the boy Gruffydd with him and ensuring his safety.

So it was that about a week after Peter regained consciousness there was a visitor to the Sanctuary. It was Luke who noticed her first as she entered the lounge accompanied by Morgan and Molly.

"Your Majesty!" he exclaimed in delight as he ran toward her, before remembering just in time who she actually was and sinking almost to his knees in a deep bow.

"Enough of that!" Queen Marie Antoinette laughed and raised him up. "We are old friends, *nes pas?* I do not expect my closest of friends to bow!" She kissed him lightly on both cheeks and the boy almost swelled with pride.

Unusually for her, Cissy could find little to say when Luke introduced the queen; she had always loved history at school and her brain had difficulty accepting that one of her favorite heroines was actually here, right in front of her. Penelope had no such trouble and chatted non-stop with the queen of France who, with her innate kindness, listened attentively to the girl, focusing her considerable charm upon her.

As for Gruffydd, he had no clear idea of who she was. He'd never even heard of France, but he was overawed by this beautiful, glamorous creature who was so far outside of his experience, and he could think of nothing to say to her. Even Peter, usually full of confidence, found himself slightly tongue-tied in her presence. When she first spoke directly to him, he had the uncomfortable experience of blushing; something he'd not done since he was a teenager.

Nevertheless, her natural charm soon put everyone at ease and there followed an evening of gaiety, excellent food courtesy of Alessandro and his cooks, and fine wine. Little did Luke know, although Morgan and Molly suspected, that this was the last time they would ever see the queen. The next day she was gone, taking Peter and Gruffydd with her, and later that day a message was received, written upon parchment.

The message was short, three words only.

The demons approach.

*   *   *   *

Meter after meter, the long, unwieldy column of the Demon King's army snaked its way across the countryside, moving with agonizing slowness until finally it crossed the border into England. There were few to watch it pass, for most living creatures, be they animals, birds or people, had long since fled, never to return. Those too foolhardy or too slow to run were captured and used for food or sport. This army devoured everything in its path and behind it lay a wide swathe of dead ground that marked its progress. Later, long after the war had ended, few would be willing to dwell near that region which came to be known as the Path of Death.

Demons came in all shapes and sizes, though most were bent and misshapen as if whoever or whatever first created them had played a cruel and macabre joke. They had varying degrees of intelligence, usually quite low but what they lacked in brains they made up for with cunning. It was quite impossible to trick a demon, just as it was impossible to befriend one; they had no morals, no concept of goodness and there existed within their withered souls not a shred of warmth toward their fellow creatures. Apart from their inherent cruelty and hatred of humans, demons had but one other thing in common; they loved to fight.

From the beginning of the long journey to the end, they

squabbled and fought, murdered each other in full view or secretly in the dead of night. They started fights merely so they could lay wagers on who would live or die. There were no rules, no laws; the strongest prevailed, the weakest did not. The path became littered with bodies that rotted where they lay and poisoned the earth beneath them. Many hundreds of the Demon King's army were lost in this way, but what did that matter when these unlucky few provided sport for the rest? And what did it matter, when it counted its numbers in tens of thousands?

And so, at last it reached the outskirts of London and there it waited while the Demon King's eyes feasted greedily upon his prize. The inhabitants of the city whispered fearfully and wondered what would befall them. Soon, inevitably, their whispers reached the ears of those within the Sanctuary.

*   *   *   *

For the rest of that day, and those that followed, there was frantic activity in the Sanctuary. Everyone was busy, for most would be involved in the fight in one way or another.

Except Penelope. She, of course, would take no part in the battle and the following morning she would leave the Sanctuary. Molly had decided it would be too frightening for the girl to accompany Queen Marie into what was, after all, another dimension in time. This was a view with which Penelope thoroughly disagreed, but nevertheless other arrangements had been made and so, not being needed anywhere else, she decided to pay one final visit to her favorite place: the library. And then, as time for those within the

THE SANCTUARY

Sanctuary began to run out, Penelope began to read.

Part Three

THE SANCTUARY

Chapter 36

Penelope may only have been nine years old (nearly ten) but she'd played a big part, by means of an ancient piece of knowledge that had somehow magically appeared on the internet, in helping to cure Peter Simpson.

A studious child, always with her nose in a book, she'd spent countless hours in the vast library of the Sanctuary, lost in stories of wizards and witches from years gone by, tales of long dead heroes and heroines, their exploits keeping her enraptured for hours on end.

Now though, the time was fast approaching when she would have to leave the Sanctuary, perhaps forever. For even she knew, young as she was, that the chances of defeating the Dark Wizard, or rather the demon army he brought with him, were slim.

So, her search became increasingly frantic for there were scant hours remaining, searching for something, *anything* that might tip the balance in their favor. In the weeks since she first entered it, she'd already leafed through most of the books in this library she'd come to love so much, and nothing stood out in her memory.

Now there were only a handful of books she'd not looked

at, but as she picked yet another she immediately felt a shiver of excitement run down her spine. *This book is different, I know it!* She leafed eagerly through the dusty old tome, which at first glance appeared to be full of the kind of stories she'd read in all the other books. But then she came across something different.

It was the story of a place ruled by a warrior queen, a story to keep a young child enthralled. This queen had every quality necessary to appeal to Penelope's romantic vision of what she herself would be like if she were a queen in a magical land. Beautiful and strong, brave and fierce, cruel and ruthless when needed, but also capable of great compassion and kindness. The queen in this story was head of an army, only one hundred strong, but who could not be defeated. And best of all, her realm could only be reached by magic!

Penelope read the story twice and felt herself drift into a daydream where she was the warrior queen riding across her lands, righting wrongs and protecting her subjects. She was dragged from her reverie by the sound of Alessandro ringing the dinner gong. She ignored it and continued to read for another ten minutes until it sounded again, impatiently this time, or so it seemed to her.

Penelope stood without taking her eyes from the page, trying greedily to cram in a few more lines of the story, and as she did so a scrap of paper fell from the pages and fluttered to the floor. She picked it up, hurriedly placing the book back on its shelf, and looked at it curiously, turning it over in her hands. At first, she thought the paper was blank and was about to screw it into a ball and throw it away, but some instinct made her pause. She looked again more closely and realized there *was* something written there, but no matter how much she squinted, the words, impossibly tiny, were far too small to read, even with her sharp eyes.

And there was the dinner gong again!

The meal seemed to take an age. Why did adults always insist on talking, asking you if you were okay, what you've learned today, what you've been up to? They meant well, she supposed, but honestly, dinner could be finished in half the time if they'd just shut up!

But at last, it was over and she could escape back to the library, pausing only to sneak into Morgan's chamber and borrow the big silver magnifying glass that she knew he kept in the top left-hand drawer of his desk. She gripped it tightly, moving it back and forth and squinting through the glass as she struggled to bring the words into focus. But now she had it! The words were revealed, large and perfectly readable.

It was a spell! She knew it at once and shivered with excitement and fear at the realization that the queen and her magical land were real, not just a story! Unbidden, an idea came to her, but she pushed it to the back of her mind almost immediately, for the implications were simply too daunting to contemplate.

This had all happened two days before and Penelope had spent the time since then in an agony of indecision. But now she realized the time was fast approaching when she'd have to decide what to do, for the information she'd read would potentially save countless lives. Indeed, it might help determine the fate of the whole world. But young Penelope was troubled, for surely this was not something she could do alone? After all, this wasn't just any old spell, something simple and easy like the ones she'd seen Cissy trying to do when she sneaked in on her lessons one afternoon.

No, this wasn't like those spells at all.

This one was different. Dangerous.

This spell contained the knowledge to enter Queen Aeryn's world.

*   *   *   *

Preparations for the battle were complete. Cissy and Luke could practice no more and were spending the evening watching TV or playing the Xbox. They managed to push their fears aside for the moment and were relaxed, laughing and joking like two ordinary teenagers without a care in the world.

Molly, though, was preoccupied and moody, quite unlike her usual, irascible self. She sat quietly watching the two of them, her eyes downcast to hide the sorrow in them and the tears that threatened to come at any moment. The old witch was the least sentimental of people, but her guilt threatened to crush her spirit.

Damn you, Morgan, damn your prophecy! We should have let them be! They're just children!

She sighed. It was no one's fault, she knew; it was simply how things were meant to be. If they didn't make a stand, defeat the Dark Wizard, then the entire mortal world was doomed anyway. There was no point in thinking like this, and she stood, hoping to distract herself. "Come on then, show me this Xbox thingy. I keep asking you both to teach me but you've never bleedin' bothered. Bleedin' inconsiderate of you, I call it!"

Cissy and Luke stared at her in astonishment before shifting to one side so she could squeeze between them on the settee. Molly

THE SANCTUARY

had never, ever shown the slightest bit of interest before now. Luke grinned and passed her one of the controllers; he winked at Cissy as he explained the buttons.

While this was going on, Morgan was occupied in a much more serious undertaking out in the passage-between-the-worlds; he was placing dynamite. Or, at least, the *wizard* equivalent of dynamite; tiny spells, each one easy to concoct in itself, but dozens of them placed all along the passage and in the circular room beneath the lamp post. At the moment of his death these would detonate and destroy all traces of the passage-between-the-worlds and the way into the Sanctuary; perhaps a few demons might have found their way into the passage by this time, and he gave a mirthless smile at the thought.

The Sanctuary itself would remain intact, for it was inviolate and could not be destroyed. The magic that had made it, so many centuries past, was too powerful. The hope remained therefore that one day, many years in the future perhaps, new wizards would appear to rebuild and carry on the fight.

And what of Wallace, the dourest, but also the kindest of wizards? He was to be found in his beloved training room, polishing and re-polishing weapons until they shone brightly, painful to the eye in the electric light. In a complete reversal of his usual pessimism, the old wizard had hopes they might succeed against the Dark Wizard. More than anyone, he knew just how formidable Luke had become; not that the boy could do this alone of course, but Molly had told him Cissy was pretty damned good with her wand too. Allied with the might of Morgan and Molly, and he himself, surely they at least had a chance? Truthfully, he couldn't really

THE SANCTUARY

understand why Morgan was so pessimistic.

Wallace, however, had yet to see the size of the Demon King's army.

And Alessandro? The sweet, gentle Italian would not fight. He had been instructed by Morgan not to do so. He had no skill with a sword, nor with a wand if it was to be used for killing. He devoted his magic to the concoction of the most wonderful food, and no one did it better. It would be his job to keep the company fed and watered during the battle and to provide aid and healing where needed. He was to make his escape if the battle went against them; Morgan had been clear and firm on that point.

On this evening, while Morgan wove his spells and the others relaxed in the lounge, the chef was giving his own instructions to Hans – the cook who Luke had once witnessed being chased by a knife-wielding Alessandro – and his two helpers. These three had no magic but had given long and faithful service to the Sanctuary and they would not be abandoned. As soon as word came of the demons' attack, they would escape into the passage-between-the-worlds and find their way to Queen Marie. There they would continue their service and had already been given detailed directions on how to get there and the words to speak to open the door.

After he'd said goodbye to them for what might be the last time, Alessandro went, as he did each night, to check on Penelope and make certain she was comfortable and sleeping. Morgan and Molly were a bit lax with the girl, he thought primly, and often allowed her to stay up reading long after she should have been asleep.

Sure enough, Penelope was wide awake and studying her book

intently, trying to memorize the spell she would try out tomorrow but quickly realizing she would need to write it down. There was also something she needed from the schoolroom and she waited impatiently for Alessandro to make his nightly check.

Where is he? she thought, and for the tenth time in as many minutes opened the door a little so she could peep out into the corridor. This time she had to run and jump quickly back into bed as she saw him approaching. When Alessandro knocked quietly and looked in, all he saw was the top of Penelope's fair head and all he heard was the sound of her breathing, punctuated by the occasional soft snore. Satisfied, he whispered softly, *"Buona notte, cara,"* and closed the door again.

Penelope listened for a few moments until she was sure he'd gone, then crept cautiously to the nearby schoolroom, found what she wanted and crept back, heart hammering furiously. As she sat on the edge of her bed and felt the adrenaline rapidly seeping away, she suddenly felt unutterably tired. It took all her remaining strength to set her alarm clock and get into bed, still fully clothed. Within seconds she was asleep.

But, all too soon, the strident bell of the alarm sounded and she was jerked awake. 6:00 am.

How can it be this time already? she thought, but then she remembered what she planned to do today and her stomach did a somersault in equal excitement and terror. Penelope got out of bed and splashed water onto her face to wake herself a little. She dried off, grabbed the backpack she'd found in the old cupboard beneath the main stairs and put the book inside. Then she flung one strap over her shoulder, took a last look around her room as if saying goodbye, which indeed she was, then she was ready.

Once again, she peeped from her bedroom into the corridor outside and found it deserted, as she'd hoped. The girl slipped out quietly and closed the door very gently behind her. She had planned her moment carefully; at this time of day most people would still be sleeping. Sure, Morgan might be working in his study and Alessandro would be in his kitchen preparing breakfast, but there should be nobody wandering about.

Nevertheless, she took no chances and tiptoed to the top of the magnificent, red-carpeted staircase which led down to the wide entrance hall. Penelope looked fearfully round as she made her way down, expecting to be challenged at any moment. But seconds later she had crossed the hall and, though it took all her strength, pulled open the big oak door and was in the street outside. Almost, but not quite unobserved.

It was Penelope's bad luck that Hans entered the hall just in time to see the front door click shut. Not concerned, just incurably curious – some might say plain nosy – Hans hurried to open it and have a look. Penelope was already far down the street and Hans was too short-sighted to make anything out clearly, and he was about to give it up when something made him pause. A small figure with distinctive corn-yellow hair.

It cannot be, he thought to himself. But her coat, the exact shade of red as the one Molly had bought the girl only a week before!

"*Ach mein Gott!*" he exclaimed in horror. "Penelope! *Mein kind, wo gehst du hin!*" The pot of chili con carne he had been carrying slipped from under his arm and smashed onto the steps, coating them in brown, delicious-smelling goo. His brain dimly registered that Alessandro would certainly have something to say about that as he hurried back inside, waving his arms in frantic panic.

"Morgan!" he cried and, lapsing once more into his mother tongue, "*Hilfe! Komm schnell, bitte beeilen, Penelope ist verschwunden!*"

*   *   *   *

The Dark Wizard's spy was near the end of its strength, so it was a relief when, from its position high above the demon army, London at last emerged through the mists of the breaking dawn. It had been a long and difficult journey; the demons had found great sport in hurling their spears at the crow and with their prodigious strength it had been forced to fly high in the sky to avoid them. There was one brute in particular, one of the few demons to favor bow and arrows as its weapon of choice, who had been the bird's chief tormentor. It was a great, hulking creature with massive chest and biceps and a single, large eye set slightly off-center into a forehead which protruded so far out from its head, its face was constantly in shadow.

Throughout the entire march, the demon had delighted in aiming wave after wave of arrows with unbelievable speed, and a hundred times the crow had been buffeted by the wind of their passage as they whooshed by. On one occasion, an arrow had nicked a wing, wrenching out feathers so painfully that the crow had plummeted toward the earth. For long seconds, death had seemed certain before it had somehow righted itself and managed to find a current of air that carried it to safety.

THE SANCTUARY

In truth, the bird could have followed the army's progress from afar, it was so big. But the Dark Wizard's instructions had been clear, to stay close to the head of the army and take note of all that happened. Logan was worried, wisely, of being betrayed by the Demon King, and the crow, with its customary loyalty, was determined not to let that happen. So it stayed as close as it dared, and with its acute hearing, heard every word the Demon King uttered.

But Kanzser had no thoughts of betrayal, for now that he had his army, he wanted this war just as much as Logan did. There was no plotting, no devious schemes and now that their goal was close, an air of excitement descended over the Demon King and his generals.

Satisfied and relieved, the crow was about to return to its master when it paused in puzzlement. Something was different, it thought, something had changed, but what? It took many moments for the realization to come, and when it did, the crow smiled inwardly. The sky was clear! The arrows and spears which had blighted his progress for so long had ceased! Now the demons were more interested in celebrating, and already the wine was flowing freely and drunkenness taking hold. Before long they were fighting among themselves.

The crow ventured closer to the melee, trying to make sense of what he saw, searching, ever searching. With a loud squawk of triumph, the crow spotted his tormentor, head tipped back, flagon to its mouth, wine pouring down its throat and spilling over its chest to the ground. Without hesitating, it swooped down, closer, ever closer, and as the demon threw the empty flagon aside, its

THE SANCTUARY

single eye had just a split second to see its nemesis approaching. Then the bird's fierce talons latched onto its face and, with another scream of triumph, its cruel beak plucked that single eye from its socket, leaving behind only a few bloody, stringy tendons.

The demon gave a howl of pain and staggered blindly around, arms outstretched, shouting curses at whoever had done this thing. It would have been wise to keep quiet, for after all a new eye would have grown within a few months. But it was not in a demon's nature to be passive and its cries became louder and more enraged. And those around, sensing weakness, began to gather, crowding in, getting closer. All at once the demon stumbled and as he writhed in the mud, his horned feet trying to get purchase, they fell upon him, tearing at his flesh, eating greedily until all that was left was a mound of bloody bone and tissue. The crow, its mission accomplished, simply flew away.

*   *   *   *

Unaware she had been observed or of the panic about to envelop the Sanctuary, Penelope hurried along, looking anxiously from side to side. Before long she found exactly what she needed, an alleyway that was neither too narrow nor too wide; most importantly, it was deserted. She ran quickly down, far enough to be sure she couldn't be observed from the street, then paused, heart pounding.

What had the spell said next? She tried to remember as she peered nervously into the shadows where she could hear scratching and scuffling noises. *Rats*, she thought, and shuddered.

THE SANCTUARY

Far above the alleyway, the sky was a thin strip of blue and the noises from the street were strangely muted so that she stood in near silence. The rush of adrenaline she'd experienced at the start of her adventure was wearing off and it was dawning on her she was all alone. Nobody in the Sanctuary knew where she was or that she had even gone. She would never see them again. Fighting down her rising panic, and disgusted at her own self-pity, she forced an image of Molly's kind, smiling face into her mind. She took a few deep breaths and willed her brain to work.

Find a street or passage; must be free of mortals.

"Okay, done that," she muttered. She felt in her pocket and took out the stick of chalk she'd taken from the schoolroom.

Find the center of the passage and paint a line the width of a doorway.

Well she didn't have any paint, only the chalk, so hopefully the spell wasn't too literal. Nor did she have anything to measure with. She drew the line, judging what she thought to be the center, then stepped back and looked at it doubtfully. It looked terribly thin and insubstantial; she'd been so confident earlier, but now she was equally certain her plan would fail.

Although it had been only minutes, it seemed to the girl she'd been gone for hours and she expected to hear sounds of pursuit at any moment. She hurriedly fished out the piece of paper and stood facing the line, toes almost but not quite touching as instructed. The spell was long and some of the words were difficult, but she'd copied them carefully. Now she spoke them with equal care.

Almost instantly, the shape of a doorway formed. It was filled with a shimmering light, beyond which could be seen not a dirty

THE SANCTUARY

brick wall but fields and hills and sky. It reminded Penelope of a day trip she'd once had in Yorkshire when she and her mother had stood behind a waterfall and gazed through the cascading torrent at the beautiful, rugged countryside. Looking through the doorway was just like that day, she realized.

Now, although Penelope wouldn't have known the word to describe it, she was aware of the tangy ozone smell that accompanied all spells.

'The more powerful the spell the more disgusting the smell' was a proverb all novices learned from an early age. The smell from this one was very strong indeed and it immediately assaulted Morgan's nostrils as he charged through the front entrance of the Sanctuary. It also told him exactly which direction to take. The wizard rushed down the street, closely followed by Wallace, Luke and Cissy; Molly followed a dozen meters behind them, already panting heavily.

Morgan rounded the corner into the alley and stopped abruptly as his brain registered the scene before him. It took only a split-second to take in the girl, the doorway, the shimmering light. Morgan knew exactly what it was and what she was about to do.

He shouted, horror stricken, "Penelope, don't!"

Her head turned toward him and then he was running, frantically trying to reach her in time. But invisible hands seemed to claw at his shoulders, impeding his progress so that he appeared to be moving in slow-motion. The girl ignored him and turned slowly back to the doorway. She took a deep breath and gathered her courage.

Then stepped forward.

THE SANCTUARY

"No!"

Penelope had only an instant to hear Morgan's agonized shout before it was abruptly silenced. The door behind her disappeared and she was cut off from her own world forever.

*   *   *   *

The Dark Wizard paced his lonely mansion as he awaited the arrival of the demon army. Since his last encounter with his prisoner, he had not returned to the dungeon below, for something about the man disquieted him.

When I defeat my brother and am lord of the mortal world, you will not dare defy me, he thought sourly, *then you will not speak to me in that mocking way, for I will cut out your tongue. You will not look at me with such disdain, for I will put out your eyes.*

The thought cheered him a little and served to take his mind off his concerns about the Demon King. Would that vile, disgusting thing betray him? Would he even turn up? Once Morgan was dead, there would be the question of how to deal with Kanzser, for deal with him he must. Logan wasn't sure yet how he would get rid of him; it would be no easy task, but he would find a way.

He allowed himself to daydream for a while, but he couldn't prevent his thoughts returning to the prisoner. *What was it about the man?* he wondered. *Why does he disquiet me so?* Perhaps it was because he sensed the man was old, much older than he appeared. And perhaps he had an uneasy suspicion that the man who called himself the Landlord had power, lots of it, latent, just waiting to be picked up again.

THE SANCTUARY

The Dark Wizard was many things. Stupid he was not.

Then, suddenly, the bird was there, and Logan forgot all about the man in the dungeon. *The Demon King has come!* Elation surged through him. *He has not betrayed me.* He hurried outside to where his carriage waited, horses already harnessed, their hooves pawing impatiently at the ground. *Now, Brother, let us see who is the most powerful!* The journey this time was a short one and as he approached Ludgate Hill, even Logan marveled at the size of the demon army, which stretched almost as far as the eye could see.

As his approach slowed, one of the Demon King's protective guard stepped out in front of the carriage, holding up an imperious hand and forcing the horses to rear up. As the carriage came to a sudden stop, Logan was flung onto the floor, ending up in an undignified sprawl, legs in the air. He scrambled quickly to his feet and stepped from the carriage, scowling, wand in hand. When he saw the cause of his abrupt arrival, he gave the merest flick of his wand, enough to fire a bolt of white heat that made a perfect hole in the demon's abdomen. For a split-second, Logan could see right through before the hole filled with guts and gore and the long sausage of the creature's entrails spilled out onto the floor.

If the Demon King was at all annoyed by this casual murder of one of his own, he did not show it. Instead he gave an ironic bow and gestured for Logan to join him.

"Welcome, wizard!" The insincerity in his voice was sickening. "Are you ready to fight?"

Logan inclined his head, not trusting himself to speak.

*   *   *   *

"No! No! No!"

Morgan's companions stared in shock as he knelt and pounded with his fists the spot where Penelope had stood only moments before.

"Don't! It's okay!" Luke approached cautiously. "We can get her back. Wherever she went we can go after her, can't we?"

Morgan's head whipped up and he glared at the boy; Luke took an involuntary step backward. So great was his anger that tiny forks of lightning sparked from his eyes, creating a neon-blue halo around his head.

But to Cissy even that wasn't the worst thing as she looked in horror at the tears coursing down Morgan's face.

"Morgan, don't! Please don't!" She moved to comfort him. "Luke's right, we can—"

"You don't understand!" It was almost a scream. "None of you do!" He coughed violently, great retching coughs that went on and on until eventually he vomited onto the cobbles. Suddenly all the anger seemed to leave him, and he sat back, exhausted. He looked at them and now his eyes were dull and lifeless.

"You don't understand," he repeated, "she's gone to the world of Aeryn." His voice was a flat, weary monotone. "Nothing can save her; she's probably dead already."

"That's enough of that," Wallace intervened sharply. "Pull yourself together, man, we can just recreate the spell, follow the girl into Aeryn's land, and bring her back safely." Morgan shook his head, but Wallace was having none of it. "Nonsense, of course we can. You're not just any wizard, you're Morgan, you can do anything you choose. Now get yourself together, look at the example you're setting these youngsters!"

Morgan smiled sadly and looked gratefully at his old friend, understanding his clumsy attempts to help.

"I said you didn't understand, Wallace. Aeryn allows nobody to leave her realm should they be so foolish as to enter. Sure, we could go after Penelope, but then we'd be trapped too. Why do you think there's no entrance from the Sanctuary into her world? It would be too dangerous. I had it moved and hidden centuries ago in case anyone came upon it accidentally."

Molly stared at him and the realization that Penelope was truly lost slowly dawned. But there would be a way, she knew, there always was. *Morgan could always find a way!* But even she was alarmed at the depths of hopelessness she saw in the old wizard's eyes.

"C'mon," she ordered, "let's get you back in-bleedin'-side."

THE SANCTUARY

Chapter 37

Penelope wasn't dead.

In fact, at that moment she was sitting on a hillside with the sun beating down and the grass around her swaying in the gentle breeze. Butterflies fluttered above and bees buzzed and crawled all over a lavender bush not far away. There was a nearby stream and birds chirping and singing in the trees. The heat of the sun, the sound of the water, the humming of insects, all had a soporific effect that sent the girl into a dream-like state, and presently she fell asleep.

She might have slept the afternoon away had a noise not pierced her subconscious and awakened her. It was the sound of somebody shouting, faint at first but becoming louder as consciousness returned. Penelope sat up, rubbed her eyes and looked around.

"Help!" The cry came from somewhere down the hill. "Help!"

She stood quickly and shielded her eyes against the sun. She could vaguely make out a small figure in the distance where the stream flowed into the valley. The cry for help came again, then again, seeming louder now she was fully awake. As her eyes adjusted, the scene clicked abruptly into focus and it was enough to send her racing down the hill in a panic.

Although the stream was narrow, the slope was steep so that the water ran quickly. As it leveled out, the natural geology of the valley floor had collected the water into a large pool before the stream continued on its way. In the center of the pool was a small boy, no more than five years old. His arms thrashed against the water and even from her position, high on the hillside, it was obvious to Penelope that he was drowning.

"Hold on!" she yelled as she careered down the hill. "I'm coming!" She was running so quickly her legs could hardly keep up. Within seconds she'd covered half the distance and now she could clearly see a girl, older than the boy by the look of her, hopping by the edge of the pool, still shouting for help.

"Hold on!" she yelled again, and the girl looked up in surprise.

"Oh hurry! Do hurry!" she screamed. "My brother! He can't swim!"

Penelope had almost reached the bottom, but as the grassy slope leveled out and became gravel and loose stones, her feet flew out from under her and she fell heavily. Momentarily dazed, she looked at the large rip in her jeans and the blood seeping through from the nasty graze on her thigh. It wasn't so long ago she would have burst into tears, but that was – almost literally – in a different lifetime, and now she barely gave it a second thought. She was back on her feet and ran the last few meters to the edge of the pool, just in time to see the boy slip under the surface. And remain there.

Penelope wasted precious moments waiting for him to reappear, but all she saw was a stream of bubbles rising to the top. Suddenly unsure, the girl could see nothing past the glare from the sunshine reflecting on the water.

"Sebastian!"

The scream shattered her uncertainty and galvanized Penelope into action. She clambered onto a nearby boulder and, from her new vantage point, everything below the surface of the pool became visible. The water wasn't actually very deep, and the boy could be seen floating just below. His long blonde hair streamed out in all directions, waving like golden seaweed, his eyes open but unseeing.

Perhaps he's already drowned, she thought desperately, then, forgetting she'd been the only one in her class at school who'd not learned how, she executed a perfect dive into the pool. With a few swift strokes she reached the boy, hooked her arms round his chest and pulled him above the surface. It seemed to take an age to get to the edge, for her strength was almost spent, but the girl was able to wade into the shallows and help drag her brother up onto the grassy bank to safety.

Penelope could only lay there, chest heaving, utterly exhausted, but the boy still hadn't moved and, summoning the last of her strength, she dragged herself over on her hands and knees. She wasn't entirely sure what to do but, copying what she'd once seen on TV, she straddled him and pushed firmly between his shoulders.

"Will he live?" The girl's voice was barely a whisper. Her face was heart shaped, eyes large and corn-flower blue. Her skin was smooth as porcelain but marred by the dirty tracks of her drying tears. Penelope thought she must be about her own age.

THE SANCTUARY

"Please save him," she entreated, but Penelope was unable to answer, her own breath coming in great heaving gulps as she pummeled the boy with increasing frustration.

"Come on," she gasped, "breathe!" and as if in answer the boy coughed once then vomited a stream of shiny bile. Penelope's fist was raised to give him one final blow when she heard approaching horses.

*   *   *   *

Aeryn, Warrior Queen, swung her sword in a wide, scathing arc toward her sister's head. A mere second before it could cleave her in two, Daraproud raised her own sword and met the blow in a loud clash of steel, then in the same movement, whirled and aimed a thrust to Aeryn's midriff, which the queen could only avoid by springing backward on the tips of her toes.

Sisters were rarely less alike in appearance – in fact the only feature they shared were their eyes, which were oval in shape, and dark brown, like pools of melted chocolate. Aeryn was tall and muscular, her nose just a little too large in a face that was handsome rather than beautiful. Her hair was fair, and she wore it in two thick braids, which hung to her waist and writhed and twisted as she fought so that they resembled golden snakes.

Daraproud's hair also hung long although it was twisted into a single braid and was black, shining like polished anthracite in the torch-lit room. She was shorter and less muscular than her sister, and her features were perfect, almost doll like, breath-taking in her beauty. It would be a mistake, though, to assume her gentle aspect meant weakness, for there was a steely determination about her which, combined with her speed and skill, made her a worthy opponent.

Aeryn was powerful, stronger than most men, and her skill as a fighter was legendary. And when the battle was real, not just practice like this one, she fought with the fury and intensity of the berserker, and enemies quailed before her onslaught. But now she had stopped abruptly and was perfectly still, the great jewel-studded broadsword again raised as if about to strike.

Daraproud took advantage of what she thought was a momentary and very unusual lapse in concentration and thrust her own sword into the protective leather jerkin that covered her sister's breast.

"I've told you before about letting me win sister," she protested. "I don't…" She paused as Aeryn frowned and shook her head. She watched as her sister lowered her sword and lay it on the purple velvet cushion within the carved wooden case that was its home. The rubies adorning its hilt and the emeralds embedded into the upper part of the blade still shone as brightly as they had when the sword had been forged more than five thousand years ago.

Since then it had been handed down through many generations to each successive queen of this land. No other was permitted to touch it and the punishment for doing so was death; this was a law as ancient as the sword itself. Now Aeryn stroked its blade with reverence before closing the lid of the case and striding out onto the balcony. As her gaze swept intently over the vista before her, she was dimly aware that her sister had come to stand beside her.

"Someone has entered our land, Daraproud," she said, a note of disbelief in her voice. "For good or evil, I do not know but—"

THE SANCTUARY

"Impossible! No one has been able to enter this land since… since…"

Aeryn interjected quickly to avoid *that* particular name being uttered; no one had dared do so this last hundred or so years.

"Nevertheless, I felt a disturbance, a moment ago, exactly the same as *he* used to cause, and I tell you, someone has used magic to enter our land!"

Daraproud knew it was pointless to argue even though she felt her sister must be mistaken. The words of the spell that would allow such a thing were long gone, had been taken by *him*. Daraproud's mind would not allow her to even think the name of the man who had caused such heartache so long ago and it was inconceivable that he could have returned for he had been banished from the kingdom. He would not dare defy that command; would he? And why? What reason would he have after all these years? No, Aeryn was mistaken, she had to be.

Her thoughts were interrupted by a man appearing on the balcony; it was the young Prince Dominic. He greeted his mother respectfully, then grinned at Daraproud, for despite the difference in their ages – she was thirty-five while he was just nineteen – they were more like close friends than aunt and nephew. He began telling them of the new stallion he'd bought yesterday at the markets in Chiang. His enthusiasm was infectious and they both listened to him prattle on about the magnificent beast. Dominic was a pleasant young man, handsome and with an open, honest face. He was easy-going and good-natured, totally unspoiled by his rank, yet tough and ruthless when necessary.

He was still waxing lyrical about the stallion and, truthfully, the discussion would normally have captured his mother's interest, for she herself was a fine horsewoman, but she was distracted, still thinking of the disturbance she had felt.

"Dominic," she interrupted, "I have a task for you."

She was still on the balcony, alone now, when the drawbridge far beneath her lowered and her son, at the head a small troupe of soldiers, galloped out of the castle. She stood there long after they had disappeared down the slope, and as she brooded, she became aware of a feeling in the pit of her stomach. It was as unwelcome as it was, initially, unrecognizable, and when she did realize what it meant she tried to thrust it angrily aside, for she abhorred any sign of weakness.

It was a very long time since Queen Aeryn had felt anxious.

THE SANCTUARY

Chapter 38

The soldier took in the scene at a glance. In an instant he had dismounted, and the tip of his sword was at Penelope's throat. "Harm him and you will die." His voice was deep and harsh and when she looked into his cold, gray eyes she had no doubt he meant it.

"I wasn't…I mean, he was…"

"Silence." The man hardly raised his voice, but he didn't need to, for its tone demanded absolute obedience. "You will not speak." He turned to his men. "Take her." Almost before she could react, Penelope found herself sitting on a horse, hands bound, held firmly in the grip of a steel-clad soldier.

"Oh, but—" the boy's sister tried to intervene, but she was silenced with a gesture.

"I would suggest, Angelina, that you save your explanations for the queen. She will wish to know why you placed her son in danger." At this, the girl's face went a distinct green color and her words petered out as she subsided miserably into silence.

Horrible man, thought Penelope. But then the soldier knelt before the boy and a remarkable change came over him as he gently brushed a few strands of wet hair from his face.

"Are you hurt, Sebastian?" His voice was so tender and full of love that Penelope looked at him curiously. Sebastian shook his head and the man smiled. He gathered the boy into his arms and lifted him into the saddle of his horse. "Come, you shall ride home with me." His eyes, which moments before had been cold and unrelenting, were now full of warmth.

As they rode, Penelope took in the magnificence of this land. To one side, there were gently rolling hills that stretched, mile upon mile, in a thousand hues of green. Dotted here and there were forests of larch and pine, others of stately oak and elm. Through it all ran rivers and streams, which flowed in the distance and glittered like silver threads in the sunlight.

And in the other direction, the ground was rockier, more rugged, rising steadily before exploding into snow-capped mountains that looked immeasurably tall, even from so far away. It seemed to Penelope that the colors were brighter, richer somehow than any she'd seen in her own world. And the flowers, oh the flowers! They were everywhere, absolutely everywhere, so that the air was redolent with the heady aromas of every rich and expensive perfume ever created. And above it all hung the huge fiery orb of the sun, with its golden rays that shone in a cloudless sky of an impossibly beautiful shade of blue.

Gradually Penelope became aware that the girl was speaking.

"But, Dominic," she tried to say but he held up a hand.

"Enough, Angelina!" His voice was exasperated rather than angry, and he spoke in hushed tones so as not to awaken the boy, who had fallen into an exhausted sleep almost as soon as they'd begun riding. "I've already told you to save your explanations for our mother." Then he saw her misery and relented. "Try not to worry. It would seem your carelessness has done no real harm." He turned to Penelope. "As for you," his said, and again his tone was grim, "you will answer to Queen Aeryn. I suggest you throw yourself upon her mercy."

The words 'Queen Aeryn' conjured a vision somewhere between Snow White's evil stepmother and the Wicked Witch of the West. But despite her fear, Penelope was suddenly angry and fed up. Hadn't she just saved a little boy's life, for goodness sake?

I'm nine years old, she thought, *I shouldn't have to put up with this nonsense at my age!* She fixed him with a long, glowering stare and uttered a single word. "Whatever."

Her defiance was marred somewhat by the fact that her clothes were still dripping wet and her hair hung in lank strands that stuck to her cheeks. Nevertheless, he was startled, unused to being defied like this, particularly by a child. Then the moment for a witty retort passed and he lapsed into silence, but his curiosity got the better of him.

"What is your name?" The words sounded harsher than he'd intended and she reacted sharply.

"None of your business."

The man smiled to himself. *She really is the fiercest little thing!*

"I'm sorry," he said. "I am Dominic, Prince Dominic, son of Aeryn, queen of this land." *It will do no harm to remind her who she's dealing with and the trouble she's in,* he thought. But the more he cast his mind back to the earlier scene, the less inclined he was to think the girl had meant to harm Sebastian. It wasn't the first time, after all, that his brother had fallen into a river; the boy had a rare talent for getting himself into scrapes of all kinds that usually ended with him needing to be rescued. He felt a little guilty for the way he'd reacted. *She's just a child, for goodness sake; what was I thinking!*

"What's yours?" He gave a reassuring smile.

She hesitated but recognized the peace offering. "It's Penelope," she said, and tentatively returned his smile.

"And where did you come from, Penelope? It is unusual to find strangers, children in particular, walking alone in this land."

"I…I…" Suddenly she was unsure what to tell him. She could hardly say, 'Oh, I cast a magical spell that opened a door into your world and I just walked on through!' In the end she stayed silent and he didn't have time to pursue it, for just then the ground rose sharply, taking them out of the valley in which they'd been riding for the last hour. They crested the hill and paused to allow their horses rest. Penelope saw that the ground in front dipped sharply into another valley before rising again into an even larger hill about a kilometer distant. And as her eyes followed the rise, she gasped at the sight of what was, presumably, their destination.

She had seen pictures of castles of course – Edinburgh, Stirling, Caenarfon to name but three – and she'd been to a few smaller ones when she was younger, for her mother had loved history as much as her daughter. There'd even been that memorable school trip to see Dover castle only last year!

But this one dwarfed all of those both in size and beauty. It was built from huge blocks of rich, golden stone, which seemed to shine in the strong sunlight and hurt to look at. Even from this distance, there was the impression of immense grandeur, the walls stretching on and on, becoming hazy and indistinct in the distance and soaring upwards, high into the cornflower sky. At intervals, and at each corner, the walls were interrupted by towers, circular in shape, rising far, up beyond the battlements. Each of these was topped with a roof of dark gray slate which rose into a steep point. On top of each point was a white flagpole with a pendant that fluttered gaily in the breeze.

She turned to Dominic, her eyes questioning.

"Yes, that is my mother's castle, my home." He nodded, his voice full of pride. "Our home," he amended as Angelina cantered up to join them.

The girl smiled at Penelope before turning to her brother. "She really wasn't going to harm Sebastian, she saved his life, he was drowning!" Before he could reply she hurried on, "Will Mother be really angry? How can she be when Penelope saved Sebastian's life? It's not right! I really think—"

"Stop! Angelina, it's alright, truly it is." The girl was becoming slightly hysterical. "If what you say is true then Penelope has nothing to fear." *Although she will have to account for how and why she dared enter this land uninvited,* he added silently to himself. "Don't worry, Sister, our mother is stern, but she is fair; you know this to be true." He ruffled her hair. "Come on, I'll race you!"

His feet jabbed his horse's flanks and he was away at top speed down the slope. Angelina gave a shriek of delight and followed, catching and overtaking him a hundred meters later as he slowed and allowed her to win. His men, caught by surprise, had to scramble to catch up and as they did so, Penelope, still in the grip of the soldier, stared curiously at Dominic.

He was hard to fathom, she thought, one minute stern and forbidding, the next acting like a child having fun. She decided that, on the whole, she quite liked him after all.

Now the ground began to rise again, and their progress was slow, but eventually they reached the top and Penelope saw the castle was protected by a deep ravine. At their approach, a drawbridge lowered and, as they crossed it, the great iron portcullis lifted slowly with a great rattling of chains. They rode beneath a stone archway and Penelope found herself in a small, cobbled courtyard. As she stared up at the soaring walls, she thought she saw someone watching from one of the many windows that lined the walls. But then the figure moved back into the shadows and Penelope wasn't sure if she'd imagined it.

They halted at last and almost immediately several people came running from different directions and Dominic gave a series of orders. A woman, middle-aged and clearly one of the palace servants, possibly some kind of nurse-maid, Penelope thought, took hold of Sebastian and quickly ran with him into the palace. Another lifted Angelina from the horse and led her away, but the girl resisted.

"What about Penelope?" she insisted. "What's going to happen to her?"

"Peace, Angelina, if she has done nothing wrong, she has no reason to be afraid. And nor have you."

"But…"

"No buts, Angelina." Dominic was becoming exasperated and

trying not to show it. "Go to your room now, clean up, rest a while." He dismounted and gave her a brief hug. "You've had a busy day, so why don't you relax and I'll see you later at dinner." He nodded to the woman then turned away.

Even still, the girl clung on stubbornly. "I want to know what will happen to her!"

"Angelina, for the love of—" He stopped and drew a deep breath, then went on more softly, "Penelope will be housed in one of the upper chambers and later she will meet our mother." He nodded curtly to the nursemaid. "Now please just go, I have things to organize." The woman gripped the child's hand more firmly, but this time Angelina didn't resist. She allowed herself to be led away, not before flinging one last comment over her shoulder, "See you at dinner, Penelope, and try not to worry!"

Penelope had been unable to hide the sudden spasm of fear at the mention of meeting the queen and Dominic must have noticed, for he smiled kindly and touched her arm gently. "Don't worry, my mother can be fearsome, but she is no monster. I think you will have nothing to fear from her." Penelope nodded, grateful. "One of my men will escort you to your chamber. I would give you the same advice as my sister: relax for a while and try not to worry."

A short time later, Penelope found herself in a large room, carpeted and simply furnished. In it was a bed, a table and chair, and little else apart from a long, narrow settee of the style that would be known as a *chaise-longue* if this were France. Covering much of the stone walls were huge tapestries, clearly very old, depicting hunting scenes and battles. The room was clean, comfortable and, thankfully, nice and warm.

Not long after she'd been locked inside – and the door *was* locked, she'd tried it – it opened again and she was provided with dry clothes. These fitted her perfectly and were similar in style to those of the women she'd encountered when they'd arrived at the castle. Not long after, a youth not much older than herself arrived with food and drink, which he placed on the table. Penelope tried to engage him in conversation, but he ignored her and disappeared without speaking. Although she heard the click of the lock, she tried the door again, but to her frustration it didn't open. Hunger soon outweighed her annoyance and she sat at the table to devour the meal.

Every half hour or so the door opened, and the same boy looked in, presumably to check she was still there and hadn't miraculously flown from the room, and just as quickly left again, closing and locking the door before Penelope could make any further overtures. She looked out the window, banging the palm of her hand against the glass in frustration. All she could see were fields and hills that went on and on, far into the distance.

And for the first time she felt truly frightened. Nobody knew where she was and she had no idea how to return to her own world, the spell hadn't told her that. Sure, this was no dark, dank cell but it was a prison nonetheless; what if the queen intended to keep her here forever? She tried to remember Dominic's reassuring words, tried to focus on the fact that she'd saved Sebastian's life. *The queen should be thanking me, not keeping me prisoner!*

Penelope forced herself to calm, taking deep breaths and waiting for her furiously beating heart to slow down. *Of course I won't be kept prisoner, idiot!* After all, she hadn't done anything wrong, had she? *Apart from coming into Aeryn's world without permission,* an unwanted voice in her head reminded her. She ignored it, telling herself she was being ridiculous and that she had nothing to worry about. Penelope sat at the table and began to plan what she would say when the summons came.

*   *   *   *

In an attempt to distract herself from this strange, unwanted emotion, this disquiet she felt, Aeryn turned her thoughts to the three children who had come to mean so much to her. *Though Dominic can no longer be thought of as a child,* she thought with pride.

He had been born in the land that neighbored her own, a harsh, unforgiving place whose overlord was cruel and corrupt, ever eager to extend his borders. The frequent wars between the two had gradually diminished her army and soon she feared they would be overrun. The men who died or were killed could not be replaced for no new sons had been born to the women of Aeryn's land for a very long time.

Dominic's parents had been simple folk, poor farmers who had instilled their own code of decency into their son, a decency he continued to exhibit now, long after their deaths. But they had been foolish, a little too vocal in their criticism of the corrupt regime that condemned them to a life of toil and hunger. In time, their muttering reached the ears of their overlord and from that moment their fates were sealed, throats cut silently in the night while their son slept in the adjacent room.

So the ten-year-old Dominic had been forced to fend for himself for six long months until, in the middle of the harshest winter for a century, he was taken in, half-starved and desperately malnourished, by one of the many rebel groups who resisted the overlord. For the next two years he flourished, becoming stronger and sturdier as he learned the art of guerrilla warfare. And so it was that one day, when Dominic was fourteen, he and his group found themselves fighting alongside Queen Aeryn and her soldiers. But the group, which had operated in the shadows for so long, were less well-versed in hand-to-hand fighting and they'd been wiped out, all but Dominic, who was left once more bereft and alone.

And it was now that his life changed forever. Aeryn had learned of his plight and, as reward for his service, he'd been invited to return with the queen and live in a new land. In reality, it was not sentimentality that drove her, but rather the need for someone to act as regent until a replacement could be found, in the event of her death, That person should be brave and strong, yet kind and compassionate, intelligent and loyal. Aeryn sensed that, young though he was, this boy fitted the bill perfectly.

The boy had not required long to make up his mind. Aeryn smiled as she remembered how eagerly he'd accepted her offer. He'd soon proved her right; her two younger children adored him, and her own love for him had become as strong as that of a mother to a natural son.

But thinking of him inevitably led to thoughts of Angelina and Sebastian, brother and sister, also orphans of the war with the overlord. They had arrived a year or so after Dominic, having been found by Daraproud, huddled together, with Angelina desperately trying to shield her baby brother from the battle that raged about them. Her own motherly instinct aroused, Daraproud had refused to return without the two terrified children.

Aeryn wondered idly where Angelina and Sebastian were, for she'd not seen them since they'd breakfasted together that morning. She knew she was lax in allowing the two of them to roam far and wide, but they'd known such heartache in their short lives, and soon Angelina must begin the task of preparing to be a queen.

Sebastian was perhaps the luckier of the two, she mused; only females could rule in this land, never the male. Ordinarily it would have been Daraproud who stood as heir to the throne, but her sister didn't want it; was violently opposed to the idea, in fact. And so, unless the impossible happened and Aeryn were to have a child of her own, the mantle of Queenship would one day fall to Angelina.

Just then, there was the clatter of hooves on the cobbles outside. She looked down into the courtyard and saw her son in the act of lifting Sebastian from his horse, and there was Angelina and… who was that? She was about to hurry and find out when she heard footsteps running up the steps to her chamber.

After a hurried greeting, Dominic sat and described the events of that day. Her heart quailed when she heard of Sebastian's lucky escape from drowning. Not lucky, she realized; he owed his life to this mysterious girl.

Who was she? Where had she come from? Aeryn's earlier disquiet returned as she sensed she would not like the answer.

"Give me time to change," she told him, "then bring the girl to me."

Chapter 39

An hour later, Penelope was summoned for an audience with the queen. In the short time she'd had to contemplate the coming confrontation, she'd imagined what she would say to the queen, how she would humbly ask for help whilst politely pointing out that the Aeryn owed her a massive favor. If that didn't work, she might even point out that as a mother, she'd been very careless to allow a small child to play near water, particularly when he couldn't swim.

In her mind she practiced the exact tone of voice she would use, a mixture of sternness, utter un-answerable-back-ness, with a slight hint of patronizing sweetness mixed in for good measure. She wasn't sure she could manage to hit the exact note necessary and she tried to remember how her old school headteacher had always done it, just before she doled out punishments to any pupils unfortunate enough to get on the wrong side of her. She had always managed to set that particular tone *perfectly*.

In any case, she'd probably end by giving a gentle but firm reminder that if she, Penelope, hadn't happened to stumble *accidentally* into this world at the exact moment young Sebastian was drowning, well the consequences didn't bear thinking about, did they?

That was what she'd practiced, and now that the moment had arrived, she'd forgotten all of it. The servant led her along a series of corridors and down several flights of steps until before them were a pair of huge, wooden doors which reached right up to the ceiling far above. As they approached, they swung silently inward, although by what means Penelope could not see, for as she stepped with trepidation into the room, she saw it was quite empty.

It reminded her of the training room at the Sanctuary, except it was ten, no, a hundred times grander! First of all, there was its sheer enormity; she literally couldn't see where it ended. Then the seemingly never-ending line of windows on each side which, like the doors, reached up to the ceiling. Each was covered by curtains of some sheer, gossamer-like material which diffused the sunlight from outside, giving the impression of a gentle mist cloaking the room.

Penelope walked further inside slowly, drinking in the atmosphere, which felt somnambulant, like lazy Sunday afternoons, in the absolute silence of the place. She approached the nearest window and brushed an idle hand against the material, reveling in its softness. Almost immediately the curtains ruched upwards and to the side, followed in turn by all the others, and the room was flooded with sunlight.

Revealed in all its magnificence, she saw the walls were made of plaster, blinding white in the now sunlit room, and that every centimeter was covered in intricate carvings depicting, she would later learn, the history of Aeryn's world, reaching back many thousands of years. The floor was the wood of ancient oak trees, so highly polished that everything was reflected up at her so that, if she looked down, she was overcome with vertigo.

"Beautiful, is it not?"

The words startled her and she spun around quickly. There, only a handful of meters away, stood quite possibly the loveliest yet most frightening woman Penelope had ever seen. She was tall, long-limbed and her hair fell to her waist like shimmering liquid gold. She wore an ankle-length dress of deepest green that hugged her figure, accentuating the muscles beneath.

But her eyes were the most arresting feature of all and they seemed to see right inside Penelope, stripping her naked so she had a sudden urge to hide. Yet they gave nothing away; indicated neither friendship nor displeasure, no clue as to what fate she may have planned for the girl. Penelope had the uncomfortable impression that those eyes were capable of displaying intense love or implacable hatred and she hoped fervently she would never experience the latter.

"Welcome to my home, Penelope, is it?" Her voice was rich and deep. When she received no response, the queen went on, "Angelina has informed me of what happened, as has Dominic; it does appear that you saved my son's life today."

Penelope nodded, dumbstruck by the sheer presence and charisma of this woman.

"Although I'm forced to wonder if you are responsible for him being in the water in the first place?" As Penelope looked at her in surprise, Aeryn's gaze turned cold and her next words were full of foreboding. "Perhaps my son arrived just in time. Perhaps you are a spy or an assassin. Perhaps you pretended to save him when you realized you had been caught?"

The incongruity of her own suggestion struck Aeryn forcibly and she had an insane urge to laugh; never had anyone looked less like an assassin than this little girl. But Penelope reacted as if stung.

"No!" Despite her nervousness she found her voice and the word was flung angrily at the queen. "He was drowning, and I saved him!"

Her honesty was so transparent that Aeryn nodded, satisfied. "I'm sorry," she said, "I had to be certain. But I believe you, Penelope, and I owe you a debt I can never repay; as does Sebastian." *And Angelina,* she added wryly to herself. "At tonight's feast you will be guest of honor at my table." She smiled reassuringly. "Perhaps then you can explain how you happened to be in my land." The words were phrased as a gentle admonishment, but Penelope sensed they were anything but.

"You will have to return to your own world tomorrow, I'm afraid, but in the meantime might you like to spend time with my daughter, Angelina? You are of similar ages, I should think." And that was that. Interview finished. The queen nodded in what was clearly a dismissal and swept past her toward the door, motioning for the same servant to escort Penelope back to her chamber.

And that's all the thanks I'm gonna get? The queen was almost at the door.

"They need your help!" she managed to blurt out at last, her anxiety making her voice high-pitched and shrill. Queen Aeryn turned to stare at her in amazement.

THE SANCTUARY

*   *   *   *

Molly and Morgan were still arguing, as they had almost constantly since Penelope's disappearance.

"You cannot abandon that girl to live out her life in some place far away! It's immoral! Bleedin' hell, it's not like it's even just a foreign country, is it? It's a foreign bleedin' world!"

"You dare preach morals to me?" Morgan's eyes flashed dangerously. "You think I want to abandon that little girl? You think I don't suffer the torments of the damned when I imagine what she might be going through at this very minute?" He was truly angry now and in danger of losing control.

Luke and Cissy looked on in distress but dared not become involved, and Velveteena and Moth hadn't been seen for hours. Even Wallace held back, reluctant to take sides, although he was inclined to agree with Morgan. In any case, he knew his old friend was faced with an impossible dilemma and was glad the decision was not his to make.

"If you're suffering so much, do something about it!" Molly fired back.

"No, Molly! This debate has gone on long enough. I cannot and will not risk the lives of many to save one! It's the most difficult of decisions, but while I'm leader of the Sanctuary it is mine to make!"

Before she could respond, the front door of the Sanctuary exploded in a shower of wood and stone. Morgan's wand appeared in his hand without conscious thought as he leaped forward and peered cautiously around the shattered doorway. He could see nothing at first, but as the dust cleared he was able to make out a solitary figure standing in the street.

To the others he said softly, "Get your weapons, quickly, he will not be alone." Then he stepped outside to face his brother. "Seriously, Logan? You couldn't just ring the doorbell?"

The Dark Wizard sneered. "Always the joker, dear brother, always the joker." He put his own wand back in his pocket and folded his arms in a deliberate display of bravado. "I wonder if you'll be laughing once you've met my friends."

In turn, Morgan replaced his own wand. "Friends? You have *friends?*" It could have been a joke but there was not a trace of humor in his voice and his eyes were chips of ice. "Even if you defeat me today, do you really think the Demon King will let you have the power you crave?" He strode forward into the street until only a few meters separated them.

"Well?" he called loudly, looking beyond Logan. "Is that really your intention, Kanzser? Will you concede such power to my brother? Go meekly back to your lair without reward?" His voice was deliberately mocking, hoping to goad the Demon King into revealing his position, but the only reply he received was that of his own words echoing back. "Don't be a fool, Logan, join me and together we will defeat this tyrant," he urged in a low voice. "We have been enemies for too long! It's time to forgive and forget!"

For a split second, he fancied there was longing in his brother's eyes and his heart leaped. *He's going to listen! Perhaps it is truly not too late!* But then the shutters came down once more and his brother's face closed.

THE SANCTUARY

"Logan, please." He stepped forward and instantly the Dark Wizard's wand was at his throat. Morgan nodded sadly and took a careful step backward. With sudden clarity he knew there could never be peace between them.

He turned and, with shoulders slumped, trudged forlornly back to the Sanctuary, then stopped in surprise. Before him were his companions, weapons in hand and ready to fight. So silently had they gathered neither he nor Logan had noticed. His shoulders straightened once more, and he smiled.

"Good luck, my friends." Then he took out his wand and, cloak swirling around his feet, spun to meet his fate. "So, brother dear," he asked conversationally, "exactly where are these friends of yours?"

In answer, the Dark Wizard turned and looked to where distant figures could be seen in the gathering gloom. Morgan watched as they grew rapidly larger and now, accompanied by the rhythmic sound of tramping feet, the demon army approached.

*   *   *   *

"They need your help!"

Queen Aeryn supposed she should have been offended. Indeed there were those who, in the past, had paid for such insolence with their lives. But the sight of this girl, this *child*, facing her with hands on hips was almost comical. *And that expression on her face! So angry! So determined!* Aeryn fought down the urge to laugh at the incongruity of it. And it had taken courage, she conceded, impressed despite herself. Courage was a virtue she valued in others above all else. Anyway, she did owe the girl a debt.

"Enough," she commanded, having only half-listened to Penelope's impassioned entreaties. She had enough troubles of her own without interesting herself in those of a child from another world. "I have some sympathy for your friends and the evil they face from this…this Dark Wizard, but they are not my concern. And do not forget you have entered my realm uninvited, the punishment for which is death. Always." She paused long enough for this to sink in. "But I owe you the life of my son. For this I allow you to live and I allow you to leave. Take this chance while you are able and remember there are not many who have been so lucky."

"It's not enough!" the girl persisted stubbornly. "It's not even close! How can you see your son live but let others die? It's not fair! It's wrong! You know it's wrong!" Penelope was shouting now, uncaring of the consequences, and she stamped her foot angrily. The guards who stood at intervals around the room each stepped forward, alert for trouble.

Aeryn stilled them with an impatient gesture. *How much harm could a nine-year-old girl do her, for goodness sake?*

"It's not fair, I tell you! Luke and Cissy will be killed, Molly and Morgan too! It's not fair!"

Aeryn was inclined to agree, it *wasn't* fair. When she thought of how close Sebastian had come – and according to Angelina it *had* been close – she wanted to prostrate herself before the girl and weep with gratitude. But to display such weakness would be fatal, she knew, for there were always those who waited in the shadows, ready to pounce and steal her throne. Over the centuries there had

THE SANCTUARY

been many who'd tried and failed.

No, she mused, *they tried and died.* Then Penelope's words penetrated, and she looked at the girl sharply. "What were those names?" she demanded. "Quickly, tell me!"

"Er, Luke and…"

"No, the others!" Aeryn towered over her, suddenly more frightening than at any other time since Penelope had arrived.

"M– Molly and Morgan, they…"

But Aeryn had already turned away. "It can't be," she breathed, "it's not possible." She turned to the girl. "Leave me," she commanded, "I have to think." There was something in her voice that warned Penelope it would be unwise to argue.

Less than an hour later, there was a knock at the door to her chamber and Dominic entered.

"Make ready," he told her shortly, "we depart in five minutes." He turned to leave but she stopped him hurriedly.

"Leave? Where to?"

The entreaty in her voice shamed him, for he was not a cruel man, and he sighed. "I am to take you back to the place where we first met, by the pool. Queen Aeryn will meet us there. She will open the door into your own world; you will pass through and never return."

He forestalled her protests. "Penelope, I would not have you think us ungrateful. We can never, ever repay the debt we owe for Sebastian's life." He paused as he struggled to find the right words; such displays of emotion didn't come easily to him. "Please, there are things you don't understand, reasons why the queen will not, cannot help your friends." He was saved further explanation by

THE SANCTUARY

the sounds of shouting from the castle battlements. He ran from the chamber and up the narrow stone stairwell to the top of the keep.

His mother was already there, staring down in amazement at the figure who stood, demanding entry, on the drawbridge far below.

THE SANCTUARY

Chapter 40

They were holding their own, this small company of wizards, witches and mortals and the street was littered with the bodies of hundreds of dead and dying demons. The cobbles were awash with blood that collected in glutinous puddles on the uneven street, and in these puddles floated hands and arms, sliced from their owners by the flashing swords of Wallace and Luke. In the chaos, decapitated heads rolled and were kicked around like macabre footballs.

Wallace's prediction had proved accurate and Luke did indeed make a fearsome opponent. Those long, countless hours spent in the training room now bore fruit and his enemies had no answer to his skill. Fighting alongside his mentor, they cut such a swathe through the unrelenting hordes that they threatened to reach the Demon King himself, though he watched the battle in safety, far away down the length of the street.

Molly's wand jabbed and darted faster than the eye could follow, sending out stream after stream of argent fire that inflicted terrible injuries on her enemies.

At first she tried to protect the teenagers by keeping as many demons from them as she could. This was soon impossible as she was beset all around by a dozen assailants who, because of her size and generally scruffy appearance, were stupid enough to underestimate her.

They joined the countless others who had done the same across the centuries. All had died, for Molly had been taught by the best, the most talented teachers the witches council had to offer. Catching sight of Cissy she relaxed a little when she saw the girl, like Luke, was doing okay.

In fact, Cissy had grown in confidence by the minute. When the demon army had appeared, she'd never been so terrified in her whole life. But when her first blow found its mark, felling the demon who charged at her wielding a wicked looking scythe, all her fears had melted away. Now she dodged and whirled, her ability technical rather than spectacular, but still remarkable for one with so little training.

Even Velveteena and Moth got in on the act, flying and buzzing, worrying and distracting, using their swords not to kill – they were too small for that – but to scratch and cut, pierce and blind. This last one proved to be their most effective tactic, flying side by side like a pair of fighter planes, swords outstretched, aiming for the eyeballs, which gave a satisfying *pop!* as they burst with a gush of white goo.

Leading them all was the mighty wizard Morgan, and watching from his vantage point next to the Demon King, Logan knew he could never defeat his brother. Only the demon's iron grip prevented him from making his escape there and then.

But the company could not keep up this pace! An hour. Two,

three. The battle raged on and seemed to pass in the blink of an eye. Still the demons came and, at last the company were tiring. Wallace, with his old leg wound, could barely turn quickly enough to meet the thrusts of the demon's weapons. Already he had suffered a nasty gash to his arm which bled profusely and weakened him further. Luke found himself protecting his mentor as much as himself and he also was panting heavily, his strength waning fast.

Cissy was doing better, for her wand was not as heavy as a sword. But as yet another hour passed, she saw her companions' struggles and the never-ending numbers of the demon army and wondered if it would ever end. Gradually, a cloak of hopelessness descended upon her and, inside, she started to panic.

Only Molly and Morgan remained strong, doling out death and destruction without faltering. Nevertheless, the demons sensed the tide turning and, at Kanzser's command they surged forward with a great roar. Instantly the company was forced back and the demons began to come at them from the sides as well as the front, attempting to envelope them in a pincer movement.

"They're trying to encircle us!" yelled Morgan. "Wallace, to the left! Luke, the right! Cissy, help them!" He knew, if the circle was completed, it would be the end.

For a while Morgan's tactic worked and they were able to beat the demon's back a little. But as the fighting became increasingly desperate, slowly and inexorably, the circle began to close. Now the company had to protect their backs as well and there were just too many. Suddenly, the demon circle snapped together and the demons roared again in triumph.

THE SANCTUARY

The tiny company were squeezed together, forced to fight back-to-back. It was a miracle that none had fallen, but now it was only a matter of time. In the distance, Morgan caught a glimpse of Kanzser striding confidently toward them, certain of his victory.

THE SANCTUARY

Chapter 41

Velveteena and Moth had done their best, of course, injuring as many demons as they could. But really, that was not their role. They had a much deeper purpose. They'd observed the battle from above and delayed as long as they dared, until both understood that the destruction of the Sanctuary was imminent.

And now the real reason for the faeries appearance was finally revealed. Molly had been naive in thinking they had agreed to come merely to turn the pages of a book. That was far too menial a task, which is why, as every witch knows (except for Molly, apparently), that particular spell never works. Faeries were never summoned unless they wanted to be!

But there was a prophecy that one day soon there would come one with powers to exceed all others. The origin of the prophecy was so lost in the mists of time that nobody, not even Morgan or his grandfather or his great, great, great…well you get the picture. The prophecy went that far back. Nobody remembered that it was first spoken not by wizards or witches, but by the Faer Folk.

And the time for that prophecy to be fulfilled had arrived at last. So they had come, that mischievous pair, children in their own world but old, oh so very old, in human years. They had come to speak a word. Simply that, just a single word.

Velveteena and Moth abandoned their game of who could ruin the most eyeballs; they'd long ago lost count in any case. Their time had finally come; instinctively they knew it. Savoring the moment, they flew high above the scene of the battle, so high that those below looked like toy figures, arranged as part of a child's war game. They hovered for a moment, then zoomed back down again. Aiming for two from the hundreds still crowded into that narrow space.

Two only.

Two teenagers. And now, oblivious to the battle that raged about them, they flew to circle first around Cissy's head, then Luke's, then Cissy, then Luke. Backwards and forwards a dozen times.

But this was no game. No, this was making sure, because to make a mistake now, to speak the word, *that* word, into the wrong ear, after so many millennia? The disgrace! But really, the faeries knew who it would be. They'd always known, almost from the moment they'd arrived. The time since then had been spent making sure. Oh, and playing of course.

Fairies do love to play most of all.

But now Velveteena and Moth were deadly serious as they looked at each other and came to silent agreement. Hand-in-hand, they flew until they hovered next to one of the teenagers' ear and leaned right in. And then, loudly and clearly, they spoke the word.

Instantly the battle slowed, seeming to stop completely. Senses became hyper-vigilant and reactions ridiculously instantaneous. A spear, thrown hard and fast, could be caught, *caught in mid-air,* and thrown back with the utmost ease! No doubt similar feats could be achieved with the plethora of other weapons favored by the demons. Not that there was any need.

Not when one had…*a wand!* And not when the merest idea of a command was enough for it to obey. Cissy absorbed all of this in a heartbeat and then…she attacked.

Her speed was frightening as her wand sent out cascade after cascade of white-hot light in all directions. The demon hordes broke and scattered in panic before the onslaught. And as they ran, they died, five, ten, a score at a time as the light seared into their flesh like a laser, cutting through sinew and bone.

Molly paused and looked on in amazement, almost paying for it with her life as she narrowly dodged a poison tipped spear. She dispatched her assailant with a casual flick of her wand.

"Help her!" she yelled. "She can't do it all by her bleedin' self!"

The others renewed their attack, which had started to wane, with vigor. Now Cissy matched even the great Morgan for speed and skill, and together they were an unstoppable force that the demons were quite unable to match. Even Wallace and Luke, whose arms had begun to feel like leaden weights, felt new energy coursing through their veins. They wielded their swords with such deadly accuracy and skill, hacking, cutting and slicing, that their enemies quailed before them.

And so the demons died in their hundreds, the bodies piling one on top of another so that the living had to climb over them. But for each one that fell it seemed there were another ten to take their place. There was no sign of their numbers dwindling and nor would there be; the Demon King, by his evil machinations had made sure of that, had ensured there would be an endless supply of meat to be thrown to the wolves.

For Kanzser could not lose this battle, *must not lose this battle!* Oh, it was nothing to do with the pact he had made with Logan. The Dark Wizard meant nothing; he would easily be removed once he'd defeated the real enemy. No, it was Morgan.

Morgan! Accursed Morgan, so long a thorn in the Demon King's flesh! Only he stood between the Demon King and his ultimate desire to rule the world of mortal men. For centuries Morgan and his forbears had fought him, thwarted and prevented him achieving his goal. For a time, the Demon King had sought to use the brother, but Logan, despite his undeniable power, was flawed, weak, and weakness was of no use to the Demon King.

No, Morgan must be removed once and for all, so Kanzser had gathered this army, one so vast, numbering not thousands but tens of thousands, that no one, not even Morgan, could withstand it. Now he stood and watched the progress of the battle with satisfaction. It did not matter that the bodies were piled high, numbering thousands already. For eventually Morgan must tire; he could not keep up this relentless pace forever. Even the girl – *Logan should have killed her when he had the chance!* – even she, with her newfound power, would weaken eventually. And when they did…

But Morgan could not know any of this, nor could the others. Not even the faeries knew for sure. But they suspected something of the sort and their senses, their infallible instincts, were screaming to them now.

The child! Something must be done about the child!

"You can't win! The enemy's number is too great!" The faeries delivered their message to Morgan, each taking turns in breathless, high-pitched voices, in equal measure agitated and excited.

"You must go now!"

"While Cissy's power is still at its height!"

"You see that the demons cannot touch her now, but she is young, her body will tire and she still has much to learn!"

"Go now while she is still strong!"

"You must rescue the child!"

"Her purpose is unclear to us, but our senses tell us she has some part to play and that without her, you cannot win this war!"

Morgan, who had earlier withstood the force of Molly's anger and refused to leave, suddenly understood the truth of their words. *How could I have been so blind? Why did I not follow the child immediately?*

Without further thought, he made his decision. "Retreat! Everyone, back inside the Sanctuary!"

If the others were surprised at the command, just as they had the upper hand once more, they didn't show it, and obeyed instantly.

"Quickly! Inside, everyone." Morgan pushed the last of them through the door to safety and slammed it behind him.

"Morgan?" Molly panted. "Why now, when we were winning?" She looked around at the others. "You all fought so bravely. Luke, what a battle! And Cissy! That was just amazing, seems like it's you after all—"

"Penelope," Morgan interrupted. "She's gone to seek aid from Aeryn. Why, oh why didn't I realize?" He thumped his forehead angrily. "Look, Aeryn will not help us, but I must bring Penelope back and get her into the safety of the mortal world. Just in case we…" He left the sentence unfinished.

"Rest, recover. Alessandro will bring food. Soon the battle must begin again, but we are safe for now; the demons cannot enter here." And, before anyone could react, he was gone.

Back in his chamber, Morgan quickly prepared the spell that would take him to Aeryn's realm, then he spent precious seconds pondering his return.

For a return it was. There had been a time when he was welcomed in that land. But that was many years ago. When he had loved Aeryn.

And she had loved him.

Chapter 42

"Morgan," she whispered, unaware she had spoken aloud. Her son had an arrow notched and ready. "I can reach him from here, Mother, just say the word."

Aeryn lay a hand hurriedly on his forearm. "Be still, Dominic, let us at least see what he wants." *He's here for the child, not for you.* The thought entered her head unbidden and lodged there, stubborn, immovable. To the guard she said, "Allow him entry."

Nearly two centuries had passed since she had last seen him and now she drank in the sight as she stood in the secret anteroom and watched him from behind the gilt framed two-way mirror.

He hasn't changed much, she thought, *hair a little grayer perhaps but still looking good.* She allowed herself a tiny smile as she imagined running her fingers through that hair as she'd done so often long ago. She shook her head to rid herself of the memory, for such thoughts could serve no purpose now. But almost at once it was replaced by another as he paced around the room. *Always so impatient, so restless,* she mused, remembering how he'd never been able to sit still for very long.

Abruptly Morgan ceased his pacing and looked directly into the mirror, and she had the uncomfortable feeling he was looking right at her. Then, as if to prove her right, he spoke. "If you've seen enough, Aeryn, perhaps we can get down to discussing why I'm here?"

The words were loud in the stillness of the room and, despite herself, she jumped slightly and her face reddened.

Damn him, she thought, *damn him for his arrogance, for always being right!* She left the room and spoke tersely to the guard who waited nearby.

"Let him wait another hour, then bring him to the throne room." She paused. "Make that two hours."

She'd done it on purpose of course, kept him waiting for so long. He walked through the doors of the throne room, determined not to give her the satisfaction of seeing how irritated he was. But he stopped as he saw her sitting there in all her finery. Her beauty quite literally took his breath away. But then, it always had. To hide his confusion, he sank into a deep, slightly ironic bow of obeisance.

"Your Majesty," he intoned gravely.

It had been worth getting dressed up, she mused with satisfaction, noticing his reaction, although she was glad she'd resisted wearing her crown; it always made her feel vaguely ridiculous.

"Morgan," she said carefully and politely, "how nice."

"I'll come right to the point," he told her as he approached without being invited to do so. The guards who flanked the throne lay their hands on their sword hilts.

"I wouldn't bother if I were you," he told them, "you'd not even get close." Morgan wasn't usually so rude or so arrogant but really, kids today…

"What do you want, Morgan?" She was equally amused and annoyed. He was about to answer when she was suddenly angry. "Actually, why *are* you here? Two hundred years and you think you can just waltz in here without a by-your-leave?" Now she was on her feet and shouting. "Just who do you think you are?"

"I didn't just waltz in here as you so eloquently put it; you invited me in," he pointed out, "then you opened the door." His tone, rather than the words themselves, only served to infuriate her more, as it had been designed to do.

"I didn't mean into the *palace*," she howled. "I meant into my realm! You arrogant, annoying, *pig-headed*…I mean, it's not as if you can just take a wrong turn and end up here! It's not a case of 'oops sorry, I must have had the map upside down!'"

She was panting now, which had turned her cheeks a most appealing shade of pink, he thought, but still she hadn't finished. "Two hundred– well, one hundred and ninety-six years, eight months and three days, give or take." Her eyes flashed, and there was hurt there. "Soon forgot me, didn't you!"

But now he was angry also, although his brain had time to register satisfaction that she knew the exact length of time. As he himself did. "And whose fault is it that it's been one hundred and ninety-six years and, whatever, whatever? Who put a spell on your borders so I couldn't get back in? Eh? Eh? Forty years it took me to break that spell, *forty years!*"

"Oh, forty years was it?" She adopted the most sarcastic tone she could manage. "So what about the other one hundred and sixty? You've not exactly been in a hurry to get here, have you?"

"I have my pride," he answered stiffly, the anger gone as swiftly as it had arrived. "And you're wrong," he continued softly, "I didn't forget you." He looked into the dark depths of her eyes, still as vivid and deep and beautiful as the day they'd met. "Not a day has gone by that I haven't thought of you." He gave her just long enough for that to sink in. "Now where is the girl?"

Completely wrong-footed, she became defensive. "Don't worry, she's been well looked after. I know I have something of a reputation, but *really?*" Her voice dripped with sarcasm as she imagined him hanging in chains in one of her dungeons, shut off from the sunlight, begging her to set him free. She savored the image and embellished it a little by adding red-hot branding irons and other forms of torture, purposely designed for insufferable, pig-headed wizards.

The sound of him speaking dragged her from her daydream.

"Excellent, so if you'll just fetch her we'll be on our way."

She couldn't believe what she was hearing. "That's it? After all these years, that's *it? Fetch her and we'll be on our way?*" She gave a near-scream of frustration and to the nearest guard shouted, "Get the girl then escort them both from the castle and out of my realm!" She walked, almost ran, from the room, her dignity in shreds. Then she stopped abruptly. "And make sure they leave! And if they're not gone in five minutes then…then; I don't know, execute them both!" She paused again. "No, not the girl, just *him!*"

The door to the throne room opened and Dominic entered,

THE SANCTUARY

followed closely by Penelope. When she saw the wizard, she stared open-mouthed for a second then ran down the room and flung herself into his arms.

"Morgan! I knew you'd come; I knew it!" She turned to Aeryn, eyes shining. "This is Morgan, the friend I was telling you about!"

"Really?" she replied acidly. "You do surprise me."

Penelope was oblivious to the sarcasm or the atmosphere in the room. "You will help us, won't you? The others are in trouble; please, you must help us now!"

The refusal was already forming on her lips but the words had brought the wizard back to his senses. *The battle! His friends were waiting while he dallied here, flirting and fooling around.*

He broke in. "No, Penelope, the queen cannot help us, and we must leave at once. You were brave and very foolish to make the attempt,"—he smiled at her—"but it was always doomed to failure." He looked at the queen. "Isn't that right, Aeryn?"

She met his gaze proudly, for she had nothing to reproach herself for. The squabbling of mortal men and women was no longer of any concern to her. Too many of her subjects had died in the past, fighting on Morgan's side against his half-wit brother. It was one of the reasons, no, the *only* reason she had banished him from her realm, though it had broken her heart to do so.

No, she had nothing to reproach herself for. In the last few minutes she'd acted like a silly schoolgirl, so overwhelmed had she been to see him, but she was a queen, respected and feared in equal measure across the land. She needed no one, had ruled alone and supreme for centuries, would do so for many more.

Addressing Penelope, she said, "I thank you again for the life of my son, but the debt between us is repaid. I, in turn, give you *your* life by allowing you to leave. And yours." She lifted her head proudly as she turned to Morgan. She gave him a long, hard stare, trying to imprint his image onto her mind, for she knew she would never see him again.

"Leave my realm and do not return. Ever." She swept from the room and did not turn around, even when Dominic shouted, "Mother, wait!"

She could not turn. Would not let them see the tears that were already coursing down her cheeks.

THE SANCTUARY

Chapter 43

As soon as they'd left Aeryn's castle, Morgan quickly brought Penelope up to speed. She was distressed to learn the battle was already in full flow. *If only I'd been able to persuade her to help us,* she thought.

Now they were back in the Sanctuary, but instead of heading back out to re-join the battle, he took her to his chamber and had her sit at his desk. He took out pen and paper and scribbled quickly. When he'd finished, he rummaged in one of the drawers and fished out a scruffy, tea-stained envelope. He sealed the note inside then added an address and handed it to her.

"The door in the big lounge, the one directly above the settee, the purple one not the orange?" he raised an eyebrow and she nodded. "It's not locked, go through, it leads into the passage-between-the-worlds." She nodded again. "Good, now listen carefully; follow the passage to the end, it's about a kilometer or so, that's all. You'll come to a circular room. There's another door set halfway up the wall, don't worry there's a ladder." He stopped and looked suddenly worried. "You're not afraid of heights, are you?" He was relieved when she shook her head. "Good, so climb the ladder and go through the door."

He rummaged in yet another drawer. "Where is it?" he muttered softly. "I know I chucked it in here somewhere. Ah!" He produced a small, intricately wrought silver key. "You'll need this," he said, "make sure you keep it safe. It was made by an Elven locksmith more than two thousand years ago and is quite irreplaceable." He hustled her out of the room, and they hurried down the staircase that led to the lounge.

"Now," he gave his final instructions, "the door leads into the mortal world. When you get there, cross the road, and be careful, it's around…"—he took out his fob watch—"midday in the mortal world. Make sure you look both ways, the traffic in London is mad, simply mad. Never should have invented the automobile in my opinion, horse and carriage was a much more civilized means of transport, I've always thought."

Penelope didn't bother to answer but simply stood there, hands on hips and waited.

"Yes, well," he continued, slightly embarrassed, "cross the road to the bus stop on the other side. Make sure you do or you'll end up going in the wrong direction."

"*Morgan,*" she said in an exasperated tone, "don't be an old fusspot, I do know how to catch a bus, I *am* nearly ten!"

To the best of his knowledge, the most powerful wizard in the last five hundred years had never been called an old fusspot before. He chose to ignore it and was about to continue when realization of what he was actually saying hit Penelope.

"Wait a minute, you're sending me away?" she said incredulously.

"I thought I was going on some kind of, I don't know, secret mission or something, but you want me to leave the Sanctuary? Why would you do that?" Despite her bravado she could feel tears welling in her eyes and she *really* wanted to let them fall. Instead she got angry. "Why would you send me away? What did I do wrong?" And now the tears did come. "I know I went to Aeryn's land without permission, but I was trying to help, truly I was. And what about Peter? I helped with curing him, didn't I?" She was no longer shouting, and the tears were falling freely. More quietly she said, "I thought I was part of the Sanctuary? Like Cissy and Luke? Not as important as they are obviously, but still…"

Her voice trailed away and she looked up at him, her eyes big and round and unhappy. She sniffed loudly then her voice cracked as she begged, "Please don't send me away."

Morgan felt tears pricking the back of his own eyes and he knelt before the child, gathering her into his arms. He hugged her tightly for a moment, not even minding she was getting snot on the shoulder of his robe. Then he regarded her earnestly.

"Penelope, listen to me carefully, I'm going to say something very important and I need you to understand. Can you do that for me?" She wiped her eyes, then her nose on the back of her sleeve, and nodded. "Good girl." He handed her a big white handkerchief. "Now first of all, you *are* part of the Sanctuary just like Cissy and Luke, like Molly and me and everyone else. You're equally important as the rest of us, do you understand?" She nodded and gave a tremulous smile. "Good, now listen. You're quite right when you say you're almost ten and that means you're old enough to hear this."

She nodded again, but more doubtfully this time; suddenly she was afraid of what he might say.

"Penelope, we may not survive this battle, probably will not survive it." Her hand flew to her mouth and she began to deny it, but he continued, "No, it's true and you must listen for I have a task for you. The demon army is huge, the Demon King has worked some kind of spell which is beyond my understanding and his army of vile creatures just keeps on attacking, wave after wave of them, never tiring, never ending. We kill them in their hundreds, thousands even, yet still they come."

He stopped, trying to gauge her reaction but she was quite calm now and he allowed himself a momentary burst of pride. "And we are few, Penelope. Yes, we are powerful but that is not enough. Soon we will become exhausted and we will falter. And we will lose. For many centuries I have fought the Dark Wizard, fought the Demon King and I have always prevailed. But this time…"

He stopped. What else was there to say?

He looked at the girl he had become so fond of, pleased to see her eyes were dry and she had herself under control. "This will be the last battle," he admitted, then he stood and became business-like. "Now, there can be no more delay. Go to the address on the envelope, it's the home of Cissy's parents, Charles and Lucy. They will look after you and there are instructions in the letter for Charles and for yourself. The number 86 bus will take you there." A thought struck him, and he delved into a pocket and gave her a handful of coins.

She looked at them then handed them back. "Roman."

He glanced down and saw the head of *Vespasian* looking

sideways at him.

"Sorry," he grunted and drew out a five-pound note.

"Penelope, Charles must deliver a message to Aeryn and you must go with him." He saw her eyes widen in surprise. "He doesn't know the spell to get there, but you do!"

She nodded proudly.

"And, more importantly, Aeryn knows you." Morgan didn't allow her to interrupt for he was anxious now to re-join his companions. "Charles isn't the most accomplished wizard, and he's likely to get himself killed before he has a chance to deliver the message. That's why you must go with him. Aeryn will not harm you or any friend of yours. I know her well and yes, she can be tough, ruthless sometimes; she has to be. But she is not cruel, and she is not a murderer."

She nodded her understanding. "But what's the message? Why do we have to go there?"

"Tell her…tell her that the Demon King has won, that the Sanctuary is no more. Tell her that I and my brother are dead."

The girl gasped, not understanding, and he explained.

"We will be defeated, Penelope. Oh, we will fight, of course we will fight! But in the end, we cannot prevail. In the end we will lose and when that happens the Demon King will not allow Logan to live. But that is not what is important. It is vital that you tell Aeryn that soon he will rule the mortal world and she must act to save it. She has no liking for what goes on outside of her realm, but you must convince her. For it is my belief that once he has subdued the world of mortal men the Demon King will not be content, and in his greed he will move next against her realm. She must be ready, and she must act. Quickly!" He knelt again and hugged her briefly. "Do you understand?"

She nodded, but absently. The talk of Aeryn had triggered something, some memory. What was it? She didn't know. Something at the back of her mind, tantalizingly close, something important. *What was it?*

"Penelope, do you understand?"

She looked at him and nodded again.

"Good, it's all in the envelope anyway. Now go. Through the door into the passage."

Penelope climbed onto the back of the settee, opened the door then stepped into the passage. She looked back to see Morgan was already striding from the room. She pulled the door almost closed but didn't allow the latch to click shut, then she sat in the passage with her back against the wall and had a think. After about ten minutes, she opened the door again and jumped back into the lounge.

Penelope was a responsible girl and she would deliver the message. But only if she had to. She found it hard to believe Morgan would lose, despite what he'd told her, and she would not abandon her friends until all hope was gone.

THE SANCTUARY

Chapter 44

"Sister, I am ashamed." A deep frown marred Daraproud's features as she strode into the queen's bedchamber uninvited and unannounced. "I never, ever thought I would say this but..." She stopped in shock as she took in the pale, bloodless features, the puffy eyes, the ruined make-up and the black streaks that ran down her sister's cheeks where the kohl she wore on her eyes had run. "Aeryn, I..." Her words dried up; it was the first time she could remember her sister looking anything other than perfect.

"Did I do the right thing, Daraproud? Will I ever see him again?"

The queen's younger sister sighed and sat on the bed beside her. "Truthfully, Aeryn? I'm not certain you did. I know Morgan came because of the child but..." She hesitated, not wanting to upset her sister further.

"Go on, nothing you say could make me feel any worse," said Aeryn. "You were always wiser and less hot-headed than I."

Less pig-headed too, thought Daraproud, *you and the wizard are well-suited. You've both wasted the last two hundred years with your stubbornness.* Aloud she said, "I think Morgan wanted to ask for your help but couldn't."

"Why not? He should know he can ask anything of me, and I would grant it." The only reply was a delicately raised eyebrow and a very slight disapproving purse of her sister's lips. "Well, perhaps you're right," admitted Aeryn, "but anyway, why would Morgan need help against his brother? He never has before."

Daraproud shrugged impatiently. "I don't know, maybe it's the demons. There have been rumors."

Aeryn thought for a moment before disregarding it. "No, that can't be it. It would take more than a few demons to stop Morgan."

"So will you help him after all? Will you use our army against the demons?"

Aeryn shook her head. "Sister, you know I cannot. The curse…"

Daraproud nodded, but remained silent, neither judging nor condoning, full of understanding for the moral dilemma her sister faced. With the passage of time, Aeryn's army now numbered little more than eight hundred.

The silence went on as Aeryn fought her conscience.

"I cannot," Aeryn repeated at last, her voice almost a whisper, "I will not command men to fight for a cause that is not theirs, one that is not even in their own world."

Daraproud remained silent.

"I cannot risk depleting our army further, thus leaving our own borders vulnerable."

Still Daraproud did not speak.

"We don't have enough men. Sister, answer me!"

Now Daraproud finally lost patience. "We don't have enough men?" she exploded. "We don't have enough *men?* We never will until you marry!" She jumped up from the bed and paced, hardly able to contain her anger. As she did so the pins holding her hair came out and it fell to her waist in a shimmering black cascade.

"And as Morgan is the only man you've ever looked at and you didn't even see *him* for two hundred years, we're kind of screwed, aren't we? The menfolk continue to die out because neither I nor any other woman in this land can bear children until the curse is broken! And thanks to your stupid pride it has endured far too long! So what does it matter if the army disappears now or in a hundred years, five hundred? Tell me, Sister, *what does it matter?*" And now the real reason for her anger was revealed. "Aeryn, he was here. *He was here and you sent him away!*"

The queen didn't answer but turned to look out of the window and survey this land she ruled. This land she loved so much. For a long time, there was silence, broken only by the ticking of the clock. It was already long past midnight.

Eventually she faced her sister. "Daraproud, send someone to the barracks. Find out who has a taste for killing demons. I want fifty volunteers saddled and ready to move out at dawn."

*   *   *   *

Penelope went straight to the library and pulled books from the shelves. *What was it she'd read? What couldn't she remember? It was in one of these books, she was certain of it!*

Hour after hour she looked through book after book while

whatever it was she was trying to remember nagged at the back of her brain. It was something she'd read and taken little notice of. *Why, oh why, hadn't she taken more notice?* Half a dozen times she nearly had it but every time, at the last second, the thought ran away like a cat after a rat.

Eventually, tired and frustrated, she left the library and climbed the stairs to the top floor landing from where she could observe the battle through the window. She was scared, not of what she might see but of who she might not. Would all of them still be there, fighting for their lives? What if someone had been killed? She couldn't bear that.

Please let them all be alive, please let them all be alive, she repeated silently, over and over like a mantra. When she reached the landing, she was surprised to find it was night time. Clouds hid the moon and it was difficult for her to make anything out in the maelstrom of the battle below.

* * * *

For hours, the battle had raged once more. Luke was so exhausted he could barely lift his sword and the battle had merged into a nightmare of noise and sweat and blood. Beside him Wallace fared little better. His skill with a sword was legendary, but battles weren't supposed to be like this. They were supposed to last an hour, maybe two or three at most. This one though had gone on for hour after interminable hour and still the demon hordes came. It was a miracle they'd survived this long, he knew, and now he was tiring, near the end of his strength.

THE SANCTUARY

"Luke, you must rest!" Wallace commanded. "Go back to the Sanctuary for a while! Go on!"

In answer, Luke heaved his sword into the air and swung it – another demon head flew from its body. Molly, on the other hand, was indomitable. She was long past exhaustion and her movements were purely automatic, instinctive. Her wand flashed in all directions, faster than the eye could follow, killing all who dared come near.

But she too could not last much longer; she knew the end was inevitable and that it would come soon. Even in the turmoil, she had time to feel regret for Cissy and Luke, for two young lives that would be lost. And it was anger that sustained her, fury that the Dark Wizard had brought them to this. *He* was responsible for the fact that her friends and two children she loved as if they were her own, were all going to die today. Molly looked across the battleground, over the heads of the demon army, to where the Dark Wizard stood, his arm still firmly in the grip of the Demon King.

Then some instinct made him look up and their eyes locked. And he smiled.

And Molly went incandescent with rage. She rushed forward, screaming incoherently, and with a wide sweep of her wand she took out a dozen demons at once. In no time she'd gone twenty meters, thirty, forty, leaving a trail of dead and dying behind her. For a minute it seemed as if she might actually reach the Dark Wizard, and for the first time since the battle had begun, he took out his own wand.

Then Molly slipped. Her legs simply disappeared from under

her and she fell flat onto her back with a painful thud, her wand flying from her hand. The nearest demon gave a howl of triumph and raised its own weapon high above its head. It was a mace, a cruelly spiked ball of iron on the end of a thick chain. The creature swung it around a couple of times to gain momentum and Molly lay there, helpless to prevent it. As the ball began its descent, she watched it detachedly, noticing how the spikes weren't distributed quite evenly, how some of them were rusted. *Or was it dried blood?* she wondered.

The demon's head shattered like a melon smashed by a hammer. The mace fell to the ground and she had to fling herself to the left to avoid it, then to the right as the demon came crashing to the ground. As she did so, her fingers closed around her wand. A spark of hot fire scattered the demons who were already crowding round, intent on the kill, and it gave her time to see who had saved her.

Not Cissy or Morgan, they were too far away and busy with their own problems; same with Luke and Wallace. *But who was it?* She peered through the darkness. *Alessandro! What the bleedin'...?* she thought, utterly amazed. Alessandro was about as good with a wand as she herself was at cooking; in other words, not that great. And it was true that he had struck more by chance than skill, or perhaps some divine providence had guided his aim. Alessandro had taken in the scene at a glance, given a panic-stricken flick of his wand in her general direction and succeeded in reducing the demon's head to mush.

Now, as she made her way frantically toward him, she could see he was jumping around like a cat on a hot tin roof, sending bolts of lightning in all directions, panic rather than skill keeping the demons away. In truth, he shouldn't have even been there, but it was his conscience that had driven him from the temporary safety of his kitchen and out into the street, into that noisy, terrifying nightmare. He was no coward, it was simply the knowledge that he had little skill for fighting that had kept him from the fight, but eventually his mind was made up.

Quickly he had donned body armor, grabbed his long-forgotten wand from the back of a drawer, then ran downstairs into the ruined entrance hall. Taking a deep breath, he muttered a quick prayer then stepped outside. The very first thing he'd seen was Molly laying on the ground and a huge demon standing above her swinging a fearsome looking weapon above its head…

*   *   *   *

Despite the darkness, a little electric light was cast through the windows of the Sanctuary onto the street below, enough for Penelope to witness what was happening.

She saw Wallace and Luke side by side, battling valiantly, their swords glinting silver in the light and shining crimson from the blood of the slain. She watched in amazement as Molly was transformed. *Could this really be the same fat, occasionally irritable but always reliable Molly?* She watched, transfixed, as the witch twisted and turned, jumped and crouched and spun in rapid circles whilst her wand emitted a continuous, coruscating barrage of fire.

Her attention turned to Cissy, her dear, gentle friend who

secretly she loved most of all. But now she was different, *powerful*. Penelope had heard the stories about a prophecy and wondered. It couldn't be Cissy the legends talked about, could it? Surely not? It wasn't possible!

And Morgan, dear, kindhearted, no-nonsense, sometimes intimidating Morgan. Now he was revealed in his ultimate, supreme power and his anger was terrible to behold. No creature, no matter how big, how powerful, could face him. No! Not even the Demon King himself could have withstood the mighty wizard Morgan this night.

For a long time, Penelope let herself hope they might win. But from her vantage point high up in the Sanctuary she could see far down the street and beyond to where thousands of creatures still gathered, ready to take the place of their fallen comrades.

It's impossible, she thought, and her heart sank as she realized with sudden horror that Morgan had been right, that there was no way they could win. A sob caught in her throat and she wept as the realization dawned that all her friends were about to die.

I have to leave, she thought hysterically, pacing backwards and forwards on the landing, panic-stricken not through fear for herself but that she might fail to deliver Morgan's message, might let him down. Yet it was hard to drag herself away, it felt like she was abandoning them. But at last she knew she had to go, could delay no longer.

She cupped her hands against the glass and, through her tears, tried to make out each of the people she had grown to love so much.

As she saw them fighting for their lives, she blew each of them

THE SANCTUARY

a silent kiss; Luke, Molly, Wallace, Alessandro, Cissy, Morgan. She couldn't see the faeries but she knew they were there somewhere. She hoped that they at least would escape and return to their own world.

"Goodbye," she whispered, "I'll never forget you." And at last the little girl, brave beyond her years, turned away…

… just as the night was bathed in bright sunshine.

THE SANCTUARY

Chapter 45

Across the dark sky was a huge rent, like a gash in the fabric of time, and through it poured an army of soldiers on horseback. A new sound drowned out that of sword on metal, grunts and curses and the lament of the dying: the sound of iron on the cobbles of a London street as the hooves of more than fifty horses clattered into the fray, trampling all in their path. And these were no ordinary horses, these were the famed *destriers,* horses bred especially for war, well-muscled and agile, strong and brave.

It was as if the entire scene had been floodlit, and from the upstairs window Penelope could see everything highlighted in stark relief. It was impossible to make out features beneath the immaculately polished helmets, but she knew with certainty who had come.

"Aeryn," she breathed, then gripped with sudden excitement, "Aeryn!" And there she was! It had to be her! The golden circlet that adorned her helmet was unmistakable! And beside her rode Dominic, with his golden hair flowing around his shoulders. And another figure, slighter in build, a woman, jet black hair tied into

THE SANCTUARY

a rope that reached to her waist.

These three rode ahead of an army that was small but deadly. Demons scattered in panic and deserted the battlefield. Those of the Sanctuary were rejuvenated by the arrival of Aeryn and her soldiers, and redoubled their efforts. Soon it became a rout as the demon army died in its hundreds and the rest of it ran.

"I knew you'd come!" Morgan shouted with a grin as Aeryn abandoned the pursuit and cantered back to the Sanctuary.

"Then you knew more than I," she replied, and her visage was stern and unsmiling. But then, unable to maintain the pretense, she removed her helmet and returned his grin. For a long moment, the others ceased to exist as they gazed at each other, then suddenly they were embracing and laughing. Just as quickly they separated, embarrassed, and both made a show of introducing their companions.

"The girl!" exclaimed Aeryn suddenly. "Where is she?" She gave Morgan a hard look. "I liked that girl, she showed great spirit. I hope you have made certain of her safety?"

"Of course!" he replied, indignant. "She is far away by now and quite safe."

Penelope, from her vantage point saw what those below could not; something that chilled her to the bone. The demons, they were massing together again and had begun to march. But now their approach was more ordered and organized.

Why? she wondered, and then saw the reason and her blood froze. *They're being led by the Demon King.*

Penelope forgot her intention to leave and tried to think. She had to remember this lost detail, she had to! Somehow, she knew it was vital! It was there, tantalizingly out of reach! She could have cried with frustration and, to make things worse, the rent in the sky sealed itself shut and her eyes, temporarily blinded by the bright light, could make out nothing below. But as she peered through the glass, desperately trying to make out what was happening, the wind changed direction and the clouds, which had covered the sky like a thick blanket, shifted and the street was bathed in yellow moonlight.

Thank goodness the moon is nearly full, she thought, and all at once that tantalizing clue edged a fraction closer. *The moon…something about the moon…blood moon! That was it! The blood moon!* She forced her mind to stop racing and to concentrate, making herself remember: Molly, newly returned from her adventure, told her story, boasting a little…

"You should've seen it, the blood moon, I never saw anything so bleedin' beautiful. The whole countryside like a big, red sea…"

And the contempt in her voice as she'd spoken of the demon. "Bleedin' terrified it was, couldn't disappear quick enough. Said the blood moon is fatal to demons." And, laughing, she'd joked, "Shame we can't make our own blood moon."

… can't make our own…

… make our own…

The cogs in Penelope's mind clicked into place. It was like fitting that final, satisfying piece into a jigsaw as at last she remembered. *Aeryn has the power to conjure a blood moon!*

THE SANCTUARY

*   *   *   *

It didn't take long for the demons to rally and resume their attack, and the Demon King immediately sought out Morgan. The creature gave a wild howl of triumph as he spotted his enemy and raced toward him, axe high above his head. His own demons scattered before his charge and those not quick enough were simply barged out of the way if they were lucky or, as he became increasingly desperate to reach his foe, were dispassionately killed with a thrust of that massive, viciously curved blade.

Morgan stood and watched, arms folded, as Kanzser approached. Despite his casual stance it seemed to those who saw him that the wizard grew taller and broader, that he exuded an aura of invincibility and power. Even more disconcerting to his enemies was the slight but unmistakable smile on his face as if he relished the coming fight.

He remained perfectly still until the Demon King was almost upon him, then his wand was in his hand. As the axe arced down, a stream of blue fire leaped from the tip of the wand and met the razor-thin edge of the blade, stopping it in mid-air. Kanzser stared at the wizard in shock. His muscles bunched and he used all of his strength to break the axe free, but it wouldn't budge. The demon grunted with effort as he strained, yet the wizard hardly seemed to be trying at all; for the first time, the Demon King felt a twinge of fear.

With a sardonic smile, the wizard extinguished his fire, taking Kanzser by surprise. With all resistance suddenly gone, he was unable to prevent the axe continuing its descent and crashing to the ground, causing sparks to fly off the smooth cobbles. But Kanzser was lightning fast, and as the next blast of fire hurtled toward him, he smashed it away with the axe.

Now it was Morgan's turn to be surprised, and it slowed his reflexes; only by a fraction but long enough for Kanzser to attack. The wizard was forced to retreat under the ferocity of the Demon King's blows, only just managing to block each one with the fire from his wand. But, prematurely sensing victory and still unable to believe he could lose, Kanzser grew careless and overconfident. Arrogantly showing off to his men, he raised the axe, then, as it began its descent, he tossed it deftly into his left hand.

The delay gave Morgan the chance to send a bolt of fire toward the demon's chest, but he was off balance, trying to avoid the axe, and the bolt hit Kanzser with a glancing blow that left a long, angry burn but didn't penetrate the thick, scaly hide. He gave a howl of pain and retreated a little to inspect the damage, turning away from the wizard as he did so. Morgan was alert for the trickery that followed, but even he was surprised at the speed with which it came.

Staggering slightly, Kanzser stumbled as if in great pain, and in the instant his back was turned, he transferred the axe back to his right hand then spun, still half-crouched, and sent it hurtling through the air toward the wizard. So quickly and skillfully executed was the maneuver that even Morgan was unable to release a blow of his own before the axe, perfectly aimed, was shooting through the air with bullet-like speed. To the wizard, it appeared to be moving in slow-motion, twenty meters away, fifteen, ten. He watched it with horrified fascination, his entire being frozen, his wand still only half raised to counter the threat.

Desperately, he closed his mind to his impending death and let instinct take over as the axe, now only five meters away, looked certain to bury itself in his chest. At last, with barely a millisecond to spare, Morgan willed a blast of lightning from his wand and it slammed into the side of the blade, diverting it a fraction. The change in direction was just enough and the axe shaved the side of the wizard's head, slicing off the tip of his ear before burying itself dead center in the forehead of one of the demons watching behind.

Meanwhile, busy as he was fending off his own assailants, Luke could still take a second to appreciate what he was witnessing. Skilled as he had become, he realized he was a mere novice in comparison to the newly-arrived woman and her companions. *If I practiced for a hundred years I might be half as good,* he thought as he neatly dodged an approaching demon and dispatched it with a deft flick of his sword. There'd only been time for the briefest of introductions before the demons were upon them again and now he was aware of dozens of blades all around him, flashing, cutting, thrusting and slashing at lightning speed. And the woman, Queen Ar…something, was most frightening of all, he thought, as she whirled and jumped and somersaulted, delivering death to all who came near.

For every demon Luke could kill, ten fell to her sword, but what really unnerved him were the noises she made as she fought, grunts and snarls that fell from her lips, feral and vicious in nature. She wore a look of intense ferocity, a complete, implacable hatred of her enemy, that did as much to strike terror into their hearts as did her sword.

Those at either side of the queen fought with no less speed and skill. The man – Dominic, Luke recalled – had been polite and soft spoken, almost diffident when Morgan had introduced him. And the woman, what was her name? Luke couldn't remember, but she was beautiful, with her long black hair and her kind, gentle features. There was nothing diffident or gentle about them now though and the three of them together formed a terrifying killing machine which cut a wide swathe through the demon ranks. Then the men on horseback overtook them on either side, galloping at great speed to flank the enemy and it became carnage as fifty of the huge *destriers* wreaked havoc, kicking and biting or goring with the cruel spikes attached to their foreheads.

Heart pounding at his narrow escape, Morgan took advantage of the now weapon-less Demon King and assailed him with a barrage of blue fire that the creature could only deflect with his armor-clad arms. Around him, his army saw their master in trouble and began to panic and run. Sensing victory was near, Morgan's companions found new energy and the battle, which had hung in the balance an hour before, now threatened to become a rout.

Escape was suddenly all that mattered as demon killed demon in their desperate attempts to flee. But in the confusion, Kanzser was able to retrieve his axe and he fought on, still locked in mortal combat with his great adversary. His anger at his fleeing army was terrible and he screamed curses at them. It was enough to halt their flight and they regrouped to once more face their enemy; better to fight and perhaps die now than face the Demon King's

THE SANCTUARY

wrath and certain death later.

Beyond them, keeping a prudent distance and making sure he didn't get too close to the actual fighting, stood Logan, watching in trepidation as the battle wore on. A half-dozen times he jumped onto the carriage and grabbed the reins, ready to spur his horses into action, only to jump down again as the battle once more appeared to swing in his favor.

Then he'd seen the girl, somehow filled with unnatural power, fighting side-by-side with his brother. *How? How was it possible? She couldn't possibly...the prophecy! Could that really be it? Was it she and not the boy?* And the Dark Wizard had truly felt fear. *I should have killed her!*

He'd barely had time to take it in when the sky had rent open and he had watched, first in disbelief then despair, as this new army, small but deadly, had cut through the demon ranks. For a time, it had seemed that Morgan must once again prevail, but when the Demon King himself had challenged the wizard there had been renewed hope. *Kill him,* he had willed, silently at first then aloud. "Kill him! Kill him!" Then, when Kanzser had thrown his axe, he had prayed its course would stay true only to curse as once more his brother's infernal luck came to his aid.

Now though, it seemed the demon army was gaining the ascendancy again. Some of the *destriers* had fallen, brought down by spears flung from a distance, their tips coated with lethal poison. Even as Logan watched, another horse fell and a horde of demons were on its rider, hacking and stabbing. Despite the distance, the Dark Wizard could see the blood and gore spraying upwards and he looked away with distaste.

And now the girl was tiring at last, that much was obvious, and the boy was nearly spent. The woman and the two who fought beside her were still creating havoc, causing dreadful carnage and... *Where was the old witch? There! Still going strong!* Logan looked away in disgust; he hated Molly almost as much as he did his brother. Elsewhere he saw yet another *destrier* fall, and another. The demons had regrouped and were taking control at last. He hardly dared look to where the Demon King had been, but yes! There! Kanzser was still battling and as long as he prevailed, the demon army would stand firm.

"Not long now, dear brother," he gloated, speaking aloud, "your end has almost come at last."

Chapter 46

It had been an impossibly long and difficult journey, full of hardships that had tested him to the limits of his endurance. Only instinct had guided Oscar's way and only determination and a fierce longing to see his friend again had given him the strength he needed. On the way, there had been many dangers and it was nothing short of a miracle that he'd survived; or perhaps some unseen guardian had watched over him, never allowing the hazards he faced to be more than his increasingly battered spirit could endure.

There had been the river, swelled with recent rains that had turned it into a raging torrent. When he'd tried to cross, the treacherous currents had swept him far away, depositing him at last, half drowned and exhausted, miles out of his way.

And more than once he'd been confronted with wild animals, angry, snarling creatures, themselves trying to survive. Time and time again they'd chased him, occasionally surrounding and attacking so that he barely managed to fight his way free. On yet another occasion he'd lost the path and traveled many days in the wrong direction, hunger making him weak and disoriented. Perhaps worst of all was the loneliness, that dull, aching longing for someone just to shield him and offer comfort and protection.

But now he was almost at the end of his quest; his friend was near, he could sense it! But the city frightened him, its many buildings closed in on him, claustrophobic and forbidding, its smells putrid and disgusting. How he longed for the sweet aromas of the countryside, for the rugged mountains of his native land. It was night and he cowered, wet and cold, in a deserted alley behind a rotting midden, the stink that emanated from it penetrating his skin and coating the roof of his mouth like grease. It invaded his nostrils and he thought he might never smell clean air again.

He could have attempted to find somewhere better, but the noises of the night were unfriendly and alien and he was too scared to move. So, he lay there and waited for this long night to end, tired, cold, frightened until at last, he fell into a fitful doze.

* * * *

As soon as the realization hit her, Penelope didn't hesitate, running down the wide, sweeping staircase toward the ruined entrance of the Sanctuary. But when she reached it and looked out into the pandemonium on the street, she was horrified. From the safety of her upstairs window it had all looked bad enough, but nothing could have prepared her for this noisy, chaotic mess, for the screams, the squealing of the horses, the sound of metal on metal, the stink of sweat and dirt and blood. Her spirits quailed as she backed away into the relative safety of the dimly lit entrance hall, and it took all her nerve not to run back up the stairs and hide.

Then she remembered the doorway into the passage-between-the-worlds, and she remembered the mission with which she'd been entrusted. *I could leave now,* she thought, *nobody would blame me.* She tried to shut her ears from the noise outside, close her mind to what was happening. *Morgan told me I had to leave.*

And she might well have done just that had another thought not popped into her head. *They aren't my family; I don't owe them anything.* She stopped abruptly, utterly appalled and ashamed. *They're the only family I have, and I owe them everything!*

Hardly realizing she had moved, she found herself outside and in the thick of the melee. Recklessly she pushed in between legs and barged any obstacles aside, keeping as close to the ground as she could to avoid discovery. As she did so, some sixth sense alerted Molly and she stared at the girl, horrified, then made her way toward her, still flinging bolts of lightning haphazardly behind her as she ran.

At the same time, the girl was spotted by Velveteena and Moth who zoomed over to help. Their wands weren't powerful enough to kill, but they could still maim and distract the demons. Meanwhile, Penelope was desperately trying to reach the spot where she'd last seen the queen. For that was all that mattered now; all their efforts came down to this moment. She *must* reach Queen Aeryn.

*   *   *   *

"We are being overpowered!" Morgan gasped. "We must do

something!"

"I'm doing my best," Aeryn panted back, "why don't *you* try harder?"

"Don't be so damned touchy, I didn't mean…"

"If you two want to stop arguing for a minute, there's a battle to win?" Cissy sprinted past in pursuit of a demon, who she quickly caught and dispatched before turning and giving them a wide grin.

Aeryn gave Morgan a look that said 'That girl is definitely much too big for her boots.'

"We can't fight them all and our strength is waning," Morgan shouted and Aeryn looked around at the mass of heaving, fighting flesh.

"I know, but we can do no more!"

And indeed, it was true. Dominic fought tirelessly, encircled by at least a dozen enemies but managing to fight his way free. Daraproud, more naturally skilled and infinitely more flamboyant, whirled and spun, her sword dealing death and destruction with lightning speed. At one point, Aeryn could swear she saw her sister run a couple of paces up the wall then flip backwards to land behind the group of demons that had assailed her. With a triumphant scream, she spun full circle and decapitated half a dozen heads with one sweep of her sword.

Aeryn had time to smile and shake her head ruefully; her sister's style was unorthodox, certainly risky and absolutely designed to show off to whoever might happen to be watching. But the smile faded as, further away, she saw Wallace, looking much older these days, she reflected, and clearly nearing the limit of his strength. Beside him it looked like the boy Luke could hardly swing his sword either. And there was Molly, dear Molly; Aeryn had always liked her, bad tempered and irascible though she could sometimes be. She was also tough as old boots and continued to send out wave after wave of lightning bolts from her wand. But her movements seemed oddly static as if each one was automatic, a supreme effort of will, and her face was bright red, sweat pouring down it. Aeryn knew she couldn't last much longer.

We are almost overrun, she thought as despair threatened to engulf even her. But just then she felt a tug on her sleeve, and she glanced down, incredulous at what she saw. "What are you doing here? Morgan, why are you allowing this child to be exposed to such danger?"

"I didn't—" he began but Penelope interrupted.

"Never mind that! You have to conjure a blood moon, it's fatal to demons!"

Morgan was puzzled. "Pen, what are you talking about? Why are you here?"

"I read it in a book in the library." She was almost desperate in her hurry to get the words out. "Aeryn has the power to change the moon, to summon a blood moon!"

Molly reached them and began yelling furiously at either Penelope or Morgan, or probably both. "What the bleedin'—" But the girl's words stopped her. "Is this true?" She spoke sharply to Aeryn and when the queen reluctantly nodded, she turned to Morgan in excitement. "Demons cannot withstand the blood moon. I heard one of them telling Logan, back at the cave, the blood moon is fatal to demons!"

Morgan felt a rush of excitement. *This was it! This was victory!* He turned to Aeryn, his eyes shining. "Will you make the attempt?"

And she, unable to refuse him this chance, nodded slowly, not quite able to meet his gaze. "I will make the attempt," she agreed, "but first, hold me, Morgan, hold me like you used to."

Molly snorted impatiently. "This is hardly the bleedin' time…"

But the wizard, perhaps sensing something was amiss, shushed her and drew Aeryn to him. She reveled in his closeness for a moment, breathing in the heady aroma of his skin. And then she whispered in his ear.

He stepped back and his face was ashen as she ordered, "Protect me." He and Molly obeyed immediately, standing at either side of her and circling slowly, clockwise, fighting off any enemy who came near, giving her the space she needed.

At first, he fought in a kind of dazed stupor, unaware of his movements as her words reverberated around his head, before they jumbled together into a loud, roaring cacophony that filled his ears.

I may not survive this, but remember I always loved you. It repeated over and over. *May not survive this…survive this…always loved you…may not survive this.* Morgan thought he might go insane with the horror of it and a demon almost broke through, forcing him to pull himself together as he killed it with uncharacteristic viciousness. He stared at Aeryn who, in that moment, was magnificent, arms held aloft, fingertips pointing to the sky as the incantation left her lips.

Even then he might have prevented her, despite all that was at stake, but it was too late. The words were faint at first but quickly became stronger as their power took hold. Soon they rolled across the battlefield and the surrounding buildings shook from the vibrations, the sound of their windows shattering was like the cracking of a thousand whips. The fighting slowed as demons paused to look fearfully up at the moon which was already turning pink, and as they did so, many were blinded by the millions of shards of glass which fell like a storm of glittering ice.

The Demon King was the first to react and he raced toward one unfortunate soldier who, sat astride his destrier, was also distracted by the moon. In a single fluid movement, Kanzser buried his axe deep into the man's chest, dragged him from the horse and leaped into the saddle. He grabbed the reins and sank the pointed tip of the axe into the beast's flank so that it screamed in pain before jerking into a crazed gallop.

The whole thing took only seconds, yet in that time the redness of the moon had deepened, turning crimson, and demons began to die horribly. They died in their hundreds at first and then in their thousands, catching fire from the inside so that gouts of flame spilled from their mouths and lit their eyeballs from behind, giving them, ironically, a truly demonic appearance. The air was soon filled with agonized screams as their flesh shriveled and blackened so that one could almost feel sorry for them…almost.

Logan crouched behind the wheel of his carriage, more in danger now than at any other stage of the battle as demons spontaneously combusted all around him. He saw the Demon King riding frantically toward him astride a huge horse and he ducked. But Kanzser was intent only on escape and swept by without even noticing him.

Logan waited until he was out of sight before stepping from

the shadows, then he stood, bathed in the red moonlight and looked around at the vast carpet of dead, at the ruination of his dreams. In the distance he could see his brother, surrounded by those sycophantic fools he called friends. For a mad moment he considered going over and challenging him, but deep down he knew he could not win, not this time. In his madness, the Dark Wizard didn't understand that if only he had tried to make peace he would have been forgiven, even now, after all the death and destruction he had wrought.

He had to get away, he knew; the battle was lost and nothing remained for him here. He turned toward his carriage, but before climbing up he took a small object from his pocket and considered it for a moment. It was a small glass vial, exquisitely cut and centuries old. As he turned it around between his thumb and forefinger its many facets sent beams of crimson moonlight shooting in all directions.

Would I dare? Can I really do it? Shivers of fear ran down his spine at the thought of what he contemplated. Impulsively, before he could change his mind, he removed the stopper and held the vial aloft for a few seconds before replacing it and putting it back inside his cloak where it lodged, hot and heavy against his chest. He climbed into the carriage, but the street was so clogged with bodies it was useless to try and leave that way. He sighed; he would send for the carriage later, but in the meantime it would be a long walk home.

As he trudged forlornly away, all around his army continued to burn and only the quickest survived. But these were few, those with enough intelligence to seek out the shadows of the neighboring streets. Even the Demon King was hard pressed to escape the fatal light which grabbed at his horse's hooves for kilometer upon terrifying kilometer. In the end he was saved only by the dawn, but by that time his army, which an hour ago had numbered tens of thousands, was now less than a hundred. And as he reached his mountain retreat at last, the Demon King roared his anger at his hated enemy.

"Morgan!" he cried. "Morgaaaaan!" His lament echoed far along the passageways of his domain, but there was no one to hear. No one but himself.

Chapter 47

It was all over and they had won. All around, the charred remnants of the demon army gave evidence of the completeness of their triumph. The sun shone high in the sky and it was going to be another unseasonably warm day. But the victory felt hollow, empty, for Aeryn was dying and Morgan's heart was breaking.

For a time, she had been invincible, or at least she had appeared so, as the words of the spell resonated from her lungs and rapidly became louder and stronger. Her power was impossible to resist, and the moon began to turn, first a slight shade of pink, then red and finally that deep crimson that was fatal to the demon kind.

But as the object of the spell was achieved it exacted its price, as all spells of this kind must. The ancient magics, and this was one of the oldest, demand the ultimate sacrifice in return for revealing their secrets. And so, as the moon turned crimson, Aeryn's voice faltered and the words, no longer needed, faded into nothingness before she collapsed, unconscious to the floor.

As the last of the demons perished, the others had returned to the Sanctuary, unaware of Aeryn's plight, and Luke and Cissy had gone with Alessandro to help bring some much-needed refreshments.

"How many?" Dominic laughed as he pulled off his helmet and scratched his itching scalp furiously.

"Absolutely no idea!" Daraproud returned his grin. "I lost count after the first dozen or so!" She pulled off her own helmet and, in doing so, dislodged the pins which had held her hair into a rope so that it cascaded over her shoulders and down her back. Alessandro, who was entering the room at that exact moment, armed with drinks and food for the victors, stopped abruptly and stared, transfixed, almost dropping the tray and struggling to balance it again. *Santa madre di Dio!* he thought. *Never have I seen such a beautiful woman!*

Daraproud noticed his reaction and a faint smile crept over her face, barely touching her lips. Then slowly and very deliberately she turned her back on him and, without a word, walked toward the door.

So, he said to himself with a smile, *let the games commence.* He grinned openly as she opened the wrong door, one that led to a broom cupboard. She closed it, cursing inwardly, and reached for the identical one next to it and hurriedly left the room. As she left, Alessandro had time to see the blush rise rapidly up her neck to her ears.

No, he thought, *it is not a contest you can win, my beautiful one.*

*   *   *   *

Morgan knelt beside Aeryn and shouted her name, shaking her, gently at first but with increasing violence as if by doing so he could miraculously bring her back to him. Her skin was deathly pale, and it felt so cold!

He knew that hardly a spark of life remained; perhaps it had already gone. *No! I won't allow it! I refuse to let her go!* Desperately his fingers probed her wrist, searching for a pulse but without success. He moved to her neck, pressing, stroking…still nothing. He peered intently at the smooth skin, hoping for a sign but… *Wait! It was there! The merest pulsing of that delicate blue vein!* It was weak and faint to be sure, but she still lived!

"Do something," he entreated, and Molly thought despairingly that she'd never before heard such pain in a voice. "Molly, please do something!"

She knelt beside the prostrate body of the queen and took hold of her hands. She was immediately shocked, then frightened by the fragility of the life she sensed there.

"Molly, hurry!" He gripped her shoulder painfully and she shrugged it away. She felt consumed by terror for the responsibility being placed upon her. Every instinct she possessed screamed at her to run and hide. *I can't do this,* she wailed inwardly, *I do not have the skill!* And even as these thoughts entered her head they were drowned by the voice of her old mentor and teacher Siwaraksa.

You can! You can! The words reached across the ages as clearly as if Siwaraksa stood beside them. *Remember your teaching, child, you have the knowledge to save her.*

Amused, despite the situation, at the memory of how her old teacher had always her called her *child*, long after that were actually true, Molly felt her nerves calming.

THE SANCTUARY

I ain't been a bleedin' child for a long time, Siwaraksa. She chuckled to herself. As her breathing steadied, she distanced herself from her surroundings and it seemed that she and Aeryn were cocooned, cut off from everyone and everything, even the noise of the few demons who were slow to die was muted.

Molly closed her eyes in concentration and the words she needed came unbidden to her lips, as clear in her mind as when she'd learned them centuries ago. But the spell was long and, as the minutes ticked by, she could sense the inner struggle that raged within Morgan as he battled not to intervene, to force her to be quicker.

At long last she'd uttered the last word. Molly opened her eyes and looked fearfully at Aeryn. *What if it hasn't worked? What do I bleedin' tell Morgan?* She stared at the unmoving body for long seconds, which quickly turned into minutes, willing it to live and trying to delay the moment when she would have to face Morgan and tell him she had failed.

But Morgan had turned away, unable to bear the pain. All that had happened, the defeat of the demon army, the salvation of the Sanctuary and of the human race; he had been triumphant, but now all of it had turned to ashes. He crouched, back turned to them as great, heaving sobs wracked his body. Molly hovered uncertainly, wanting to offer comfort to her friend whilst knowing nothing she could possibly say would make amends for her failure.

Then suddenly, Aeryn drew in a long, shuddering breath. Her eyes flickered open, panic stricken as they roved round and round, from one side to another. She struggled to sit up, but Molly was at her side instantly and restrained her gently.

"Take it easy, Queen Aeryn." She grinned. "Just rest awhile."

"Morgan, where is he?" Already she could feel her strength returning. "Where is my Morgan?"

But the wizard was already there, great gasps of relief making it almost impossible to speak as he wept tears of disbelief. "Here, Aeryn, I'm here." He sat beside her and grasped her hand tightly in his. "Don't try to speak."

"My Morgan." She relaxed a little at the sight of him and settled her head in his lap. "I dreamed I was dying," she said softly, "I didn't want to die…"

"Hush," he told her, "you very nearly did." He stroked her hair softly. "It was Molly who saved you."

"Molly?" She turned her attention to the witch. "I don't underst…ah, Siwaraksa, it was she who taught you."

"Yes, it was," Molly said, "many, many years ago."

"Yes, only Siwaraksa would have the knowledge to create such a spell." She smiled gratefully and took her hand. "Thank you, my friend, you truly are a remarkable witch."

"You're welcome," Molly replied, embarrassed. "Are you strong enough to move yet?"

"Of course! Help me up!"

"Wait," Morgan intervened. "The blood moon. How?"

Aeryn smiled. "Ah, Morgan, you should allow me some secrets." But seeing Morgan wasn't pacified, added. "It was Cornelius, many centuries ago. He taught me the spell."

"Cornelius!" Morgan exclaimed. "But why?"

She shrugged. "He was a frequent visitor to my land, long ago, in happier times. He wanted someone to have the knowledge, so

THE SANCTUARY

he told me. He foresaw a time when it might be needed. He was right, wasn't he?"

Morgan nodded, slowly. *Really, was there no end to Cornelius's power?*

"Come on, Aeryn, if you're ready?" said Molly. "We should go inside."

She was unsteady on her feet but she leaned heavily on Morgan's arm for a moment and found her strength quickly returning. "Help me inside, my love," and she looked at him almost shyly, the term of endearment sounding strange to both of them.

"Slowly then." He smiled down at her, but for once the smile didn't reach his eyes. Despite his relief that she would live and despite the love he held for her, her endearments troubled him, for he knew their happiness together could only be fleeting.

Soon they were back inside the Sanctuary. Dominic stared at her in alarm and moved quickly toward her. "Mother, what's happened?"

She held up a hand to forestall him. "A slight mishap that's all." She squeezed Molly's hand in warning, hoping she wouldn't give away the lie. She went on quickly, "But it reminds me, why aren't you seeing to our dead, Dominic? They deserve to be treated with honor, as I'm sure you know."

Dominic blushed with shame. "I'm sorry, Mother, I didn't think of it, I'll go now—"

"No," she interrupted, "I spoke harshly, I'm sorry. It was unfair, and you deserve your time to celebrate." She smiled at him almost shyly for she'd never found it easy to give praise. "I'm proud of you, more than I can say, Dominic, and of Daraproud too." She looked over the gathered faces. "Where is she, by the way?" As her gaze passed over them in turn, it was Alessandro who blushed, but she didn't notice. When nobody answered she shrugged. "All of you, I'm proud of all of you; everybody fought bravely."

She stopped, suddenly self-conscious at her little speech, but then she grinned, and her eyes shone.

"We won." Aeryn sounded as if she could hardly believe it and she beamed at her son. "*We won!*"

THE SANCTUARY

Chapter 48

Oscar emerged from the alley in the gray light of dawn and looked cautiously around. With his acute hearing he'd heard the sounds of the battle far across London without understanding what they were. But the screams and the noises of animals in distress had been almost too much to bear and it had been a fitful night's sleep. Then there'd been that strange red light which had bathed him and everything around for a while. Curiously though, this hadn't scared him for he'd sensed the light was not evil, would do him no harm.

Now there was no noise and the city was cloaked in a curious silence that the dog found almost as frightening. More than anything he wished himself far away, back in the countryside of Wales that he loved so much, back with the Landlord and the simple life they had led before the tall stranger had invaded their lives.

As the stiffness in his limbs eased and he moved more freely, the sun appeared above the tops of the buildings and Oscar's spirits lifted. Today he would find his friend, he was sure of it! He gave an excited bark, then another and another, then he broke into a run, heading in the direction that instinct told him he should go.

Still far away across London, the Landlord, with his unnaturally acute hearing, jerked his head up at the sound. "Oscar," he breathed, then, "Oscar!" He jumped up toward the window and, grasping the bars, pulled himself up in the same way Peter Simpson had done many times during his long imprisonment in that very same cell.

"Oscar!" He yelled as hard as he could. "Here, boy! Oscar!" Almost at once the Landlord realized there was no way he could be heard. He knew the dog was still far away and that Oscar's hearing was in no way as acute as his own. Oscar couldn't hear his shouts but… He dropped down and stood in the middle of the cell, then placed the middle and forefinger of each hand into his mouth and blew.

The shrill blast was so high pitched as to be inaudible to human ears, but half the animal inhabitants of London heard it and wondered. Cats stirred from where they lay beside their firesides and looked lazily around, annoyed at being disturbed. Stray dogs ran toward the sound, individually and in packs, while their domestic brothers and sisters pawed at doors and whined to be let out.

Rats paused in their scavenging while mice in their cozy nests quivered with fright. Far away in the woodlands on the northern edge of the city the inhabitants of a large badger's sett stirred sleepily and wondered what had disturbed them. In the more densely populated areas near the center of town, wily old foxes, bold even in the light of day, halted their mischief and stood dead

THE SANCTUARY

still before prudently slinking away to their dens to await the safety of nightfall.

Much closer to the Landlord's cell, pigeons roosting on a nearby ledge startled into the air, while across the street, a chattering of starlings, taking advantage of the last warmth from a large, steeply sloping roof, swarmed to join a vast murmuration that swooped and swirled in a beautiful, perfectly choreographed gray cloud.

But then, one by one, the inhabitants of London, those that could hear the whistle, realized it carried no threat. Cats tucked their heads back atop their paws, stray dogs returned to their business while those who lived with humans ceased their pawing and whining. Rats resumed their scavenging while mice stopped their quivering. Badgers went back to sleep and wily old foxes sat in their dens and contemplated more mischief.

Pigeons returned to their ledges and starlings, a few at least, returned to their roof although most preferred to continue with their amazing aeronautical display.

And Oscar, cheered by the sound, lengthened his stride until he could not possibly run any faster, eager to be reunited at last. And not a moment too soon, for the Dark Wizard was already on his way home as the little dog turned at last into the ruined gateway of the old mansion. At once he began to bark, high-pitched yapping sounds, irritating to some perhaps, but music to the ears of the Landlord.

"Oscar!" he yelled, and this time the dog did hear him, and he began running this way and that, searching for a way inside. Backwards and forwards he went, circling the whole building as the Dark Wizard drew ever closer, but there was nothing; no open window, no holes in the brickwork.

Increasingly panic-stricken now, for he could somehow sense the impending return of the tall man who'd frightened him so, Oscar was at a loss to know what to do next. What he wanted to do was curl up in a corner somewhere and hide, but he would find a way inside if it was the last thing he did. He was about to try yet again when something caught his eye; a small head peeping out from a hole in the ground. In happier times he would have taken great delight in chasing one of these particular creatures, but now he approached cautiously, not wishing to scare it away. Nevertheless, the head ducked into the hole as he approached, but immediately popped up again as if to make sure he was still coming.

The hole was a tight squeeze even for a small dog like Oscar, but it widened almost immediately once he was underground. The rabbit turned once to make sure he was following, then it scampered away, its white tail bobbing up and down in the darkness, and Oscar was forced to run to keep up. The route twisted and turned as the rabbit led him through the maze of tunnels and soon he was hopelessly disoriented and very hot, for there was little air.

The warren was large and tantalizing smells drifted to his nose from the tunnels he passed on each side; normally he would have loved to explore, but now he was intent only on finding the Landlord's prison. Was this creature leading him there, he wondered, or was it playing some kind of game? He pushed to the back of his mind the thought that it might be a servant of that tall, frightening human.

The tunnel continued to twist this way and that, sometimes

widening, at others becoming so narrow he thought he would suffocate. The smell of a thousand rabbits, at first so wonderful, now clogged his nostrils and made him feel slightly sick. He was just beginning to think he really had been tricked when his sensitive nose picked up a different scent. He barked in excitement and his companion turned and shushed him furiously.

"Be quiet, you foolish creature," it hissed. "We do not know whether the Dark Wizard has returned and we do not want to alert him of our presence!"

Oscar understood the tone if not the words and he growled apologetically, but his tail quivered with excitement as with each step the scent grew stronger. Moments later, he sensed rather than saw the slightest change in the darkness, the merest hint of light ahead, and as his eyes adjusted, he realized the rabbit was no longer there but had disappeared, unseen down one of the side passages. Then the tunnel ended abruptly, and the dog had to dig his paws into the earth for fear of going over the edge. Now the scent of his friend was extremely strong, and he barked again, but softly this time, and at last he heard the voice he had longed for.

"Oscar? Oscar, is that you? Where are you?"

Where indeed? Even though he could hear him and smell him, the dog still had no idea. But all he had to do now was follow his nose.

Near the ceiling outside the Landlord's cell was a gap in the stone, small but nevertheless a way in if not, unfortunately, a way out. Long ago, during a particularly freezing cold winter, the stone had cracked in two and in the ensuing years the pressure of the earth behind had eventually sent it crashing into the passage below. As the rabbit warren outside grew larger year upon year there came a time when, by chance, or perhaps by some ancient plan, one of the tunnels met the hole and this was where Oscar now found himself.

The dog had to squeeze his head through to have a look and his heart quailed when he saw how high up he was. Still with his head in the gap, he lay on the tunnel floor and whined miserably.

"Oscar, where are you? Can you get here?"

The voice spurred him on and he pushed himself through the hole. The edges of the stone cut into his back so that he cried softly, but he kept on pushing. As he hung there, half in and half out he had nowhere to put his front paws and could only push with his back ones. Below him the drop seemed immense and he closed his eyes tightly, wondering how he could possibly survive it, then with a final heave he was through at last and tumbling downwards. More by luck than judgment he landed on his feet, but he was still terribly winded, and it took him a while to catch his breath.

"Oscar! The key!" There was urgency in the Landlord's voice now for he also sensed the return of the Dark Wizard. And there was good reason, for their enemy was now, unbeknownst to them both, less than a kilometer away.

Oscar heard the urgency and got up, wincing at the pain, and sat in front of the door, looking up. He was an intelligent creature and he understood the key was needed to unlock the door; he just wasn't sure how to get it. He sat there making soft, high pitched whines as he tried to work it out.

"Jump, Oscar, you must jump!"

THE SANCTUARY

The dog barked excitedly as he caught the meaning at once. The lock wasn't very high, and he could easily jump that far despite his aches and pains. The first attempt was too far to the left, the next too far to the right, but the third was perfect and his jaws closed around the end of the big iron key. But he only had a split second to try and drag it from the lock before he descended again. The key didn't budge a millimeter and all he succeeded in doing was to hurt the inside of his mouth.

And now the Dark Wizard is less than a half kilometer away.
Keep trying!
Too far to the left again.
This time not far enough.
Too high!
He was getting tired now and still he didn't give up…
But now he is only two hundred meters away.
Oscar could almost taste the danger as the Landlord looked on helplessly.
Try again!
Once, twice…five times…
One hundred meters!
Six, seven…ten times…
And this time…success! Surely he'd managed to move the key? Yes! It was literally hanging out of the lock.
The Dark Wizard is home! Sshh! Be… quiet…perhaps he won't… hear you…
The Landlord banged as hard as he could on the cell door, trying to dislodge the key, but it remained stubbornly in its place. Oscar jumped again and, now exhausted, fell agonizingly short

once more.

The Dark Wizard had already decided his prisoner had to die, but he was tired from his long trek across London and it could wait until tomorrow. But then he heard the banging. *I'm not putting up with that all night,* he thought angrily, *this will only take a minute.* Forgetting that he'd planned to take his time and enjoy the execution, he took out his wand and headed for the dungeon.

Oscar jumped again, but now his paws barely left the ground.

Logan opened the door to the passage.

The Landlord, watching through the bars, saw him before the dog did and he went cold with terror, but not for himself; he knew Logan would kill him now and he didn't care but…

"Run, Oscar! Get away! Quickly!" The feeling of sheer helplessness and impotence was worse than torture as he saw the Dark Wizard run. "Hurry, Oscar, please, oh please save yourself!"

And Oscar, not for the first time in his life, it has to be said, ignored him completely. With a last, monumental effort of will and concentration, he launched himself upward, reaching desperately. He knew this was his last chance; fail now and both he and his master would die. And so he stretched, teasing every last iota from muscle and sinew.

At last! The merest contact from his toenail, only the slightest of touches but it was enough to knock the key from the keyhole and send it flying through the air, straight toward Logan's outstretched hand. With lightning speed, the Landlord closed his eyes and formed an image of the key in his mind, focusing all his will upon it. The Dark Wizard's fingers were already closing around their prize when it moved direction, oh so slightly, and spun harmlessly

THE SANCTUARY

past to clatter to the floor behind him.

Quick as a flash, Oscar darted forward, gathered it up and now he had the advantage because this was a game he and the Landlord had played many times, although never with so much at stake. But still, there was only one chance to get this right and with the key in his mouth he whipped his head sharply sideways and flung it, spinning toward the ceiling. As it descended, a long, skinny arm came through the bars of the door and deftly caught it.

Enraged, the Dark Wizard aimed a vicious kick at the dog and narrowly missed as Oscar twisted away, barking and nipping at his ankles. Logan raised his wand to blast him out of existence but before he could summon the command, the Landlord was out of his cell. He drew back a big bony fist and punched the Dark Wizard in the face, sending him sailing through the air, halfway up the passage. As he landed with a painful, bone-jarring thump on the cold stone floor, his grip on the wand loosened and it flew from his grasp. Still barking excitedly, Oscar was torn between retrieving it or greeting his beloved friend; he chose the latter, jumped into his arms and began licking his face furiously.

"Stop it, Oscar!" The Landlord laughed as he felt a tongue go up his nostril, making him sneeze, then he let the dog down. "The wand, Oscar. Quickly!"

Logan was on his knees and trying to crawl toward the wand which lay almost within reach. But as his hand reached out to take it, Oscar darted forward and grabbed it triumphantly, leaving the Dark Wizard once more sprawled on the floor. He ran back with it, but as the Landlord went to take it, he darted away again. This was another favorite game and one the Landlord normally loved to play too. But not this time; he knew the Dark Wizard wasn't defeated yet, not quite.

"Oscaaar." He used the exact tone of voice which told the dog he meant business. Oscar looked at him without relinquishing his prize for a moment then reluctantly dropped it at his feet. The Landlord ruffled the top of his head and picked up the wand, hardly able to believe his luck. "Well done, Oscar, well done indeed!"

To touch a wand not meant for you was usually a very painful experience, as Peter Simpson had demonstrated to Cissy. But all the Landlord felt as he approached Logan was the slightest tingling in his hands. Although he didn't look it, and the Dark Wizard certainly hadn't suspected it, the Landlord was far more powerful than any wand; only Morgan knew who he really was. Molly, who had been lightly scornful of him, much to the Landlord's amusement, would feel extremely embarrassed when she found out.

"Go on, kill me!" The Dark Wizard, seeing his wand in another's hand, knew that all was lost and for once was not attempting a false bravado. He fully expected to be killed, for he had no concept of mercy. But the Landlord was about to do something much worse.

"I'm no murderer," he told Logan, as he gripped the wand in both hands, "but perhaps you will wish I was."

"No! Don't!" The Dark Wizard pleaded, panic-stricken as he saw what his adversary was about to do. "Don't!"

As the wand snapped in two, the Landlord walked without a backward glance from the passage, Oscar trotting at his heels.

THE SANCTUARY

*   *   *   *

Several centuries distant, a young girl was clearing away the remains of her meal when all of a sudden, she felt very strange indeed. Dizzy and light-headed, she tried to reach a chair, the one nearest the table where she had recently shared breakfast with her grandfather, but she swayed and stumbled. As she tried to steady herself, one of the plates she carried flew from her hand and smashed into tiny pieces on the stone floor.

"*Ffwl trwsgl!*" she cried. "Clumsy fool!" And the other plate crashed to the floor as hands covered her mouth in shock. Next moment she was out of the door to the old cottage and running as fast as she could toward the village square, yelling as loud as she could.

"Ffranc, Ffranc!" She ran down a side street and around the corner, narrowly avoiding one of the village boys who was carrying a tray of newly baked bread. "Sorry, Timothy!" she yelled over her shoulder. "Have you seen Ffranc?"

It was another boy who answered. "He's at the forge talking to the blacksmith, Dai, but how are you able to—"

"*Diolch,* Toby," she shouted but didn't stop. "Thanks!" Despite running as fast as she could, the building was at the far end of the village and it was some minutes before she got there. She burst inside and for a moment was unable to catch her breath, doubled-over, gasping.

"Child!" Ffranc was alarmed. "What on earth…"

Catrin looked up at him, her eyes shining. "Grandfather, I can speak!" But she got no further as he gathered her to him and held her tight, just as the tears fell down his ancient, lined face.

THE SANCTUARY

Chapter 49

The battle wasn't long ended but Aeryn was already fretful about her own land being left unguarded. Soon she would leave the Sanctuary and return home, yet the prospect filled her with dread.

"Stay a while," her sister urged, glancing involuntarily at Alessandro who had been neglecting his kitchen shamefully while he found opportunities to steal precious moments with her. "Let us enjoy our triumph for a while."

"There is no point enjoying our triumph, Daraproud, if our own castle is taken by our enemies because we congratulate ourselves here." The knowledge that soon she would say goodbye to Morgan, probably forever, was making her uncharacteristically peevish and she cursed him silently for barging back into her life without a by-your-leave. Under her breath she muttered, "And every moment I spend here makes it all the more difficult to leave."

Quietly though the words were uttered, Daraproud heard and understood. "Have you asked him?"

"No," Aeryn snapped curtly, "I have not, and you'd best leave that boy alone too, for we'll be going soon. There's no need for his heart to be broken!"

Now Daraproud was angry. "That's none of your business, Sister. I'll do what I damned well like! And I—"

"No, that's where you are wrong, it is very much my business! And you will not, as you say, do as you *damned* well like. I am your queen; you'd do well to remember that!"

Heads were turning at their raised voices and Daraproud sank into a deep curtsy, somehow managing to put every possible ounce of hurt and sarcasm into the movement. "As you wish, Your Majesty." It was said with a wealth of sadness and Aeryn knew she was in the wrong; she had never, *ever* used her position as a weapon against her sister.

"Daraproud, I…" She faltered at the tears in her sister's eyes. "I…"

"I like him, Aeryn, *really* like him. Surely, just because you and Morgan…well, surely I'm allowed a chance at happiness?" And her sister could only smile sadly and agree.

"Of course, but what if he won't come back with you? He may not want to, you know; he is very loyal to Morgan, to the Sanctuary."

"I know, but I thought I might stick around for a while and see."

They were interrupted by a commotion across the room as a man and a boy emerged through the doorway from the passage-between-the-worlds.

"Dad!" Luke shouted in delight as Peter Simpson, accompanied by Gruffydd, stepped down into the room. As soon as possible after the end of the battle, Morgan had sent word and the pair of them had hastened back to the Sanctuary. Luke flung himself into his father's arms and they held each other tightly. Then everybody crowded around, talking excitedly, welcoming them, while the faeries zoomed about, generally making a nuisance of themselves.

After the excitement had died down a little, Peter and Luke managed to sneak away to a quiet corner to talk, and uppermost in their minds was Mrs. Simpson. Luke hadn't had much time recently to think about his mother but now the battle was finished he realized he missed her terribly and he was eager to return home. It had been much longer, of course, since Peter had last seen her.

"She's going to have quite a shock," Peter said. "I don't know how she'll take it. Not too badly, I hope. And where does she think *you've* been all this time?"

"She doesn't think anything. Morgan says she kind of knows I'm here." Luke paused, uncertain. "She's gonna be amazed when you turn up though."

"I know," he replied, worried and equally uncertain.

Not knowing what else to say, Luke was relieved when Cissy joined them. They smiled at each other, suddenly feeling absurdly shy. "Fancy the prophecy being about you, after all," he said at last.

Cissy waved a hand dismissively, feeling hugely embarrassed, particularly since she knew it was supposed to have been Luke and she wasn't quite sure how he felt about it. "Yeah, I know, weird isn't it? When will you go home then?" she asked, changing the subject. "Tomorrow?"

Luke looked at his father. "Can we, Dad?"

Peter nodded. "Yes, I think we'd both like that. What about you, Cissy? You're gonna visit home, surely?"

She returned his nod. "I'm going tomorrow too. You're both coming back though, right?"

"You bet we are!" father and son exclaimed together. "What about you?" Luke asked. "You'll come back too, won't you?" He was a little worried she'd no longer want him as a boyfriend after everything that had happened. He'd witnessed first-hand the extraordinary power she suddenly had, and he felt a little overawed. Perhaps she'd be too grand for him now.

"Well, I'll have to sell my mum and dad on the idea," she admitted. "I don't think they'll be so happy about it. But I have to return, I think; Morgan will insist on it, given all that's been going on. I expect they'll get used to the idea. Anyway,"—she grinned at Luke—"you're gonna be here so I have to come back." Peter made an embarrassed noise and moved swiftly away.

And Luke suddenly felt a whole lot better.

Just then, the door to the passage-between-the-worlds opened for the second time that evening.

"It's like Piccadilly bleedin' Circus tonight," Molly began, then stopped as a small bundle of fur leaped inside, ran barking across the room and flung itself onto her lap, licking madly at her face.

"Oscar! What are you doing here?" Then as two very long legs appeared through the doorway, she hardly dared hope, until… "Landlord!"

"Well now!" He grinned. "If it isn't the witch." He snapped his fingers as if trying to remember her name, although he knew it perfectly well. "Mandy…Milly…Molly! That's it, Molly!" He

THE SANCTUARY

took one of her hands in both of his. "How are you, my dear, safe and sound I see?"

Her reply was interrupted by Morgan's arrival. The wizard had been sitting with Penelope, teaching her to play chess, but when Oscar had bounded through the door she'd cried out in delight and ran to pet him while Morgan went striding quickly across to envelop the Landlord in a huge bear hug as Molly looked on in amazement.

"We feared the worst, old friend, we feared the worst!"

Old friend? she thought, as Morgan continued, still laughing, "What happened to you?" He sobered. "Molly told me about the destruction of…" He glanced around. "Well, you know."

"Of the portal-between-the-dimensions, you mean?" The Landlord grinned. "Don't worry, Morgan, it need not be a secret. Molly already knows about it anyway and we are all friends here."

Who is he? she wondered, sensing there were things here she didn't understand.

"And as for what happened to me, well I've been a guest of your dear brother recently." The Landlord's face darkened as he remembered his imprisonment and, in particular, the journey from Wales, which had almost killed him.

"A guest of *Logan's*?" Morgan was astounded. "Why, how?"

"Oh, no point going on about it," said the Landlord. "Oscar rescued me in the end, as I knew he would." The dog gave two sharp barks of agreement. "Oh, that reminds me." He patted first his trouser pockets, then his jacket. "I know I've got it here somewhere. Ah!" And he handed over what were now just two sticks. Morgan stared at them in amazement.

"So, his power is finally broken," he breathed at last, half to himself. "How did you ..?"

"Oh, like I said, no point going on about it. Anyway, time we were going really."

That's Logan's wand, thought Molly. *Who the bleedin' 'ell is he?*

The Landlord was about to turn and leave when a thought struck him. "You do know your brother's loss of power is temporary, don't you?"

"I think not," Morgan disagreed. "He never was as powerful as he believed, and without his wand…"

"Beware your arrogance does not become your own undoing." He sounded like a teacher chiding a naughty pupil. "Your brother can get a new wand; he can go to the—"

"To the goblins, yes I know," Morgan interrupted, "but to get to the goblins he would need to travel all the way through the land of the Necromancer, still dangerous even though he is long dead. Then he'd have to turn left just before he falls off the edge, jump down into the land of the witches, hope *they* don't catch him, and even if he managed all that, he'd still need to…"

"I *know* the way to the goblin land," the Landlord said with asperity; he was tired, and he wanted to go home.

"Of course you do, sorry." Morgan realized he'd had his lecturing head on for a moment there, quite forgetting just who he was talking to. "I forgot myself for a moment, forgive me."

Molly looked at her friend and frowned. *Who is this man!* Her curiosity was eating her up and she opened her mouth to speak. But her moment had passed. The Landlord inclined his head to show there were no hard feelings, but Morgan was still talking.

THE SANCTUARY

"The fact remains, though, that he'd have to enter the Necromancer's land and there is only a single entrance to it and that's…" He stopped himself just in time and shrugged. *Best not mention the corridor,* he realized.

"Hmm," the Landlord muttered. He also, unbeknownst to Morgan, knew about the corridor. *Keep your secrets if you will, my friend.* But he said nothing more; really, he didn't like to be involved in the affairs of wizards and witches anymore. And there'd been far too much of that recently.

"Right then, we'll be on our way."

"Won't you stay awhile?" Morgan invited. "It's been such a long time."

"Yes, please stay a bit!" Molly wanted to ask a few questions, find out who he really was. She knew by now he wasn't just an ordinary pub landlord.

"Oh, you know me, Morgan, thanks for the invite and all that, but I never was one for company really, so we'll just be on our way." He gave a low whistle and Oscar immediately left his game with Penelope and trotted over.

"Wait," Morgan said hurriedly, "the portal, can it be restored?"

The Landlord smiled. "Of course it can. It may take a little time, but it will be healed." He stepped forward and embraced his friend briefly. "Take care, Morgan." He nodded to Molly. "You too, my dear. Come and visit when the portal is fixed; I'll let you know. We can have an opening ceremony. Or something," he added a little vaguely. "Peter, nice to see you free at last and healed; nasty stuff that demon poison."

Damn, how did he know about that? Morgan had a lot of

explaining to do, Molly decided.

But now the Landlord really was leaving. He turned to go, then saw Penelope staring up at him with big, round eyes. "And as for you, young lady,"—he bent at the waist to bring his face level with hers, which meant he had to twist his body at a very odd angle—"look after them," he whispered, indicating the witch and wizard. "They're really not fit to be let loose." He winked as she put a hand to her mouth and giggled in delight.

He was almost at the doorway when Molly called after him. "Who *are* you?"

But the Landlord simply laughed and scooped Oscar up into his arms, then he stepped into the passage-between-the-worlds and was gone.

"Well?" Molly wanted an explanation. "And who the bleedin' 'ell was that?"

"Oh, he'll tell you himself someday, no doubt," Morgan answered.

"We know him." It was Daraproud who had joined them, leaving her sister upstairs in her chamber where they'd sat talking for most of the evening. "He is well known to us at the castle; he visits occasionally."

"Really?" asked Morgan, astonished.

"Really?" echoed Molly.

"Sure!" she replied. "He's been no end of help in concocting magic to aid our defenses; he is a very powerful wizard, you know." She looked at them smugly. "And sometimes," honesty forced her to add, "he just comes for a holiday."

"Hold on," said Molly, "if he's such a powerful wizard, how

come nobody's heard of him?"

"I have," Morgan pointed out.

"So have I," added Daraproud.

"Well I bleedin' haven't," she replied, "and I want to know why!"

"It's quite simple really," Morgan said, placatingly, "he just likes the quiet life. Honestly!" He laughed at Molly's look of skepticism. "He really can't be bothered with the affairs of mortals and he's quite happy to be guardian of the portal between the dimensions. I don't know how Logan managed to get the better of him, some kind of treachery I suppose. But it will have hit his pride hard and he will be anxious to make amends."

"Hmm, I see," she said, becoming calmer, "but your brother is, or was, pretty powerful though, you have to admit, Morgan."

"Yes, he was, but nowhere near the Landlord's league. He is a different proposition altogether. He's even more powerful than I am, much more so. If he had wanted to use that power to its full potential, it might have been him leading the Sanctuary, not I."

That sobered them and there was silence for a while. Molly went off to find a convenient armchair where she could have a nap, Morgan and Penelope resumed their game, while Daraproud went to watch TV with Gruffydd. Both of them were intrigued by this mortal invention and wanted to have a proper look while they had the chance. He was due to return to Wales tomorrow, a prospect which filled him with excitement, for he missed Catrin more than he'd realized he would.

As for Daraproud, she thought she might hang around a few days longer and see what happened with Alessandro. She could see him skulking in the shadows, nervously awaiting his chance

THE SANCTUARY

to approach her. There! He'd realized he'd been spotted and was coming over! She looked away and pretended not to notice. Nonchalantly, he sat on the settee next to her, as close as he dared, without making it too obvious. There was an awkward silence for a time, broken only by Gruffydd's startled exclamations as he used the remote to flick through the channels.

Desperately, Alessandro tried to think of something to say but his mind was blank. Eventually he said, rather lamely, "You have a beautiful name, *dolce signora*, does it have a meaning?" As a chat up line, it wasn't the best, but she turned toward him and smiled radiantly.

"Daraproud? It means *the star that glitters in the sky and shines the brightest.*"

He stared at her, mouth open so that eventually she had to reach out and push his chin upwards to close it.

"You don't like it?" she asked, anxious.

"I think," he breathed, "it's the most beautiful thing I've ever heard."

Daraproud blushed and he turned away, embarrassed, looking for a distraction. He grabbed the remote from Gruffydd and said eagerly, "How about some music?" Without awaiting a response, he switched channels and soon, loud, pulsating rhythms filled the air.

Across the room, Cissy and Luke were deep in earnest conversation, but every now and then the girl stole a glance at Morgan who was still patiently teaching Penelope the complexities of chess.

As Cissy watched, a worried frown creased her forehead, for

an awful suspicion was growing in her mind, one which filled her with foreboding. Although Aeryn was conspicuously absent tonight, she'd seen how the two of them were together.

Cissy wondered what that meant for the future and waited impatiently for the chess game to end so she could tackle him about it. *Surely it was way past Penelope's bedtime?* she thought, moodily.

By now, Daraproud and Alessandro were on their feet dancing wildly; they'd even pulled a reluctant Gruffydd to his feet. Putting her bad mood to one side, Cissy joined them, followed by Luke. Soon, shrieks of laughter competed with the music.

"I wish you lot would bleedin' quiet down." Molly was thoroughly annoyed at being jerked awake. "Can't a person catch forty winks around here?" But Cissy and Luke were grinning, which only made her more irritable. "Don't know what you two find so bleedin' amusing," she complained, "it's okay for you young 'uns, you've got plenty of energy."

"Sorry," they both said, deadpan.

"Well you don't bleedin' sound it," she grumbled, "you should have more respect for your elders. Honestly,"—she fixed them with a steely glare which didn't bother them in the slightest—"it's just too—"

"Bleedin' inconsiderate!" they chorused. And the teenagers burst out laughing.

*   *   *   *

"You will be here when I come back from home?" Cissy had

become tired of waiting for the game to end and had decided just to ask Morgan outright.

But he chose that moment to turn and say something to Wallace, who had just that second entered the room. *But I know he'd heard me!* Cissy looked at him thoughtfully before returning to the music. Distracted, she glanced across at Morgan for the umpteenth time and wondered why he pretended not to hear her.

That night, Morgan sat for a long time in his chamber staring blankly at the wall. He knew he should be glad they'd won the battle, and he was of course. But he knew from long experience that this was only a respite, that his enemies would come again one day; they always did.

Since the battle had ended, he'd had soldiers combing the streets, looking for the body of the Demon King, without success. Morgan could only assume he'd escaped and the wizard would have expected nothing less. And his brother? Morgan knew he would not let it be. Oh he would be quiet for a while, regain his strength, find a new wand. And then he would forge a new alliance against the brother he looked upon with such blind, unreasoning hatred.

Suddenly Morgan was sick of it all, sick of the worry, the fighting, the constant fear of betrayal, the responsibility. Yes, they'd won the battle and all his friends had come through safely, but now it all felt like such an anti-climax. And tomorrow he knew Aeryn would ask him a question, one he hoped for and dreaded in equal measure and for the life of him he didn't know what answer he would give. He sighed as he turned out the light, but after all, tomorrow was another day.

THE SANCTUARY

Chapter 50

"Will you return with me?"

Morgan looked at her sadly. "What of the people here? Molly and Wallace, my oldest and dearest friends? What of the new arrivals, Luke and Cissy, young Penelope? What of Alessandro, Hans? And what of the people of the mortal world? Should I abandon them so soon after our triumph? You ask much of me, Aeryn." He dropped his gaze. "You ask *too* much."

"And what of your own happiness?" she protested. "Don't you deserve that after all these years?" Aeryn tried not to let her anger show, but honestly this strict code of honor he followed was so *irritating*. Why couldn't he let someone else carry the burden, just this once!

"My happiness does not matter. I was put on this earth to protect the mortal world, to lead the Sanctuary." Inwardly he cringed at how pompous he sounded.

"Morgan, times change, and the time has come for Cissy to lead, she's the chosen one after all." Aeryn went on hurriedly as he tried to interrupt, "You've waited centuries for the prophecy to come true, for this chosen one to appear, and now she has. You've got to give her a chance!"

"But she's young and has had little training, it would be unfair…"

"What's unfair is that you don't trust Molly and Wallace to guide the girl, to keep her on the right path. It's no different to Dominic acting as regent to my daughter Angelina!" She knew her temper was rising, and she forced herself to take a deep breath. "And anyway, they could visit, occasionally; once, twice a year perhaps, and you could visit them!" She was pushing him too hard, but she couldn't help herself. "Morgan, we've been apart too long!"

At this, he nodded and took her hand. Encouraged, she pressed her advantage. "Just think of it, you and I together in my beautiful land, in my magnificent castle!"

Her use of the word *my* rankled a little. "Ah, to be a queen's consort…"

"No!" She realized her mistake. "We would rule as equals!"

The look he gave her was openly skeptical. "Really, Aeryn? No man has ever ruled in your land. Are you trying to tell me you would thwart custom, change the law so readily?"

"Times change, Morgan," she said again. "You are the most powerful wizard this world has ever known…"

"Owain the Original was more powerful," he demurred modestly.

She waved a hand in irritation, feeling her exasperation rise again. "Irrelevant. My point is that I would not expect, and I would not wish us to be anything but equals!" She stopped, suddenly realizing he couldn't be persuaded, would have to make up his own mind. "Please," she whispered, "please don't make me beg."

He held her close so he wouldn't have to see her eyes when he refused. But he couldn't abandon his people, he just couldn't. It was all very well for her to talk about occasional visits, but it wasn't enough. He couldn't simply let go of a world he'd strived to protect for so many years! The words of refusal were forming on his lips when he had a thought. He stepped back and looked at her for a long moment. Sensing his inner turmoil, she remained silent.

"Come with me," he said at last. He strode into the hallway and quickly down the staircase, leading her across the lounge and up into the passage-between-the-worlds, then along it to the circular room. "Before I show you this there are still no guarantees, agreed?"

She nodded but remained silent, wondering what he was planning; she sensed there was great power happening in this room. The wizard had already taken out his wand and placed its tip gently against the rough stone wall. Now he said a word, one that was drenched in magic.

Aeryn jumped back, startled as a door appeared in the wall. "Do you have to make me jump like that?" she complained, embarrassed at her reaction, and he grinned annoyingly.

"Sorry," he said, clearly not, then he twisted the large iron ring set in the door's center and pushed. It swung silently inwards to reveal only darkness beyond. He made as if to step through then paused, suddenly serious. "No one but me knows of the existence of this place, not even Molly."

She stared at him in surprise. Molly was his dearest friend and they'd been together for centuries. That Morgan would keep this secret from her... *Yet he will reveal it to me.* All at once she felt humbled as she realized the honor he paid her, realized how deep his love for her must be. As they stepped inside, her feet sunk into thick carpet while the darkness was relieved by the light of gas lamps stretching far along the narrow corridor in which she found herself. Curiously, she saw that the walls on each side were made of old, soot-blackened bricks at odds with the vibrant purple carpet, as if the passage couldn't decide whether it was indoors or out.

"Where are we?" she whispered, almost reverently, for if she had thought the circular room was powerful, in here it seemed magnified a hundred-fold. "This seems to go on forever."

He shrugged. "We are nowhere, a void in time and space, and this corridor is neither finite nor infinite. It is, if you like, a bridge between dimensions."

"Er, yes, I'm sure that's very impressive. What are you talking about, Morgan?"

He smiled. "Sorry, this is the first time I've ever had the opportunity to show this place off. I call it the Corridor of Dimensions. Okay then, think of it as a gateway…or something. Look, each of the doors is an entrance to a world, of which there are many."

"Doors? What doors…?" She stopped and looked in amazement, because sure enough there *were* doors lining the walls on either side as far as she could see, giving the effect of an impossibly long row of terraced houses. But surely, the doors… they weren't real! They had been *drawn* onto the bricks in what looked like crayon. And they were crudely done as if by a very young child, with crooked lines and door handles that were simply a rough swirl of color.

"Who made this place? You?"

He laughed. "Of course not, no one knows who made it. It's simply always been here as far as anybody knows. But it was discovered by Owain the Original after many years of searching. Its why he created the Sanctuary around it and the passage-between-the worlds, so that he could be near to this corridor. He had… reason to unlock some of these doors occasionally."

"But surely this is the true passage-between-the-worlds, if you think about it?"

"Well, yes I suppose so, except that it's a closely guarded secret, so it's never had a name until I gave it one. Passage-between-the-worlds was just a term coined by Owain, and there are doors in it too. But those lead mostly to other dimensions of the Sanctuary, other versions if you prefer to think of it that way, not, strictly speaking, to other actual worlds. But *these* doors on the other hand…"

"But they're not doors, are they? They're just drawings!"

"Oh, that's just for protection, a most ingenious form of security really. After all, if someone *did* find this corridor, we can't have them simply breaking down a door and entering its world uninvited! No, the doors are there alright, but they require very powerful magic to unlock them."

"Okaaay." She suddenly felt playful. "Let's test you." She pointed to a bright blue door. "Where does that one lead?"

"No idea."

"What about that one?" A green door this time.

"Nope, no idea either."

"You're not very good at this," she grumbled. "That brown one?"

THE SANCTUARY

"That one I'd rather not think about." He shuddered.

"Alright, last chance,"—she pointed to a door drawn in black—"what about that one?"

"Ah," he exclaimed, "now that's a most interesting one. It leads to the world of the Necromancer, long empty now of course, since the old wizards and witches, and the goblins, fought together to defeat him."

"Cool! You must tell me about that sometime!"

"*Cool?* You've got that from Cissy," he accused.

"From Penelope actually," she corrected tartly. "And that orange one?"

"That one leads to the Witches Domain, not somewhere you'd want to visit really." He was lost for a moment in his memories. "Although it used to be a pleasant place for a holiday when Siwaraksa ruled there. Molly used to visit often. It's how she learned the skills that saved your life."

Not noticing her expression had darkened as she remembered how close to death she had come, he continued blithely, "But then she was betrayed and murdered during the Ice Cloud War. Molly and I had to flee for our lives pretty sharpish. It was never the same again after that. Molly sought a safe place and came to live with me at the Sanctuary. She was only going to stay a week or so, as I recall."

Finally noticing her mood had changed, and realizing he'd been rambling a bit, he sought to distract her. "C'mon, let me show you the reason I brought you here." He took her arm and led her further down the corridor.

They walked in silence for a few minutes until a thought struck her. "What about the demon world? Isn't there a doorway into there?"

"Of course there is, we passed it five minutes ago."

"So how come Molly had to make such a long journey to get the blood thorn you told me about? Why didn't she use the door into the demon world, nip out and get the thorn then nip back in and get back here? Ten minutes, tops."

"Well for a start," he said a little sarcastically, "you don't just *nip* in and out of the demon world, you escape with your life *if* you're lucky." He lengthened his stride and moved ahead of her, speaking over his shoulder, "And I've already told you, this place is secret!"

She stuck a tongue out at his retreating back and fired a hundred poisoned arrows into it, barbed ones to cause maximum pain. Sighing because they weren't real, she had to run to catch up, then almost cannoned into him when he stopped suddenly.

"Suppose this passage wasn't kept secret anymore?" He blurted it out. "Suppose I revealed its existence but concealed all the doors?"

"What would be the point?" She sensed his agitation but didn't know what he was trying to say.

"Suppose I concealed all the doors; all except this one." He had stopped in front of a door that was drawn in a vivid shade of emerald green.

"Why? Where does this one go?" She felt unaccountably nervous.

There was a long pause until he finally took a deep breath. "It leads into your world, Aeryn."

Astounded, she found she couldn't speak, but after a moment she realized it made perfect sense. *Of course, there would be a door to*

THE SANCTUARY

my land. Why not? It seems there's a door to everywhere else! Suddenly she was scared he was going to send her back. He couldn't make her go, obviously, but she was proud, too proud to stay where she wasn't wanted.

"You couldn't use magic to open and close this door," he was muttering, "it would be too powerful, would kill any but the strongest wizard." He was talking half to himself, trying to work it out. "The door would have to remain permanently unlocked."

Now it was her turn to hesitate as his meaning began to penetrate. "What are you saying?"

"But it would still be perfectly safe from the outside world," he went on, ignoring her, "because only those who are able to enter the circular room could get in here."

"Morgan?"

He stared as if noticing her for the first time. "Would you allow it? Free access for all who inhabit the Sanctuary?"

Now it was her turn to hesitate. *Allow strangers into my land? How can I possibly?* The thought of breaking a thousand-year-old custom terrified her. *And yet why not? Times, after all, do change.*

"Will you let me create this border between our worlds?" He sounded more insistent this time, more anxious too.

All at once she felt reckless, tired of abiding by the rules. "If I do so, will you come back with me?"

He realized he'd been holding his breath, but suddenly he knew it was all going to work out and he felt the last of his burdens, carried for centuries, fall from his shoulders. He took her by the waist and drew her close. As her arms snaked up around his neck, he showed her such a look of tenderness it took her breath away.

THE SANCTUARY

"Will you come?" she repeated in barely a whisper, still hardly daring to hope.

His mouth quirked upward slightly at the corner, that smile she remembered so well.

"You know I will," he said.

Epilogue

It has been said before that one does not simply walk into the realm of the Demon King unannounced, and it had taken the Dark Wizard a long time to gather his courage. But eventually, as the days turned into weeks, and the weeks into months, he knew he could delay no longer.

Now, as he squeezed into the crack in the cave wall, he knew his presence would not remain secret for long. Sure enough, he had gone but a dozen or so paces when his path was blocked by the tall figure of a demon.

"You dare to enter this place uninvited, wizard?" The creature drew a dagger and held its tip against Logan's throat, drawing a thin trickle of blood. "Give me a reason not to kill you now!"

Logan tried to ignore the huge, raw burn that covered the left side of the creature's face and head. In the few seconds it had taken to find shelter from the blood moon, its eye had begun to melt. Then, when the demon had found the shadows, the eye had hardened again so that now it appeared to be dripping from its socket.

THE SANCTUARY

Logan swallowed the bile that rose into his throat and spoke, careful not to move and give the demon a reason to strike. "I have come to offer my services to your master, to discuss how we can avenge ourselves on the accursed wizard Morgan." The lie came easily to his lips and he gave the demon a sly, contemptuous smile. "After all, I would think he needs all the help he can get right now."

Despite its limited intelligence, the demon was forced to concede that Logan had a point. Of the tens of thousands of demons that had made up the Demon King's army, only a couple of hundred had survived. Persuaded at last, despite its misgivings, the demon turned abruptly and stomped down the passage.

"Follow me."

Logan obeyed without comment but as his footsteps took him deeper into Kanzser's realm, he smiled a secret smile and fingered the small pouch that hung from his belt, hidden from view.

*   *   *   *

Logan was different, more confident somehow; the Demon King could feel it and his misgivings grew. *What does he conceal beneath his robe?* Kanzser wondered, and his nervousness increased. Logan, on the other hand, was feeling far from nervous. In fact, he felt supremely confident as he remembered how this vile creature had manipulated and used him as a boy.

"Of course, one gains wisdom with age, Kanzser, isn't that right?"

They'd been sparring for the past half hour, attacking with

THE SANCTUARY

subtle taunts and barbs, but neither resorting to outright insult, so the need for violent confrontation had so far been avoided. Logan, of course, was savoring his moment, anticipating his coming triumph, secure in the knowledge he could not lose and that Kanzser did not yet know it.

But a fool he was not, and he lowered his guard not even for a millisecond, for he knew the Demon King was fast, that he could destroy him in the blink of an eye. But he also knew his adversary was curious, would want to know the reason for Logan's intrusion and, therefore, would not strike yet.

If the Demon King was annoyed at his name being used so freely, he didn't show it. Instead he reached for the wine flagon and poured two generous measures, one of which he proffered to Logan, who ignored it. Kanzser placed both cups onto the table, untouched.

"What do you have in there?" He could contain his apprehension no longer; whatever the Dark Wizard was hiding didn't bode well.

"In here?" Logan patted the pouch beneath his robe. "Nothing of any importance." He reached into the pouch. "Only…"—he took out the vial—"your doom."

The Demon King stared at it in horror for he knew instinctively what was inside. He moved toward the Dark Wizard. "My friend, there's no need…"

"Come no closer," Logan warned and held the vial outstretched before him. Kanzser took a step backwards.

"What do you want?" he growled. And even as he spoke, the most delicious idea occurred to Logan and a slow smile crept across his face. The Demon King saw it and trembled.

THE SANCTUARY

"I want…" He paused, determined to savor his moment, for rarely could revenge have tasted so sweet. He remained silent, allowing the tension to build until Kanzser could stand it no longer.

"Well? Just name it!" Then his voice became softer, crooning. "We will rebuild my realm together; it will be ours. Is that what you want, Logan? Name it and it will be yours."

It was a last, desperate throw of the dice, but still the Dark Wizard did not respond, and sweat formed on the Demon King's brow. "Answer me!"

Logan sighed heavily. "Such impatience, demon." He fingered the stopper of the vial idly and Kanzser watched in fascinated horror, in much the same way as one is transfixed by the stare of a cobra. But, unnerved though he was by this, it was the smile on Logan's face that was somehow more terrifying.

"What do I want?" He laughed once, and only then did the grin leave his face to be replaced by a look of pure malice. "I want you to kneel."

The Demon King stared at him in amazement. The irony of the situation was not lost on him, so he laughed. "You think you can speak to me thus, wizard?"

Once upon a time, the look of hatred on his face would have silenced Logan but now he reveled in it. He unscrewed the stopper slightly and gave the Demon King a sardonic look. The threat in the gesture was as crystal clear as the liquid inside.

"Now, demon, I believe you were deciding whether we have a deal?"

Kanzser regarded him for several long seconds, wondering if he dared defy his adversary. But the vial was refracting sinister points of crimson light through its cut glass and he knew that, for now at least, Logan held the upper hand. He fell clumsily to his knees, his gaze not leaving Logan's face, the look of hatred never wavering.

"You think I don't see the irony here? Well, have your fun while you—"

"Lower."

"Come now, Logan." He held out his arms, palms upward in a supplicant gesture. "There really is no need."

"Lower."

"Please, I—"

"You do know what's in here?" Logan interrupted, and held the vial inches from Kanzser's face so he was forced to squint. "Well? Do you, demon?"

Kanzser gave the slightest of nods, appalled at the situation in which he found himself.

"Then I would have you *prostrate yourself* before me!" With one foot placed firmly between the Demon King's shoulder blades, Logan tossed the vial carelessly from one hand to another while he squinted up at him in horrified fascination.

"Now what would you call this? Irony? Revenge?"

Kanzser's eyes followed the passage of the vial as it looped up and down, from left to right, right to left.

"I never was very good with words." The vial was in the air. "Oh, I know!" Logan clapped his hands together in the manner of someone suddenly solving a difficult problem and his quarry tensed. "I do believe it's both!" Logan affected to miss the vial, stooping quickly to catch it only centimeters from the ground, and Kanzser closed his eyes, certain the end had come. But then he felt the pressure ease as Logan removed his foot and, for a single, wild moment he thought he was reprieved. He looked at Logan with wild, pleading eyes.

"You've lived long, you know; you really shouldn't complain." The Dark Wizard was kneeling by his head and his thumb was lifting the stopper, slowly, infinitesimally upwards until it was half out of the vial.

"Please, Logan, I beg you. Don't!"

The thumb paused.

"We can rebuild this kingdom." He could barely speak, such was his agitation. "Together, we can do it together!"

"Well, it's a possibility..."

"Yes, yes!" He was sobbing uncontrollably now. "And you could be its leader! Our armies would bow down before you! Together we will sweep aside our enemies!"

"Kanzser, Kanzser, my dear friend," Logan interrupted the increasingly incoherent tirade, "I'd like to help, truly I would." He took up the edge of his robe and used it to dab away the Demon King's tears. "And your offer? Tempting." He stroked the Demon King's brow solicitously. "No, honestly, I mean it. Really, *really* tempting." Tears splashed onto Logan's foot and he wiped them away. "But unfortunately..." His thumb flicked up and the stopper flew into the air. A deep, crimson light flooded the room, joyously, eager to leave its prison.

The Demon King was already clutching his throat, gasping. Logan watched, fascinated for a moment as his eyeballs melted and his flesh expanded, the skin splitting, allowing streams of fat to ooze out.

The Dark Wizard stood abruptly, suddenly disgusted at the sight. Then, before the vial could expel the last of its poison, he tossed it through open door into the passage and deathly light flowed through the maze that was the Demon King's realm.

*   *   *   *

Many months had passed since the defeat of the demon army and after returning from their mountain hideout, life in the village, with its usual sounds and smells, had gradually returned to normal.

Gruffydd came back full of stories of his adventures, accompanied by Molly who, trying to hide the fact she desperately wanted to see Catrin again, said she didn't trust the boy to 'find his bleedin' way home again'. Her delight in finding Catrin could speak once more was matched by the boy himself who immediately set about trying to win the girl, who, by all accounts, wasn't putting up much resistance.

Molly also provided much welcome information, such as how the prophecy had been fulfilled and how Cissy had taken over leadership of the Sanctuary. Upon hearing of the rekindling of the romance between Morgan and Aeryn, Ffranc made little comment. He'd known of the ancient rift between them of course but wondered what good would come of it all, with Morgan living in another world and no longer concerning himself with the affairs of mortals.

And so, these villagers, who had endured so much, began to

THE SANCTUARY

pick up the pieces of their lives while Ffranc looked on fondly. They were a simple people who did not ask much beyond having a home to live in and to be surrounded by their friends. And in some ways, life had improved, for no longer did they have to endure occasional raids from the menace which had lurked close by for centuries, and this was a source of great joy. But Ffranc was wiser and his wisdom caused him to become troubled for he knew that the Demon King still lived, that he would rebuild his kingdom and trouble them again one day.

And what of the Landlord? Molly had related how he'd visited the Sanctuary briefly and told how he'd been imprisoned by, then escaped from, the Dark Wizard. After that, Ffranc had had no further word of his friend during all this time, but he wasn't particularly concerned; he knew he'd turn up eventually. Sure enough, yesterday the Landlord had suddenly appeared, much to the delight of the whole village, and the celebrations had continued long into the night. *There are more than a few sore heads this morning.* Ffranc smiled to himself. *And that reminds me, I must...*

But he never finished the thought for at that moment the ground shook violently beneath his feet and he was flung headlong. *An earthquake? Here? Surely not...* And then his brain caught up. *Oh, my word. By the sacred sword of Llywelyn, could it really be?*

"Gruffydd!" The old man hauled himself to his feet with an agility which belied his age and ran up the main street, just as people staggered from their homes to find out what was happening.

"Gruffydd!" He spotted the boy up ahead. "Fetch your horse!"

The boy was startled but he gathered his wits with remarkable alacrity and soon they were galloping out of the village and up the hillside. Just as they reached the crest, the ground shook again and this time it did not stop. Gruffydd clutched at Ffranc who sat in front and gathered him in his strong arms, then together they managed to slither to the ground, scant seconds before the horse reared onto its hind legs and bolted back down the hillside.

It seemed an age before the tremors subsided, but eventually they were able to stand and look cautiously around as if they expected the world to have come to an end. It was Gruffydd who noticed it first, and he turned to the old man, puzzled. "Look, Ffranc, over there. What's that?"

Ffranc looked across the valley to where the boy pointed at the mountain beyond. He stared in disbelief for a few moments before he chuckled, then laughed aloud. For there, above the lair of the Demon King, was a haze; a blood red haze. Ffranc's laughter echoed across the valley while Gruffydd stared at him in bewilderment.

"What are you laughing at?"

But Ffranc could only answer with a shake of his head as the tears ran down his face. At last his laughter subsided and he was able to speak. "What's that you ask? What's *that?*" And suddenly the tears were not of laughter but of joy. "That, my boy, is salvation!"

*   *   *   *

With a final, satisfied glance at the bloated, dying figure of the Demon King, Logan stepped away and left the room. But instead of heading upwards, back toward the cave entrance, he turned down the steep incline that led deep into the Demon King's realm.

Logan walked without stealth, for he knew none could have survived the light of the blood moon, and so it proved, as occasionally he came across corpses already starting to decay, their flesh turning to liquid and oozing onto the ground. With only a fleeting, distasteful glance, Logan stepped gingerly over each one, knowing the mess would eat through his boots like acid and strip his flesh down to the bone.

The air became increasingly hot and more rancid the further he descended and sweat poured from him. Peering around in the gloom, he tried to remember the way; it had been so long…

"Well, childling, what do you think of my realm?" The Demon King glanced slyly at the boy and rejoiced at the wonderment on his face. So easy, so very, very easy, *he thought with satisfaction.*

"It's magnificent! Are these…?" Logan paused when he saw the grin on the face of the Demon King, taking in the array of sharp, pointed teeth arranged shark-like inside the dark cavern of his mouth, and the thick gobs of saliva that drooled from the corners. "What are you smiling at?" Doubt entered the boy's mind for the first time.

"Nothing! Nothing at all!" Kanzser adjusted the grin hastily into a sincere smile, lips pressed together to hide that fearsome array of daggers that could tear a victim to shreds in seconds. "I'm just delighted you like my home. I want you to feel welcome here anytime you choose to visit."

The words stuck in his throat like vomit and he almost choked. His hooded eyes hid the deceit within. So, so difficult to pretend friendship with this young fool, *he thought, but there was no trace* of deceit when he addressed the boy again. "Now, what were you going to ask, my dear boy?"

Logan nodded, reassured. "I was going to ask about those." He pointed to the ceiling. "Are they real?"

The walls and ceiling of the rough-hewn passage were thickly encrusted with precious and semi-precious stones. The effect of the light they cast, reflected by the flames from the torches set into the walls, was eerie and disturbing.

"Of course." The fake smile remained on the Demon King's face as he reached upward. "Look." With a single, razor-sharp fingernail he prized out one of the stones and presented it to Logan.

"For me?" He was almost speechless. In his hand was a huge ruby, at least the size of a small orange, and stunning in its clarity and beauty. "You're truly giving this to me?"

"A gift to my dearest friend." The insincerity was so sickening it was almost palpable, but Logan swallowed it whole.

"Th… thank you," he stammered. "Thank you so much."

The Demon King waved a dismissive hand. "Oh, it's nothing; really it isn't," he almost simpered, his manner becoming shy and coy. "It's a mere trinket, of no importance." But secretly he thought, now you are mine.

"Nothing?" the boy went on. "It's amazing!" He would have continued had Kanzser not silenced him by placing an arm around his shoulder and squeezing gently.

"Yes," he agreed, "the stone is indeed beautiful, but it is as nothing when compared to the love I bear you." He turned away and gagged; only just able to prevent himself from vomiting.

But Logan hadn't noticed. "Truly? You feel that way?" Now the

THE SANCTUARY

look he gave the Demon King was completely trusting. And completely deluded…

Now, more than three centuries later, the Dark Wizard stood in those same passageways and tried to remember the location of the one he needed, his search becoming increasingly urgent as he sought a way out of this accursed place. As he tried to remember what the Demon King had shown him all that time ago, he pondered wryly on the naive boy he'd once been.

Well, you lost in the end didn't you, Kanzser? And despite the satisfaction he felt, a well of hatred arose in him also. *Soon you will be dead, whilst I go from strength to strength.*

That the Demon King still lived was proven by the fact that the walls of his realm had not yet begun to crumble. Even as the thought crossed his mind, there was a tremor, the floor tilted beneath him, and he was showered with loose stones and dirt.

Not for much longer. He grinned at the knowledge, but then the precariousness of his own situation dawned on him and he hurried. He rounded a bend and found himself in a huge open area.

I recognize this place. I've been here, I'm sure of it! But on that occasion he'd been dazzled by the light of billions of precious stones. Now, those stones remained but they were lifeless, though the light from a thousand torches still burned from sconces set into the walls. The place had once thronged with hundreds of demons, each one prostrated on the ground in the presence of their master.

Now only a few remained and they too were prostrated, but in death, their flesh already melting from their bones. He noticed a glow to the west of the clearing; the last remnants of the blood moon! And just before it dissipated fully, Logan saw the black archway of another passage, its entrance smaller and closer to the ground...

"Where does this one lead?" The boy had to stoop in order to peer into the inky blackness of the passage.

"Oh, nowhere of importance," the Demon King hedged, trying to sound nonchalant. "Come..."

"Can we have a look and see what's down there?" And, seeing Kanzser hesitate, "Please?"

Kanzser, full of anger inside but not wanting to destroy the boy's new-found trust, was forced to acquiesce. Together, bent almost double, they entered the passage and were enveloped in near darkness. Eventually, a slight glow became discernible, growing stronger with each step, until abruptly the passage opened out into a small cavern and Logan was forced to shield his eyes from the intense silver light that confronted them. It was some minutes before he was able to make out the outline of a large stone door, beset with strange symbols wrought from what looked like solid silver. The symbols were underlined with a thin sliver of silver giving the effect of a maze of lines forming an impossibly intricate design.

"What are those?" he breathed in wonder. "What do they mean? Where does the door lead to?"

The Demon King hesitated but could find no lie which might appease the boy's insatiable curiosity. "These are runes, ancient, magical runes which reveal the secret for opening this door. And no,"—Kanzser saw the boy was about to interrupt—"I will not divulge the secret; it is known only to me."

Before Logan could think of a response, the Demon King had stooped back into the passage and Logan had no choice but to follow. There was, however, time for one final question, but even so there was a long pause before the answer came rolling back to him, muffled in the confines of the narrow passage.

"Unless one chooses to cross the Chasm of Nothingness – and to enter Aeryn's world is a folly even I would not attempt without good reason – that door remains the only entrance to the land of the Necromancer."

Logan understood hardly any of this. He'd heard neither of anyone called 'Aeryn' or a place named 'Chasm of Nothingness'. But all children were taught of the Necromancer from an early age; tales of that almost mythical creature had been used for countless generations to threaten or instill obedience and fear.

Now the word 'Necromancer' seemed to echo loudly and clearly down the passage so that, despite the extreme heat, Logan shivered…

He was forced almost to his knees as he once more traversed the length of the passage, his limbs and back screaming in protest at the effort. There came a loud rumbling and the ground shook again. Then, unmistakably, there was the sound of falling rock in the distance and he felt another flutter of panic pass through his stomach as he redoubled his efforts to reach the cavern.

Is that the silver glow in the distance? he wondered hopefully. But he wasn't sure because now he was aware that the passage was filled with dust that irritated his eyes and caught in his throat.

All at once the world came to an end. Or so it seemed to the Dark

THE SANCTUARY

Wizard, as his senses were assaulted by a thunderous roaring, and he knew that the passage behind him was collapsing. It occurred to him that this must mean the Demon King was dead at last, but there was no time to dwell on this as he somehow ran even faster, crab-like, oblivious to the pain as his head crashed against the ceiling. He was hardly aware of it but now there *was* the glow of silver light and the passage opened out into a larger space. He instinctively threw himself to one side and huddled against the wall, curling into a fetal position in an effort to make himself as small as possible and protect his head.

It seemed to take an age, but gradually the ground shook a little less and the noise wasn't quite so deafening. Looking around cautiously, Logan found that, whether by chance or design, he had escaped serious injury, although his body would forever bear the scars from hundreds of shards of flying rock. At first, he could hardly credit that he was still alive but as the noise subsided even further and the dust cleared a little, he was able to see the reason why. Through the haze, the silver runes gave enough light to see that the passage through which he'd just come was completely blocked and that several boulders had rolled into the cavern.

His initial elation at being alive disappeared as quickly as it had arisen. Better that his end had come quickly, for now he was trapped, condemned to the slow, agonizing death of starvation. And yet, despite his predicament, he almost laughed. "Well at least you didn't beat me, Kanzser," he spoke aloud. "You died first." He giggled. "You died first!" He felt the mirth rising within him and recognized the first real signs of panic; panic that he tried to dispel by thinking of his brother.

THE SANCTUARY

Logan had never had much difficulty in feeling anger toward his twin, anger that usually dispelled any other emotion he might be feeling. Yet now all he felt was a strange, unfamiliar sadness.

We will never be reconciled will we, Morgan? It occurred to him that his brother would probably never even know what had happened to him. Despising his own weakness, the Dark Wizard was unable and unwilling to give in just yet, so he got to his feet and approached the silver light of the door. He examined the runes minutely, tracing his fingertips lightly across the intricate patterns, searching for something, *anything* that might yield a clue as to how to get out.

Damn you, Kanzser! You could have shown me the way! He slammed his fist against the door in frustration and, to his utter amazement, his hand simply disappeared into the stone. But the pain was tremendous! Burning! He snatched his hand back hurriedly.

What the hell just happened? Tentatively, he pressed his little finger against the door and once more it sank into the stone and again, *the pain!* He stepped back and regarded the door. *It must hold a secret, but how to unlock it?* Even as his mind spoke the word 'unlock', everything became clear. Beneath each of the runes was a line of silver and these lines formed a pattern.

A lock mechanism...surely...

And there, in front of him, was a perfectly described lock mechanism complete with cogs and levers and wheels, all beautifully wrought in silver. His gaze followed the design of the levers to the edge of the door and then to the doorknob. *Surely it can't be that easy...*

He reached out, took a deep breath, and plunged his hand deep into the door, grasping the knob. The pain! Unbearable! But fleeting! The Dark Wizard turned the knob and immediately he felt the door open. He withdrew his hand and hugged it to him, trying to soak up the agony. But inside his heart was singing as the door swung open and he saw the hills and sky beyond.

"Kanzser, you clever, clever…" He laughed aloud.

Then he stepped through the doorway, from the cavern which had almost become his tomb, and into the land of the Necromancer.

The End

THE SANCTUARY

THE SANCTUARY

Acknowledgements

There are so many mortals who helped get me over the line and finish this book, they'd fill another dimension in time and place.

I want to mention just a few. My heartfelt thanks go to these beautiful people.

Knun, whose love and friendship gave me the peace of mind to pick up the pieces of my work, when I thought it was lost forever. But for you, I would still be thinking what might have been.

Fi, the most amazing friend I could wish for. Her passion, common sense and determination in helping me publish this work is incalculable. As is her uncanny ability to pluck new character names out of the air instantly.

Carrie, my lovely, wonderful friend. Thank you for agreeing with my more outlandish ideas, rather than trying to rein me in. Mind you, being outlandish yourself, that really wouldn't be in your nature.

My friends and colleagues at The Horizon Centre and in particular, Claire. Thank you for your encouragement and interest

THE SANCTUARY

throughout the writing of this book. So many of you have asked, when will The Sanctuary be published? Well my friends, the answer is now!

It is one thing to write a novel and quite another to get it seen by you, my readers. Special thanks go to Paula Telizyn whose expert knowledge of all things publishing and marketing knows no bounds. Without you, this book would still be stuck somewhere in the ether.

And to you, the reader, for enjoying this book. The next instalment of the passage-between-the-worlds trilogy is coming to a universe near you in 2023.

THE SANCTUARY

THE SANCTUARY

Made in the USA
Columbia, SC
22 August 2023